P9-CFH-539

Alice Brown's Lessons in the Curious Art of Dating

Life's more exciting
when you let yourself be surprised

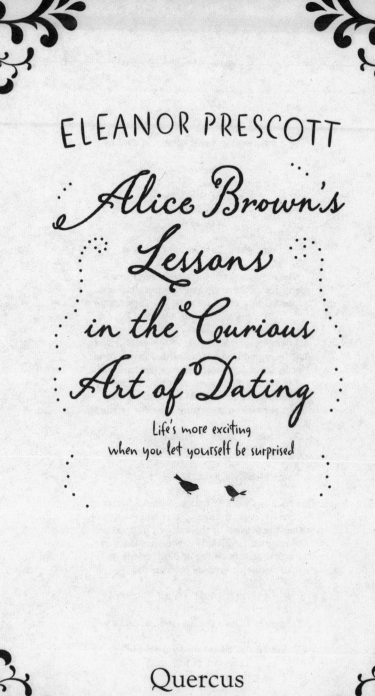

ELEANOR PRESCOTT

Alice Brown's Lessons in the Curious Art of Dating

Life's more exciting
when you let yourself be surprised

Quercus

First published in Great Britain in 2012 by

Quercus
55 Baker Street
7th Floor, South Block
London
W1U 8EW

A CIP catalogue record for this book is available
from the British Library

ISBN 978 0 85738 714 1

10 9 8 7 6 5 4 3 2 1

Typeset by Ellipsis Digital Limited, Glasgow

Printed and bound in Great Britain by
Clays Ltd, St Ives plc

For Nigel, without whom . . .

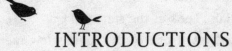# INTRODUCTIONS

'Where are all the men?' Kate whispered as she clutched her orange juice and looked nervously around the room. She tried to stop the disappointment reaching her face.

'In the pub with the normal human beings,' Lou snorted loudly. Despite already having a full glass of wine in one hand, Lou lunged at the circulating drinks tray and liberated another. 'Jesus, Kate, what the hell are we doing here?'

Kate was beginning to wonder. It had seemed such a good idea on paper. But now that she was here, in the overheated function room of the Holly Bush Hotel, she wasn't so sure.

'I'm all for doing things for a laugh, but this is beyond a joke,' Lou observed harshly. 'They're freaks, the lot of them!'

'Shhh! . . . You promised to be nice!' Kate frantically tried to quieten her. She tried to look on the bright side; after all, she hadn't expected to actually find a man *tonight*. 'They're just people,' she reasoned lightly. 'Just like us. We're all in the same boat.'

'We're absolutely not in the same boat,' Lou insisted.

'We're luxury yacht kind of girls, Kate: speedboats, cata-marans. This lot look like they're on a menopausal cruise ship with a broken rudder. Christ, it's no bloody wonder they can't get laid. Look at the state of *him*!'

Lou was pointing at one of the room's few men. Kate hadn't noticed him before. Tiny and fifty-something, he was clutching his wine like it was the last float on the *Titanic*. He was totally beige; even his skin was the colour of porridge. His only distinguishing feature was a thin veneer of perspiration on his upper lip. As Kate looked, he turned and held eye contact just long enough to show he'd overheard. Kate's heart leapt into her mouth and her cheeks tingled with shame. She quickly ushered Lou away into a corner of the room. She should've known bringing her would be a bad idea. But these were desperate times, and desperate times called for desperate measures.

As Lou busied herself with draining her glasses of wine, and the discreet tap on the shoulder and polite request that they should leave didn't materialize, Kate allowed herself to relax into some form of normality again. She ventured another look around the room. What kind of people came to a talk on 'The Secret to Finding Mr/Miss Right' anyway? She studied the groups of heads huddling around the nibbles table. Mainly they were late thirty-, early forty-something professional-looking heads, adorned with discreet highlights and the occasional expensive autumn-coloured tint. Then there were the exhausted on-the-point-of-giving-up heads, hair brushed that morning and then forgotten about, at best tucked behind ears or pulled into lumpy ponytails. And finally there was the hairdo brigade: the grittily determined, heavily lipsticked fifty-ups, with barnets carved from Elnett. Dotted amongst the sea of hair, a couple of shiny bald spots bobbed under the strip lighting, boosting the room's quota of men to a meagre handful. And steaming through the middle of it all, a red-cheeked woman with a halo of frizzy orange hair was loudly instructing everyone to visit the little boys' and girls' rooms 'toot suite', because the talk would be starting in five minutes.

Kate's eyes followed a few apologetic backs as they scuttled to the door in search of the loo. She gazed into the corridor beyond. What did they all look like to the outside world, she wondered? Would a passer-by be able to tell that everyone in the room was incapable of pulling? Was a tell-tale smell of sexual desperation seeping out, giving their secret away?

'We've got to face facts, Lou,' she declared matter-of-factly, although she wasn't sure whether she was trying to rouse her friend or herself. 'This is the level we're at. There's got to be a reason why we never have boyfriends; it can't all be down to bad luck. Maybe we're intimidating to approach; maybe we're giving off the wrong signals, or looking in the wrong places. Whatever, just like him' – she discreetly inclined her orange juice towards the beige man – 'there's something we're not doing right, and we need to find out what.'

'Speak for yourself,' Lou replied drily. 'I'm only here for the free booze. And if Twinkletoes over there really *is* my level, there isn't enough booze in the world. I'll be settling for an intimate acquaintance with my right hand for the rest of my life, and considering it a lucky escape.'

On the other side of the room, Alice hugged her cardigan around her and looked happily at the gaggle of anxiously expectant faces. She loved coming to Audrey's talks and was always the first (and only) member of staff to volunteer to help out. She'd arrive early to set up the room, unstacking the chairs, pouring the wine and checking that Audrey's lighting was kind and that her microphone was working. And then she'd open up the packets of biscuits and minia-ture sausage rolls, and lay out the brochures before greeting every member of the audience with a hello and a smile. She'd reassure them over their worries and give soothing answers to their uptight questions. Despite the regular orders barked in her direction by Audrey – and the fact that she'd never hand back the function room key before ten – Alice always went home with a spring in her step and a giddy, fluttering feeling in her tummy that was a bit like being drunk but a million times better. This was the kind of night she lived for; it was the kind of night that changed everything.

'The lavatories are in the lobby,' Audrey chivvied loudly. 'Chop-chop; you've got the rest of your lives to chatter. The talk will be starting at 7.30 prompt. Cupid won't wait for stragglers.'

Alice's smile wavered for a moment, but then her mind deliciously drifted. How many faces from tonight's throng would she see again, she wondered? How many would make it to the office next week? A lot, she hoped; as many as the books could take without bursting. She suddenly imagined the audience as a queue, starting at her desk, continuing out through the office front door and snaking the whole way around the block: a laughing, chattering ribbon of love-hopefuls, all waiting to be matched with their perfect other halves. Who knew: maybe romance might even blossom whilst they were waiting in line!

As she daydreamed, the melee of people hovering between the nibbles table and the exit shifted, and Alice suddenly caught a glimpse of two young women standing apart in the corner. One was striking, dark-haired and seemed to be drinking two glasses of wine at once, but it was the other woman who caught Alice's eye. Shorter and softer-looking than her friend, she was dressed in a smart skirt-suit and heels. But her sophisticated clothes were at odds with the expression on her face. Beneath the shiny hair and blunt, obedient fringe, her smile was clenched. Alice knew that smile. She'd seen it many times before, and at least one person always wore it on nights like tonight. Translated, it said *Be positive; breathe deeply; look relaxed*. It was a smile of jumbled-up hope, disappointment and a desperate determination to see things through.

Instinctively Alice stepped out from behind the Bourbon biscuits and started moving towards her. This woman was interesting. She was more than interesting: she was exactly the reason why she volunteered for nights like this. She had to speak to her, reassure her, make sure that she was one of the ones who made it into the office next week.

'*Alice!*' Audrey hissed violently from nowhere, making Alice jump from her path. 'Lights!'

Reluctantly, Alice faltered. The melee moved again and the woman disappeared from view.

'In your own time . . .' Audrey was eyeballing her sharply.

Alice turned back towards the electronic control panel hidden discreetly behind the nibbles table and started to dim the room's lights. The audience instantly stopped their conversations and spilled forward into the empty rows of seats. She faded up the apricot spotlight positioned over Audrey's lectern, and her boss was illuminated, revealed to the room. Alice searched the darkness to see where the woman with the smile had sat. She'd make sure she spoke to her later. Alice was a firm believer in following her instincts, and all her instincts were telling her she could help the woman with the sharp suit and soft face.

Theatrically, Audrey cleared her throat and laid her hand to her bosom. Everyone was seated and silent; the room was emphatically hers. Alice flicked a final switch and Audrey's microphone gently hummed into life. As if on cue, the audience leant collectively forward in edgy anticipation as they prepared to learn the elusive secrets to finding their Mr and Miss Rights.

KATE

'It's all the bloody *Daily Post*'s fault.' Kate picked up her glass of wine and took an angry gulp. 'If it didn't keep going on about how impossible it is to conceive after the age of thirty-five, we wouldn't even be thinking about this.'

Kate and Lou were in Luigi's wine bar for a 'Secret to Finding Mr Right' post-mortem. Kate liked Luigi's, with its battered wooden tables and soft candlelight. It had everything she wanted in a bar nowadays – booze, a seat and near-pitch-black lighting.

'*We're* not thinking about it. *You* are,' replied Lou, giving the barman her best, unmistakably lascivious look. Lou didn't believe in being ambiguous.

'Of course you are,' Kate contradicted her. 'Every woman who's in her thirties and single is thinking about it. It's *all* we think about. If you've not bagged a man and got yourself pregnant by thirty-five, you might as well skip straight to the end and reserve a single room in the retirement home.' In the half-light of the bar, Kate glowed with righteous indignation.

'But you're not thirty-five! And you're talking rubbish.'

Kate shook her head. 'Once we hit our thirties it's over. Men don't want us any more.'

'That's the spirit,' Lou deadpanned, her eyes scanning the bar for talent before settling back on the barman. He gave her a wink and twiddled – quite suggestively, Kate thought – with the beer taps.

'I'm just being realistic,' Kate reasoned. 'And the *Daily Post*'s enough to kill off anyone's positivity. It does a "time's running out" article every bloody week. You know what it said yesterday? There are twenty-eight million single women over the age of thirty-five in America, and only eighteen million single men. That means ten million women are going to spend the rest of their lives on the shelf just because of impossible maths.'

'Better cancel the emigration plans then.'

'Everyone knows that where America leads, we follow,' Kate stressed. 'The *Daily Post* says that in the next few years Britain's going to have an epidemic of single women. Apparently we've got a bleak future of longer working hours and later retirement to look forward to with none of the good stuff like babies, families and a husband to top up our pensions with. I'm telling you, Lou, *Sex and the City* wasn't a comedy: it was a warning!'

'Bollocks,' Lou scoffed. 'And since when did you believe everything you read in the papers? And what's with the hang-up about thirty-five? It's not like all the men suddenly fall off the face of the planet. Besides, we're forever hearing about those granny mums popping out kids in their sixties. When they smile you can see their dentures. You're only thirty-three and you've still got your own teeth – you've got bags of time.'

Kate twirled the stem of her wine glass. Lou was right about one thing: she shouldn't believe everything she read in the papers, not least because so many of the stories she'd planted there herself. Kate worked in PR – or 'in lies' as Lou liked to call it. She should know how much of what was written was exaggerated for the sake of a titillating daily read, because she was part of the machine that served it up. It was what she got paid to do.

But this seemed different. Surely it was an indisputable medical fact that your fertility dropped at thirty-five? And it certainly seemed that the number of men who looked your way decreased with every year you got further away from your twenties. What if it was just nature's way ... the dating equivalent of survival of the fittest? Just as the old, wobbly zebra at the back of the pack always gets eaten by the leopard, maybe men *couldn't help* getting less inter- ested in you the less able you were to breed? Could it be that – for the survival of the species – all men aged fifteen to a hundred were naturally programmed to fancy fertile twenty-one-year-olds? Judging by the number of men who'd been interested in her recently, Kate was sure this was true. Men were divining that any moment now her gums would recede and her ovaries collapse. She was, she realized with a sickening lurch, the wobbly zebra at the back of the pack. Good for a quick snack, but nothing more nutritious.

Kate looked up, ready to share this realization with Lou,

but her friend had pulled out her make-up bag and was flipping open her compact with the speed of a fast-draw cowboy.

Kate watched with a grudging admiration. She loved Lou, even though they were opposites. Lou was lots of the things she wished she could be: confident, brave, dramatic. She was the kind of woman who could emphasize both her eyes and her lips and not give a damn about whether she looked slutty. Slutty! That was another thing that Lou was that Kate wasn't. Kate admired Lou's promiscuity. She wished she could be more free and easy, but it just wasn't in her DNA. She fantasized about having reckless one-night stands in the way that Lou so regularly did. She thrilled at the idea of having sex with a stranger in an alley. But she just wasn't that kind of girl. She was more of a TV, pyjamas and early night kind of girl. And the pyjamas had to be Egyptian cotton and ironed with a crease down the front.

Suddenly she realized Lou was talking.

'For God's sake, Kate, wake up!' Lou barked as she multitasked drinking, applying sparkly black eyeshadow and simultaneously eyeing up the barman. 'You need to stop fannying about and get out there. Stop worrying about everything. You're way too young to be thinking about babies. You should be thinking about getting out of the office more. Having fun! Getting laid!'

Lou put down her make-up and looked at Kate seriously. 'I mean, Jesus, Kate, how long is it since your last shag?'

Kate choked in embarrassment.

'Use it or lose it!' Lou drained her glass and started packing away her armoury of make-up.

'You know what . . . you're right,' Kate agreed suddenly. 'Which is why I wanted to go to the talk tonight.'

'What, that pathetic excuse for dating advice?'

'It wasn't all bad . . .'

'You're joking!' Lou gawped in shock. 'It was the biggest pile of shit I've ever heard! Honestly, what was that madwoman on about? Do you think she's ever had a date in her life? And has she not heard of conditioner? I've seen better-hydrated pubes.' She poured them both another glass of wine. 'And hey; what was with you with the orange juice and the notes? You're such a swot!'

Kate coloured. 'I didn't want to forget anything.'

'It was a crappy talk, not an exam!' Lou was momentarily distracted by a bottom zigzagging back from the bar, its very drunk owner slopping his pint as he went. The bottom found its friends and sat down. Lou's eyes returned to Kate. 'And really, Kate, you've got to promise you won't do any of the things she recommended. Her advice was ridiculous. If you do what she says then you've probably already had the last shag of your life. She was a living, breathing hand-book on what *not* to do to get a man.'

'Says the woman who hasn't had a boyfriend in living memory,' Kate mumbled.

Lou's face darkened.

'Listen.' She leaned forward, jabbing a finger at Kate. 'If you want to stay single and childless and let your ovaries moss over, just like the *Daily Post* says they will, then go ahead and do what that demented woman said. It's like taking the fast track to spinsterdom. I mean, what was that rubbish about "accidentally" dropping your groceries into a man's shopping trolley? Please! I can't see anyone rushing to ask you out after you've dropped wine and Tampax on his veg.'

'I get my groceries delivered,' Kate said thoughtfully. 'The only opportunity there's the delivery man, and he's missing teeth.'

'Not to worry – there was always Audrey's brilliant suggestion of joining a club! What was it? Ah, that's right . . . Join a toastmaster's association. Fuck me, what a truly fantastic idea! I'm always hearing about young, attractive, thrusting man-about-town toastmasters. I bet their clubhouse is awash with sexed-up man-totty.'

'You're right; her advice was . . . questionable . . .' Kate paused as Lou snorted explosively. 'But that Alice lady was great. And the fact remains: we're single and we're knocking on a bit. And, as you so delicately pointed out, I'm hardly swamped with offers.'

'Swamped by your job, more like.'

'All I'm saying is, whether Audrey Cracknell is right or wrong, we're single. We're *always* single. I know you say you like it, but I don't. I'm sick of it. I don't want to suddenly wake up and realize it's too late. I want a man' – she saw Lou's eyes mentally undressing the barman – '. . . a *nice* man! Someone who isn't frightened of growing up and getting off the shagging-about merry-go-round. I want a boyfriend to take me out for dinner, to go for country walks with. Someone who's not going to be freaked out at the thought of meeting my mum. Someone to have kids with. But he's not going to land in my lap and I can't just leave it to chance. You know me; I don't like taking risks, and I can't risk getting any older and letting my face drop and my knees sag and my fertility dwindle and *still* being single. I'm not going to bang my head against a brick wall any more.'

There was a long pause. The two women looked each other in the eye, Lou's painted and kohl-heavy, bristling with scorn, Kate's more discreetly made-up in Bobbi Brown nudes, steady and determined. In the background Kate heard the owner of the bottom scrape back his chair, loudly declare he was off to 'siphon the python' and then fall over his briefcase, smacking face first into the wooden floor. As his mates burst into loud frat-boy laughter Lou broke eye contact.

'Well,' she said as she picked up her glass and drained it, '*you* might be fed up with banging your head against a brick wall, but I'm happy banging mine against my headboard, thanks. Or *his* headboard tonight, if he plays his cards right.' She picked up her handbag and headed back to the bar, her eyes fixed on the barman like a hawk focused on a fluffy field mouse.

'Same again?' she called back to Kate as she pulled out her purse and closed in.

Kate sighed, shook her head and reached for her mobile. She scrolled through her address book for a cab. All of a sudden she yearned for her bed. She looked up. Sure enough,

Lou already had her hand on the barman's chest and was suggestively fingering a shot glass. It was definitely time to go home. She pulled on her coat.

AUDREY

At exactly 8.30 a.m. Audrey Cracknell swept through the doors of the Table For Two dating agency, her coat billowing behind her. As ever, she was the first to arrive, and she had precisely thirty minutes to mentally prepare herself for the rigours of another day at the front line of matchmaking.

She flicked on the kettle and surveyed the empty office. This was her favourite part of the day, before the office became littered with staff and clients. She ran a finger over the surface of her desk to quality-test the work of the cleaners. Her finger came back perfectly pink. A burst of optimistic January sunshine filtered through the windows and bathed the room in its wash. It was a most satisfactory start to a Tuesday morning.

Audrey turned on her computer and set about tidying her desk. She couldn't countenance a messy desk. 'Always start with a clean bottom,' her father used to tell her. He'd served in the Royal Navy as a chef, and it probably applied to food hygiene but it made perfect sense to Audrey, who liked to start every day with a clean bottom.

At fifty-one years old, and a bracing five foot ten, Audrey

was what was kindly described as solid. Her bosom was a large and heavily bolstered shelf. Sturdy underwear ensured it rarely, if ever, moved. Her rounded shoulders gave way to fleshy arms that wobbled when she moved. Her frizzy, bright-orange hair sat awkwardly next to her farmer-red cheeks, like traffic lights stuck on both stop and wait.

Audrey stirred her coffee and took stock. Not only had last night's talk at the Holly Bush Hotel swelled the coffers with the admittance fees from a full house of singles wanting to discover the secret to meeting their future spouse, but according to Alice's text (which had taken Audrey several exasperated minutes to remember how to open), there'd been an exceptionally high number of converts signing up to join the agency too. And not just the online dating function, but the one-to-one optimum-fee-paying premium service! In all, there were fifteen new premium service members. It was probably Table For Two's most successful night ever.

The Table For Two dating agency was now in its eleventh year, and its eighth of profit. When Audrey's father died he'd left her a semi in the suburbs and £15,000 in cash. With her mother long departed, no siblings and a stifling job at the city council, the world had suddenly revealed itself – at the not-so-tender age of forty – as Audrey's dazzling oyster. What had seemed an inescapable path of paper-pushing and spinsterdom had suddenly widened to reveal infinite, sparkling possibility. She could go on a cruise, sell the house, lavish thousands on a chin-lift.

But what she really wanted was to be important. Although

single for her entire adult life, Audrey was nevertheless enchanted with the idea of old-fashioned courtship; of gentlemen who stood up when a lady entered a room. Plus she loved nothing more than a good nose into somebody else's business. While Audrey's own life was woefully lacking in gossip, other people's romantic fortunes were a source of intrigue for her, even if those other people were just the constant friends she found in the characters she watched on her soaps. What better way, she thought, to have an inexhaustible supply of real people's lives to feel important in than running a dating agency? And so Audrey decided to extend a plump, unmanicured toe into the invigorating waters of small business and set up her own matchmaker's bureau.

And here she was, eleven years later, still geographically living in her father's semi, but metaphorically a country mile away from her previous existence. Whereas the old Audrey had sometimes gone from one end of the week to the other without the sustaining fuel of a personal conversation, now she had hundreds of lonely people on her books, all reliant on her. And she got to hear – *first hand!* – the intimate stories of countless clients. Over the years, Table For Two had instigated 6,000 lunch dates that had led to nineteen church weddings and forty-two registry dos. And that didn't even include the online matches which – frankly – were anyone's guess. Audrey firmly believed that if you were paid peanuts, it was usually by monkeys. If a client wasn't prepared to invest in the one-to-one premium service to find a loving partner with whom to spend the rest of their lives, it stood to reason that they wouldn't be bothered to reply to a simple emailed enquiry to ascertain whether they'd left the online service because they'd successfully found a love match.

As Audrey scanned her emails, her eye was distracted by a framed photo on her desk. It was of a distinguished-looking man, dressed in a dinner suit. His jacket was open and his arm draped casually on the back of the chair next to him. He was smiling, his striking blue eyes crinkling warmly at the corners. Tied to his chair was a pale-pink balloon, and in the background a large round banqueting table was littered with the debris of a good night. Audrey had taken the photograph at the Dating Practitioners' Society annual ball years ago, and she'd kept it on her desk ever since. It wasn't the first Practitioners' Ball she'd attended with John, but it was the first time she'd taken her camera. She'd been longing for a photograph of him, and she'd finally plucked up the courage. Her hands had shaken with nerves, but miraculously the shot was perfect. Audrey looked at it hundreds of times a day. When the client on the phone described her perfect man, Audrey sometimes felt it was uncanny. It was as if her ladies could see what she was looking at, so often did their descriptions match John. She carefully traced her finger over his photograph.

'Morning!' a voice chimed across the office.

Audrey jumped. Alice was making her way across the room to her desk, her long woollen scarf trailing on the floor behind her. Audrey felt her hackles prickle. There was something about Alice that never failed to get her back up.

'Did you get my text? Wasn't it a fantastic evening?' Alice asked cheerfully as she pulled off her coat and slung it over the back of her chair, creating the day's first eyesore of mess. 'So many people, and so nice too! We all chatted for hours afterwards; it was such a shame you couldn't stay.' She pulled the lid off her coffee and blew across its steaming surface, her eyes finally resting on Audrey expectantly.

'Yes, fantastic,' Audrey murmured, trying to appear engrossed in her emails. This was one of the moments when she wished she'd invested in something more solid than glass for the partition to her office. At the time she'd thought a glass wall an ingenious idea. Not only did it create her own private office, a boss-like distance away from the open-plan area where her staff sat, but the clear pane meant she could still make sure they weren't wasting time on personal chit-chat. She'd even considered learning to lip-read for those moments when her office door was closed and she was sealed into her see-through kingdom with only muffles penetrating through.

At this particular moment, though, Audrey's door was wedged open, and Alice was peering through with all the perkiness of a cartoon bunny.

'Fifteen new premium service clients! That's got to be some kind of Table For Two record, hasn't it?'

'The premium service is the only sensible option,' Audrey lectured chillily. 'Anyone who's serious about meeting their future husband or wife knows the internet's not the place to find them. All this online dating nonsense is just a silly vogue that will soon go out of fashion. If you want a genuine love match, you do it face to face with a professional match-maker. Between the internet and all the other so-called matchmaking bureaus out there, the road to happiness can be a dangerous place. Those fifteen new clients are lucky they found us.'

'Absolutely!' Alice nodded vigorously. She seemed at a loss as to what to say next, so she bowed her head and set about her paperwork.

Audrey wondered what it was about Alice that annoyed her so. She wasn't unpleasant, she supposed, and she was helpful in her own sort of way. But there was just some-thing about her . . . She always claimed to be busy, but was forever staring out of the window in a daze. And then there were her clothes. Underneath the cardigans and corduroy there was probably a perfectly decent figure; it was just drowning in wool. Where was the girl's colour? Her vibrancy? And that hair! How old must Alice be? Twenties? Thirties? Audrey wasn't sure. But she *was* sure that, what-ever her age, Alice was too old for plaits. It was bad for business. The staff of a dating agency should be attractive, romantically successful individuals. Gentlemen clients should look at her girls and hope to be matched with a woman just like them.

Audrey grimaced and returned to her emails. Today was a good day, she reminded herself. Not only were there fifteen more clients, but there was also the matter of this year's Dating Practitioners' Society annual ball . . . and only three weeks away! The ball was the highlight of Audrey's year, and this one would be better than ever. Table For Two was finally catching up with Love Birds, its biggest rival, run by the dreadful Sheryl Toogood. The ball would give Audrey the chance to point out that Table For Two client numbers were up twenty-three per cent. She was sure Sheryl Toogood couldn't come close to matching that, no matter how hard she bluffed it.

And then there was John. She couldn't wait to have him sitting at her side, attentive and urbane. She'd have to call Geraldine and make sure the date was in his diary. She couldn't believe she hadn't done so already. She'd attend to it tonight as a priority.

There was a kerfuffle at the door and in came the rest of the Table For Two staff: Bianca and Cassandra, with Hilary, the website co-ordinator, puffing in their wake. Audrey frowned. Hilary was pregnant again, and getting larger by the day. She'd be disappearing on another stint of maternity leave soon, leaving Audrey with the double inconvenience of having to bankroll her baby-tending holiday *and* having to oversee Table For Two's online dating service in her absence. She wasn't sure which inconvenience irritated her the most.

As the morning chit-chat swirled around the office, Audrey noticed Alice staring into the distance in a dream. She bristled. It was time to get her to pull her socks up. There was no room in the world of Audrey Cracknell, Audrey Cracknell told herself, for shirkers. And shirkers who looked like spinsters were even worse.

LOU

'I'm going to do it,' Kate declared defiantly on the other end of the phone. 'And you should do it too.'

'Wha . . . ?' Lou groped for her watch by the side of her bed. 'For fuck's sake, Kate, what time is it? This had better be an emergency. Your mother had better have died.'

'Five to nine,' Kate replied matter-of-factly. Lou could hear the muted burble of the office in the background. Kate was an early riser and had probably already been at work for several hours. Lou was not what could be termed a morning person and had chosen a career in bar work specifically for the 11 a.m. starts.

'Did you hear what I said? I'm going to do it.'

Lou rubbed her eyes and fell heavily back onto her pillow.

'Do what, you mad, sleep-wrecking cow?' she yawned. She stretched out her hand to the other side of the bed. It was empty. With a wince she remembered last night.

'Sign up to the Table For Two dating agency and meet the man of my dreams.'

Lou made a strange noise, somewhere between a laugh, a yawn and a snort.

'You *are* joking, right?'

'Nope, I'm deadly serious. Their one-to-one personal service.'

'Have you been drinking?'

'Of course not; it's five to nine!'

Lou rubbed her eyes again. Some of last night's make-up smeared across her face.

'So let me get this straight. You took a bang to the head after leaving the bar last night, and you've woken up thinking that handing over God knows how many of your hard-earned pounds to that ginger-haired matron with knockers down to her knees is going to make all the difference and you're suddenly going to find a man and live happily ever after?'

'I'm not going to sign up with Audrey; I'm not completely mad!' Kate laughed. 'If she picks up the phone I'm going to hang up. No, I'm going to ring that nice Alice.'

'The frumpy librarian in the woolly socks? Smart move!'

'It doesn't matter what she looks like. It's about how she's going to open me up to new people; widen my horizons.'

Lou sat up.

'You mean lower your standards and get you dating retards! Jesus, Kate. Remember how strange the men were last night? They were so far beneath your league, they're ... they're ...' Lou threw back her duvet in disgust and got out of bed. 'This isn't funny. You've got to be winding me up. What's wrong with going to the pub or using the internet like everyone else?'

'The internet's for shoe-shopping, not man-shopping.'

'Sounds like an excuse to me.'

'It's not,' Kate replied tartly. 'I just don't want to do internet dating. It's too public, putting your profile up for everyone to see; I don't trust people's motives; they don't tell the truth. And as for going to pubs ... hey, what happened with that barman last night?'

'What? Oh. Not my kind.'

'Since when was any man not your kind?'

Lou arched an eyebrow. 'At least I have a kind. Anyway, I still don't see why you have to join a dating agency. It's a bit bloody old-school.'

'I don't want to do it fashionably, I want to do it *right*. I'm sick and tired of *working* at finding a boyfriend. I work hard all day at the office. Finding a boyfriend shouldn't feel like yet another job to be done. So I'm going to outsource. I want to pay my money, sit back and let the experts deliver some quality candidates to wine and dine me. I don't want some internet shark who's just after sex. I want someone who's serious about settling down and having a family.'

Lou chewed her lip.

'Well, you certainly seem determined.'

'I am,' said Kate in her most determined tones.

There was a long silence. Lou heard Kate fend off a colleague.

'Well, go for it then,' she said lightly. 'Good luck.'

'Do you really mean that?' Kate asked, her voice immediately vulnerable.

'Yes,' Lou replied as she groped for the bathroom light.

'If you're daft enough to shell out cash to meet balding, slopey-shouldered rejects who've probably never had a girl-friend in their lives, let alone a shag, then you're going to need all the luck you can get. They're all the same men, you know . . . on the internet or from a dating agency. They're just the leftovers because the good ones our age have already been taken. You're better off just going to a bar and pulling a twenty-four-year-old.'

Lou was suddenly struck by a flashback. What was it the barman had said last night? *Thanks, but no offence, I don't do older chicks.* No offence? Immature little scumbag. Cheeky little fucker. She looked at herself in the mirror. Older chick my arse, she thought as she checked out her panda mascara eyes and shades-of-grey complexion. She could still swing it. She just needed a pair of straighteners and a layer of slap. It was all in the presentation and the lighting. Besides, nobody looks good in the morning.

'So, come on . . . How much is this privilege going to cost you, then?' she asked aggressively.

'Three hundred, and then a hundred a month.'

'Bloody hell, Kate! What if it takes you a year to find someone?'

'It won't!' Kate replied confidently. 'I'll have professionals helping me; it'll probably all be sorted in a couple of weeks. Besides, it *can't* take that long; I haven't got the time. I'm already behind schedule.'

'Behind schedule?'

Kate lowered her voice so she couldn't be overheard.

'Well, I want to have two children, and I've always wanted

them before I'm thirty-five. Ideally there should be two years between them so they're not too close together at school, so that takes me back to at least thirty-two. Obviously I should be married first; and I've always thought my husband and I should have at least a year together to just enjoy being a couple and to have some nice upmarket holidays before the kids come along and we have to go to theme parks . . . *So that's thirty-one.* And we should have been together eighteen months before getting engaged – any longer and it looks like he's keeping his options open in case someone better comes along . . . *twenty-nine and a half.* And everyone knows you need at least another eighteen months to organize a decent wedding . . .'

'Christ almighty, am I dreaming this? Am I still asleep?'

'. . . so you can see how far behind I am!' Kate's voice was getting louder and just a little bit shrill. 'I should have met Mr Right when I was twenty-eight; I should be giving birth to baby number one now! I'm already five years late as it is, so it can't take me another year to find the right man; it just *can't!*'

The line suddenly went silent.

Lou exhaled in bewildered shock.

'Kate, how come I never knew you were mental?'

'There's nothing mental about having a life plan,' Kate replied obstinately.

For a rare, brief moment Lou was at a complete loss as to what to say.

'Lou, come on, please!' Kate implored. 'I need you to be positive about this. I'm doing a very brave thing.'

There was a pause.

'Don't suppose there's any chance you'd join with me?'

'Fuck, no!'

'Not even for a laugh?'

'If I want a laugh I'll look at myself naked. And if I want a man I'll go to a cheap bar, like any other sane woman. I, for one, haven't hit rock bottom.'

'Well, I have!' said Kate chirpily. 'And I'm going to call Table For Two right now, get them to find me a fantastic man and live happily ever after,' and she hung up before Lou could retaliate.

Lou put the phone down on the side of the bath and gave herself a long, hard look in the mirror.

'Unfuckingbelievable,' she deadpanned to the empty bathroom.

ALICE

Alice was having trouble concentrating on her paperwork. No matter how hard she tried, her mind kept wandering.

She *loved* fifty per cent of her job. When it came to interviewing new clients and discovering their dreams, she was in her element. Each client felt like a brand-new adventure, a voyage with her as captain of the ship. It was her mission to navigate them through the choppy waters of dating and into the calm of a tropical paradise where their perfect partner was waiting, probably stretched out in a hula outfit on a sun-drenched rock. The morning after taking on a new client, Alice would rush into work early to scour the files and find their romantic match. She'd lose herself for hours, weighing up each prospective partner, imagining their conversations and chewing the top of her biro as she thought through all possible pairings.

The post-date follow-up calls and the counselling for patience Alice also loved. It was all about keeping her clients positive. Positive people were attractive people, and so she saw it as her duty to keep everyone's spirits up. She phoned her clients often, meeting for impromptu coffees if their morale was flagging. When they were crushed over a false start, she was crushed too. The match, after all, had been born in her imagination. Making successful matches was the stuff that filled her dreams at night. And the whiff of romance was what made her days magical.

The paperwork, on the other hand, Alice hated. She'd never been great at knuckling down. All her life people had called her a dreamer. Alice agreed. Things were more exciting with the technicolour of a little daydreaming. It was real life, but airbrushed better.

But today was Tuesday, which was paperwork day at Table For Two. Everyone was sitting at their desks, heads bent over their screens. It was the only time the office was quiet. Even Audrey wasn't immune from paperwork Tuesdays. Alice could see her in her glass-walled office, frowning heavily at her computer.

Alice stared blankly at the figures on her own computer, willing them to make sense. It was no good. Try as she might to focus on the numbers, she couldn't help but start picturing the face of a man. Not just any man. *The* man. The one for her. She hadn't met him yet, but he was out there, she was sure of it. You had to believe that, in this line of work, she reasoned. You had to believe in Prince Charmings.

Alice's own Prince Charming was forever popping into her head. She'd met him a thousand times – sometimes in the supermarket, sometimes the swimming pool, the library, the bus stop, the pub. Other women wanted Prince Charmings with big muscles, fat bank balances and a wardrobe full of the right kind of clothes. But Alice's Prince Charming was more likely to be brandishing a charity bucket than a bulging wallet. Today her Prince Charming was a florist, delivering flowers to women all over the city. Alice imagined women sighing as they accepted his bouquets, disappointed that they were from their husbands and not Prince Charming. He'd almost run Alice over in his delivery van and would rush to check she was OK. She'd be fine, just attractively flushed and a little shaken. He wouldn't hear of her cycling home when she could be in shock. He'd stow her bike amongst the tulips and azaleas in the back of his van and give her a lift home. Thanks to his perfect mental recall and uncanny ability to predict her favourite flower, the next day she'd find a huge bunch of gerberas on her doorstep and a note asking her to dinner.

Alice sighed. That was the trouble with this job. You were paid to think about ideal partnerships all day long, so how could you not think about your own perfect date? It was like putting an alcoholic behind the bar and telling him to sit on his hands. Was she a romanceaholic, Alice wondered? Did such people exist?

She gave up on her paperwork.

'Anyone want a coffee?' She broke the silence.

'Just what the doctor ordered!' said Hilary, relieved by the distraction. 'Wanna hand?' She started to pull herself up from her seat.

'No, you stay where you are,' Alice said with a smile. Hilary beamed gratefully over her pregnant belly.

'Bianca?' Alice prompted.

'Please,' Bianca murmured without removing her eyes from her computer. Alice eyed the top of Bianca's head. The January sunshine was catching her neat rows of honeyed highlights, making her hair look like spun gold. Bianca always looked together and classy in a way that Alice simply couldn't. Even if she actually bothered ironing a shirt for work, an hour later Alice still looked like she'd slept in her clothes.

'Were you dragged through a hedge backwards this morning?' Audrey once asked her loudly across the office. 'Twice?'

Bianca, on the other hand, looked like she woke up in full, artfully understated make-up every morning, photo-shoot-ready from the pillow. With her ever-fresh hair and pearly oval fingernails, she was the kind of woman who, just by looking at her, made you feel you were somehow failing your sex.

'Did someone say cappuccino?' chirped Cassandra loudly. 'I'll have mine extra skinny.'

'I wasn't going to . . .'

'And one of those big cookies. Bugger the diet.'

'Er, right.'

Cappuccinos meant a trip to the coffee shop round the corner. Alice hadn't intended to leave the office – a Nescafé courtesy of the office kettle would have done. But at least a trip outside meant ten minutes away from the paper-work.

She pulled on her coat. On the mat the post lay ignored.

Alice scooped up the envelopes and caught her breath. There were two handwritten envelopes. She felt a thrill of excitement. Gingerly she pushed open the door to Audrey's office.

'Coffee?' Her breath was unsteady as she self-consciously put Audrey's letter on her desk. 'I'm nipping to the shop . . .'

Audrey grunted but didn't look up. Alice hovered expectantly. She'd put the handwritten envelope tantalizingly close to Audrey's line of vision. The envelope was thick and cream, and was addressed in swirly gold calligraphy. Alice had been sent one too, and she had an idea what it might be. She paused, telepathically urging Audrey to see it. Audrey's eyes were fixed on her computer.

'Looks like you've got an invitation to something,' Alice prompted. 'It's a handwritten envelope . . . with gold pen.'

Everyone at Table For Two had a keenly developed 'wedding radar', and gold pen could only mean one thing . . . nuptials! Weddings were the holy grail of the dating agency. To set up a match that ended in a wedding was the golden goose of matchmaking. It was what all the staff – and all the clients – wanted most. It was the stuff that sent the company brochure to the printers for a revamp, and it was what prompted Audrey to hang the expense and take out an ad in the local gazette – not just to lure in new clients, but to lord it over the rival agencies too. In this age of one-night stands, virtual relationships and text sex, a wedding was a modern miracle.

Audrey snapped her head up and gazed penetratingly at

Alice. Alice could almost see the words 'gold pen' sinking in.

'Yes, well, get along now.' She shooed her away.

Alice scuttled back to her desk, coat still on, and tore open her own handwritten envelope whilst simultaneously trying to spy on Audrey through the glass wall. Her heart beating fast, she yanked out the card. Her eyes danced along the words hurriedly, trying to take them in before Audrey could do the same ... 'Mr & Mrs Derek Whitworth' ... 'request the pleasure of' ... 'wedding' ... Yes, *wedding*!

Alice's eyes flew up to Audrey's office. She could see Audrey's eyes making their way across the same card, her hand creeping up to her bosom in excitement as she read.

'. . . of Jason Christopher Lee to Jennifer Lesley Whitworth.'

Jason and Jennifer! They were one of hers! Alice cried out in happiness. How fantastic! They were such a great couple. She'd set them up herself, and now they were getting married! She'd done it! She'd matched a marriage!

Suddenly Audrey shot out from her office, waving the invitation aloft.

'Ladies,' she declared loudly, a wobble in her voice and a flush on her neck. 'We have a Table For Two wedding!'

The office erupted in squeals. Cassandra and Bianca hugged each other with delight. Hilary – wedged in her seat – wolf-whistled loudly. Audrey kept waving the invitation whilst triumphantly declaring, '*A wedding, a wedding!*' Only Alice was quiet. She was staring at her own invitation, rereading it to make sure it was real.

Mr & Mrs Derek Whitworth
request the pleasure of
.... Alice Brown .....
at the wedding of
Jason Christopher Lee to Jennifer Lesley Whitworth
Bramley Church, Honey Blossom Lane
Saturday April 6th, 3 p.m.
Followed by dinner & dancing at The Rectory
RSVP

It was there in gold and cream. She'd done it. Another one of her matches had made it all the way to the altar! Jennifer had been her client for a few months, and as soon as Jason joined the books Alice had known they'd be a perfect match. And now they were getting married! Her eyes prickled with tears of happiness. She looked at her celebrating colleagues, a beaming smile on her face.

'Of course, I always knew Jason and Jennifer were the real thing,' Audrey said as she sank into the nearest seat and fanned herself with her invitation.

Bianca was rummaging in the office fridge for the bottle of cava kept for special occasions.

'I knew it the moment I set them up. I said to them, "Mark my words, I've got the perfect partner for you." A matchmaker gets a sixth sense about these things.'

Alice's smile froze. The excitement drained down her body and collected in a lump in the pit of her stomach. It had been *her* match, *her* idea. She was the one who'd phoned them and arranged the dates – not Audrey!

But Audrey was steamrollering on.

'This is my twentieth Table For Two wedding, ladies. Hurry up with that champagne, Bianca! This is what you should have as your goal when you're making matches. It's not about finding partners. It's about finding husbands and wives. Matchmaking a wedding is the crème de la crème. That's what you should aim for: crème!'

Alice numbly accepted a glass of cava. She felt sick. Audrey *knew* it had been her match.

'Of course, girls, I really shouldn't be surprised by these latest nuptials,' Audrey continued immodestly. 'After all, when I launched Table For Two, the first five matches I ever made *did* all make it up the aisle!'

'And not a single one since,' Hilary muttered darkly, loud enough for only Alice to hear. Alice smiled weakly in gratitude. At least Hilary wasn't fooled by Audrey's blatant credit-pinching. Besides, she and Hilary always shared a secret smirk whenever Audrey regaled them with this story – which was at least twice a week. It was the first thing visitors to the website were bombarded with, and it was emblazoned triumphantly across the front cover of the company brochure. The story of Audrey's matching prowess had reached such flowery Table For Two legend that Audrey was bound to have it carved on her headstone.

'To weddings!' Hilary toasted loudly, her irony unnoticed by the majority of the room.

'To my nose for a perfect match!' trilled Audrey triumphantly. 'It never lets me down!'

Bianca and Cassandra cheered.

Alice took a tiny sip of her drink. She knew the truth. And so did Jennifer and Jason.

Everyone was too busy celebrating to hear the phone ring, its sound buried beneath their hysterical chatter. Alice picked it up.

'Good morning, Table For Two,' she said hollowly.

'Is that Alice?' a nervous voice asked.

'Speaking.'

'Thank God for that! It's me; Kate, Kate Biggs ... From last night ...?'

'Oh, hi, Kate.' Alice shrugged out of her coat and laid her wedding invitation aside. 'How are you? What can I do for you?'

'I'm going for it. I'd like to join up, please!'

'That's fantastic news!' Alice said with as much encouragement as she could muster. 'Well done! You won't regret it, I promise.'

Audrey could take all the credit, Alice thought to herself. She knew the truth. And this was what the job was all about – people like Kate Biggs, and their dreams. And Alice was going to do her very best to make those dreams come true. She twisted away from Audrey's triumphant noises and concentrated on the phone call.

KATE

Kate pushed through the office door, trained her eyes on the floor and concentrated on getting to her desk at racing-driver speed. She shoved her shopping under her desk and tried to look as if she'd been rooted to the same spot for a day and a half.

She sneaked a look at her watch. Why did she feel so guilty whenever she took a lunch break? She'd only been gone for forty-five minutes: barely enough time for Julian, her boss, to have finished his starter at The Privet. Julian always took ridiculously long lunch breaks. And Kate was always working through hers. Not for the first time that day (or any day), Kate pondered the bitter irony of the fact that the more you got paid and the more senior you became, the fewer hours you bothered to work for your money.

Normal working hours didn't apply to either Kate or Julian, but in totally opposite ways. Kate was always the first to arrive at the office at 7.30 a.m., and was always the last to leave. But Julian had the working hours of a primary-school child. He'd be in by 9.00, and would spend the first half-hour perched on some unfortunate colleague's desk, arrogantly swinging his leg, chomping on a croissant and blindly spitting out flakes of pastry (Kate had frequently gone to the loo mid-morning to discover chunks of Julian's breakfast in her hair). And then he'd be off for a couple of so-called meetings, which largely involved him braying with laughter over a male client's lame attempts at humour, or flirting gruesomely with the female clients.

A hard morning of braying and flirting would be topped off by lunch, which usually ran from 12.00 to 3.00. This would be followed by a very noisy half-hour in the office, with Julian demanding to see everyone's press plans and then snorting at their ideas, before jumping into his sports car and abandoning ship. By 3.30 p.m., Julian's Blackberry would be switched off whilst he bandied some nonsense about 'brain-storming' or 'networking'. But everyone knew he'd screeched out of the car park and straight into the nearest old-boys members' bar. Or failing that, he'd be sporting a ridiculous Aran tank top whilst idly slinging a few tennis balls around a court with an ageng public-school chum.

Kate hated him.

A lot.

However, she loved her job.

A lot.

No matter how irritating Julian was, working for Julian Marquis PR was fantastic. And Kate had to admit that for the few short minutes a day when Julian put the work in, he was brilliant. Julian Marquis PR was the hottest public-relations company in the city, and to land a job there was a real career boost. The hours were exhausting, but no two days were the same, and watching Julian spin a new idea, or manipulate a tabloid editor to write exactly what he told him to, was awe-inspiring. And the thrill of seeing one of her stories in a national newspaper never failed to give Kate a soaring, bursting-with-pride high.

As Kate whizzed through her emails her eye fell on her shopping bags. She felt a small twinge of guilt at the punishment she'd just put her credit card through, but it was instantly extinguished by a surge of excitement. What woman alive couldn't be moved to ecstasy by the purchase of a cripplingly expensive but exquisitely beautiful pair of shoes? And Kate had managed to buy three new pairs this lunchtime alone! It had been a necessity. Well, one pair was, at least. She needed to look just right for her meeting at Table For Two. She'd already spent hours agonizing over what to wear. She wanted to give the right impression. She didn't want to look too keen, or too . . . *single*. She wanted to look like a successful woman; someone in control of her life; someone who men routinely threw themselves at. She wanted to look like the kind of woman who didn't need to go to a dating agency at all, but was giving it a go as some kind of modern social experiment. The right outfit, Kate believed, could say all this. And as every woman knows, a killer outfit starts with the shoes.

Kate resisted the urge to photograph her new purchases on her iPhone and send the pictures to Lou. Instead she nudged her shopping out of sight and set about applying herself to her work. Today she really had to concentrate on one of her less glamorous clients: the Pedigree Pooch account. ('It might be bitch offal to you,' Julian had stated blithely when Kate and her colleagues sighed on learning they'd won the business, 'but to me it's twelve mortgage payments and a week in the south of France.')

Kate's dog-food client had created a new variety of 'jellied meat chunks for the discerning hound' and had tasked Julian Marquis PR with devising some 'sexy' ways to promote it. Kate had had to fight not to choke with laughter when the client had come out with this, straight-faced and earnest, in the briefing meeting. But it had been even harder not to convulse (so hard it had actually hurt) as she watched Julian bend over backwards to agree that their brand-new jellied meat chunks did indeed look appetizing and that canine food had never been so mouth-wateringly gourmet.

Kate soon lost herself in thought over how exactly she could make dog meat sexy . . .

Two hours later, Julian burst back into the office, his jacket rumpled and his eyes alarmingly wide.

'Katy, darling!' he chimed extravagantly. 'What's hanging?'

Kate hated being called Katy. Only Julian did it. She'd corrected him numerous times, but it seemed to go in one ear and out the other.

'I've just been coming up with some ideas for the Pedigree Pooch account,' she managed politely.

'Ah, tempting tripe for the pampered pet. Well, come on then! Amaaaaaaze me,' Julian drooled sarcastically, dropping himself onto her desk. 'Tell me how you're going to single-handedly make us all wish we were yappy, flea-ridden lapdogs, just so we can chomp down the latest treats from Pedigree Pooch.'

'Well,' Kate started awkwardly. She could sense everyone in the office listening in. 'You know how they have farmers' markets in front of the Corn Exchange?'

'Yes, yes, yes.'

'Well, I thought we could stage a gourmet pet-food festival there instead,' Kate said tentatively.

'Go onnnnnnnnn,' Julian drawled pensively.

'Pedigree Pooch could take over the square for the day, and set up lots of stalls with chefs – real chefs in hats and chefs' whites – cooking up delicious organic feasts, all for dogs.'

There was a pause. Kate stumbled on.

'So we'd have lots of woks and top-of-the-range barbecues, all cooking different things. For instance, one chef could be cooking an organic doggy lamb stew, and the dogs could come along to sample it – once it's cooled down, of course. The chefs could talk through the recipes as they cook, so the owners could see first-hand the kind of ingredients that Pedigree Pooch use – which would all be fresh and locally sourced. And another stall could do doggy fish dishes: blackened cod, maybe? Or salmon fishcakes? And another could do doggy desserts: not sugary ones . . . They'd have to be healthy and good for dogs' teeth. So I was thinking of a doggy cup cakes, with hidden grated courgette – and instead of icing they could be topped with Philadelphia/apple purée mix. It's much lower-fat, especially if you use Philadelphia Light. I saw it on a diet cookery programme . . . For humans, obviously,' she added hastily, realizing the office had gone deathly silent. 'I don't think they do diet cookery programmes for pets.'

Julian was uncharacteristically quiet. There was a long pause. The air prickled with tension. Kate meekly added her final idea.

'And at the end of the day the dogs could go home with a bag of samples from the stalls . . . You know . . . a doggy bag.'

Someone sniggered. Kate's stomach sank.

'I don't know what you lot are laughing at!' Julian snapped back into life, eyeballing the staff aggressively. 'Katy, my darling, it's total bloody genius!'

Kate went weak with relief.

'Genius!' he whooped as he started jigging around the office. 'The Pedigree Pooch lot will expire with excitement!' He kissed the top of her head. 'Quick! Write it up and set up a meeting with the Pooch posse asap. They're going to love it!'

And he waltzed off into his office.

Kate felt almost giddy with praise. Julian liked the idea! She couldn't believe it! She looked at her watch. Maybe she'd get home at a decent time after all. She really hoped so. Tonight she wanted to finally nail down which outfit she was going to wear for her Table For Two meeting – *and* plan out the accessories. Her appointment with Alice was a few days away yet, but she liked to be prepared. After all, she had a lot riding on it: an end to Friday nights in on her own and a potential lifetime of loved-up happiness, no less! It *had* to go well.

Smiling, she turned to her computer and opened a new document.

ALICE

One of the many forms that new clients at the Table For Two dating agency had to fill in contained the questions, 'What is your ideal Saturday night out?' and 'What is your perfect Sunday morning?' While Alice could never be sure of her ideal Saturday night out, she was very clear on her version of Sunday morning Utopia ... a leisurely browse around her local garden centre.

There was something very liberating about slopping around Greenfingers in a tatty jumper and her oldest jeans. The mere sight of the orderly rows of plants – immaculately laid out like disciplined soldiers, yet rebelliously unsymmetrical like naughty schoolboys – would make Alice's spirits rise. She'd lose an hour or two wandering up and down the aisles of baby clematis or azaleas, imagining the riots of colour they'd soon burst into. As Alice looked along a row of rangy hellebores, the thought struck her that garden centres were really centres of hope. You didn't buy bulbs, you bought little bundles of optimism, courtesy of Mother Nature. All you had to do was plant them and water them and you were rewarded with beautiful explosions of colour.

Alice wheeled her pushbike up the driveway to Greenfingers and padlocked it to a railing. It was five minutes to ten, and she was the only impatient gardener waiting for the doors to open. She looked at her reflection in the glass door. Her hair was all over the place (she must have forgotten to brush it again) and she was wearing an old pair of jeans she'd got from a charity shop. Her jumper had a big hole in the front from an accident with a branch. She looked, as Audrey would say, like something the cat dragged in.

Dudley, the security guard, peered through the glass of the door and smiled at her. She beamed back at him. She and Dudley had had many Sunday morning chats before the rest of the world arrived. Like her, Dudley loved the tranquillity of the outdoor section of the garden centre. Neither of them liked the indoor area, with its piped music, bored kids and harassed parents. But outdoors, where it was cold and quiet, and the only noise was the babbling of the water-feature displays – that was what made Alice leap out of bed on a Sunday morning.

Dudley pulled back the doors and Alice headed through the shop, past the aisles of creosote and Baby Bio, and out into the courtyard. She sighed happily, drank in the atmosphere and delved into the first row of greenery.

When Alice had bought her one-bedroom garden flat on Eversley Road she'd discovered a love of gardening. It had come as quite a surprise. The flat didn't have much of a garden, just a square of paving stones and a scrawny yew tree. But the garden had two very important things going for it – it was totally private and totally hers! It became Alice's sacred space – a place for peace, quiet and daydreaming. It was where Alice could really be Alice.

Within a few months the paving stones had come up, the yew tree was coaxed into life, and borders had been created, stuffed with vibrant cascades of flowers. A friend had helped Alice haul home a two-metre free-standing window box and she'd filled it with fragrant flowers and herbs. In summer, when the French doors in her bedroom were open, Alice could lie in bed and breathe in the warm scent of lavender.

Alice spent a contented hour humming amongst Green-fingers' bedding plants, filled her bike's pannier basket with greenery and headed home. As she cycled along she felt happy. She loved her job at Table For Two, and had some great clients. She believed in good karma and happy endings, and that nice things happened to nice people. It wasn't often that she got a client she didn't like – weirdly, Audrey always seemed to want those clients for her own list – but when she did, she found them very hard to match.

Alice turned into Eversley Road and pedalled hard to get up the hill to her flat. She grimaced. She was embarrassed to admit it, but Audrey intimidated her. She knew Audrey didn't like her. Alice did her best to be friendly, but when-ever she spoke the words seemed to die in her mouth. She'd witter, desperately trying to fill the yawning silence whilst Audrey eyeballed her with derision. It had always been the same, and Alice had been at Table For Two for years. Six months into her job, she'd considered leaving. But she liked her clients too much. Clients come and go – or they should if she matched them successfully. The problem was that Alice *always* had clients she liked. She didn't want to abandon them before she'd fixed them up. And as fast as she fixed them up new clients would come in. Before she knew it all thoughts of leaving had been forgotten.

Alice reached her flat, dismounted her bike and carried the plants inside. She looked at her watch. Good – she had enough time to potter in the garden before cooking the Sunday roast. Ginny was coming round at three with Dan and the baby. Happy in the knowledge that she had a couple of hours of green-fingered pleasure ahead, she stepped into her garden with a smile.

KATE

Monday morning had finally arrived.

Kate took a deep breath, smoothed down her brand-new Reiss skirt-suit (nothing she already owned was quite right, she'd decided), and walked purposefully through the doors of the Table For Two dating agency. Inside was an open-plan office with several women talking busily on the phone. There was no nice, safe reception desk to walk towards, so Kate loitered awkwardly by the door, rocking unsteadily on her new heels.

Eventually the woman at the nearest desk put down her phone and smiled.

'Yes, love. Who are you here for?'

'Alice.' Despite her best intentions, Kate's voice still came out sounding nervous.

The woman twisted and looked across the office. As she moved, Kate noticed her belly. She was pregnant: hugely pregnant! Good, Kate thought excitedly. This was exactly the result she'd be paying for: a fast ticket through the games and nonsense. She'd obviously entered an arena of success. This was a place where women found boyfriends who became husbands who became fathers. She hoped this success was infectious – ideally, airborne and immediate.

The woman turned back.

'She's on the phone. Pop yourself down on the sofa and make yourself comfortable. She won't be long.'

She pointed towards a seating area that Kate hadn't noticed before. Kate backed awkwardly into the sofa and tried not to look nervous.

The pregnant woman immediately immersed herself in another phone call. Kate peered surreptitiously around. She'd been wondering what a dating agency would look like. Last night, just as she'd been drifting off to sleep, she'd been struck by the sudden, terrifying thought that it would have huge mugshots of its clients on the walls – like a giant police line-up of the most desperate people in town. The thought had kept her awake for hours. But there was no such gallery of shame. In fact, it looked disappointingly normal.

Suddenly the door swung open and a delivery man burst in, brandishing a super-sized bouquet of flowers. He loitered, his head and upper body almost entirely obscured by the enormous, cascading blooms. Seconds passed. And then a loud knock made Kate jump in her seat, and the bunch-of-flowers-on-legs headed over to an area separated from the rest of the room by a glass wall. Rapping imperiously on the pane was Audrey Cracknell. Barely pausing in her telephone conversation, she ushered the walking flowers in, accepted them without so much as a blink and dismissed the delivery man with a wave of her hand. Kate felt a momentary sense of relief that she wasn't signing up with Audrey today. There was something utterly terrifying about her. But the relief was immediately followed by awe. This was a place where women were sent bouquets of flowers from their admirers: *even women like Audrey!*

'Hello again, Kate.'

A friendly looking woman stood in front of her, smiling kindly.

'Alice!' Kate jumped up and nervously started pumping her hand. She was then led across the office into a small room, where Alice shut the door behind them. The room contained two wicker armchairs and a low coffee table, empty but for a laptop, a bunch of white flowers and a box of tissues.

'Are they in case I cry?' Kate laughed awkwardly, pointing at the tissues.

'Well,' Alice began gently, 'the interview room is where we find out about you, the things you like and what you want for yourself. Some people find it difficult, especially if they've been looking for a partner for a long time.' She caught sight of Kate's stricken face and smiled. 'Don't worry. Most just find it really exciting to think about the people they're going to meet. Right! Let's get started, shall we?'

As the minutes passed, Kate relaxed. She hadn't been wrong about Alice; she liked her. She couldn't imagine going through this process with Audrey. The very thought of opening her heart to her was terrifying. But Alice wasn't scary; she was nice, warm; she exuded kindness. She was a bit scruffy and could really do with a tailored jacket and a pair of sheer tights – and those shoes were a bit . . . vintage. But she had great cheekbones, fantastic skin and she seemed really on the ball. And she was very easy to talk to. So easy that Kate found herself saying way more than she'd intended. Over the weekend she'd carefully planned her interview strategy: she'd be articulate and in control; she'd impress Alice with her calm sophistication and snappy dressing. But now that she was here she couldn't stop gabbling. It was as though her brain had lost control of her mouth, and her tongue had escaped on a frenzied rampage; she couldn't shut up!

'If you could describe your ideal partner,' Alice asked, taking advantage as Kate paused for air, 'what would he be like?'

'Well,' said Kate, wondering how much detail to give. 'I'd like him to be tall . . . dark . . . good-looking. He'd have a nice smile, maybe with dimples. And a strong jaw; clean-shaven. Straight white teeth. The kind of teeth you get from having a brace when you were little. And blue eyes, I love blue eyes. He'd have a good job, the kind of job he has to wear a suit for. I guess he'd be a manager, or some kind of entrepreneur. He'd have a car, obviously, but nothing too flashy. Maybe an Audi or a Saab. Not a BMW; they're too obvious. He'd be a really good boss, kind to his staff. He'd have a decent income. Six figures and prospects to be on the board. Not that I'm a gold-digger or anything. I love my job! It's just, I want us to have a nice house and go on nice holidays, and not have to worry. Besides, men should be ambitious; it makes them more manly, don't you think? And I've always fancied St Lucia. So a good work ethic's a must. Oh, and he's got to be sporty, but not sport-mad; so he'd go to the gym but definitely wouldn't be glued to Sky Sports all weekend. He's got to like kids and want two of them: a boy and a girl, ideally. Oh, and he'd need to be a family person – you know, nice to his mum, happy to pop round to the in-laws for Sunday lunch. And he won't have too much of a past. He'll have had girlfriends, but not too many. I definitely don't want a stud.'

There was a pause.

'That's quite specific,' Alice said diplomatically. 'Would you say you're open-minded?'

'Oh yes!'

'Good, because my job is as much to make people more open-minded as it is to deliver a selection of perfect partners. We all dismiss people because they don't tick our list of ideal boxes. But some people aren't finding partners because they've got an image of a perfect person in their head, and nobody else will do. But that person is a fantasy; no one in the real world could ever measure up. And so when someone nice comes along who doesn't quite fit the fantasy, they don't give them a chance. Which is a shame, because that person could actually be *perfect for them*.'

Kate looked chastened. 'It was just a wish-list,' she offered limply.

'Good! Because life's more exciting when you let yourself be surprised.'

'Surprises are good!' Kate agreed quickly.

'So, Kate,' Alice continued, 'what's your history? Have you had many boyfriends?'

Kate blushed. 'Three. It's not a great track record for a thirty-three-year-old, is it? I don't know why there haven't been more. I know my hips are too wide and my bum's a bit big. And I'm not blonde. But I'm a good listener. And I've got a good job, and I'm well read. And I go out – all the time! Well, some of the time. Actually, every now and then. But what I mean is, it's not like I'm staying at home being miserable. I'm out there doing all the things you're supposed to do to get boyfriends. But it's just not happening.'

'You've probably just been unlucky,' Alice said sympathetically.

'Yes!' Kate jumped to agree.

'But we're going to change that.'

'Great! I'm not a freak, I promise! I mean, I've had sex with more than three people.'

'I don't really need to kn—'

'It's seven. I know even that's not many. If you divide seven men between the sixteen years since I first, well, you know ... it averages at 0.44 partners a year. It's not even half a man a year! It's not like I've got a problem with men or anything. It's just they're like buses. I mean, you wait for ages and ages, and when one does finally come along you can't get on. And that bit about them coming in threes, well, that's just a myth, isn't it?'

Kate paused and the room went silent. Mercifully it was Alice's voice she heard next.

'I'm sure you've had your fair share of opportunities. It's probably that those opportunities weren't right, so you didn't notice them as options.'

'Do you think so?' Kate leapt on her theory hopefully.

'Absolutely,' Alice said firmly. 'And it's my job to sort out who your right man is – and to make sure you recognize him when you meet him. The rest will be plain sailing.'

Kate grinned with excitement and relief.

'Well, Alice,' she said, 'I'm putting myself in your hands. Do you have anyone for me?'

'Definitely,' Alice replied as she leaned forward and opened the laptop.

LOU

Lou's bar – or rather, the bar where Lou worked, because although she managed it with a monarchical air, it wasn't actually *her* bar – was a basement affair. With no natural light, and stairs that twisted at a blind angle on their way down from street level, Lou often thought how advantageous it was that the lack of windows, coupled with the stairway security camera that gave notice if anyone was on their way down, afforded her ample opportunity to get up to mischief. Which was exactly what she was doing at 5.05 p.m. on a deserted Monday evening.

Standing behind the bar, Lou felt Tony's hot breath against her ear as he pumped away behind her, punctuating his thrusts with the words, 'God . . . you drive me . . . wild . . . you dirty . . . horny . . . *filthy* little bitch.'

Lou, her knickers around one ankle and her hands steadying herself by gripping the Bishop's Finger beer tap, was keeping an eye on the security camera. Not that it mattered much. If anyone happened to come down the stairs unnoticed, both Lou and Tony were fully dressed from the waist up, and pumping actions and flushed faces apart, she was sure she could concoct a story about problem pipework to explain their suspicious body language. Besides, Lou could offer the unexpected guest a drink whilst she nudged her knickers under the dishwasher, buying Tony just enough time to waddle into the back room and pull up his trousers.

Not that Tony would have thought that far ahead, Lou mused. Men rarely did. She braced herself as Tony's pummelling became faster and more forceful. His lips moved right up against her ear.

'Tell me how much you want me to fuck you,' he commanded. 'Tell me how you touch your pussy and think about me.'

'I want you to fuck me. I touch my pussy and think about you,' Lou echoed mildly as her stomach was rammed rhythmically against the drip tray, slopping beer over the sides with each thrust. Tony emitted a guttural, strangled sound before crumpling into the back of her neck. Lou could feel the sweat from his forehead smear against her skin.

She let a few seconds pass.

Then she pushed away, stepped into the right leg of her knickers, and pulled her skirt down from where it had been bunched around her waist. Turning away from the security camera, she surveyed Tony as he leaned sweatily against a fridge, trousers around his ankles, his member already shrivelled within its plastic coating.

'Tony,' she asked casually, 'have you ever wondered what would happen if your wife popped in and caught us?'

'Christ!' he spluttered. 'She'd tear off my balls and

microwave 'em.' He snapped off his condom and threw it across the length of the bar into the bin. Lou scrunched up her face in disgust.

'And then she'd be straight round to her lawyer to screw me for every penny I have and make sure I never saw the kids again.' He hoisted up his trousers and helped himself to a beer from the fridge. 'I'd probably lose this place.' He looked around the bar. 'She'd turn it into a tanning shop just to fuck with my head.'

Lou started to fill a bucket so she could mop the floor between Tony and the bin. She might be loose, but she was hygienic.

'So why do you do it?' she asked as she squirted in the bleach. 'Why risk it when you could lose so much?'

Tony moved close and groped her backside, his fingers exploring forwards into the flesh between her legs. 'Because you're so fucking hot, I can't keep my hands off you,' he letched into her ear. 'You're all I think about when I . . .'

'Seriously, Tony.' Lou pushed away and turned to face him. 'Why, when you've got two kids and shedloads of money to lose, let alone *a wife*, why do you risk it? I'm curious.'

Tony shrugged his shoulders and swigged from his bottle.

'Because I know Suze. She'd never tear herself away from the beauty salon long enough to come here. I'm so far down her priority list it's a fucking joke. I'm bottom of the pile, behind throwing my money away on designer handbags, getting her hair done and spending all day in the gym; then it's the kids, the car, the dog and *then* me.' He sniffed. Lou wished she'd never asked.

'In the six years we've been married she's never once "popped in", which is why' – he stepped towards Lou again and started rubbing her rhythmically – '. . . I can spend quality time on staff relations.'

Clinging to the mop handle, Lou felt her nipples harden. She couldn't help herself. She knew Tony was a prat. She also knew he'd fire her without a second thought if she started giving him grief. But that was fine; she was using him just as much as he was using her, and bar jobs were easier to pick up than thrush. Besides, she liked shagging the boss. It meant no-strings, high-risk sex (highly prized requisites in her book) and an elevated status in the work-place. And it also made going to work each day a little more bearable knowing that, if the night was quiet and the condi-tions were right, she might get a sneaky shag.

A sudden noise interrupted them as Jake and Paul, two of the bar staff, clattered down the stairs. Tony turned and stalked, beer in hand, into the back room. Lou gave the floor a quick mop, and then talked them through their duties for the night.

By eight o'clock, Tony was ensconced in the back room, pretending to do paperwork, but actually watching the soaps, and Lou was perched on a stool at the end of the bar sipping a white-wine spritzer. Lou never drank at work. Spritzers were at least fifty per cent non-alcoholic so didn't actually count. Lou's definition was that if it didn't give you a hangover it wasn't really drinking. A movement on the security camera caught her eye. It was Kate.

'Nice threads!' Lou eyed Kate's outfit appreciatively as she walked up to the bar. 'Just finished work?'

'Yep. And I'll have what you're having, thanks.' Kate nodded towards Lou's glass.

'But it's only a spritzer!'

'And it's only a Monday night!'

'Suit yourself.' Lou shrugged and slid off her bar stool. 'So how was work?'

'Good. Julian actually liked one of my ideas!'

Lou snorted. 'Julian likes *all* your ideas. That's why he keeps promoting you. That and because he knows he's got the world's biggest workaholic on his payroll.'

'Anyway.' Kate sipped her drink. 'That wasn't the only reason it was a good day.'

Lou lifted an eyebrow in anticipation.

'I had my induction meeting with Table For Two this morning,' Kate said lightly, before bursting into a huge grin. 'And it was brilliant!'

'Brilliant?' Lou fought to keep the sarcasm out of her voice.

'I was sooo right about Alice; she's amazing! She was really interested in *me*, and what I like, and the kind of man I'm after. I really think she's going to find me someone. Not just someone; *the one!*'

Lou added more wine to her spritzer. She suddenly felt the need to actually taste the alcohol.

'Uh-huh,' she said tightly.

'She showed me pictures of the men on their books, and you know what? Some of them were really hot! There were some really handsome men with proper jobs and eyebrows that didn't meet in the middle and everything!'

Lou smiled thinly.

'So, anyway, I pointed out a few I liked, and Alice has given me a form to fill in to help her narrow it down some more. And once I've sent it back to her she's going to work out a match. She said I should have my first date next week!'

'Next week? It's a bit sudden, isn't it?' Lou's voice sounded strange.

'Now I've set the ball rolling I want it to be tonight!' Kate was fizzing with excitement. 'And it's going to be a real old-fashioned date; you know, dinner in a restaurant. They recommend you don't go to pubs, as there's nothing to do with your hands other than drink, and you'll get too drunk to remember any of it. Apparently your first date should be over lunch, but I'd never get away from work. So I've told her I can only do dinners and that I want to start asap. I can't wait! It's so exciting!'

Lou quietly sipped her drink and looked at her friend, who she'd never seen look so energized or so beautiful. She had a strange sinking sensation. This wasn't the Kate she knew. She didn't like this Kate. Or this dating agency idea, for that matter. It just seemed so, so . . . Lou didn't know what. But she knew she didn't like it.

AUDREY

It was fast shaping up to be one of those days. First Audrey had slept through her morning alarm. She couldn't think how it had happened, as she prided herself on being a 'morning person'. She'd dressed in a hurry and it was only as she was scuttling out of the front door that she'd noticed the ladder in her tights. She'd chased back into the house and had only just made it to work on time, her hasty journey giving her painful indigestion which three cups of chamomile tea had so far failed to ease.

And on top of all this, she'd had the misfortune to take a phone call from Maurice Lazenby, Table For Two's longest-serving client and a whinger of epic proportions. As any matchmaking bureau chief knows, male clients are hard to come by, so shoddy manners and diva-like complaints are tolerated with gritted cheeriness. Men must be retained at all costs. If female clients ever found out quite how low the male-to-female client ratio was, Audrey doubted they'd ever join at all. So, she forced herself to breathe deeply and give him the soft-handed treatment she'd spent so many years perfecting.

'Well, Maurice,' she explained once there was a suitable

gap in his diatribe, 'the other women we've shown your profile to haven't been interested in meeting you. You're not their type.'

'What do you mean?' Maurice asked peevishly.

Audrey sighed. Technically Maurice was Alice's client. Alice should already have managed his expectations.

'Women like sporty men, high earners; men who are interested in animals and children and do all those fashionable, dangerous hobbies with parachutes and aeroplanes and funny bits of elastic. The ladies you're after are the crème de la crème. They're looking for men who'll whisk them off for a surprise trip to the ballet . . .'

Audrey could hear Maurice start to interject.

'. . . in Paris,' she added heavily. 'Now, Maurice, I know you'll thank me for telling you this, I'm not one to soft-soap. You need to lower your sights. Now, are you sure you wouldn't like Alice to organize another rendezvous for you with Hayley? The veterinary nurse with the funny finger. I'm sure *she'd* be amenable for a second date.'

Eventually an exasperated Audrey had handed Maurice over to Alice to pacify. He knew he was supposed to speak to her anyway, so heaven knows why he was bothering her with his whining.

By eleven o'clock Audrey had taken refuge in her glass-walled office. She propped open the door – all the better to eavesdrop on the staff – and pretended to busy herself at the computer.

'Phone call for you, Audrey,' Hilary called out from across the office. 'It's Sheryl Toogood on line three.'

'Oh, God, what does *she* want?' Audrey grumbled, her fleeting peace shattered. She closed her office door. Conversations with Sheryl Toogood were awkward enough without the staff hanging on her every word.

'Good moooorrrning, Audrey,' Sheryl cooed. No one made as much of a meal of their vowels as Sheryl Toogood. Audrey could imagine her sitting in her office, all smarmy insincerity in a low-cut top.

'Sheryl,' she replied tartly through gritted teeth.

'How aaaaaare you? How's business?'

'Booming,' Audrey jumped in, pleased at the unexpected opportunity to boast. 'We've just heard that we've matched another wedding!'

'Oh, well done you! I know how you love a chance to dust off your hat and hurl some confetti.'

Audrey hesitated, not sure if she was being patronized or not. 'How are things at Love Birds?' she diverted.

'Oh, frightfully busy, as ever,' Sheryl gushed. 'I took on a new consultant last month: Matteus. He's an internet dating specialist and very easy on the eye. He's upped our online traffic by twenty per cent *and* brought in a dozen one-to-one clients too! We're rushed off our feet. Every restaurant in the city has one of our couples dining there this evening.'

'Very nice.' Audrey forced the words out.

'I know,' Sheryl replied immodestly. Audrey could hear the synthetic swoosh of Sheryl's tights as she crossed her legs.

'And how's your little online dating thing going, Audrey? Managed to increase your thumbprint yet?'

Audrey could hear the squeak of a barely suppressed snigger. She flushed angrily. Sheryl would never let her forget her little gaffe. How was she supposed to know that websites had footprints? She wasn't up on all the technical jargon. The blasted website. She'd only set it up because all the other agencies had them.

'Look, I'll cut to the chase, Aud,' Sheryl continued before Audrey had had a chance to think of a cutting reply. 'I'm sure it hasn't escaped your notice that it's the DIPS ball next month.'

'Absolutely not!' Audrey exclaimed. DIPS was shorthand for the Dating Practitioners' Society. Audrey never used abbreviations herself; they were an insult to the Queen's English.

'I trust you'll be coming?'

'But of course!'

The date had been etched across Audrey's consciousness from the moment it had been set. It had been the lone entry in her diary for months, and she'd spent every moment between turning out her bedroom light and slipping into sleep savouring the very thought of it. It was, after all, a guaranteed evening with John.

'As you know,' Sheryl continued, 'I was nominated as this year's event organizer. Such an honour! A real compliment to the standing of Love Birds, don't you think?'

'Well, I don't think the two are totally—'

'. . . So, as the ball organizer, I was taking a look through the RSVP list and noticed that I haven't received your cheque yet. And I thought to myself, oh, that's strange! Audrey's normally such a prompt payer! I do hope Table For Two hasn't got a cash-flow problem?'

'No, of course not! What a funny idea! Ha ha ha.' Audrey forced a fluttery laugh. 'It slipped my mind, that's all. I'll get the cheque off right away.' The cheek! But what a mistake! She couldn't imagine how she'd forgotten. It was unthinkable.

'So, I'll put a little question mark by your name for now.'

'You'll have the cheque first post tomorrow,' said Audrey firmly.

'And I do hope you'll be bringing along that dishy husband of yours?' Sheryl cooed stickily.

Audrey's senses sharpened instinctively as though detecting imminent danger. Her chest went tight and her neck began to flush.

'Such a charming man: so attentive. I'd keep a close eye on him, if I were you,' Sheryl continued. 'Pay him some proper attention. As I tell my clients, you've got to work at keeping your man. Wow him every now and again. If you don't, there are plenty of others who will. If I had a man like John I'd keep him on a very' – her voice became thick with suggestion – '. . . short . . . leash.'

She laughed crudely.

Audrey felt sick.

'Yes, well . . .' She felt Cassandra and Bianca's eyes boring through the glass at her. Really, could she get no privacy in this office at all? And what was Sheryl getting at exactly? Why was she talking about John getting away, and what did she mean by a leash? Was there something that she knew? 'I really don't think I have any cause for concern,' she snapped defensively.

'I'm sure you're all the woman John needs,' Sheryl gushed unconvincingly.

'Right, well, if that's it . . . Because I'm really rather busy.'

'Yes, I think that about wraps things up,' Sheryl replied lightly. 'So I'll keep an eye out for your little cheque.'

'I'll attend to it immediately. Right, well, goodb—'

'. . . Just *one* more thing, Audrey,' Sheryl interrupted slowly. 'You haven't let me know which one of your girls you'll be bringing. You do have that complimentary ticket, you know, for a "matchmaker in the making".'

'Oh, golly. I'd forgotten.'

'You'd forgotten that too? I need names by close of play. Just pop me over an email and I'll make sure Sienna sends her an invitation. Such a treasure, Sienna! I don't know how I ever got by without a PA. You still don't have one, do you? Anyway, must dash, Aud. Ciao.'

Audrey put down the phone and took several deep breaths. She could feel her neck burning. Sheryl was a nasty black cloud in the perfect blue sky of the Dating Practitioners' Society ball. She was bad enough on the phone, but even worse in the flesh. And what a lot of flesh. Not that Sheryl was large – far from it. It was just that she never wore enough clothing. Her bosom was always on display, thrust into a too-small top that was invariably hot-house pink. And she'd teeter around on stilettos – some-times without tights! And she was a terror around men. Always tossing her bottle-blonde hair at them, or leaning close to whisper some crude indiscretion. And what was all that stuff about John? Was he the latest man Sheryl wanted to get her talons into? *Her* John? But John was far too refined to go for a trollop like Sheryl. Wasn't he? Audrey felt her indigestion burn again.

After ten minutes of strenuous paper-shuffling Audrey felt calmer. Of course John wouldn't go for a strumpet like Sheryl. She could flirt all she liked, but John would stick by her side. She knew she could rely on him, despite their current – *temporary* – status. She touched her neck. It was feeling cooler already.

All that remained was for her to decide who to take to the ball as her 'matchmaker in the making'. It was a Dating Practitioners' Society tradition that each of the major dating agencies brought along a young, aspiring matchmaker. It was a way of showing them the big league of matchmakers, and inspiring them to work their way up through the ranks. A silly tradition really. She'd much prefer an evening away from her girls and their inanities. But still, traditions were there for upholding. Audrey peered at her staff and wondered who to take.

Her eye fell on Bianca. If she had to pick a favourite it would be her. She was the kind of girl who threw on a pashmina and looked just right. She wasn't the sharpest tool in the box, but she was from a good family, had gone to an excellent boarding school, and always sat neatly with her knees together.

She turned to Cassandra. Cassandra was well enough bred and a keen horsewoman, but had a tendency towards bandy-leggedness. A bit too Zara Phillips and not enough Middleton sister. But all in all, not too bad a sort.

Then there was Hilary. Hilary had been her very first member of staff and knew almost as much about Table For Two as she did. She'd been to the ball several times, pre-children, when she still had a waist. But she was eight months gone now, and an assault on the eyes. She couldn't possibly take her.

And finally there was Alice, who was staring out of the window in her customary dreamy manner. Alice had been at Table For Two for donkeys' years and still hadn't been to the ball. Bianca and Cassandra had both been – Bianca twice – even though they'd worked at Table For Two for far less time. Audrey sighed. It was no use; she knew it would have to be Alice. She just hoped she wouldn't embarrass her. She was bound to turn up in some sackcloth-and-ashes outfit and stick out like a sore thumb. She could just imagine Sheryl raising her eyebrow. And Barry Chambers was bound to crack a joke. She's an albatross around my neck, that girl, Audrey thought bitterly.

She opened her office door and summoned her in. Alice jumped in her seat, knocking her papers to the floor. Audrey watched as she scrambled to pick them up. Her eyes fell on Alice's feet. What was that ugly, clumpy footwear she had on? Was it ... Was it a pair of *clogs*? Audrey stared in horrified disbelief. Words failed her. She returned to her office and sat down heavily.

Well, Alice would have to buck up her ideas and her appearance if she was going to come to the Dating

Practitioners' Society annual ball, Audrey thought angrily. She groped in her handbag for her chequebook. Hang the post; she'd get Alice to take the cheque round to Love Birds straightaway. On second thoughts . . . Maybe Alice and her footwear should be confined to the office; best not give Sheryl any more ammunition. Just because she was event organizer this year – the power was clearly going to her head. Audrey's own head was throbbing viciously. She touched her brow and winced.

Yes, it was definitely one of those days.

KATE

Kate was resisting the urge to break into her emergency Kit Kat.

She'd never been a believer in the adage that rules were there to be broken (unless the rules were for a diet, in which case all bets were off), but as she slaved over her Table For Two 'All About You' form she began to wonder whether honesty really was the best policy.

Kate had always been great at passing stuff. She had a formula: work hard, revise diligently, get top marks at the end. But this was something else. There were no crib notes on how to pass a dating agency questionnaire, and every question asked led to a million more. Even something simple like 'What kind of music do you like?' was a minefield. Should she fess up to a list of ballads and cheesy big-night-out tunes, or should she plump for something more credible – an obscure Mercury Prize nominee? Which looked best? Did 'fun' translate into 'bimbo', and 'arty' into 'bore'? What kind of music did men *want* her to like? This wasn't a questionnaire at all; it was a deadly game of dating Russian roulette.

She grabbed her phone.

'Am I spontaneous?' she demanded the moment Lou picked up.

'Is it in the schedule?' Lou flashed back. It was 8.30 and the bar sounded hectic behind her.

'I can do spur of the moment! What about that time we got drunk in the pub next to the station and ended up partying in Edinburgh?'

'That was ten years ago; I rest my case. That's six pounds twenty, mate.'

'What about my favourite book ...? Do you think it sounds better to say *Wolf Hall* or *The Blair Years*?'

'Are you doing your dating agency form, by any chance? Christ, just put the *Kama Sutra*. Nobody'll say no to that. D'you want it on the rocks, gorgeous, or as nature intended?'

'This is so hard! I mean, what do men want you to put?'

'The *Top Gear* Annual? I dunno, Kate. You joined the agency; you work it out.'

Kate put down the phone and frowned. One of the reasons she'd joined Table For Two was precisely to avoid this kind of form. She hated them. They cast you in iron and forced you to lie. She'd never told Lou, but she *had* tried online dating sites before – though she'd never got further than the profile questionnaires. It wasn't *just* their limiting multiple-choice answers, it was where the forms went when you'd finished that put her off. She didn't want her profile uploaded into some cyberspace catalogue of the unpullable. Anyone could log in and judge her: clients, exes, old school-mates ... *Julian*. It was humiliating. And then there were the questionnaires themselves. It was bad enough to be asked your income and your views on politics ... but your age? Your exercise regime? Your *weight*? And even if she shaved off a stone and said twenty-something, she still had to tick her body shape. Was she skinny, athletic, curvy or cuddly? Skinny and athletic were obviously out; but was cuddly just code for obese? And did curvy mean Kelly-Brook-voluptuous or lard-lady dressed in a tent? Why couldn't they just put in a box for a passable size 12 on top but needing work down below? Didn't they know that by ticking curvy she might be limiting herself to the heavyweights and the feeders?

The whole thing had been enough to put her off. And OK, so the Table For Two 'All About You' form wasn't exactly a walk in the park, but at least it wasn't about her body. And at least it would be private.

She struggled through the next few questions before picking up her phone again.

'OK, so for "What couldn't you live without?" I've put morning espressos and my iPad.'

'More like Zara and Reiss,' Lou scoffed.

'Speaking of which ... on a scale of one to ten, how wrong is it to put shopping as my hobby?'

'It's beyond wrong.'

'So what *should* I put?'

'Five-aside and three-in-a-bed? Sorry mate, the Speckled Hen's off.'

'Maybe I should put baking – men love women who cook. Just look at Nigella ...'

'For fuck's sake, Kate. Why don't you go the whole hog and say sock-darning and washing-up?'

Kate ignored her. 'How would you describe my style?'

'Certifiable?'

'I've put Danni meets Christina Hendricks. Do you think men will get it?'

'Yeah, all the gay ones. Look, Kate, it's heaving down here tonight. It's wall-to-wall blokes, and they're all drunk and vulnerable. I've got everything from geek-chic to beefcake. Forget all this dating agency rubbish. Get your arse down here and start batting your eyelasles. You'd have to be a nun with halitosis not to pull in here tonight!'

Kate frowned distractedly at her computer.

'No, I've got to finish this form. I promised Alice she'd have it by tomorrow.'

'Come here and you won't need the form, or Alice!'

'I think I'm going to put Ibiza as my favourite holiday destination. It'll make me sound fun.'

'Christ, Kate, if you're going to do this agency bollocks, you might as well tell the truth. You're not a clubber and you don't even *like* fun! Put shopping in New York; put facials in an alpine spa; put *a bloody fortnight in Cadbury World*! At least then you might get matched with someone who actually suits you.'

Kate put down the phone and thought. Maybe Lou was right, for once. Not about going to the bar tonight, but about telling the truth. Being honest was frightening, but if she was paying £300 to join the agency and £100 a month, shouldn't she make sure she got what she wanted? And besides, wasn't the whole reason why she was doing this because she no longer had time left to waste? She couldn't afford to be matched with the wrong kind of man. Every day was yet another day closer to being thirty-five.

She didn't have time to lie.

She deleted her answers and started again.

ALICE

If she didn't share her big news soon she'd burst.

Alice whizzed through the streets, pedalling as hard as she could, the wind making her clothes puff out around her as though she was cycling in a fat suit. Her tyres screeched as she took turns without braking and sleeping policemen at full pelt. Eventually she made it home, whipped out her mobile and dialled Ginny's number.

'Hello?'

Alice's ears were instantly filled with the sound of Scarlet, Ginny's baby daughter, wailing.

'Is this a bad time?'

'It's always a bad time.'

Scarlet gave a scream that could shatter glass.

'Guess what? Audrey's invited me to the Dating Practitioners' Society annual ball!' Alice shouted excitedly over the din. 'I'm going as Table For Two's "matchmaker in the making"!'

'About bloody time too!' Ginny cheered triumphantly. 'Cinderella's finally going to the ball – and on the arm of an ugly sister!'

'I can't believe it! It means the society think I have potential!'

'Alice!' Ginny scolded. 'You've got so much potential it must leak out of your ears at night! I can't believe Audrey hasn't taken you before, the miserable witch. But maybe it'll give you the chance to bond a bit; speak as equals.'

'Mmmm, maybe,' Alice said doubtfully. Her spirits sank. She hadn't thought as far as enforced socializing with her boss; and there wasn't a snowball's chance in hell Audrey would suddenly treat her as an equal. Still, at least Audrey's husband would be there. She always made them sound like the most perfectly matched pair of lovebirds ever to have shared a branch, so they'd be bound to spend the evening glued together. And that meant Alice would get the chance to chat with the other dating professionals. She couldn't wait!

'So what are you going to wear?' Ginny interrupted her thoughts. 'Is it black tie?'

Alice felt panic prickle in her throat.

'I didn't ask. Do you think it's important? I was just going to wear a skirt and top.'

'Of course it's important!' Ginny laughed. 'It's your big chance to be taken seriously. You can't turn up in a skirt and top if everyone's in evening dresses. You've got to dress appropriately. And yes' – Ginny laughed as Alice began to protest – '. . . that *does* mean you've got to wear make-up! *And* heels! *And* get your hair done!'

Alice felt sick.

'I don't see why I can't just go as I am. I'd feel like an idiot in a dress and high heels.'

'Tough!'

'I don't even own any heels,' she mumbled forlornly. 'Or a dress.'

'Alice Brown! How can you get to the age of thirty-one and not own a pair of heels?! You ought to be ashamed of yourself!'

Alice did feel a small twinge of shame. But you couldn't ride a bike in heels, or run for the bus, or take the short cut across the grass in the park. Heels were for ladies; real ladies who wore tights the same colour as their skin and didn't cut their nails with kitchen scissors. Ladies like Bianca. Oh God, why hadn't Audrey invited Bianca to the ball instead? Maybe it would be better all round if Alice didn't go at all.

'Saturday!' declared Ginny decisively. 'Whatever you're doing, cancel it. Dan can babysit. You and I are going shopping for an outfit.'

'OK,' Alice agreed meekly.

'And that means dress, shoes, accessories and handbag.'

'Surely I don't need that much!'

'They're just the basics, for God's sake!'

Alice had a terrifying vision of herself. There was a reason why she didn't own any ladylike clothes and it had something to do with the fact that they made her look like a cross-dresser.

'We're going to get you a knock-'em-dead outfit,' Ginny enthused. 'You're going to be the belle of the ball.'

'Ah, well, I don't really thi—'

'Alice!' Ginny interrupted sharply. 'This kind of stuff's

supposed to be fun! Most women list shopping as a hobby, for God's sake! Going to the ball is your golden opportunity. You're going to have a great time, you're going to look fabulous, and everyone's going to realize what a brilliant matchmaker you are.'

'OK,' Alice mumbled uncertainly.

'Jesus, cheer up!' Ginny laughed in exasperation. 'This is *good* news!'

Alice put down the phone. Her joy at going to the ball had evaporated. Only the sick-making ordeal of having to truss herself up, coat herself in make-up and do small talk with Audrey remained. She didn't think she could do it – any of it. Maybe she should just tell Audrey she had an appointment, a family commitment, an evening funeral to go to . . . anything rather than go to the ball.

KATE

If the character of rooms could be likened to people, Kate thought, then the reception area at Pedigree Pooch was an elderly gentleman scholar.

More of a fusty gentleman's club than a waiting area for a dog food company, Pedigree Pooch's reception area took itself very seriously indeed. There was none of the minimalist furniture or funky artwork that the receptions of Julian Marquis PR's clients normally sported. Instead, Kate and Julian were sunk deep within two antique leather armchairs, listening to the hypnotic tick of a grandfather clock and eyeballing dusty paintings of the revered (and all spookily similar-looking) Laird family, the original founders of Pedigree Pooch.

Julian blew his nose noisily. He was clearly bored, and Pedigree Pooch was not a place where things happened quickly. They'd been waiting for ten minutes with nothing to divert them but yesterday's paper and the ticking of the clock. And Julian was the kind of man who never sat still. As he stuffed his handkerchief back in his pocket he rolled his eyes at Kate and squirmed in his squeaky leather chair.

Suddenly the silence was shattered by a phone. Julian's mobile was always ringing, so it took Kate a few moments to realize it was hers. She dived into her handbag, scattering pens and notebooks in her haste.

'Hello?' she whispered and smiled apologetically at the frowning receptionist.

'Morning! It's Alice from Table For Two.'

'Oh, hi!' Kate replied tightly. Already Julian's ears were flapping.

'Ah ... I'm guessing you've got an audience.'

'Correct.' Kate tried to sound businesslike to throw Julian off the scent. She saw him pick up the newspaper and pretend to read. He was a terrible actor. 'But please: go ahead.'

'Well ... I've got a potential date for you!'

Kate held her breath in excitement.

'He's called Sebastian and he ticks a lot of your boxes.'

'Has he ... ?' Kate tried to think of some unsuspicious words. 'Has he *approved the artwork*?'

'Yes! He's seen your picture and he's keen to meet as soon as possible.'

Kate's heart leapt. She wanted to jump out of her seat and dance right in the middle of reception, but instead she uttered a tight little 'Uh-huh' and tried to keep the excited wobble out of her voice. In the corner of her eye she could see Julian desperately trying to earwig. He was leaning so close he was practically falling out of his chair.

'That sounds like a positive development,' she managed, neutrally.

'I'm emailing you his photo, so take a look and let me know what you think. But I'll just talk you through a few of his details, if that's OK?'

Kate nodded wordlessly. She had a date! Her first date! She felt giddy with excitement.

'He's thirty-seven, and just like you wanted, he's tall, dark and handsome. He's been with us a few months, and all the ladies we've matched him with so far have thought he was . . . and I quote . . . '*gorgeous!*' You also said you wanted someone who wore a suit to work, was a manager of some kind and drove an upmarket car. Well, Sebastian's a trust-fund manager, so that ticks a few more of your boxes. I don't know what kind of car he drives, but he's just got back from two weeks' skiing in Val d'Isère, so he ticks the sporty box too. Oh, and you mentioned you'd like a man with good teeth, so when I last met him I sneaked a look and I'm pleased to report they're white, straight, and in the right places!'

Kate blushed, remembering her list of preferences.

'He suggested you meet at The Privet for dinner. Do you know it?'

Kate gasped. Did she know it? The Privet was *the* place to eat and had a waiting list a mile long.

'God, yes,' she said a little breathlessly. 'That's, err . . . That would be most acceptable.'

She did her best not to giggle with glee. Beside her, Julian made a great show of looking at his watch. The receptionist took the hint, lifted a telephone and started making barely audible enquiries. Kate didn't have much time left.

'Well, thank you very much,' she said to Alice. 'You have my go-ahead to proceed.'

'Don't you want to wait and see his photograph?'

'No, everything sounds in order.'

'Great! I'll call him straightaway. Shall I tell him 8.30 at The Privet on Wednesday?'

'Anything I should know about?' Julian pounced nosily the moment Kate hung up.

'No, everything's in hand.' Kate smiled, doing her best to look calm and controlled whilst her insides did cartwheels. She had a date! A date with a tall, dark, handsome man who – if she wasn't very much mistaken – sounded like a filthy rich studmuffin to boot! *And* he'd seen her picture and it hadn't put him off! She could scream with happiness. Julian peered at her inquisitively, but luckily a thick, oak-panelled door swung open and Geoffrey Laird stepped into the room.

'Terribly sorry to have kept you,' he apologized. 'We've had a few issues with canning. But we're all intrigued to hear your ideas for dragging Pedigree Pooch into the present and sexing us up!'

Julian slapped Kate's back matily.

'Geoffrey, trust me,' he bragged, 'you won't be disappointed. My girl Katy's come up with a cracker.'

'Splendid!' said Geoffrey, rubbing his hands together in anticipation as he ushered them into the boardroom.

AUDREY

Although she was her favourite employee, it always irked Audrey that Bianca would, without fail, ignore the ringing phone and start shutting down her computer at 5.26 p.m. every day. She was as regular as clockwork – a trait that ordinarily Audrey admired in people, but one that on *her* time and at *her* expense never failed to gall. Office hours, as per the contract, were clearly stated as 9.00 a.m. to 5.30 p.m. with an hour for lunch. This daily early abandonment was not just irritating but, surely, in a legal sense, some sort of dereliction of duty. And of course, wherever Bianca led, Cassandra followed. Audrey had tried to admonish Bianca about her timekeeping and the kind of example it set to the staff, but she'd looked at her so sweetly and with such confusion that Audrey had felt like a heavy-handed prison warden. Audrey really didn't want to upset her (she liked to run a happy ship at Table For Two), so over the years she'd resigned herself to bidding a premature goodbye through gritted teeth.

And so, as Bianca calmly ignored the ringing phone at 5.27 p.m. Audrey bore down and tried to breathe steadily until Alice tore herself away from her files, groped for the receiver and put Audrey out of her misery.

'Bye, everyone,' Bianca called, and she breezed out in a waft of perfume.

This was followed immediately by the harsh scraping sound of a chair being pushed back.

'Yes, night, chaps,' Cassandra barked.

Audrey dismantled her rigor mortis smile as she heard Cassandra's noisy footsteps along the hall. A few moments later the sounds dissipated and the gentle hum of the office resumed. Audrey took a calming glance at John's photograph on her desk, and returned her focus to her computer screen.

Now where was she? Ah, yes! Max Higgert. Max was a handsome, unassuming architect who no doubt earned a six-figure income. Such a prize for the agency! Men like Max didn't fall into your lap and onto your books very often. Thank goodness for long working hours and a shy disposition, or he'd have been snapped up years ago. He was a man with education and taste, who spent his working days considering clean lines and beautiful aesthetics. Audrey had caught him halfway through his enrolment interview with Hilary and had immediately whisked him away to the more rarefied confines of her office (where he'd no doubt been impressed by her glass wall). Max Higgert was someone who should have first-class Table For Two treatment, and not be bothered by the unclean lines of the pregnant eyesore that was Hilary Goggin.

Audrey clicked open a file and browsed the profiles of Table For Two's choicest lady clients.

Serena Benchley? No, too old.

Lorraine Hendy? Too obvious. If she knew gentlemen – and Audrey was quite sure she did – then Max would want a more discreet woman; a lady in the true sense of the word.

She clicked through a few more files. Kate Biggs's profile filled her screen.

What about her, the new girl Alice had taken on? Audrey's mouse hovered over Kate's picture. She was the right age, and pretty enough. None of that awful orange fake tan that so many young women slathered themselves in these days. University-educated too. Audrey scanned Kate's details. No. She clicked out of her file. She was one of those PR girls. PR girls were, in Audrey's book, a rather brazen bunch. Not for Max at all. Audrey clicked on.

Helen Oxford? No: bad teeth. So long! They must be forever getting caught in her lipstick.

Abigail Brookes? Not with those roots.

Lisa Jenkins? Too thick.

Jennifer Baxendale? Too thickset.

Catherine Huntley?

Della Bosworth?

Audrey sighed. There were so many average women to wade through. Nobody in the matchmaking business ever dared say it, of course, but it was true. Lady clients always moaned about the lack of good, available men, but they only had themselves to blame. Why was it that so many women thought it acceptable to wear jeans and trainers these days? Audrey was convinced that the rise in single women was in direct correlation to the plummeting of dress standards. In the 1950s a woman was always impeccably turned out, and you didn't get too many of them harping on about their biological clocks. Women these days simply didn't put in the effort. If a lady wanted to attract a man she had to give out the right signals: look smart, keep her hair styled, wear heels, limit her drinking, refrain from smoking in public. Women these days were too interested in 'being themselves'. Either that or they were too busy with their careers. And what kind of woman listed 'going to the gym' as a hobby? Audrey always despaired when she saw a client write this on her application form. Really! Did women really think this was what men wanted? A grunting, muscular Serena Williams with a career more high-flying than their own?

Audrey drained her teacup and set it back on its saucer. She knew what Max wanted. She knew better than he knew himself. He'd been rather vague. 'Kind' was the only criterion he'd come up with. But Max should have a discreet, well-groomed partner, willowy and graceful. Someone he could rely on to say the right thing when she accompanied him on important work events. Audrey knew this woman – she could see her! The problem was, she couldn't see her in the Table For Two files. There were too many tattoos and divorces in there.

She'd sleep on it, she decided. And then she'd call Max in the morning to talk him through a few choice selections. She'd knock his socks off with her ladies, come hell or high water. She wasn't letting a client like Max Higgert get away.

Audrey looked up. She hadn't noticed Hilary leaving. Only Alice remained, bent studiously over her paperwork, her hair piled onto her head and held in place by a chewed biro. Audrey shut down her computer, squeezed into her coat and headed for the door.

'Goodnight, Alice,' she called out frostily.

There was no response. Completely lost to the world, Audrey thought. The place could burn down around her and that girl wouldn't notice.

Audrey strode out of the office and immediately came face to face – as she did every night – with the insult that was Alice's bike. If there was one single thing that could dampen the pleasure of knowing she was on her way home for an evening of uninterrupted BBC television programmes, it was the sight of Alice's bike, manacled to the railings like a rusting suffragette. Audrey had never known an item scream 'romantic failure' quite so loudly. Why couldn't she get the bus to work like any normal person? No: sensible, practical Alice had to ride a clapped-out pushbike and leave it padlocked right in front of the door. And to top it all, it was accessorized with the ultimate stamp of spinsterdom: a pannier. *A pannier!* What must the clients think?

Audrey straightened her mac and powered in the direction of the bus stop. Mentally she was already pouring her first sherry of the night.

ALICE

On Saturday morning Alice wheeled her bike through her front garden and headed into the city centre to meet Ginny. She wished she didn't feel such dread. Normally her spirits would soar at the prospect of spending the day with her best friend. But today was being rudely gatecrashed by the unwelcome guest of shopping.

Alice wasn't exactly a 'shopper'. For her, a trip to the shops was only brought about by absolute necessity, like an empty fridge and impending starvation. And today was to be dedicated to the very worst kind of shopping: shopping for clothes. Shopping for clothes meant looking in mirrors. Alice hated looking at herself in mirrors and didn't keep one in her flat. It's what's inside that counts, she reasoned defiantly as she pedalled along. When Mr Right shows up he's not going to scarper just because I forgot to brush my hair that morning or didn't get around to ironing my skirt. Love conquers all: even mismatched outfits and saggy jumpers.

All too soon she arrived at the shops. She padlocked her bike and made her way to the boutique where Ginny had decided they'd meet.

'Morning!' Ginny chirped, her arms already laden with clothes. 'I've found loads for you to try on. There's the peach taffeta with the sweetheart bow, the sheer lemon minidress with matching knickers, and the plunge-front satin in scarlet; you won't be able to wear a bra with that one.'

The blood drained from Alice's face.

'Don't be daft!' Ginny laughed. 'I think a nice, safe little black dress is more your thing.'

Relief flooded through Alice's body.

It was short-lived.

'I thought you said women went clothes shopping for fun,' she growled several hours later as she discarded the umpteenth dress and reached for her jeans.

'Obviously they've never been shopping with you.' Ginny slumped on the changing-room floor in exhaustion. 'Right, so you've hated pretty much everything so far.' She darted a murderous look at Alice. 'But the things you've hated most have been tight, feminine, or shown more than a millimetre of flesh. So what have we got on the plus side?'

There was a very long pause.

'Well, you don't have much up top ...' Ginny mused finally, nodding towards Alice's bust, '... but you're slim, toned, and you've got great legs. You know, maybe you could pull off a backless dress?' She sounded positive for the first time in hours.

'A backless dress?' Alice echoed in alarm. 'Aren't they a bit dangerous?'

'They're dresses, not hand grenades!'

'Well, a bit revealing, then?'

'Nope, that's the whole point. You're not showing your legs or your boobs, just a back. Who cares about a back?' Ginny leapt up. 'Stay there! We're going to crack this.' And she darted back out to the shop floor.

Alice forlornly undid her jeans.

Two minutes later Ginny zipped Alice into a backless satin dress. 'You know, the dress would look a whole lot better if you took your socks off,' she said sarcastically.

Reluctantly Alice bent down and pulled them off.

'That's better!' Ginny sounded cheery. 'Look!'

Alice turned and looked at herself in the mirror. And to her great surprise she didn't hate what she saw. From the front, she was covered up. The dress started at her collarbone, and although it was sleeveless, it hugged her armpits so that her chest was completely hidden. And the hemline was just below the knee. If only the dress had a back, it would be perfect.

'And if you could just stick these on' – Ginny reached behind her and pulled out a pair of peep-toe stilettos – 'it would look twice as good again!'

Alice eyed the shoes suspiciously. They looked hazardously high. Surely you could break your ankles in those. But she caught a glimpse of Ginny's face. It wasn't a face to be messed with. She backed into the changing room, sat down and wriggled her feet into the shoes.

Instantly her feet became ladies' feet, not her own feet at all. Her foot contorted into a delicate, ladylike arch and her toes winked flirtily out of the peep toe. Gingerly she stood up. She felt the spindly stiletto heels wobble a bit and then settle. It wasn't exactly comfortable, but it wasn't the razor-blade experience she'd been expecting either. Like a baby giraffe she took a few uncertain steps.

'Bloody hell!' Ginny exclaimed, a hint of marvel in her voice. 'I think we've done it!'

She stepped forward, scooped Alice's hair off her shoulders and held it loosely on top of her head.

'Look!' she commanded.

Alice blinked. She couldn't believe it. The person blinking back at her was a woman: an actual, feminine woman! The long expanse of skin from her hairline to the base of her spine looked lean, healthy and – Alice blanched as she even thought the word – *sensual*. The dress tapered to reveal shapely, bicycle-toned calves that led to the sexiest pair of feet Alice had ever seen. The shoes were amazing. Her feet had somehow transformed into film-star feet. It was a miracle!

Her eyes met Ginny's.

'I'll take it,' she heard herself say. 'All of it.'

Four hours, five hundred pounds and two bottles of Sauvignon Blanc later, Ginny and Alice were back at the bicycle stand, cheeks flushed with alcohol as late-night shoppers milled around them. Alice didn't normally drink much, but the dress and shoes made her look like another person, and that person liked to celebrate eye-wateringly expensive shopping with a generous helping of booze. After the purchase of the dress and shoes Ginny had propelled Alice into yet more shops to buy 'vital' ball stuff, including deep-red nail varnish, some dangly earrings and a small black handbag. Finally Ginny had marched her into a lingerie boutique.

'I've never seen your underwear drawer, but I'd stake my life on there being nothing in it worthy of being worn under your new sexy dress.'

So Alice had left the shop the slightly embarrassed owner of a pair of ridiculously overpriced, unfeasibly flimsy, but secretly thrilling tiny black knickers.

'I don't know how you're going to get back home,' Ginny laughed as she surveyed Alice's mountain of shopping bags. 'I don't think shopaholic sex goddesses normally travel by bike.'

Alice swayed slightly.

'I'll just hook them over the handlebars,' she muttered. 'Of course, it'd help if the handlebars would stay still.'

Ginny sniggered.

'Anyway,' Alice continued, 'shouldn't you be getting back to Dan?'

She thought she saw Ginny grimace, but she couldn't be sure. She could see at least three Ginnys, so maybe it wasn't fair to judge. She turned to her bike and tried not to wobble as she awkwardly lifted her leg over the saddle.

'Alissssssss, darrrrrling!' a voice trilled from the mass of bodies on the pavement. Alice froze momentarily with her leg in the air.

A pair of breasts in a low-cut emerald-green dress emerged from the crowd.

'Alisssss Brown, how lovely to see you,' said the breasts. They were framed by a fake-fur jacket and topped off by long blonde hair tonged into curls. 'I thought it was you hiding behind all those shopping bags, you naughty girl. Audrey's obviously paying you too much!'

'Er . . . hello . . . Ms Toogood.'

'Sheryl, please!' Sheryl Toogood touched Alice's arm conspiratorially. 'And what have you been up to?' she asked lasciviously. 'Have you been buying yourself a little outfit for the DIPS ball?'

'My friend Ginny has been helping me,' Alice mumbled awkwardly. Ginny was eyeballing Sheryl with a mixture of horror and awe.

'How sweet.' Sheryl threw a brief semi-smile at Ginny. She stepped closer to Alice and lowered her voice conspiratorially. 'Can I just say how deliiiiighted I was to hear Audrey was bringing you this year. And about time too! Many's the time I've said to Audrey, "Aud, why have you brought that dull little Bianca again? I'm sure she's an adequate matchmaker, but she's never going to fire off more than a couple of Cupid's arrows. Why don't you bring that wonderful Alissss? I'm sure she fires off arrows by the quiverful."'

'Well, um, that's really nice of you, Ms Toogood. But Bianca's a great matchmaker.' Alice tried to move but Sheryl gripped her arm.

'Sheryl, please. And nonsense! Credit where credit's due. I've got spies all over the city and I hear great things about you! It seems you're the engine that keeps Table

For Two afloat. Without you they'd be scrambling for the lifeboats.'

'I don't think that's really true . . .'

'You know, Alisssss, we must do coffee. I've been meaning to have a little tête-à-tête with you, matchmaker to match-maker.'

'Oh?' Alice replied in astonishment. 'Well, yes . . . that would be very nice.' Nice? It sounded terrifying! What on earth could Sheryl want to talk to her about?

'Well, that's settled. I'll get Sienna to arrange it. But it needs to be hush-hush; no telling Audrey. She'd only come along and ruin our fun.' Sheryl burst into peals of laughter.

'Um . . .' said Alice. Much as she disliked Audrey, she was uncomfortable with the idea of going behind her back.

'Well, I must run.' Sheryl was already clip-clopping away. 'So lovely to bump into you and your little friend. I'll look forward to that coffee. Don't let me down, Alissss.'

'I won't . . . Sheryl,' Alice called out awkwardly. But Sheryl and her breasts had already been swallowed up by the crowd.

Ginny let out a low whistle.

'What on earth was that?!'

'That was Sheryl Toogood,' Alice mumbled, still peering at the spot where Sheryl had disappeared. 'She runs another dating agency – Love Birds. Audrey can't stand her.' Why had Sheryl come to talk to her? She hadn't realized Sheryl even knew her name.

'I can see why!' Ginny laughed. 'What a snake! The way she was gripping your arm . . . She was like a boa constrictor and you were lunch.'

Alice shuddered at the thought of Sheryl slowly squeezing the life out of her, smiling with her glossy red lips. What had Sheryl wanted? And why did she want to meet up?

'Still, she was right about one thing,' Ginny continued.

'What?'

'About you being the powerhouse at Table For Two! See?' She nudged her friend. 'That's why you're going to the ball. Everyone knows you're a brilliant matchmaker. And that's why she wants coffee with you. You're hot property!'

Alice stared thoughtfully in Sheryl's direction. That wasn't it. But what on earth was Sheryl playing at? She was too tipsy to work it out. But she was sober enough to know something wasn't right.

LOU

It was Saturday night and the bar was heaving with punters. Lou loved Saturday; no other night was like it. Work stresses were long forgotten and everyone was dressed up and determined to have fun. Heads swivelled as everyone weighed up who to try their luck with first. Lou loved the nakedness of it. On Saturday night the whole world was on the pull, the bar was sticky with hormones, and the customers would be three-deep, all vying for her attention. Saturday nights made her feel powerful. No girl in the world got as much attention as a flirty barmaid on a Saturday night.

Lou was already several hours of pint-pulling and eyelash-batting into her shift and it was time for her break. Tony had the night off and was dragging himself around the city's lap-dancing bars with his mates. He'd doubtless be back at closing time, hoping for an illicit nightcap of X-rated exertions before he returned home to the sterile charms of Suze. Lou smiled. Tony was nothing if not predictable.

Normally Lou spent her break on the pavement, chain-smoking her way through three or four cigarettes in quick succession. But Tony's absence was an opportunity for a more gentrified fag break, so she poured herself a spritzer and made her way to his office. The roar of the bar muffled as the door swung closed behind her. She leaned back in his chair, put her feet on his desk and lit her first cigarette. She eyed the '*It's against the law to smoke on these premises*' notice that hung above his desk and exhaled extravagantly.

Her eye fell on the security camera that was trained on the bar area. It showed a sea of bodies all clambering in the direction of the beer pumps. It was a scrum out there, she thought; a delicious, orgiastic scrum intent on nothing more complicated than booze and sex. She felt a sudden surge of fondness for her fellow man. This is what it's all about, she thought as she sipped her spritzer and drew on her cigarette. This is what it all boils down to: drinking until you're uninhibited enough to do your mating dance and bag a shag for the night. Because Saturday nights are just long-drawn-out mating dances – Mother Nature at her purest; the one night a week dedicated solely to the procreation of the species. Men were so simple, she thought. You only had to dance the mating dance and they were yours.

Lou took a swig of her spritzer and thought about Kate. Kate had never got the hang of the mating dance. She was too self-conscious. She didn't get that it was just a few shakes, pouts and struts; that men only needed the smallest whiff of encouragement. Kate was always worried about something: the size of her hips, her garlic breath, the man's intentions ('but he's only after a one-night stand,' she'd whinge dolefully). But she was missing the point. Nature wasn't bothered about getting things 'just right'. If you thought too hard about attraction it was gone. Lions didn't pontificate over which member of the pride to fuck.

But now Kate had ducked out of the mating dance entirely, getting so-called professionals to analyse the players and serve her up a mate. It was wrong. It was messing with nature. Attraction was raw and earthy and about the here and now. Even if the here was just here, and the now was right now, and the mate you'd so carefully chosen the night before had scarpered by morning. That was life. You didn't see jungle animals holding hands and twittering poetry.

Lou took a last glance at the security camera and drained her drink. Her twenty minutes were up; it was time to re-enter the jungle. She reached for her make-up bag. The jungle could wait a few more moments. There was no way she was stepping back into battle without another layer of warpaint.

ALICE

Someone had once told Alice that in order to be beautiful a woman had to suffer. At the time Alice had thought it ridiculous. She was from the tub-of-E45-and-an-early-night school of beauty. All those women who subjected themselves to painful waxing and peeling were mad. But now, having spent her Sunday practising walking in a pair of toe-wrecking, arch-snapping, spine-realigning heels (and still loving them at the end of it), Alice was beginning to understand what that person had meant. And now she was recovering with the aid of her foot spa and a mug of PG.

She sighed and thought – for possibly the thousandth time that day – about the ball. Any ideas she'd had about begging Audrey to take Bianca instead had vanished the moment she'd trotted up to the till at the boutique and handed over her plastic. Now that she had an outfit to wear – and not just any outfit, the greatest outfit of her whole, entire life – she was actually looking forward to it. All day she'd kept opening her wardrobe just to peek at her dress. She'd slip it out and hold it against herself, trying to remember what it had looked like in the full-length mirror.

When it got dark she turned on the lights and left the curtains open so she could see her reflection in the window. Every time she saw herself her breath quickened. Could she really pull this off?

Alice gently moved her feet in the water, letting the bubbles tickle along her soles. Of course, she'd also had at least thirty fantasies this afternoon alone about what would happen if the ball night was also the night her Prince Charming decided to show up (well, that *was* what they're supposed to do at balls). Obviously everyone in the room would be clamouring for his attention. But he'd only have eyes for Alice, whose hand he'd take and kiss before leading her to the dance floor. It was the full Cinderella moment, except that there was no chance she was leaving one of her new peep-toes behind!

But there was an obvious flaw in this fantasy. Alice already knew the men who'd be at the ball; they were all DIPS members and – if the meetings were anything to go by – they'd all be spending the evening engrossed by Sheryl Toogood's cleavage. Of course there could be a few other men, but they'd be the 'plus ones' of DIPS members and therefore not in the market for over-imaginative, romance-aholic matchmakers, no matter how well shod.

So Alice had had to content herself with the far more problematic fantasy of meeting Prince Charming on the way to the ball. So far the best she'd come up with was that he was her bus driver, or maybe a kind-hearted passenger on his way to help out in a soup kitchen. He'd look up from his battered paperback, readjust his glasses and be dazzled into a love stupor by the vision of Alice in her ball outfit. It would be a fatal case of love at first sight. It almost worked, she thought as she hugged her knees together and wiggled her much-improved toes in the foot spa. Until he looked down. There was no way Alice would manage tottering to the bus stop in her heels, and even *her* powerful imagination stopped short of the hero scooping up the heroine in a backless dress and grubby trainers.

'Oh well,' she thought as she clicked off the foot spa and reached for a towel. She'd just have to meet Mr Perfect another night. It was a shame though. Now that she'd seen herself in heels and a posh frock, even she knew she'd have her work cut out getting Prince Charming struck by a thunderbolt and pledging his undying love whilst she was wearing a cardy.

AUDREY

'Max, good morning! How are you?'

Audrey was using her best telephone voice and was smiling into the receiver. Years ago she'd paid an exorbitant fee for a session with a life coach. All the other agency owners were doing it and she was damned if she was going to be left out. He'd been a total waste of money, and the only thing she could remember was his instruction to smile on the telephone. Smiling softened the vocal cords; people were more likely to do business with you, he'd promised. Audrey didn't like to do it if the girls could see. But this morning she was smiling most determinedly for Max Higgert.

'Ah, Audrey.' Max sounded tense. 'I'm well, thank you. And you?'

'Oh, I'm marvellous,' Audrey simpered. So few clients bothered with basic courtesies. She'd somehow known that Max was a cut above. 'I just thought I'd give you a tinkle to see how your lunch date with Penelope Huffington went yesterday. She's a dream, isn't she?'

'She was ... um ... a lovely woman. Very, er ...'

'Educated!' Audrey gushed. She'd scoured the agency books to find the right lady for Max, and Penelope was perfect.

'Yes, very well educated.'

'And elegant!'

'Ah, yes.'

'And cultured!' Audrey played her trump card. Men like Max prized a cultured woman.

'Very! I felt like the village idiot!'

'So you liked her then? You clicked? I knew you would!'

'Ah . . .'

'I *knew* you'd have a marvellous time!'

'It was very nice, Audrey, but, um, well, it wasn't quite what I'd hoped for.'

Audrey blinked. 'I'm sorry?' Her smile dropped a notch. Max coughed.

'Well, as I said, or you said, or one of us said,' he faltered, '. . . she's charming and educated and cultured and prob-ably perfect for very many people. But, ah, I don't think I was her cup of tea, actually.'

'You're quite wrong. I've had her on the phone already. She asked me to organize a second date.'

'Oh, right. Well, that's very flattering. That she wanted to meet again, I mean. And please, tell her thank you. But . . .'

'She comes from the Whitting family, you know, the merchant bankers? They own the Whitting Country Club. Such lovely people. They've had money for generations. And Penelope's a great lover of the arts, always attending launches and exhibitions. And she helps out at the cathedral with their fundraising concerts. She does so much for charity, Penelope. Such a wonderful woman!'

'Yes, certainly. But I'm afraid I don't think we're right for each other.'

'Oh, don't be silly! You're a perfect match.'

Audrey's smile clattered around her jawbone. Bugger smiling; her muscles hurt.

Max continued nervously. 'Actually, I was wondering if there was anyone else you had in mind. Someone *not* so educated and cultured and accomplished.'

'Oh.'

'Someone warm ... and kind. Someone a bit more ... *normal*!'

'Right, I see.' Audrey patted her hair in bewilderment. 'But well-groomed though? And elegant?'

'Well, I don't really ...'

'Someone who can entertain your clients and accompany you to dinner parties?'

'That's not quite wha—'

'Of course, Penelope is a little uptight. Actually, I've always thought she was a bit of a cold fish; a bit too eager to talk about her charity work. It does get a bit vulgar when she flaunts it in your face. But don't worry! I've got just the woman for you!' Audrey started to swivel purposefully in her chair again. 'She's a perfect match. In fact, that's why I'm phoning – to see if I can arrange a lunch date. Her name is Hermione Bolton King. She used to be married to a fabulously successful stockbroker and did very well out of the divorce. She's got a six-bedroom house on the Holly Bush private road. You know, with the fountain and the electric gates?'

A few minutes later Audrey put down the phone having secured Max's permission to instigate a date with Hermione. Honestly, he could have sounded a bit more enthusiastic, she thought bitterly. She couldn't think why he hadn't liked Penelope Huffington. She'd put a lot of thought into that match; he could at least have given her a second try. But never mind; he'd adore Hermione. And what an impressive house Hermione had, with its conservatory made entirely from hand-blown Venetian glass. Max was bound to be impressed!

She looked at her watch and frowned. It was 11.30. Where the devil were her flowers? They'd normally arrived by 11.00.

She swung open her door and bristled into the main office.

'Is everything all right, Audrey?' Bianca asked sweetly.

There were no flowers anywhere.

'Yes, yes.' She forced a civil tone, casting her eye around the flowerless desks. 'Right, well, I'm very busy.'

She sailed back into her office and shut the glass door behind her. If the flowers hadn't arrived by midday she'd have words with that florist.

She decided to cheer herself up by calling President Ernie. Audrey believed it a business imperative to keep up a personal relationship with the Dating Practitioners' Society president.

Audrey had first met Ernie when Table For Two was in

its infancy and she was a rookie matchmaker. Ernie had already been in the business for twenty years, and what he didn't know simply wasn't worth knowing in the first place. With his silver-grey hair and taut figure he cut a dash at the Society meetings and was always full of clever ideas about how they could pull together. He was touching sixty now, and Audrey was dreading the day he decided enough was enough, and retired.

'Audrey, how wonderful to hear from you!'

'Good morning, Mr President!'

Despite Ernie's protestations, Audrey insisted on addressing him this way. A world without hierarchy was a world going to the dogs.

'So, you've heard the news about Nigel at Cupid's Cabin then?' he gossiped importantly.

'Which news in particular?' Audrey tried to keep her tone light. She hated to look anything less than one hundred per cent informed on industry tittle-tattle.

'Well, you didn't hear this from me, but I know I can trust you. Nigel's laid off Beverly!'

This *was* exciting news. Audrey was glad she'd phoned.

'He's got so few clients now,' Ernie continued blithely, 'and they're deserting him in droves. Sheryl at Love Birds has been getting several disaffected Cupid's Cabiners banging on her doors each morning. I tell you, Nigel's in hot water. He'll be out of business by the ball.'

'Goodness!' exclaimed Audrey dizzily.

'I'm surprised you've not had any of his Cupid's Cabiners over your way . . .'

'But of course we have!' Audrey blustered. 'I just didn't want to rub poor Nigel's nose in it. The last thing he'd want is everyone gossiping.'

'I quite agree.'

'But isn't it awful? What do you think has gone wrong over there?'

'Far be it from me to speculate, but I bet it's got something to do with what's going on at home. Nigel and Marjorie have been having problems. Apparently Marjorie's developed a roving eye and Nigel's jealous of any man she comes into contact with. He won't leave the house in the morning until the postman's been and gone. Business is bound to suffer!'

'Of course!' Audrey agreed vigorously.

'You know as well as I do, Audrey, you can't be in the business of creating love at work unless you've got love at home. Else it's like a vicar losing the Lord, or a policeman waking up one day and deciding he's going to be an anarchist. Without a happy home life your matchmaking mojo's gone. We owe it to our clients to make sure our own domestic situations are in order. A happy marriage makes for a happy bureau makes for happy clients; that's what I say!'

'Quite! So, you think Nigel's lost his matchmaking mojo?'

'I'd put money on it!'

'Heavens!'

'But where there are losers, there are also winners; Sheryl's really cleaning up! You've got to admire her!'

Audrey made a small coughing noise that could be taken as a rough approximation of agreement.

'Of course, we'll have to be terribly discreet at the next Society meeting and pretend we don't know. Mum's the word!'

'Absolutely, Mr President,' Audrey gushed.

'Anyway.' Ernie moved glibly on. 'I hear you're bringing Alice Brown to the ball as your "matchmaker in the making".'

Audrey's senses went on high alert. She strained to hear mockery in his voice.

'Quite right too!' Ernie continued emphatically. 'I hear great things about young Alice. She's quite the rising star!'

Audrey looked across the office towards Alice. She was wearing another of her porridge-coloured cardigans with what appeared to be her mother's blouse. Surely Ernie couldn't mean it. He had to be pulling her leg.

Audrey put down the phone, feeling unsettled. There was a knock at her glass door and Alice inched gingerly in, manoeuvring a heavy bouquet.

Audrey raised her hand to her chest in theatrical surprise.

'Oh, that silly man!' she said in her best fluttery voice. 'He's such a hopeless romantic. I keep telling him to stop, but he keeps on sending them!'

'They're beautiful,' smiled Alice. 'Your husband must love you very much.'

'He does.' Audrey shot her a peculiar look and clutched the flowers to her bosom. She dismissed her with a wave of her hand. She needed to think and that cardigan was giving her one of her heads.

KATE

Kate slammed the front door of her city-centre apartment and hurtled down the stairs. She hated being late.

Although she'd planned to leave work at six, take a leisurely bath and slowly apply her make-up, there'd been a last-minute client crisis and she hadn't left until nearly 7.30. She'd been too late to pick up her carefully selected outfit from the dry-cleaners, so was going to have to make do with an old favourite standby. Her fantasy preparations scuppered, she'd grabbed a quick shower, sprinkled her hair with talc and then spent her last valuable minutes ransacking her bedroom, frantically searching for her tummy-tightening pants. It hadn't been an ideal start to the night.

As she powered in the direction of The Privet she tried not to dwell on the fact that this was her first date in nearly two years. Sebastian was a terrifying reintroduction to dating; every time she thought about him her stomach buckled with fear. When she'd opened her email from Alice she couldn't believe what she saw. Sebastian wasn't a man; he was a god! His photograph had been taken professionally, and he was looking to the left as if he was being called by a group of glamorous friends. The angle perfectly showed his straight nose, immaculate jaw and dark, luxuriant hair. He looked like he should be dating a film star, not wasting time with a size-14 nobody with talcum-powdered hair and support pants.

With a flush Kate remembered the photo Sebastian had been sent of her. It was a snap from a package holiday she'd been on with Lou five summers ago. It had been taken from quite a way away and was a bit blurry, but she'd picked it because the distance and her tan made her look ten pounds lighter.

Kate hurriedly turned the final corner and The Privet loomed intimidatingly before her. There was no going back now. This could be it, she thought giddily – the end to her single existence and the beginning of her new life! A life that begins with a date at The Privet and ends in a detached four-bedroom house with a gorgeous husband, two kids and a golden retriever!

'Do you have a reservation?' A tall, snooty woman eyed Kate suspiciously.

Kate cleared her throat and tried to speak assertively.

'Yes, I'm here to meet Sebastian Lincoln.'

The woman raised an eyebrow.

'Mr Lincoln?' She gave Kate a quick but unmistakable once-over. 'This way.'

Meekly Kate followed her as she swept into the dining area and snaked deftly between the tables. Kate eyed the tiny gaps between the tables with a sinking heart. Her hips were too big for a place like this; she was bound to knock something over. But the woman was disappearing quickly and there was no choice. So she took a deep breath and ploughed ahead, squeezing herself in every time she approached a table. She noticed diners removing their wine glasses from her path whenever she loomed close.

Suddenly the snooty woman stopped.

'Your table, madam.'

The woman melted away and Kate was confronted with the in-the-flesh reality of Sebastian Lincoln.

'Katy.' Sebastian nodded at her briefly but didn't get up. He was studying the wine list. Kate paused, debating whether to point out he'd got her name wrong (too aggressive, she decided; not cool). She hastily dropped into the empty seat and pretended to look at the menu. She tried to control her breathing. Sebastian was a vision of physical perfection.

'Bring us the '68 Chateauneuf-du-Pape,' Sebastian commanded a hovering waiter.

The waiter nodded and withdrew before Kate could say anything. She could have kicked herself for missing her chance. What with the power-walk to the restaurant and a mouth parched dry with nerves, she was dying for a glass of water.

'The lobster here is divine,' said Sebastian, looking up and surveying Kate as though deciding whether to make a purchase. She blushed as his eyes moved blatantly around her body. 'Of course, the venison's delicious too, but I always find it a little ... *heavy*.'

Kate ignored his emphasis on the word *heavy* – she was probably being paranoid – and tried to smile. Her lips stretched dryly over her teeth. 'Lobster it is, then!' She'd always wanted to try lobster, and being at The Privet with the world's most handsome man seemed as good a place as any to do it. Besides, the menu said it came with chips.

The waiter reappeared and filled their wine glasses. Kate looked at hers dolefully. Red wouldn't have been her colour of choice. It always left a black ring around her lips, staining her teeth grey and making her mouth look rotten. It was hardly conducive to an end-of-date kiss (she blushed at the thought that she might be kissing Sebastian in a few hours!). But she daren't ask for white now he'd already bought a bottle. She'd just have to nip to the Ladies after each glass and scrape her lips with her fingernail.

'You're a lot bigger than in your photo,' Sebastian remarked suddenly. 'More weathered.'

Kate gasped. She mumbled something about it being an old photo.

'Yes, there seems to be a lot of that,' Sebastian drawled. 'Every woman I've met through Table For Two is at least five years older and ten pounds heavier than her photo.'

Kate's cheeks stung as though slapped.

'We all like to think we're still twenty-one,' she joked weakly.

'Mmmm.' Sebastian managed to sound both sceptical and bored at the same time. Thankfully, he changed the subject. 'So you're the PR girl, aren't you?'

'Yes,' said Kate, taking a sip of wine to steady her nerves

and deciding to overlook the patronizing use of the word 'girl'. 'I'm an account director at Julian Marquis PR.'

Sebastian raised his eyebrow. 'Julian Marquis? Jules and I go way back. We were at Oxford together.'

Kate froze.

'We go skiing every Christmas. We always stay at a fabulous lodge with twenty or so close friends and hole in for the holidays. The piste was perfect this year . . .'

But Kate wasn't listening. Beneath the fixed smile she was smarting. Tonight was fast turning into a disaster. First of all, she couldn't believe he'd mentioned her size. Was she really so big? She knew she wasn't skinny but was she really so fat that it was the first thing someone noticed about her? And then, could Sebastian have made his disappointment in her any more obvious? And finally, to top it all, Sebastian knew Julian. They might talk. She'd never live it down if Julian found out she'd joined a dating agency.

She took a large gulp of wine, and then followed it with several more. The more Sebastian talked, the more she gulped. By the time the waiter brought them their lobster – just as Sebastian's story was building to its climax of how he'd heroically tackled a black run in only his second-best pair of skis – she realized she was overdue a trip to the Ladies to scratch the black ring from her lips.

'Excuse me.' She hastily bundled towards the toilets, leaving a mid-flow Sebastian alone with his crustacean.

In the dimly lit sanctuary of the Ladies Kate eyed herself in the mirror. Sure enough, she looked like she'd been eating dirt. Her gaze fell lower and she surveyed her dress miserably.

She knew she'd been in a rush, but why on earth had she decided to wear this one? No wonder Sebastian was disappointed. She looked enormous, like a sack of spuds in heels. Miserably she took a deep breath and headed back into the restaurant.

Back at the table, Sebastian was attacking his lobster with the precision of a ravenous surgeon. Between his hands a set of silver utensils flashed ominously. Kate looked down at her plate. Next to her lobster lay a fork, some kind of nutcracker and a long pointy prong. There was no knife. She looked at her lobster. It was still in its shell, all eyes, claws and tentacles. With a heavy heart Kate realized there must be an art to eating lobster, some secret posh way to break open the shell. She began to sweat.

She munched a few chips to buy time. She sneaked a look at Sebastian to see what he was doing, but whatever it was, he was doing it too fast for her brain to process.

As Sebastian cracked and speared and chomped on his dinner, he kept up an endless one-way conversation about the state of the stock market and the importance of his job. No conversational effort seemed to be required from Kate, so she concentrated on working out how to tackle her dinner. She noticed Sebastian's eyes were locked on his dissection; he wasn't looking up.

The coast was clear.

Swiftly Kate picked up her nutcracker in one hand, lifted the lobster with the other and awkwardly tried to jam it into the jaws of the cracker. But where to crack? Not the head; too brutal. And the belly was too big. She decided on a leg. She balanced it in the nutcracker, clenched and pressed down as hard as she could. There was a loud crack and a shard of lobster shell shot off her plate and onto the carpet beneath the next table. Kate held her breath and looked at Sebastian. He was busy recounting how much money he'd made that day and was mercifully oblivious. With relief Kate picked up her skewer, hoping to spear a piece of meat. But her crack had peppered her lobster with shell shrapnel. Warily she skewered a small section, put it in her mouth and crunched. It was like eating a fish-flavoured pincushion. One of the shards cracked noisily between her teeth. Awkwardly – she couldn't spit it out, not at The Privet – she took a big gulp of wine and swallowed, feeling the shell scratch her throat on its way down. She forlornly tried to bury her ruined feast under her chips.

'Did madam not like the lobster?' the waiter asked as he cleared away their plates. Kate blushed.

'It was delicious. I'm just . . . full.' She quickly rubbed her stomach, hoping it wouldn't betray her by rumbling.

'Would you like to see the dessert menu?'

Kate straightened in her seat in anticipation. The Privet's puddings were legendary. She'd always fancied trying their legendary 'Death by Chocolate' cake served with black fig ice cream. But Sebastian waved the waiter away.

Kate's heart sank. Tonight had been a total disaster. She picked up her wine glass and drained it. Sod the black lines, she thought recklessly. The chances of Sebastian wanting a goodnight snog were zero.

Eventually the bill came. Hurrah for old-fashioned

convention, Kate thought, as the waiter delivered it to Sebastian. There was no way she was shelling out £80 for four chips. Sebastian made a great show of dropping a platinum credit card on the table. He didn't leave a tip.

Moments later they were standing in the cold air outside.

'Well, it was very ... interesting ... to see you in the flesh,' Sebastian said stiffly. The word 'flesh' hung between them. Kate winced. So much for her goodnight kiss. A taxi magically appeared beside them.

'I'll call Table For Two with my feedback,' he muttered as he swiftly bundled in. 'Isn't your name Biggs?' he called from the safety of the back seat. Kate heard him emphasize *Biggs*. She nodded miserably.

Sebastian smiled, as if confirming something to himself. 'Drive on,' he instructed the driver. And in a cough of exhaust he was gone and Kate was alone on the pavement.

AUDREY

Audrey always looked forward to the bimonthly meeting of the Dating Practitioners' Society. It was a chance for the agency heads and staff from not just the city, but the whole county, to network. The meetings were held on the last Thursday of every other month, and all the agencies switched off their phones, shut down their offices and made their way to Society headquarters. No matchmaking took place for a hundred miles. It was as though Cupid had gone on a mini-break.

On the stroke of 2.15 p.m. Audrey shut up shop and led her girls on the short walk across the city centre to Society HQ for the 3 p.m. start. She liked to arrive promptly; it sent out the right signal. And besides, it gave her the opportunity to chat with President Ernie, matchmaking professional to matchmaking professional. But today she was irked to see that Sheryl Toogood and the Love Birds team were already there. Sheryl had bagged the seat next to Ernie and was sitting with her shoes off and her legs curled cat-like beneath her.

'Aud!' Sheryl tore herself away from her tête-à-tête with Ernie. 'So glaaaad you could make it.'

Audrey bristled. Since when was it Sheryl's job to welcome her to the meeting? And when in her eleven years of Society membership had Audrey ever not 'made it'?

'Good afternoon, Miss Toogood, Mr President,' she replied coolly. Someone had to keep up standards.

Like giggling schoolgirls, Bianca, Cassandra, Hilary and Alice surged ahead, dumping their coats on seats and nattering with the Love Birds staff as they swarmed around the tea urn, selecting their biscuits. Audrey noticed all the seats nearest Ernie were now taken. She pursed her lips and pretended to busy herself reading the Society notice-board.

There was a noise at the door and Barry Chambers and his team from A Fine Romance entered the room, shortly followed by David Bennett from Perfect Partners and Wendy Arthur from Loving Liaisons. The noise level rose as people greeted each other and helped themselves to tea.

'Audrey!' Wendy broke away from the hubbub and made a beeline for the noticeboard. 'You look well. It's lovely to see you. How are you?'

'Fine,' Audrey muttered. Wendy always monopolized her attention at Society meetings. She only had a tiny agency. It irritated Audrey that she considered herself in the same league.

Wendy stirred her tea excitedly. 'And how's that nice husband of yours?'

Audrey studied Wendy closely for an edge to her enquiry. 'Fine.'

'And how's business?'

'Booming.' Audrey gave her standard answer. The Society was friendly on the outside, but she wasn't fooled. Beneath the veneer everyone was out to expand their client lists . . . even small fry like Wendy.

Wendy inched a little closer.

'Have you heard about Nigel?' she whispered conspiratorially, and dunked her Hob Nob in her tea.

Audrey was thrown, torn between her promise of secrecy to Ernie and her dread of looking like the last to know. She wrestled with herself for a moment.

'But of course!' she burst out knowingly. 'What carelessness to take his eye off the ball like that. Such an amateur mistake! But his loss is our gain. We've been inundated with disaffected Cupid's Cabiners.'

'Ooooh, us too.' Wendy nodded eagerly, sounding less than convincing.

Audrey raised an eyebrow in what she hoped was her most witheringly sceptical manner.

'Are you all right, Audrey?' Wendy looked frightened. 'Gosh, for a minute there I thought you were having a stroke.'

Fortunately they were distracted by a small movement at the door as Nigel crept in looking pale and worried. Audrey saw Alice walk over and give him a cup of tea, her hand touching his arm as she said something supportive. Audrey frowned. How did Alice know about Cupid's Cabin? It couldn't possibly have been from Bianca; she'd expressly told her that the news was secret. But it seemed as though the whole matchmaking world was in the know. Did nobody know the meaning of the word 'discretion' any more?

'Ladies and gentlemen,' Ernie called. 'Can everyone take a seat, please? Let's get started.'

Irritably Audrey noticed that the only remaining empty seat was between Alice and Wendy. Reluctantly she wedged herself between them.

Standing at the head of the room and dressed in a dashing grey suit that made his silver hair shine, Ernie skilfully called the room to quiet.

'Right, well, thank you for giving up a precious afternoon in the office . . .' (There was a cheer from the minions.) 'There's not too much on the agenda today, so we'll keep it short. Obviously the topic on everyone's lips is the forthcoming DIPS ball . . .' (another cheer) '. . . so without further ado, I'd like to hand you over to Sheryl Toogood, who's doing a marvellous job of organizing this year's event.'

There was a hearty thunder of clapping and Sheryl stood up. Audrey rolled her eyes. Sheryl was wearing a baby-pink suit with an offensively short skirt and a perilously low neckline. Barry Chambers and David Bennett suddenly snapped to attention. Of all the men in the room only Nigel seemed *not* to be transfixed, his attention rooted instead on a spot in the middle of the carpet.

'Firstly' – Sheryl paused dramatically – 'Ernie and I are both deliiiiighted by how many new faces will be coming to the ball as "matchmakers in the making". What a crop of talent we have in this room!' she chirped, and slowly, very deliberately she looked straight at Alice.

Audrey's mouth fell open in surprise. Surely she must have been mistaken. But next to her Alice squirmed in her seat and started to blush. Audrey was incredulous. Why on earth was Sheryl looking at Alice? What did she mean? And what was it she'd said? *Ernie and I are delighted.* So that's what they were gossiping about earlier! They were sniggering about Table For Two's 'matchmaker in the making'. Audrey's neck flushed and her temper flared. She knew she shouldn't have invited Alice to the ball. Well, she wasn't going to be a laughing stock. She'd had enough of Alice showing her up, with her stupid bike and saggy cardigans. She'd call her into her office first thing tomorrow and tell her there'd been a mistake. And then she'd invite Bianca to the ball instead.

Audrey looked down. Her knuckles had gone white. She forced herself to breathe deeply.

Eventually, as the minutes passed, some of Sheryl's words filtered through.

'And so the prize will be presented,' Sheryl announced, her bust wobbling with excitement, causing Barry Chambers and David Bennett to shuffle strangely in their seats, 'by our very own local celebrity, top soap actress Lucy Lucinda!'

Audrey snapped to attention.

'Prize? What prize?' she hissed at Alice.

'For Bureau of the Year! It's starting this year. Ernie's going to pick the winner.'

Audrey blinked in disbelief. A prize! Why hadn't she heard about this?

'Thank you,' Ernie said smoothly as Sheryl reluctantly

relinquished the floor. 'I'm sure everyone would agree that this year's ball looks like being better than ever. Thank you, Sheryl, for your sterling efforts.'

Ernie rattled through another couple of items of business before asking: 'And finally ... membership updates. Does anyone have any staff changes to report to the group?'

All eyes turned to Nigel who was still contemplating the carpet.

Silence.

'Ahem.' A small cough came from the front of the room. 'Actually, I do.' Sheryl Toogood was on her feet again. 'Ladies and gentlemen, I'd like to introduce Matteus.' She stretched a baby-pink talon towards an over-groomed but undeniably handsome young man. Matteus stood and bowed to the group. Out of the corner of her eye Audrey saw Cassandra elbow Bianca and mouth 'cor!'. She pursed her lips. Why must her girls show her up at every opportunity?

'Matteus is new to the area,' Sheryl continued, 'but he comes with a fantastic CV. He's fresh from the management team at the dating website dating4desperates.co.uk!'

There were gasps of admiration. Dating4desperates.co.uk was the biggest internet dating site in the country. It bagged more new members in a week than all of the DIPS agencies managed together in six months.

'Of course, we all know that matches made by professional matchmakers are far more likely to lead to love than the DIY jobs made online' – Sheryl played to the audience with a knowing smile – 'but the depth of Matteus's experience, not to mention his strong interpersonal skills' –

Cassandra nudged Bianca again; even Wendy had started fanning herself with her agenda – '. . . make him the ideal new addition to the Love Birds team.'

'Hear, hear!' Ernie led a round of applause and Matteus smiled winningly.

There was a pause.

'Anyone else?' Ernie asked. Again everyone's gaze fell expectantly on Nigel. Again Nigel seemed oblivious, locked in his own personal misery.

'In which case' – Ernie sounded disappointed – 'that wraps things up.'

The room sprang to life with women charging towards Matteus. They flocked around him, with glossy eyes and pink cheeks. Even Wendy joined in. Audrey frowned and then suddenly realized the stampede had left no one between herself and Nigel. Slowly, sorrowfully, he turned towards her, opening his mouth as though to speak. Audrey jolted. He couldn't possibly talk to her. Failure was infectious and she couldn't be seen to be socializing with a sinking ship.

'Oh, Mr President!' she called out hastily. 'May I have a quick word?'

Ernie was deep in discussion with Sheryl and looked vexed at the interruption.

'In private,' Audrey said pointedly, steering Ernie away from Sheryl and into a quiet corner.

'Yes?' he asked distractedly.

'Mr President, it's about the ball.'

'Yes?'

'About my "matchmaker in the making".' She moved to block his wandering eye line. 'I was wondering if I might change my mind? I want to bring Bianca.'

She had his attention now. He eyed her beadily.

'But Bianca's been before. Several times, if I recall. And besides, Alice has already been invited.'

'Yes, but I hadn't realized the significance of my choice.'

Ernie looked at her closely. Audrey tried to look wronged.

'I hadn't grasped what a professional endorsement it was to be invited as the "matchmaker in the making".'

'But Sheryl was very clear about it.'

'Not clear enough,' Audrey replied emphatically, happy to have an unexpected opportunity to drop Sheryl in it. 'And bringing Alice would send the wrong message to my girls.'

'But you can't invite her and then change your mind!'

'Oh, don't worry about that!'

'Think how demoralizing it would be for the girl!'

'I don't think it would be that ba—'

Ernie was looking angry.

'No, Audrey! I won't allow it. Alice is a genuine talent. And, really ... I didn't think you had it in you to be so cruel.'

He turned away, leaving Audrey feeling ticked off. It wasn't fair. Why was it that everything her girls did or said somehow reflected badly on her?

Ernie was back in huddled conversation with Sheryl, and the other society members were still fawning over Matteus. Only Audrey and Nigel stood outside the throng. Without moving her sight line a smidgen – eye contact could be read as an invitation for conversation – Audrey marched back to her seat, collected her belongings and steamed towards the door. She left the chatter of the meeting behind her and set a steely course towards the bus stop.

ALICE

It was Friday afternoon and Alice was hard at work staring out of the Table For Two window.

Friday was always the busiest day of the week, when most clients had their dates. The Table For Two staff would be in a flurry of phone calls, hastily arranging restaurant bookings and giving last-minute pep talks to jittery clients. Alice's job became part organizer, part counsellor and part mum, giving verbal hugs down the telephone and waiting nervously while her brood of clients tottered bravely into the world of dating.

On this particular Friday, Alice's phone calls had all been made, and plans were complete for myriad dinner dates to take place across the city over the weekend. Everyone knew their rendezvous times and destinations; photographs had been emailed and backgrounds given. Although the rest of the Table For Two staff were still busy, Alice's phone was silent. She looked at her watch; half past three. She grinned. She had a blissful couple of hours to spend matchmaking. She took a deep breath and closed her eyes.

Alice loved matchmaking. Alongside pottering in her garden, it was when she felt most alive. She had a special routine. First she cleared her head and blanked out the sounds of the office. She'd imagine she was in her garden, the sun on her face, the grass beneath her feet and birdsong in her ears. She'd breathe deeply, letting the stress of the day melt away as her muscles released their tension. She knew she must look odd; Audrey and the others probably thought she was asleep. But she didn't care, and she never heard their comments anyway. She'd be in the matchmaking zone, a silent, romantic place where negativity couldn't enter.

Within a minute or two she'd be ready. Sometimes she'd open her eyes and stare unseeing out of the window. Sometimes she'd forget and keep her eyes closed. The casual observer would never guess what rich and vivid activity was taking place inside Alice's head. The magic of match-making was buzzing in her brain.

When Alice made matches it was as though she led her clients into a bright, colourful movie where everything was better, nicer and more romantic than real life. Everyone had shiny hair and flattering outfits. It was a world just ready for people to fall in love.

Alice's matchmaking would begin. She'd start with the man. She'd picture him in the restaurant, smartly dressed and totally at ease. He'd be excitedly awaiting his date.

Next Alice would pick a woman who, hunch would tell her, might be a match. She'd watch her enter the restaurant and remove her coat. She'd look stunning: the best she could possibly be.

The couple would greet each other and he'd pull out her chair when she sat down. They'd smile at each other happily, both thanking their luck at being set up with someone so attractive. And then they'd start to talk.

This was the crucial part of the date. Would conversation flow? Would they find common ground? Would they even need to? Maybe they'd delight in being opposites, be enthralled to meet someone whose life and interests were so different from their own? Some people craved similarities, others difference. It was only when Alice watched their date unfold in the private confines of her mind that she knew whether the match would succeed.

Sometimes the dates broke down between the main course and the dessert. Polite enquiries only carried them so far. So the couple would thank each other for a lovely night and head home. Alice would see them safely to their doors, and then return to the restaurant, clearing the table and setting the scene for a new date and another partner.

But sometimes – the best times – the date in Alice's head fizzed and sparkled with romance. Conversations cascaded into each other, smiles lingered well beyond their cause and Alice would burst from her reverie to excitedly scribble down the match.

This was what had happened when Alice had imagined the meeting between Jason and Jennifer. There'd been so much chemistry she'd practically felt the air catch light around them. And now they were getting married! Alice felt something deeper than pride. It was the ownership a painter feels for his work of art.

Alice loved to sink into her imaginary restaurant and made matches whenever she could; in quiet moments at work, evenings when the office was empty, or at weekends as she weeded her garden. Every Monday she'd have a long list of dates to organize, each born in her imagination. It was her fantasy list, her list of romantic hope. At this stage none of the relationships had yet happened; they were just twinkles in Alice's eye. But in her mind they already blossomed. And when the relationships finally took seed in the real world, blossom so many of them did.

Alice's consciousness was gradually permeated by a ringing noise. As the noise became more insistent, the restaurant began to break up around her. She tore her eyes away from the window. She was back in the land of the office and the phone was ringing. The last remnants of the restaurant disappeared and she reluctantly picked up the phone.

'Can I speak to Audrey Cracknell, please?' a male caller asked.

'I'm afraid she's out,' Alice answered. Everyone had sighed with relief when Audrey declared that she was going out and wouldn't be back. She'd been in a terrible mood all day. Alice wondered if it was something to do with yesterday's DIPS meeting; she'd seen Audrey leave early, her neck flushed and her face tight.

'Can I help? I'm Alice.'

'Oh, um. I'm not sure. Ah. Well, maybe. Er. Actually, yes. My name's Max, Max Higgert. It's, ah, it's about the dates

I've been on. Um, well, the dates I've been sent on by Audrey.'

Alice listened.

Twenty minutes later she put down the receiver. She wanted to help but it would be tricky.

What Max had eventually told her was that he wasn't being matched with the kind of woman he wanted. He wanted a kind, caring woman; someone homely and unaffected to share cosy nights in front of the TV. But Audrey kept fixing him up with rich, socially aspiring, designer-clad women; the kind of women who made trophy wives and ruthlessly hunted for solvent husbands; the kind of women who made Max run a mile.

Alice couldn't help herself. She knew it was office suicide to meddle with Audrey's matchmaking. It was fair enough for the staff to dip into each other's client lists, but Audrey's own list was sacrosanct. But Alice knew she wouldn't be able to sleep at night if she just stood by and watched the path to true love being bulldozed. Wasn't the whole point of her job to make perfect matches? Cupid wouldn't stow away his arrows just because his target wasn't on the right list, and neither should she. She looked out of the window and started building the restaurant again.

A few minutes later Alice clicked back into the present with an energetic snap. It was 5.27. She rushed over to where Bianca was shutting down her computer.

'Bianca – please – can I ask you a favour?' Her words tumbled out hastily. Bianca was already buttoning her coat.

'It's about one of Audrey's clients; Max, the architect. I've found his perfect match and I need you to suggest her to Audrey.'

Bianca turned her big blue eyes on Alice and blinked blankly.

'Why don't you suggest her yourself?'

'Because she won't listen if it comes from me! She'd dismiss it out of hand, even though I think they're made for each other. *Especially* because I think they're made for each other!'

'Audrey's not like that!' Bianca said with a little gasp. 'If it's a good idea she'll listen.'

Alice almost laughed out loud.

'I'm sure you're right. But I can't risk it. Max *has* to meet this woman. She's his happy-ever-after!'

The two women smiled at each other; matchmakers couldn't help but go mushy at the thought of a happy-ever-after. Alice let Bianca's romantic nature take hold for a moment, and then pushed home her advantage.

'Audrey listens to you. She'll take it seriously if she thinks it's your idea.'

'But I don't want to take your credit—'

'Take it! Please – have it!'

'Well, if it's what you really want . . . And if it's going to make Max happy . . . I'll do it. I'll suggest the match to Audrey.'

Alice encircled Bianca in a huge hug. 'Thank you! You won't regret it, I promise!'

Alice could only hope she wouldn't regret it either.

AUDREY

Audrey carried her dinner tray into the kitchen and poured herself an extra-large sherry. Pickles the cat twisted around her ankles, rubbing his marmalade hairs into her tights and purring contentedly. Audrey carefully carried her glass back into the living room and settled into her favourite armchair. Her armchair was the only seat in the room that was ever sat on. Her three-person sofa was as plumped and pristine as the day it had been delivered to the house, eleven years ago. Audrey hadn't even taken its plastic cover off for the first few years, and even now she couldn't remember the last time she'd sat on it. And she never had house guests. There was never anyone to invite.

Audrey's armchair, on the other hand, had seen sustained action. Its arms were slippery and balding and several springs under the cushion had gone, but it was as comfortable as a pair of slippers and as welcoming as a hot bath. Audrey spent a lot of time sitting on it; seven evenings a week if she wasn't giving one of her 'The Secret To Finding Your Mr/Miss Right' talks. Once upon a time the armchair had been dusky pink, but over the years it had muted into the colour of butterscotch Angel Delight and had moulded exactly to the contours of Audrey's bottom. In front of her chair was a small pouffe, decorated with a dusting of Pickles's hair and scarred with two deep ruts where Audrey's feet rested.

Audrey took a long sip of sherry. Her favourite detective show wasn't holding her attention tonight. Her mind kept wandering, and the plot had become incomprehensible. Audrey firmly believed that the careful watching of detective shows was far better than any of those expensive brain-training things they sold on the television. A detective TV-show viewer needed to stay on her toes. A diet of *Morse*, *Cracker* and *Prime Suspect* reruns kept her mentally fit and sharp as a button. Apart from tonight, that was. Tonight she was fuzzy and diverted.

She lifted her sherry to her lips. Pickles suddenly jumped onto her lap, causing Audrey's sherry to slop against her lip, leaving a sticky alcohol moustache. She felt a flash of irritation, but as soon as she felt it, it passed. She couldn't be angry with Pickles. He was her constant companion, her one true friend. No matter how trying her day at work, he was always waiting for her at home, purring happily merely to be in her presence. Pickles made Audrey feel loved, and in return, she extended him a rare tolerance. They were in it together, she and Pickles.

As Pickles kneaded her lap, Audrey stroked his fur absent-mindedly. Her fingers took their familiar path down his back, from just under his ears, along the sides of his spine to the tip of his tail, before starting again at his ears. Within three or four strokes everything was forgotten. All Audrey could see was John.

Whenever Audrey daydreamed about John, she always pictured him in her life, not his. That she imagined him relaxing with a whisky in her living room, or crashing pans in her kitchen as he cooked them a romantic meal, was only natural. She'd never seen John's house. She didn't even know where he lived. Whenever she tried to bring it up he'd say something vague like 'not far away', before smoothly bringing the conversation back to her.

Audrey's evenings with John took place entirely within neutral domain. They'd meet on the safe territory of her doorstep. In her excitement she'd get dressed early and then wear down the carpet between the kitchen and the front door, nipping fortifying sips of sherry in the former and peeking through the mottled glass of the latter. She was always ready and waiting for their dates, and never had any reason to invite him over the threshold and onto the fertile ground of her hallway.

Once John arrived he'd kiss her hand in greeting, drive to the ball venue, and then, once the evening was over, drive her home again. He'd never come in when she offered a nightcap. He'd decline graciously, saying, 'Something I've learnt over the years is when to call it a night on a great evening. And that's what this has been . . . a great evening.'

So Audrey had very little geography to go on when placing John within her dreams.

But the one place she did know – and know very well – was the inside of his car. The fluttery nerves she got before their evenings together would soften as soon as John opened the Audi's passenger door and she slid inside. The car advertisements on TV were right to be seductive, she thought. John's car was a perfect, purring machine. From the understated layout of the dashboard to the cream leather seats, everything about the car made Audrey feel protected. She'd smooth her hand along the inside of the door, savouring its solidity, as John walked around to the driver's side. She'd breathe in the car's smell and quietly thrill at the muted power of the engine as John pulled away from her street and towards their evening ahead.

This was the ground zero of her fantasies. Not the racy dreams of the younger woman; Audrey dreamt of domesticity and partnership. She pictured John picking her up from work on a rainy afternoon; of him driving them to the Lake District for a romantic weekend; of the contented routine of a Saturday-morning trip to Waitrose.

Too shy in the early stages of the evening to look directly at John, Audrey would sneak glances at his hands, so manly as he turned the wheel, transporting them through the dark streets of the city. Sometimes – if it was summer – he'd wear a short-sleeved shirt, his jacket waiting neatly on the back seat. Then Audrey would see his forearms, surprisingly muscular; his skin so even and vital-looking that she ached to lean across and touch it.

These were her favourite moments. Audrey prided herself on being in the driving seat of life, but the excitement of a man driving her around the dark city made her feel so feminine. What surrender! She'd catch a glimpse of her reflection in the passenger window and be taken aback. The wrinkles were gone, the years of disappointment wiped out; she looked innocent and girlish, like a teenager on her first date.

Audrey stirred herself. The detective show had finished and the ten o'clock news was drawing to a close. On her lap Pickles lay still, his eyes closed. She looked at her half-drunk sherry. It was too late to finish it now; it was time for bed. Gently she lifted Pickles to the floor and brushed down her skirt. Cat hair floated in the air around her.

ALICE

Alice blew across the surface of her cappuccino and did her best to avoid looking at Sheryl's breasts, straining to escape from their leopard-print blouse. If Alice raised her eyes to look above them she knew she'd see Sheryl smiling wolfishly over the top of her skinny latte, her lips sticky with scarlet lipgloss. Alice wondered whether Sheryl ever wore a polo neck, or any item of clothing that didn't display a large 'V' of cleavage. Didn't her breasts ever get cold? Alice was huddled in two layers of jumper. Surely Sheryl's breasts must cry out for a day off; a little time out from being displayed to the elements? They must dream of being wrapped in a nice, soft turtleneck.

Alice blew on her coffee again.

'So, Alice.' Sheryl licked her lips and set down her coffee cup. She minutely straightened her skin-tight skirt. 'I don't believe in beating about the bush. For a long time now I've been hearing what a faaabulous matchmaker you are. I'd like you to come and work for me.'

Alice made a funny choking sound.

'I'd like you to resign from Table For Two with immediate effect and join us at Love Birds. Naturally I expect your clients to follow you.'

Alice tried not to let her mouth flap open.

'Just like that?'

'Just like that.' Sheryl gave a small, pouty smile.

'But what about Audrey?' Alice asked in bewilderment. 'What about my contract? I've made promises.'

'Promises are made to be broken, every woman knows that. There isn't a contract in the world that can't be got out of and I bet Audrey's are as holey as fishnets. I can get our lawyers to give yours the once-over. I see no reason why you can't start at Love Birds on Monday.'

She gave Alice a penetrating look.

Alice clung to her coffee cup and concentrated on Sheryl's knees.

'I, uh, I'm not sure what to say,' she mumbled.

'Say yes. Whatever Audrey's paying you I'll double. And I'll make you my bureau deputy.'

'Wow.' Alice's mouth fell open again. Double her salary? She'd be rich. She could buy every plant in the garden centre. She could even buy herself a greenhouse; she'd always wanted a greenhouse! And bureau deputy . . . ? She'd almost be in charge. Never in her wildest dreams – and some of Alice's dreams could be quite wild – had she imagined she'd ever be as senior as that. It was amazing! 'That's . . .' – she grinned broadly, unable to believe her own luck – 'that's very generous of you.'

'I'm not a generous woman; I'm a businesswoman. You are a valuable asset and I need a strong wing-commander to keep on top of the one-to-one clients whilst I concentrate on expanding our web service. Online dating's a cash cow, and I intend to milk it dry. So . . .' – Sheryl leaned towards Alice like a cobra leaning out of its basket – 'as one businesswoman to another, what do you say?'

Alice's brain was whirring. A businesswoman? She'd never thought of herself as that before. Could she really do this? Could she work for Sheryl and be a . . . a matchmaking *high-flyer*?

'Um, Ms Toogood, thank you,' she mumbled in a daze. 'Thank you for having such faith in me . . .'

'It's not faith.' Sheryl picked up her coffee cup. 'You can bring me clients, earn me money.' She took a sip, her eyes fixed on Alice.

'But what about Audrey?' Alice said again as her bubble suddenly burst. 'I couldn't just leave her. She was the one who gave me my first break, my first matchmaking job. And now she's taking me to the ball as her matchmaker in the making; I shouldn't repay her like that! And she'd never let me take my clients . . . and I couldn't possibly pinch them.'

From across the table she could hear Sheryl tut as she uncrossed her legs with a noisy nylon swoosh.

'They're not Audrey's clients, they're yours! You move and they'll follow. They don't want to be stuck with an old battleaxe like Audrey. Would *you* let her sort out *your* love life? Trust me; they'll be like lemmings off a cliff!'

'But they're people with lives and dreams!' Alice protested. 'Not possessions to be carted around or chips to be gambled with. And I couldn't leave Audrey in the lurch. I'd need to give her plenty of notice so she could get everything sorted. A few months, at least.' Alice saw Sheryl look away, a peculiar expression on her face. 'Audrey hates recruiting new people,' she explained. 'By the time anyone started it would be too late. Budding relationships would have lost momentum. My clients would go back to being single and thinking they were stuck with it. And Audrey would be in a terrible way with the extra workload.'

Sheryl rolled her eyes.

'Audrey's tough. Like a cockroach.'

'I'd need to give her at least six months. Otherwise it's not fair.'

'Oh, Alice, how sweet!' Sheryl gave a brittle laugh. 'Life as a big, bad grown-up isn't fair. Sometimes the big kids nick the little kids' sweets.'

Alice blushed and dropped her eyes to her coffee. 'It would be the right thing to do,' she said quietly.

'The right thing to do!' Sheryl threw up her hands in exasperation. 'Next you'll be telling me you set up couples because you think they'll fall in love!'

'Of course! That's the whole point, isn't it?' Alice answered in astonishment.

Sheryl stifled a small, hard smile.

'Alice, my dahhhhling, that's the *secondary* point. A lucky coincidence, that's all. We're all in it – me, Audrey, even you, although you obviously can't see it yet – to make money first, matches second. There's no point being the world's best Cupid if you can't pay the mortgage! We're not in this out of the goodness of our hearts; all the love stuff's just window dressing. We're here to make a profit. Nobody makes a deliberate love match until they've screwed at least six months' fees out of a client. It's financial madness to give them their little happy-ever-afters too early.'

Alice stared at Sheryl. She couldn't believe what she'd just heard. Surely everybody tried to help couples find love? That was the whole point of being a matchmaker! Making bad matches just to keep the fees coming in was horrible; it made her feel dirty just thinking about it.

'Audrey doesn't do that,' Alice asserted very definitely.

'Doesn't she?' Sheryl needled.

'Of course not!' Alice was shocked by the very idea. 'She wouldn't! And besides, everyone knows she matched her first five clients so well they all got married.'

Sheryl smirked.

'Everyone knows three of them were already dating, and all five are long-since divorced.'

Alice gasped in horror. Already dating? And *divorced*? Surely not! Audrey had never said. But then again, would she? She always got a bit funny at any mention of the 'D' word, so much so that they'd all learned not to say it out loud in the office.

'Besides,' Sheryl stirred her coffee slyly, 'has Audrey ever been that efficient since? She was wet behind the ears back then. I bet she doesn't match anywhere near that quickly these days. In fact, I bet she hardly makes any successful matches at all.'

Alice opened her mouth to spring to Audrey's defence,

but then slowly closed it again. It was true that Audrey's matches invariably failed. Clients stayed on her list for ages; some of them had been there for years. But Alice had always thought it was because Audrey wasn't very in tune with people, not because she was doing anything dodgy. Then she thought about Max Higgert and how he wanted one kind of woman yet Audrey seemed determined to match him with another.

Sheryl sighed and softened her voice.

'Look, Alice. I think it's wonderful that you have high ideals; that you *believe* in the calling of matchmaking. I can use this idealism. You can handle the dreams and I can handle the bank balance. You're just what I'm looking for.'

Shakily Alice put down her coffee cup.

'I don't think I'm right for you,' she said quietly.

'Nonsense.' Sheryl tossed her hair. 'Now listen to me, Alice. I'm used to getting what I want, and I want you working for Love Birds within the fortnight. The look on Audrey's face would be priceless.'

Alice tried to interject but Sheryl pushed on.

'Look, you can hide behind your morals, but when was the last pay rise the battleaxe gave you? Has she ever given you one? Everyone knows Audrey likes keeping you at the bottom of the pile. But I'm offering you a one-hundred-per-cent rise and the chance to be my number two! Love Birds is growing; it's got a future. Audrey's a dinosaur; she's heading for extinction.'

She reached for her coat and handbag.

'I need to think,' Alice said unsteadily to no one in particular. The room seemed to be spinning. The whole world seemed to be spinning.

Sheryl stood up. She towered threateningly above Alice in her stilettos.

'You can think, but don't you dare say no, young lady. Offers like this don't grow on trees. I'll give you a few days but no more. Life's there for the taking, Alice' – Sheryl threw on her coat with an impatient flourish – '. . . so take it!'

She turned on her heel and clip-clopped malignantly out of the coffee shop, letting the door bang noisily behind her.

JOHN

It was nine o'clock and John had already skim-read the paper. He was sitting at his kitchen table, sipping coffee and gazing out at the garden, when the phone rang. It was Geraldine.

'Morning!' she chirped. 'Good news: I've got another booking for you. It's from a regular.'

His heart sank. He knew exactly what was coming. He'd been lucky to have escaped for so long.

Geraldine continued. 'It's Audrey Cracknell. She's got another of her Society balls.'

John breathed tightly and tried to keep his voice even.

'That's great, Geraldine.' Somehow he managed to sound halfway sincere. 'At the Town and Country Golf Club again?'

'Got it in one. Hold on, let me grab the details.' As he heard her rummaging amongst her papers he tried to resist the feeling of being forced into a small, tight box.

'Here we go,' she chimed. 'You're to pick her up at 7.30 p.m. next Thursday. It's a black-tie event, and she wants you to wear your cornflower-blue cummerbund. Apparently it matches your eyes! Dinner will be provided, and it should be all over by midnight.'

'No problem.' He tried to be light. 'I'll look forward to it.'

'You're a poppet,' laughed Geraldine gaily. 'That's why they all keep coming back for more.'

He rang off.

'Bugger!' He swore out loud, causing Buster, his black retriever, to lift his head from his basket. Audrey was one of those clients who made his normally pleasant job deeply unpleasant. Even in the safety of his kitchen he could picture her face as she lingered interminably in his car whenever he dropped her off at the end of an evening. She'd look up at him with a monstrous coquettishness, like an overgrown teenager waiting for a Mills & Boon kiss.

John had tried to rationalize why he hated his end-of-night goodbyes with Audrey, and he'd got it down to this: wide-eyed girlishness was wrong on anyone too old to be called a girl. Women in their thirties and above were attractive precisely because they weren't wide-eyed; they'd lived a bit. They had stories and opinions and battle scars and triumphs. And their experiences had taught them to hold themselves high, to rein themselves in and not to hyperventilate whenever they were within touching distance of a man. John had met many women through his work: some very experienced with men, others who hadn't had a partner in years. But they all had dignity, or at least an inner braking system that stopped them crossing an invisible line. When Audrey turned in his passenger seat and looked up at him through quivering, fluttering eyelashes, all he could see was her mountainous bosom heaving up and down and he'd wonder if her heavy breathing would steam up the car windows.

John shuddered.

He hated to admit it, because he prided himself on liking women – he'd chosen his job precisely *because* he liked women – but Audrey Cracknell made his skin crawl. Of course he could never bring himself to kiss her goodnight, not even on the cheek. So he'd smile, tell her he'd had a great evening and hold her gaze just long enough for her not to feel dejected. Then he'd touch his foot ever so slightly on the accelerator, just enough to suggest the idea of his leaving. Once she was on the pavement and the passenger door was finally closed he'd drive away sedately. But as soon as he turned out of her road his foot would hit the accelerator hard and he'd drive home like a reckless boy racer. It was the relief of getting away.

John tipped the remnants of his coffee down the sink. Buster's collar jangled as he followed him around the kitchen, hoping for a walk. John ruffled Buster's head distractedly. He cursed himself for not telling Geraldine he no longer wanted Audrey's bookings. He'd been meaning to for years, but hadn't had the heart to do it. He wasn't a fool. He could see what Audrey felt for him and what their evenings meant to her. He'd have to be blind, deaf and stupid not to.

John pulled on his muddy gardening boots. Buster would have to wait. The garden beckoned.

* * *

Later, after two hours of furious digging, he felt better. He breathed deeply and drank in the fresh winter air. It was hard to stay angry when surrounded by nature. He picked up the stick that Buster had dropped at his feet and tossed it high into the air. Buster caught it with a soggy snatch of his jaws.

He'd made his decision. He would have his evening with Audrey, and he'd be the consummate professional. Only this time he'd make damn sure he rang Geraldine straight afterwards to tell her that when it came to dinner dates with a certain overly hormonal lady, he was no longer on the menu.

He nodded firmly. That was it: the plan. Thursday's ball at the Town and Country Golf Club was Audrey's last supper. And the cummerbund was staying where it belonged – in the loft.

'Come on, Buster,' he called cheerily, picking up his spade and heading back towards the house, a small but definite spring in his step. 'It's time for your walk.'

AUDREY

'Hayley?' Audrey echoed incredulously. 'The veterinary nurse? With the funny finger?'

On the other side of Audrey's desk, Bianca shifted her weight and nodded nervously.

'Whatever makes you think they'd be a good match?'

Bianca glanced briefly through the glass wall towards the open-plan office as though searching for an answer.

'Instinct,' she replied. 'I just know they'll be a perfect fit.'

'Well,' said Audrey in surprise as she removed her glasses. 'A perfect fit! Bianca, I must say, you surprise me. You can obviously see something the rest of us can't. But what can a woman like Hayley offer a man like Max Higgert?'

Bianca faltered for a moment, as though trying to remember something.

'Softness. Max works hard all day, dealing with clients and workmen. Everybody demands something from him. But when he comes home in the evening, he wants someone different. Someone soft and caring. Someone *un*demanding.'

Audrey harrumphed.

'Hayley's very caring,' Bianca added hastily. 'She looks after sick animals!'

Audrey peered at her sceptically.

'But she's a veterinary nurse. Max is a high-flyer. No, I just can't see how it could work. I'm sorry, Bianca, but you're barking up the wrong tree.'

'But maybe that's why it could work. If Max wanted a high-flyer, wouldn't he have found one by now? He must meet dozens every day! Maybe he wants the opposite.'

'What, a low-flyer?' Audrey snorted. 'Well, Hayley certainly fits the bill there!'

Bianca looked towards the open-plan office. In her peripheral vision Audrey noticed Alice grinning like a lunatic.

'Please, Audrey. I've got a very good feeling about this. If I'm wrong, I'm wrong. But Max seems like a nice man; I don't think he'd hold a mistake against us.'

Audrey eyed her beadily.

'Against *me*,' Bianca added contritely.

Audrey gave a big sigh. 'Well, all right,' she conceded. 'But only because it's you. I'll call him in a moment.'

'Thank you, Audrey!' Bianca flashed a smile of gratitude.

'Yes, well. Now, get back to your work, please. I've got things to be getting on with. Oh, and send Alice in.' She dismissed her with a regal wave of the hand. She didn't see the surreptitious nod Bianca gave Alice as she pulled the glass door closed behind her.

Hayley Clarke! Well, Bianca was either a matchmaking genius or she was losing her marbles. But if the girl felt passionately about the match she wouldn't stand in the way. Besides, she'd been running out of women to pair Max with.

There was a timid knock on the door, and Alice edged mousily in, tugging at today's ensemble of shapeless, colourless knitwear. She looked at her expectantly.

'So.' Audrey patted her hair as she collected her thoughts. 'As you're no doubt aware, it's the Dating Practitioners' Society annual ball on Thursday.'

Alice smiled and nodded.

'You *have* bought a new dress, haven't you?' Audrey asked sharply.

'Oh yes; it's lovely!'

'And it's new? Not from a charity shop?'

Alice looked confused.

'I got it from the new boutique on King Street. The one Lucy Lucinda opened.'

'Wonderful,' Audrey said with an unmistakable note of relief. She shuffled her papers officiously. 'Now, I just wanted to run you through a few dos and don'ts for the evening. Obviously I'll be arriving with John, so I'll meet you inside. You do know it's at the Town and Country Golf Club, don't you? I must insist you take a taxi to the venue.'

'Oh, Audrey, that's very kind but most unnecessary.'

'It's very necessary. I insist.'

'Well, thank you ver—'

Audrey held up her hand to silence her. She wasn't being benevolent. She didn't want Alice to show her up by arriving by bike.

'Just make sure you keep your receipt. And if you're going

to tip the driver, do it with your own money. I'm not a charity.'

Alice nodded keenly.

Audrey pressed on. 'So you'll be sitting at the top table with John and me, President Ernie and his wife Patricia, Barry Chambers from A Fine Romance and his wife Eileen, and Ms Toogood from Love Birds and her partner, Brad. Don't you think you should be writing this down? I don't want you embarrassing me by forgetting the name of somebody's spouse.'

Alice delved into her jumper, pulled out a dog-eared notebook and biro and scribbled diligently.

'Oh, and that new boy from Love Birds will be there too to make it an even number. I can't remember his name. Mathis? Something like that.'

'Matteus?'

'Yes, yes. And I don't want you going all gooey-eyed over him. I saw the reaction he got at the meeting last week. Most distasteful. I'd never seen such a display of hormones.'

Alice laughed.

'Don't worry; he's not my type.'

Audrey eyed Alice. Even she had seen that Matteus was very good-looking. A bit slimy, and rather heavy-handed with the aftershave, but definitely the sort women seemed to go for. Alice, on the other hand, was a drab little wallflower, the kind of girl who'd get lost on a magnolia background. 'No, I don't expect he is,' she said dryly.

'There will be no discussing of clients,' she continued bossily. 'Remember ... there's no such thing as a cross-bureau friendship. Everyone must be treated with suspicion.'

Alice nodded.

'Might I remind you of the confidentiality clause in your contract? Loose lips sink ships, young lady.'

Alice blinked and nodded again.

'With that in mind, you will moderate your drinking. I will be most displeased to see you drunk. I suggest a water course after each glass of alcohol. Do you know what that is?'

Alice nodded.

'That's one glass of water to every glass of alcohol consumed,' Audrey steamrollered on. 'That way you'll stay in control of your faculties and we'll stay in control of our client list.'

Audrey noticed that Alice was looking at her peculiarly. 'Was there anything else?' Alice asked.

Audrey fiddled with her glasses and tried to think of something.

'No, that will be all.'

Audrey frowned as she watched Alice shuffle back to her seat and resume staring out of the window. She couldn't remember why on earth she'd invited her to the ball or, for that matter, why she'd let Hilary talk her into hiring her in the first place. It had been the last time she'd ever taken Hilary's advice and she'd never risked going on holiday since. Such a mistake, that fortnight on the Norfolk Broads when she'd left Hilary in charge. It had rained every single day, and when she'd returned to the office she'd found

Alice manning the phones. Hilary had put up such a persuasive argument for keeping her – something about numbers being up and the clients being happy – that she'd agreed to it. It had been the only day Alice had ever come to work looking smart. The moment she had her feet under the table her steam iron had mysteriously disappeared. Audrey wasn't sure that happy clients had been worth it. She watched unhappily through the glass wall as Alice absentmindedly pulled a biro from her hair. She sincerely hoped Alice had booked a pre-ball trip to the hairdressers. Slowly Alice began to use the end of the biro to scratch at the nape of her neck.

Audrey turned away. She couldn't bear to see any more.

ALICE

'She said *what*?'

Ginny's voice sounded incredulous over the background of Scarlet's ear-splitting wails. It was ten o'clock. Scarlet was obviously having a difficult night ... *again*.

'She said no matchmaker makes a deliberate love match until they've screwed at least six months' fees out of a client,' Alice repeated as loudly as she could without actually shouting into the phone.

'That's awful! Do you think it's true?' Ginny bellowed back at her, trying her best to have a normal conversation as though a screaming infant wasn't really breaking several health and safety decibel limits whilst pummelling angrily against her shoulder.

'It can't be. It's immoral. And besides, if Ernie at DIPS knew anyone was doing it he'd shut them down.'

'So you reckon it's just Love Birds, then?'

'It must be,' Alice replied uncertainly. 'I can't believe Audrey would do it too. I mean, I know she's a ...'

'Brute? Ogre? Sociopath?'

'... bit of a grump, but she's as happy as anyone when

we make a good match, especially a match that ends in a wedding.'

'Yeah, sweetness and light, that Audrey,' Ginny said sagely. Alice heard her fob baby Scarlet off on Dan. Suddenly the sounds of howling receded. Alice's ears tingled as they re-adjusted to normal sound levels.

'Audrey's got her bad points, but she's not like Sheryl,' she reasoned, as much to herself as to Ginny.

Ginny laughed. 'Not corrupt; just crap.'

Her statement hung heavily between them. Alice stared thoughtfully into space.

'So what about Sheryl, then?' Ginny broke her reverie. 'You going to take her up on her job offer? Double your salary ... offers like that don't come around every day of the week.'

'I don't see how I can,' Alice replied glumly. 'Not now I know about her tactics. I couldn't do what she does; I couldn't do that to the clients. Can you imagine how awful it must be for them, to have six months of wrong dates?'

'Most people have *years* of wrong dates out in the real world.'

'But that's the point; it's my job to take them away from all that. I couldn't deliberately make them unhappy when I know I could make them happy.'

'But what about making yourself happy, Alice? What about the money and the promotion and the greenhouse? What about getting the recognition you deserve after all these years?'

Alice thought for a moment.

'Could you do it, Gin? Knowing what we know, could you really take Sheryl's job and sleep well at night?'

'You're asking the mother of a one-year-old whether I'd sleep well at night? I'd sell my soul to the Devil for eight hours, earplugs and an empty double bed.'

'An *empty* double bed?'

'Oh, you know; space to stretch out and not to have to fight for the covers.'

'So, is that a "yes"?'

'Yes! No! Oh, I don't know.' Ginny sighed. 'Look, Alice, you've got to do what's right for you. You're a brilliant matchmaker whose talent is being ignored by a bitch of a boss with the social skills of a third-world dictator. You can stay where you are and keep getting trodden on, or you can jump ship and get your talent recognized by a *new* bitch of a boss with the morals of an alley cat. The choice is yours, but it's pretty obvious to anyone who's ever met you which one you're going to choose.'

'I choose the clients,' Alice said simply. 'Which means I choose Audrey. At least she's honest.' She didn't want to contemplate the lurking fear that Audrey might not be. She didn't even want to air the suggestion out loud.

'Bang goes the greenhouse,' warned Ginny.

'Bang goes the greenhouse,' Alice repeated solemnly.

LOU

Lou almost didn't pick up the phone. It was 11.30 p.m. and she couldn't be bothered to do small talk with anyone beyond ten o'clock at night. Unless the small talk was in a bar with a bloke and might end in a shag. But if she was wrapped in a blanket, knocking back a bottle of red and chain-scoffing Mars bars in front of a late-night TV programme about an ill-fated, surgically enhanced Italian porn star who swapped a life in blue movies for the world of politics, then small talk was definitely off the agenda.

But the ringing was very persistent.

It had to be Kate.

Without tearing her eyes from the TV Lou groped for the phone.

'I've just had the second worst night of my life!'

It *was* Kate.

'Obviously *nothing* could be worse than my date at The Privet with Sebastian. But tonight was a close second.'

Above the breathy panting on the TV Lou could hear Kate was short of breath too. She was obviously in a rush to impart gossip.

'So, I had my date with Michael tonight. You know, the owner of that internet start-up company?'

'Uh-huh.' Lou had long since discovered that phone calls with Kate often required minimum input from herself. Sometimes she could go for half an hour without uttering anything that would qualify as a full Oxford-English-Dictionary-recognized word.

'Well, after my date with Sebastian, Alice suggested I pick the venue this time. So I told him to meet me at Luigi's.'

Lou topped up her glass. It was clearly going to be a classic Kate call: a minute-by-minute account of her night.

'So there I was, at 8.30 p.m., *as agreed*. No sign of him. So I waited. And waited. You'll never guess what time he turned up!'

'Ummm,' Lou hummed, her mouth full of wine.

'Nine o'clock!' Kate retorted angrily. 'Nine o'bloody clock! The cheek of him! He was lucky I was still there! I'd felt such an idiot sitting on my own, everyone thinking I'd been stood up – me included!'

Lou tutted. The Italian porn star was meeting a white-coated specialist who was telling her that, for medical reasons, her fourth breast enlargement had to be her last. Lou goggled at her mammoth breasts. They looked like spacehoppers with nipples. She was mental if she wanted them bigger.

'So, he eventually turns up and witters some excuse about work being busy and it being hard to get away. I mean, tell me something I don't know! *My* work's busy. *I* find it hard to get away. It doesn't mean *I'm* thirty minutes late. "And

besides," I said, "aren't you the boss? Can't you just dele-
gate, or something?" Except obviously I said it much nicer
than that, because I don't want him to think I'm one of
those women who gets stressed about everything. And he
just looks at me with this sad little smile, and then his
Blackberry rings and he *only bloody takes the phone call*! At
five past nine! When he's just turned up ... *late* ... for a
date!'

'Bastard,' Lou muttered automatically. The porn star was
going for more surgery regardless.

'So I sat there, trying to smile and look relaxed, and he
eventually gets off the phone and buys me a drink. And we're
just starting to talk about what he does for a living and the
phone rings again ... *and he takes it*! We're twenty minutes
into the date and already he's spent ten on the phone!'

Lou tsked and took a large bite of Mars bar.

'Anyway, after that we eventually get to talk a bit, and
he's really nice, you know. Handsome, although tired-
looking. And clearly he's very clever because his business
is doing really well. So I think, well, maybe I'll let him off
being late and taking the calls because he's obviously got
ambition and is going places. So I went to the loo to check
my hair but when I get back he's got his laptop out and is
fiddling around with some spreadsheet. Apparently he'd
just had an idea to add to a presentation he's giving
tomorrow, and if he didn't add it in at that very moment
he'd forget it. So I sat there and watched him tapping keys.
And the next thing I know he's answering his emails too.
He keeps apologizing, saying that this is the price of owning

your own company, but meanwhile I'm sitting there like an idiot, staring at the lid of his computer and wondering when our date is actually going to begin.'

'Nightmare,' said Lou hollowly.

'So, around ten-ish he finally puts the computer away and we get some more drinks and start to talk. And I'm thinking to myself, well, I can see why you needed to join Table For Two. I asked him how many nights a week he worked late, and he said "all of them". "But what about girlfriends?" I asked. "Ah, yes," he said. "I haven't been very good at keeping them." Apparently none of them last longer than a couple of weeks; they all get fed up and scarper. Funny that! Anyway, he offered to walk me home, and I thought, why not? He's very handsome and I've always wanted a boyfriend who owns his own business. But the minute we leave, his phone rings, and he's talking to some bloke called Mo who runs his Japanese office *all the way home*. He doesn't even hang up when we reach my front door! He just puts Mo on hold! Can you believe it?'

Lou took her cue and exhaled loudly in sympathetic exasperation. The porn star has made it all the way to the Italian parliament where she looks very fetching in a collection of tight suits and schoolmistress glasses. But it's bad news on the health front. One of her implants has leaked into her bloodstream. Doctors have told her she's only got months to live, but she's battling courageously on, keeping her political appointments and not letting the public know how ill she is in case the outcry of sympathy gets in the way of her doing her important political work.

'And then he leans over, kisses me on the cheek and says, "Great night, let's do it again soon." Great night? What planet is this man on? He spent most of the night effectively in the office! It's no wonder he's single! He's got no time for a girlfriend. His girlfriend is his job!'

'People in glass houses,' Lou muttered darkly.

'What?' Kate was too indignant to hear. 'I'm going to ring Alice and tell her to have a word with him. He's never going to find someone unless he switches off his Blackberry. She's got to help this man. He's so good-looking but he's wasting the best years of his life!'

Lou smiled evilly. 'It's going well then, Table For Two?'

'Oi! I don't want any of your negativity! It's just a couple of false starts, that's all. You can't expect to pick up a tennis racket and serve an ace straight off.'

'Right.'

It was too late at night for unexpected metaphors. The Italian porn star had kicked the bucket and was being given something akin to a state funeral. Thousands of mourners were filing past her open casket, gazing upon her immaculately made-up face and doubtless wondering how the officials were going to force the coffin lid down over her gigantic knockers.

'I've got complete confidence in Alice,' Kate protested passionately.

'Whatever you say,' Lou agreed blandly, and drained her glass.

AUDREY

Audrey carefully hung her dry-cleaning on the coat rack and closed her front door behind her. She sighed. It had been a pig of a day. Hilary had inconsiderately scheduled a midwife appointment for mid-morning, so Audrey had not only been landed for a few hours with the management of the website and its inevitable accompanying headache, but she'd also compounded her misfortune by picking up a ringing telephone only to discover Maurice Lazenby on the other end. In the words of Cassandra, she'd been well and truly *Mauriced*; forced to endure his latest tales of dating woe for forty endless minutes. The only bright part of the day had been her conversation with Max Higgert, who'd been surprisingly enthusiastic about a potential date with Hayley the veterinary nurse. Audrey still had her doubts about the wisdom of the match. She only hoped Hayley would have the good sense to keep her hand in her lap. Goodness knows what Max would think if he caught a glimpse of her defective digit.

But tonight was not a night for wrestling with the love lives of her clients. There was much to do. The Dating

Practitioners' Society annual ball was just twenty-four short hours away!

Audrey fussily smoothed down the polythene around her ball gown. The dress was a floor-length petrol blue, generously cut and a long-term faithful. Mid-length sleeves and a sensible neck hid her problem areas of chunky arms and a crêpey chest. Audrey still needed to press her cream stole, but she'd already confirmed her appointment to have her hair set tomorrow lunchtime, and she'd brushed her best suede courts at the weekend.

Still in her coat, she reached for the telephone.

'Hello, Geraldine? Audrey Cracknell here. I'm just double-checking that everything's tickety-boo for John Marlowe tomorrow evening ... I need him at 7.30 prompt. Yes, I know I've told you this before ... Yes, it probably was twice.'

Audrey's gaze drifted to her reflection in the mirror above the telephone stand, and she pushed her unruly orange hair into place. It never did have any shape or texture. Years ago someone had cruelly remarked upon her follicular similarity to Arthur Scargill. It still rankled.

'Now, it's a black-tie event,' she continued into the telephone, 'and I'd like John to wear his cornflower blu— Oh, I mentioned that too? Well, jolly good. Better to be safe than sorry ... Right, well, goodbye.'

Audrey sailed into the kitchen, her coat billowing in her wake and Pickles mewing at her heels. Tomorrow would be perfect, she thought. Her ample breast was already aflutter at the thought of opening her front door and seeing John on her porch, already leaning forward to kiss her hand in greeting. He was such a handsome man. A handsome *gentleman*, she corrected herself as she pulled a ready meal for one from the fridge. She didn't know how she would have endured so many Dating Practitioners' Society balls had it not been for him. He played his part to perfection, fetching drinks for the other ladies, swapping jokes with the men and nodding in shared memory of their recent holiday stories, fictionalized by Audrey for the group. After the first couple of years she hadn't even needed to ask him to wear a wedding band.

Audrey picked up a fork, stabbed at the cellophane covering her ready meal and slung it into the microwave.

Yes, she and John were such a natural couple she really could see no reason why they weren't actually together. He'd accompanied her to every function since she'd set up her own business. It wouldn't have done for word to get around that someone who made a living by ending people's single status was actually single herself. So she'd taken matters into her own hands and – after securing written confirmation from Geraldine that John wouldn't accept bookings from any other matchmaking professionals, thus guaranteeing secrecy over the true nature of their rela- tionship – she ordered herself a gentleman friend for the evening. How was she to know that everyone would presume they were a long-standing couple? And why shouldn't she let them think that? After all, it was they who'd jumped to conclusions. She hadn't actually lied.

So over the years they had, to the outside world at least, become Audrey and John; Audrey and John Cracknell. It was such an easy falsehood to slip into, and over time she'd come to think of John as hers. Well, he was, in a way. And she was sure it was what he wanted too, despite his old-fashioned insistence on remaining firmly inside his car when he dropped her off at the end of their evenings. But he too must feel a quickening of the breast and a short-ening of breath whenever they said their goodbyes.

The microwave pinged loudly. Audrey shuffled her ready meal onto a plate, placed a knife, fork and a small glass of sherry on a tray and carried it into the living room. She was so excited she wasn't sure she'd be able to eat. But she'd give it her best shot and treat herself to just a small amount of *Morse* before she pressed her stole and gave her feet a soak in the foot spa. Then she'd give herself a mani-cure. Nothing too flashy. Just a nice tasteful pearl. John would like that.

ALICE

Alice burst through her front door and pulled off her cycling helmet, revealing bright red cheeks and flat, sweaty hair. This 'being-a-lady' stuff was far more complicated – not to mention expensive – than she'd imagined.

Buying the dress and shoes had been one thing, but now it was all getting way too silly. Everything cost a fortune and every task (like the choosing of nail varnish) led to another task (the need to file and shape her nails). It was like a nightmarishly feminine version of Russian dolls with endless primping, preening and plucking. And if the pre-ball preparation scared her, the prospect of actually going to the ball was hanging over her like the countdown to major surgery without anaesthetic. Alice was beginning to wonder if Audrey had only invited her to the ball as an ingenious form of torture.

The latest ball emergency was down to the wholly ridiculous question of make-up. Or, more specifically, Alice's eleventh-hour realization that she didn't own any. Earlier that afternoon Hilary had casually asked how she was going to do her make-up for the ball. Nobody had ever seen Alice in anything more than a watery stroke of mascara and a smudge of Vaseline. The colour had immediately drained from Alice's face. Make-up was a brand new hurdle to stress about. A quick straw poll of the office (thankfully Audrey was out) revealed that even Cassandra thought it inconceivable that Alice could attend the ball without wearing at least basic cosmetics. The trouble was that the ball was twenty-four hours away, and Alice didn't know where to start.

Back in the safety of her flat, she dropped her carrier bag of newly acquired make-up onto her armchair and heard the little pots of creams and colours clink expensively together. She'd spent the last few hours lumbering awkwardly around the alien environment of the cosmetics counter, avoiding the eyes of the scary-looking make-up girls and feeling like Crocodile Dundee as she peered at tubs of light-reflecting-this and cashmere-finish-that. She looked wistfully at her bag of purchases; bang goes another hundred pounds.

Alice checked her watch. Time was marching on. She still hadn't cooked or eaten dinner, let alone shaved her legs, washed her hair or spent the two hours it took her to apply unwonky nail varnish. And now she had the added complication of having to practise putting on make-up too. The evening was suddenly looking very short.

She pressed her hand against her stomach, trying to calm her nerves. It was hard to know what she was most scared of.

First was the dread of having to engage in small talk with Audrey.

Then there was Audrey's list of rules to follow. There had been so many, she could barely remember them, let alone avoid breaking them.

Plus there was the crippling fear of being seen in public in her new dress and heels. It was one thing swanning around her flat, imagining herself as a femme fatale, but actually wearing it all outside her front door as plain old Alice Brown . . . ? She was bound to trip in her heels and look like an idiot.

And now there was the added worry of badly applied make-up (why hadn't she been practising since the age of thirteen like everyone else?).

And to top it all there was the excruciating prospect of seeing Sheryl Toogood again.

Immediately after her chat with Ginny, Alice had burned the midnight oil, carefully composing an email to Sheryl. She'd politely thanked her for her offer but respectfully declined the job. The more she thought about Sheryl's bad-matches-for-more-money scam, the sicker she felt. She dreaded seeing her again. Sheryl wasn't the type to take rejection, even if it was only from Alice.

She'd just have a liquid dinner tonight, she decided as she rummaged in the kitchen for a bottle of wine. She was too nervous to eat. It was all she could do to pour the wine into a glass. For a moment she was tempted to drink straight from the bottle.

AUDREY

Audrey swept into the Town and Country Golf Club, her arm hooked around John's and her head held high. Her petrol-blue ball gown swished elegantly around her ankles. In her mind's eye she and John made quite an entrance: distinguished-looking, slightly regal. She liked to think the other society members considered them the elder statesmen of courtship. They were a couple maturely in love; none of the outward gushiness of young passion, but rather the deeply felt, discreetly displayed, late-blooming love of, say, Charles and Camilla. Audrey had developed quite a soft spot for Camilla over the years. She was no oil painting, granted, but she always got her grooming spot on.

Audrey nodded grandly to various Society members as she and John made their way to the bar. She always felt like a woman on John's arm. It was the only place in the world where she glowed. She felt the electricity at the point where his dinner jacket met her arm. Tonight was her birthday, Christmas and Easter Sunday all rolled into one. Tonight she wasn't just Audrey, she was one half of Audrey and John.

Suddenly a dark cloud appeared in her sight line. Audrey frowned. Why was Sheryl Toogood always the first person they bumped into? And what in the name of heaven was she wearing?

Audrey let her eyes adjust as she took in the spectacle of Sheryl's outfit. She was poured into a very low-cut silver dress with Perspex heels and a silver clutch bag. She dripped with sparkly diamonds, the only splashes of colour being her fuchsia-pink nails and matching glossy lips. Sheryl looked, Audrey noted with a purse of her own coral-coated lips, like a two-bit Las Vegas showgirl. Either that or an Argos chandelier.

As Audrey swept her eyes up and down the offending outfit her eye suddenly fell on Sheryl's middle. This section wasn't made from the same shiny material as the rest, but was a sheer silver chiffon. Sheryl was showing her midriff! Audrey was aghast. Nobody *but nobody* above a certain age should show their midriff! Audrey wasn't sure what that age was, and was dimly aware that a few years back it had been all the rage for young ladies of a questionable class to reveal their tummies. Even so, if she had to put a safe number on when the optimum midriff-showing age was, she'd probably plump for eight. Audrey felt a small rush of triumph. Sheryl had blown it. She looked like a dog's dinner! Whatever hopes she had of getting her Barbie talons into John – and that was clearly what she wanted – were well and truly dust.

'Oh, Sheryl!' Audrey gushed. 'I nearly mistook you for a Christmas fairy!'

'Oh, Auuuudrey,' Sheryl retorted. 'That dress looks just as good as it did last year!'

Audrey felt the first prickle of a flush on her neck. There was a poisonous pause, before John stepped gallantly forward.

'You can't improve a classic,' he said supportively before turning politely to Sheryl. 'Lovely to see you again, Sheryl. Audrey tells me you've organized tonight; you must have been busy.'

'Well, yes, John, I *have* been busy,' Sheryl simpered, 'but it was nothing I couldn't handle. Although I could have done with Love Birds being a bit quieter!' She tapped his chest flirtatiously with a hot-pink nail. Audrey didn't have her glasses on but she swore she was sticking her chest out at him as she spoke. 'Business has gone aaabsoluuuutely stratospheric. You know, if we don't win the "Bureau of the Year" award tonight, I'll eat my tiara!'

'Well, we'll see about that,' Audrey cut in brusquely. She turned to John, trying to make sure his eyes were on her and not on the sparkly Ms Toogood. 'Did I tell you, darling?' She tried to make the 'darling' sound casual, but even to her ears it sounded awkward. 'We've posted our biggest profits *ever* this quarter! And President Ernie referred to Table For Two in the last Society newsletter as *a temple of excellence* and *one of the last matchmaking bureaus to honour the time-old traditions of client service and discretion* . . . Oh!' She broke away from the conversation with a start. Alice had silently joined the group. 'Alice!' she exclaimed gracelessly. 'You look . . .'

'Foxy!' said Sheryl with a low wolf whistle.

The two women suspended hostilities to survey Alice. Audrey stood with her mouth hanging open, but Sheryl peered at Alice shrewdly, appraising her like a prizefighter sussing out his opponent. Several long seconds passed. Alice seemed to be vainly searching for a neutral spot to look at.

'Alice!' said John suddenly, breaking the awkward silence again. Everyone had momentarily forgotten he was there. 'I'm John. I'm so pleased to finally meet you.' He shook her hand warmly. 'Audrey's told me so much about you.'

'Oh!' Alice said shyly. 'Thank you. Lovely to meet you too. We're all very impressed by the beautiful bouquets you send Audrey.'

Audrey saw confusion fly briefly across John's face.

'Yes, well, I see you got here in one piece,' she interjected.

Sheryl was still appraising Alice. 'My, my!' she drawled menacingly. 'What a dark horse you are, Msssss Brown. We'll have to keep a closer eye on you in future.' And she gave Alice what could only be described as 'a look'.

Audrey blinked in incomprehension. She didn't have a clue what the 'look' was meant to say. She just wanted Sheryl out of John's sight as fast as possible.

'Yes, well, don't let us keep you, Sheryl. You must have a million things to do.'

Sheryl's eyes broke away from Alice. 'You know, Audrey,' she said amiably, 'for once, you're absolutely right! I must check that Lucy Lucinda' – she flashed a smile at John – '. . . our *celebrity guest* – has everything she needs. You know, refill her glass, plump up her cushions, top up her Botox.

I left poor Brad looking after her, the darling. She was ever so taken with him; she's probably eaten him alive!' She turned to John, her chest provocatively extended. 'John, gorgeous to see you again! And Audrey, may the best woman win!' And she sashayed swiftly away.

'Win what?' Audrey thought bleakly and she instinctively tightened her grip on John's arm.

A waitress walked past with a drinks tray. As John claimed a couple of glasses of champagne for the women, Audrey became aware of Alice again. She was hovering awkwardly, groping for something to say.

'I'm sure Table For Two stands a very good chance of winning Bureau of the Year,' Alice managed meekly.

'Good chance?' Audrey bristled. 'We've got far more ABC1s than Sheryl. Her clients are positively downmarket.'

'I didn't know that kind of thing mattered,' Alice said innocently.

'Of course it matters!' Audrey scoffed. 'Class always matters.' She beamed at John and then deliberately let an awkward silence settle.

Alice took the hint.

'Well, I'm sure you didn't invite me here for the free drink. I must go and network. Nice to meet you, John.' She smiled, turned and made her way into the crowd. As she left, Audrey caught a glimpse of her bare back, lean, toned and surprisingly youthful against the black satin of her dress. It looked . . . *sexy*.

'Oh!' she exclaimed with a small choking sound.

'Are you all right, Audrey?' John asked in concern.

'Perfectly, thank you,' she replied tartly and steered him into a quieter corner where they had less chance of being disturbed by tantalizing views.

Three glasses of champagne later the toastmaster called everyone to the great hall for dinner. Audrey always thought it preposterous that a golf club should call its draughty canteen a 'great hall'. But tonight, in her favourite dress and feeling like a Hollywood film star as John put his hand gently on the small of her back and guided her towards their table, she decided to overlook it.

As she struggled to catch her breath under the heat of John's touch, they found their table in prime position in front of the stage. Whilst John shook hands with their fellow diners Audrey took the opportunity to inspect the place cards.

It's a commonly known fact that whom one is positioned next to at dinner is a direct reflection of one's standing. She peeked at the place card next to her. Surely there had to be some kind of mistake! She looked again. She'd been placed next to Matteus. *Matteus!!* Her blissful mood shattered. A woman of her standing should be seated next to President Ernie – *or at least President Ernie's wife*. Not Matteus! He wasn't even a bureau deputy. He was just the latest bit of fluff employed by Love Birds, and probably via Sheryl's grubby casting couch at that. And worst of all, he wasn't even a real matchmaker. Didn't he just do the silly web-dating stuff? He barely qualified to be at the ball at all.

The small prickle of rash on Audrey's neck, that had been

cooling since her earlier run-in with Sheryl, flared angrily again. She drained her champagne glass angrily. Oh, how Sheryl must have laughed over this little stunt. She'd been dumped in the networking equivalent of Siberia.

Audrey suddenly realized her jaw was clenched, and that John might see it in his peripheral vision. She tried to relax. She heard the end of a joke that John was telling Barry Chambers, and forced out a shrill laugh. John looked at her and Audrey pushed her lips into a rigid grimace that she hoped would pass as a smile. John smiled and turned back to Barry. Audrey sat down heavily.

She looked around the table to see where everyone else was sitting. Of course, Sheryl had awarded herself prime position, tucked between Brad and President Ernie, with a direct view of the stage. It was the golden ticket of place settings. Next to Brad was Alice (*Alice! Even Alice had a better seat than her!*), then Matteus, then Audrey and John (Audrey's back was square to the stage). Barry Chambers, his wife Eileen and President Ernie's wife, Patricia, completed the circle.

Sheryl was making the most of her access to President Ernie's ear, and was whispering something that caused him suddenly to lean back and roar with laughter.

Audrey squeezed her fist in frustration, her coral-painted nails cutting white half-moons into her palm. She barely noticed John refilling her glass, or a waitress placing her dinner before her. The sight of a preening, flirting Sheryl Toogood filled her vision.

At that moment Matteus arrived.

'Audrey! Ciao!' he beamed, swooping down to kiss her on both cheeks. Audrey's neck flushed deeper. The audacity, she thought, as she awarded him the tiniest of nods. He probably wasn't even Italian or Spanish or whatever it was he was passing himself off as. He sounded distinctly Estuary to her. *And* he was late.

Audrey went back to glaring at Sheryl, who had momentarily abandoned Ernie's ear in favour of Brad's, which she was brazenly nibbling. Brad was one of those men, Audrey noted, who probably spent several hours a day at the gym, and several more gazing at himself in the mirror. He was a man far too intimately acquainted with hair gel. *And* he was orange.

Audrey took a large sip of champagne and threw a tight smile at John. Sheryl's hands were becoming increasingly animated and were flitting all over Brad. It was putting Audrey off her dinner. Sheryl leaned over and whispered something to Brad, who grinned crudely and licked his lips in an obvious sexual gesture. Audrey felt a stab of indigestion. Really! This wasn't the way to behave at a professional function. And Brad was far too young for Sheryl, and vain and shallow and vacuous to boot. Not a man at all. More like an over-pumped, over-groomed male bimbo, and probably as thick as custard.

Audrey viciously shovelled a roast potato into her mouth and sneaked a glimpse at John. Unaware of either the rage bubbling next to him or the Bangkok floor show in front, he was politely making conversation with Eileen Chambers. Audrey tried to concentrate on feeling proud. John was the polar opposite of Brad: handsome, intelligent and discreet. And he was hers and hers alone, if only for a few hours and at quite a substantial price. She felt a sudden rush of love for him. She knew that, deep down, he too was longing for the day when they could throw caution to the wind and abandon the rigmarole of invoices and dealing through the chaperone of Geraldine. He too must surely wish for a time when they could officially be together. Holding her breath and steeling her nerves, Audrey let the champagne get the better of her. If Sheryl Toogood could get away with her *Kama Sutra* manoeuvres on the other side of the table, then surely Audrey could manage a little discreet but cosy intimacy too?

Dizzy with excitement she moved towards John and attempted an affectionate half-nuzzle into his arm. In an ideal world John would have responded with spontaneous tenderness, put his arm around her and drawn her in close for an embrace. But in an ideal world Audrey wouldn't have been naturally clumsy or unknowingly drunk. Her off-balance lurch wouldn't have caught him by surprise, her alarmingly heavy nosedive wouldn't have cronked his funny bone and shot his fork out of his hand, whizzing it violently through the air, only narrowly avoiding a collision with the chandelier earrings of President Ernie's wife. In an ideal world Audrey's unprovoked nuzzle wouldn't have looked to all and sundry like an ill-aimed headbutt. Alarmed, John broke away from his conversation and twisted in his seat, only to see Audrey finish executing a manoeuvre that looked like a drunken attempt to wipe her nose on his sleeve.

'Audrey, are you all right?' John sounded alarmed.

Embarrassed, Audrey swiftly pulled up, turned away from John's worried expression and launched into animated conversation with Matteus. As Matteus started twittering his CV at her, and John hesitantly resumed his conversation with Eileen Chambers, Audrey did her best to ignore both the slick of coral lipstick that was smeared across John's sleeve and the spot in the centre of her forehead that throbbed from its thumping connection with his elbow. Physical pain and cosmetic damage were easy to blot out. What was more difficult to ignore was the unending cackle coming from Sheryl's side of the table.

ALICE

Alice was doing her best to see her champagne glass as half full. As instructed, she'd been careful to pace herself, making sure she didn't drink too much and bring to life Audrey's determined premonition that she'd shame the good name of Table For Two. Under any other circumstances she'd have described her mid-filled champagne glass as half empty. But tonight, against all the odds, she was doing her best to keep positive. Her glass was half full. She straightened in her seat and tried to look like she was having the time of her life.

The truth was that nobody had spoken to her for several minutes now. On her left Brad was busy being groped by Sheryl, and Alice was finding it hard to keep pretending she couldn't see what was happening beneath the table. Every now and again Brad and Sheryl would emit a dirty-sounding laugh, or break off to share a joke with Ernie, but it had been a long time since Brad had said anything at all to Alice. It was probably just as well. When he'd last spoken to her he'd been so flirtatious she hadn't known how to respond and had taken so long to think of a suitable answer that he'd got bored and turned away.

Besides, being invisible to that side of the table was probably a good thing, Alice told herself as everyone chatted busily around her. She'd always found Sheryl intimidating, with her chink-proof confidence and planet-sized ambition. But now that Sheryl had let her in on her dastardly matchmaking secret, Alice was officially on her radar, and that was a frightening place to be. Whether she'd wanted it or not, she now had information on Sheryl – information given only on the understanding she was coming to work for her. But Alice had turned her down, and Sheryl wasn't the type to live and let live. Waiting for her punishment was an agony … but nothing compared to the agony of working out what she should do with her newly discovered secret.

She couldn't do *nothing*; clients were suffering. And OK, so they weren't *her* clients, but worrying about them was keeping her awake at night nevertheless. Wasn't it her moral duty to put things right … ? But how? Who should she tell? Audrey? Not likely. Audrey was just as intimidating as Sheryl, and to tell her would also mean admitting she'd committed professional treason and gone for a coffee with Sheryl behind her back. And besides: what if Audrey was in on the matchmaking scam too? No, she needed to be sure of Audrey's innocence first. But if that took too long, who else could she tell? Ernie? He *was* the DIPS president, after all, and a man of unimpeachable standards. And he'd practically written the book when it came to matchmaking. *But*, Alice thought, watching Sheryl squeeze Ernie's arm as they laughed at a joke only they could hear … *but* … it would just be her word against Sheryl's. Why on earth should

Ernie believe a mousy little employee from a mid-ranking agency over the high-profile, high-achieving owner of the city's fastest growing bureau?

Alice took another sip of champagne and forced herself to smile, as though she was part of the general mood of merriment in the room and not just a bystander to it. Well, what had she expected? she asked herself harshly. Of course she was going to be ignored by most of the table; they were matchmaking heavyweights. She was disappointed with Matteus, though. He was the only other person who was neither a bureau chief nor a DIPS spouse, and she'd hoped for a bit of solidarity. But Matteus had arrived late for dinner, tossed a brief 'hello' in her direction, and then spent the rest of the meal either waxing lyrical about himself to Audrey, or heckling Ernie over-familiarly across the table.

So instead Alice had spent the meal feeling like a cross between a gatecrasher and a gooseberry. She looked around for a waitress to top up her glass. She needed a drink. But the waitresses were all busy elsewhere. So she looked at Audrey, who was staring at Matteus with fixed, glassy eyes as he loudly told her about his boundless professional achievements. But Alice knew all of Audrey's expressions – especially the negative ones – and the look she was currently sporting told her that she wasn't listening to a word he was saying. This was probably because, unless Alice was very much mistaken, Audrey was well on her way to being three sheets to the wind. Oh, the beautiful irony of it! Alice suppressed her first genuine smile of the night.

Her thoughts drifted to John. He seemed nice. Much nicer

than she'd expected Audrey's husband to be. He was younger than she'd imagined too, and actually very handsome. She wondered what he saw in Audrey; they seemed such a mismatched couple. She tried to think nice, positive thoughts. Love was always perplexing. So many couples who shouldn't match on paper fell wildly and permanently in love. That must have happened to Audrey and John. And Audrey must have plenty of good points – even if she did keep them hidden. Maybe she was a fantastic cook, or a kind and supportive partner, or even – the very thought made Alice feel queasy – an amazing lover. Maybe that was it! Maybe Audrey was red-hot between the sheets! How else could she explain handsome, polite, gentlemanly John being married to her bullish, diplomatically disastrous boss?

At that moment John looked up and caught Alice staring at him. He smiled. Alice buried her eyes in her plate, her cheeks burning. She tried to remember what her face had been doing whilst she'd been looking at him. What if she'd been imagining Audrey as a red-hot lover just as he'd looked over? What if he could tell?

She pretended to be lost in a minute examination of her plate. A few moments later Sheryl's voice cut through the hubbub of the room.

'Of course, we're all so professionally remiss!' she could hear Sheryl saying. 'We pride ourselves on our ability to find people love, yet we happily sit here with a singleton in our midst!'

Alice felt an ominous sense of discomfort.

'I mean, here we are – *at a ball*, for God's sake – and we

have our very own real-life Cinderella at the table.' Sheryl emitted a laugh that could cut glass. 'How ironic that little Alice Brown finds love for everyone else, but can't find it for herself! We should all make it our mission to sort out Alice's love life and find her a man. It's a matter of professional pride! We can't have one of our own left on the shelf!' She laughed cruelly, and several other voices chuckled along with her.

Alice felt herself burning from the tips of her ears to the ends of her fingers. She couldn't believe Sheryl was saying these things! And how did she know she was single? Had Audrey told her? Alice felt so mortified it took her breath away. She could hear her heart thudding loudly in her ears.

'Audrey!' Sheryl called out. 'Yes, earth to Audrey! Don't you find it a business liability having a spinster on the staff? What must your clients think?'

Why was Sheryl doing this? Why was she being so nasty? Was *this* how she was going to get her revenge . . . by humiliating her and exposing her as a romantic failure? She was being vicious; a bully. But why wasn't anyone stopping her? Alice peeked at Ernie. He'd always been so nice, going out of his way to compliment her on her matches. But tonight his face was ruddy with booze and he seemed too busy watching Sheryl's chest as it heaved and sparkled and spilled over her dress to leap to Alice's defence. Even Audrey didn't have anything to say. Audrey always had a few cutting words to hand whenever Sheryl was around. But typically, when Alice really needed her, Audrey sat immobile, her face as red as a beetroot and her mouth firmly shut.

'Still, at least we all know she's a faithful employee,' Sheryl continued bitchily. 'Part of the Table For Two furniture, aren't you, Alice? You know, Alice is actually in this for the love, everybody. She really believes in matchmaking, don't you, sweetie? She thinks it's her calling; her raison d'être! Every morning she gets up and pedals her little heart out on that funny old bike of hers, really believing it's her role in life to shoot her arrows and make everyone fall under Cupid's spell!'

Alice felt sick. She looked at her lap. Her red nail varnish looked ridiculous on her hands. What had she been thinking, dressing up like this? Who did she think she was, trying to pass herself off as a glamorous woman; as a professional, respected matchmaker? Everyone knew she was just plain old Alice Brown. Plain old, *single* Alice Brown. So pathetic she couldn't even find herself a man.

She suddenly became aware of somebody else speaking – somebody who wasn't Sheryl. It was John.

'Well, I think that's the best possible reason to be a matchmaker,' he said calmly, his blue eyes evenly holding Sheryl's. 'If I was ever to join a dating agency, I'd want Alice as my matchmaker. I don't know her very well, in fact I've only just met her tonight, but I can tell she's a woman of honesty and integrity, with a good heart. And they sound to me like the very best qualifications for a matchmaker.'

The table had gone quiet. Even Sheryl had stopped in her tracks.

John continued quietly, brushing some crumbs from the table as he spoke.

'And if she's single, that's nobody's business but hers. Somebody out there will consider it his lucky day when he finally gets to meet Alice.'

John turned to Alice and gave her a reassuring smile.

'Thank you,' she silently mouthed to him, before scraping back her chair and excusing herself from the table. She blindly made her way as fast as she could towards the ladies' toilets, barely caring how she was walking in her high heels. She didn't care if she fell over and broke her ankle, as long as she got far enough away from the table before she did it. As she hurtled through the great hall, she felt a tear slip down her cheek.

With a sob of relief she finally burst out of the great hall. The ladies' loo was in sight, but so too was the cloakroom. Without a moment's hesitation Alice collected her coat and shot out of the building.

There was a taxi rank at the bottom of the entrance steps, and Alice took several hurried gulps of air as she waited for the first taxi to move forward. Her muffled sobs hung like white clouds in the cold night air. The clamour of the ball continued behind her, its merriment suddenly sounding cruel.

'Alice, wait!' a voice called out.

She turned. John was hurrying down the steps towards her, his dinner jacket flapping open in the night air. She hastily smudged away a tear.

'I want to apologize for everyone's behaviour in there,' he said hurriedly, concern etched on his face. 'I'm ashamed to be sitting with them – all of them.'

Alice tried to meet his eye, but embarrassment and tears got the better of her, so she concentrated instead on his feet. Mortified, she saw a big fat tear roll down her face and splat onto his shoe. 'Thanks for . . . you know . . .' she mumbled, pointing vaguely in the direction of the great hall, hoping it would distract him from the wobble in her voice and the wet patch on his foot.

There was an awkward pause, and then he handed her his handkerchief. Without looking at him, Alice accepted it. Despite her best efforts, more tears were escaping; a particularly large one was wobbling precariously on the end of her nose.

'Look, are you alright?' he asked kindly. 'Would you like me to take you home? My car's just over there.'

'No!' she blurted in alarm. 'I mean, yes! Yes, I'm alright, and no, thank you; I'll be fine getting home.' That would go down like a lead balloon with Audrey – her husband escorting her least favourite employee home. 'Shouldn't you be getting back to Audrey?' she asked, briefly raising her eyes to the middle distance to show she was OK, and blinking heavily to try to keep everything in check. Her taxi was alongside now. She held out his handkerchief to him.

'Yes, I suppose I should,' he replied and pushed it gently back towards her. 'Please, keep it.'

'Thanks,' she sniffed. And then she turned and bundled into the car. The sounds of John and the ball died around her. As the taxi pulled away, her body sagged with relief, and she gave in to her tears. Slowly, between gasps for breath, she wiped her make-up onto John's handkerchief. The cosmetics looked toxic on the pure white linen. More than anything in the world, she longed for a bar of soap, a face-cloth and her pyjamas. And never to see anyone from DIPS again.

JOHN

John sat down and tried to conceal his anger. Thankfully everyone was busy. Audrey was bombarding Barry Chambers with rosy statistics about Table For Two's success, confidently predicting her own victory with the 'Bureau of the Year' award. Somehow John doubted she'd win. He didn't know much about matchmaking, but he sure as hell knew Audrey didn't have either the finesse to cut it as a successful businesswoman, or the empathy to be a matchmaker. He'd never met anyone who was less of a people person than Audrey. There couldn't be a woman alive less likely to fulfil people's romantic fantasies.

John frowned. Why hadn't Audrey stood up for Alice? Why had she sat by and let her be mauled? What kind of woman was she? He'd always thought she was lacking in manners, but this lack of kindness was something else.

He looked up. On the other side of the table Sheryl was pretending to hang on Ernie's every word, but it was clear to John what she was up to. He could recognize a player at three hundred paces. Sheryl was deliberately inclining her body towards Ernie at precisely the angle to give him a perfect view of her cleavage. For his part, Ernie was enjoying the scenery. His poor wife, Patricia, was ignored and forgotten, staring miserably at the remnants of her crème brûlée. John considered striking up a conversation with her, but suddenly he felt very tired. He looked at his watch. He reckoned he had about another hour before he could drive Audrey home and forget about the whole sorry evening.

Suddenly a bright spotlight rolled onto their table, causing him to blink. The spotlight fixed on Sheryl, reflecting off her dress in a thousand shiny shards that fell across the great hall in a myriad of diamonds. She looked like a giant glitter-ball. Overacting her surprise and throwing kisses to the other tables, Sheryl rose to her feet.

'Oh, for the love of God!' exclaimed Audrey ungracefully, banging her champagne glass down onto the table as the room rose to its feet.

'She's only bloody won!' shouted Barry Chambers. 'Love Birds have won! Good on yer, girl!' He put his fingers to his mouth and gave a piercing wolf whistle.

Sheryl headed towards the stage, directly behind John and Audrey. As she passed them he felt her run her finger suggestively across his back. Surprised, he looked at her, but her attention was set on the stage and an underdressed, undernourished blonde clutching a trophy and smiling a rigid showbiz smile. She had to be the celebrity actress, John thought. She had the air of someone being paid to be there. He recognized the expression; he was wearing it himself. Sheryl, on the other hand, looked as if she was born to be under that spotlight, lapping up the attention like a dancer in a gentleman's club.

'For heaven's sake!' Audrey muttered loudly and rolled her eyes. She reached for the nearest champagne bottle and savagely refilled her glass before reluctantly joining the rest of the room in standing.

As Sheryl started her acceptance speech John looked at Audrey. Her face was pinched and her lips were small and bitten together. It wasn't the face of a good loser. With her malevolent expression and her petrol-coloured dress she looked like an angry oil slick. Tonight had been one of the most unpleasant evenings of his working life, John thought. He was definitely calling Geraldine tomorrow to tell her that he would never escort Audrey again. Not even if his life depended on it.

Sheryl's speech was coming to an end. John joined in the applause as she slowly sashayed off stage, eking out every last nanosecond of attention. With a start he realized she wasn't heading back to her seat. Still illuminated in the outer reaches of her spotlight, she stopped right in front of him.

'Aren't you going to give me a congratulatory kiss?' she demanded over the noise of the applause.

The prospect of kissing Sheryl was as appealing as putting his face into a nest of rats. And he certainly didn't want to do it in front of Audrey who was, after all, his paying client. He quickly weighed up how to decline politely.

Luckily, Audrey jumped in, her tone bossy and proprietorial.

'I don't think that would be appropri—'

Completely ignoring her, Sheryl took John's head in her hands and pulled him forcefully towards her, planting a hard, lingering kiss on his lips. His head pounded under the pressure of her vice-like grip and the insistent squirming of her lips. He tried to pull away. He could hear Audrey gasp in horror. Eventually, Sheryl released him.

He turned to Audrey, his face full of apology. She was his client, and shouldn't be expected to witness behaviour like that. But Audrey wasn't looking at him. She was looking at Sheryl, and she looked ready to murder.

'Sheryl Toogood, you're nothing but a common tart; a cheap, brazen whore!' Audrey's face and neck were covered in an angry red rash, her expression beyond fury. 'You think of nothing but sex, sex, sex. You disgust me!'

Sheryl gave a little smirk, and pointedly wiped the corner of her lips with a manicured finger.

'Love and fidelity and marriage mean nothing to you,' Audrey thundered. 'You're more interested in notches on your bedpost. Don't you know men don't like that kind of thing? Decent men, I mean, not the kind of male bimbos and flopsies you surround yourself with. You need to grow up, cover up, and stop acting like a teenage slut. You're not fit to win the award. You're an embarrassment to the Society!'

'Now really, Audrey, you've gone too far.' Ernie was on his feet, swaying tipsily, and waggling his finger in Audrey's direction. 'I demand you apologize to poor Sheryl at once. We all think she looks very lovely tonight; like a diamond.'

John looked at Audrey, who was staring at Ernie aghast. Her mouth was open in surprise and dismay.

There was a long pause. Sheryl shifted insolently, a contemptuous smile on her lips as she inspected Audrey and waited for her apology. It clearly wasn't coming.

It was time for action.

John put his hand under Audrey's elbow and gently tried to steer her away.

'Right everyone,' he said pleasantly. 'It's been a lovely evening, but it's time Audrey and I made tracks.'

With relief he felt Audrey rock on her axis.

'See you all again next year!' He threw a broad smile in the direction of the table, turned and headed out, half guiding, half scooping Audrey up by the elbow. Thankfully she moved with him.

He manoeuvred her out of the great hall, past the cloakroom and straight to his car.

AUDREY

Audrey stared blindly ahead as John steered the Audi in the direction of home. The muted hum of the engine gave a deceptive air of peace. Neither had spoken since getting in a full ten minutes ago. It was only now that her Sheryl-inspired rage and her sense of betrayal at the hands of President Ernie had subsided, that Audrey realized John was angry. There was none of his normal, easy conversation. Instead he drove in stiff silence, his brow furrowed and his profile unforgiving. Audrey's anger instantly dissolved into panic. John couldn't be angry with her? He was never angry. He was always kind and calm. Her mouth went dry and her stomach lurched.

She cleared her throat and tried to think of something jovial to say, but nothing came. Instead she miserably watched his hands turn the wheel, each movement taking her closer to home, each gear-change hastening the end of the evening.

Audrey felt sick. She'd longed – yearned – for tonight for so long. But something had gone wrong. And whatever it was, it was Sheryl's fault.

All too soon they arrived home. With a sinking feeling Audrey noticed that John didn't switch off the engine, or undo his seat belt, or turn in his seat to look at her. It was over, she thought desperately; the evening was over. There were no more precious minutes to be had. Not for several months anyway. Not until a suitable work occasion beckoned, and that could be ages.

'Coffee?' she suggested in panic.

'No.' He sighed heavily. There was an awkward pause. 'You surprised me tonight, Audrey.'

'Me?'

'I . . . I didn't know you were like that.'

'Like what?' Audrey demanded, suddenly feeling very small. John's eyes were fixed on a point the other side of the windscreen.

'So . . . hard. So devoid of compassion.'

'It was Sheryl,' Audrey said hurriedly. 'She deliberately provoked me. She always does.'

'No, it wasn't Sheryl. Look, forget it. It's not my place to say.'

'Not your place to say what?'

An ominous silence fell.

'Please . . . I want to know. I *need* to know what you're thinking!' But even as she said the words she wasn't sure she wanted to hear the answer. It was all wrong. This wasn't how the story was supposed to go. She waited breathlessly for his reply.

But John just looked ahead for a very long time.

'Sorry,' he said eventually, 'but I've got an early start in the morning.'

Audrey nodded dumbly. She was dismissed.

She groped for the door, still hoping he'd change his mind and flash one of his vintage smiles that made his eyes crinkle and her stomach flip. But his eyes were fixed on the road.

Audrey climbed out of the car, murmured a tiny, contrite 'thank you', and gently closed the door. She walked slowly up the drive, drawing out each step as long as possible to give him the chance to call her back, catch her up, toot his horn, anything. But before she'd reached her front door she heard his car pull away and just the discreet murmur of the engine lingered in the night.

With a trembling hand she pulled out her house keys. And then she was in the house, the door was closed behind her and John was elsewhere.

She went straight to the bedroom. Pickles was asleep on her bed and barely stirred as she walked in. She went over to her full-length mirror and looked. She wanted to see herself – not in the way she normally did, checking her skirt was straight or that there was no lipstick on her teeth. She wanted to see what John saw. She wanted to see her: Audrey Cracknell the client, the woman.

She looked. She kept on looking.

And then she unzipped her dress and stepped out of it. She slipped off her shoes and placed her swollen feet on the flat, carpeted floor.

She was in her underwear, tights and make-up. She looked again.

She didn't like what she saw.

Her tummy bulged over her sensible underwear and her thighs stuck tightly together from abdomen to knee. Her chubby arms stuck out wider than her shoulders, making her silhouette soft and egg-shaped. She had none of Sheryl's hard, aerobicized lines. Even her bosom, certainly as large as Sheryl's, was saggy and misshapen. Sheryl's bosom was pert and pneumatic: an enticing pillow that called men to it. Audrey's bosom was like two lumpy spuds hanging in a pair of popsocks.

Audrey looked at her face. Her hair – immaculate when she'd left the house at the start of the evening – was frizzy again; wild and more orange than ever. There was a small red mark in the middle of her forehead from her disastrous meeting with John's funny bone. Her make-up looked painted on, like brittle gloss paint cracking at the edges. Her mouth was small, so small she could hardly see it. Too tiny and clenched to be kissed.

This is it, she thought. This is me. She suddenly felt overwhelmed. There was no escaping this woman in the mirror. This was her, Audrey Bridget Cracknell. Fifty-one years old and twelve and a half stone; a workhorse, held together by sheer grit and support underwear. Was this a body that could wear a silver dress? Was this a body that stirred men to defend her? No wonder John had made his excuses. He could have any woman he wanted. Why would he choose this?

On the bed, Pickles woke momentarily, yawned, licked his paws and fell back to sleep.

In front of the mirror a small shiny tear collected in the corner of Audrey's eye. Eventually, a long time later, when the night-time chill finally permeated her misery, she put on her nightie and went to bed.

KATE

Kate got to the café early and sat at a corner table. It was nearly 3.45 p.m. and the place was full of parents treating their children to a post-school slice of cake. Young, excited faces were greedily steaming up the glass on the cake cabinet, trying to decide which sticky treat to plump for. Kate smiled at their agony as they carefully weighed up the iced doughnut versus the chocolate eclair.

'I must hurry up,' she berated herself sternly.

It wasn't that her biological clock was ticking, exactly; it was more that she had a rising feeling of panic and a growing sense of time marching on. It felt like someone, somewhere, was laughing at her; and slowly, but ever so surely, they were feeding her life plan into a paper-shredder. Despite Lou's constant reminders, she wasn't just thirty-three; she was thirty-three, five months and one week. *Hell, she was almost thirty-three and a half.* Things were getting serious; thirty-five was just five hundred and sixty-nine days away. If she wasted a moment more she'd run out of time; venues might be fully booked; she might have to go registry office; two kids might turn into one, *or maybe even none*. She needed Alice to work her magic, and fast.

It was three whole weeks now since Kate had joined Table For Two, and so far she'd had only two dates. Everything was happening too slowly. Her date with Sebastian had been a disaster, and the one with Michael not much better. She'd always known she'd have to kiss a few frogs, even with the frog-filter of Alice, but at this rate it could take her months to find a boyfriend. She needed to step things up. She needed Alice to sort her out with two dates a week – *three!*

'Hello.' Alice was hovering at the side of the table, looking pale and tired. Kate hadn't even noticed her come in. She rose in greeting.

'Alice! Thanks for coming. Can I get you a tea?'

A few minutes later both women were installed behind teacups. Kate immediately got down to business.

'So, let's speed things up, shall we?' Alice suggested once Kate paused for breath. 'Actually, I've already got someone in mind for your next date. Here he is: date number three!'

She pulled a piece of paper from her bag. Kate eagerly skimmed the sheet. Date number three was called Harvey. His picture was ten-out-of-ten handsome and a quick scan of his details revealed that he regularly holidayed in faraway luxury locations and drove a Maserati. He looked promising.

'There's something I wanted to ask.' Alice's voice broke Kate's reverie. 'It's about your criteria.'

'Yes?' Kate lowered the paperwork.

Alice looked awkward. 'Well . . . I was wondering if you'd changed your mind?'

'What do you mean?' Kate asked, an alarm bell going off inside.

'Well, are you still looking for all the things in a man that you originally specified?'

'Of course!' What was Alice getting at? Was she saying she hadn't been good enough for Sebastian and Michael? Had they complained about her? Had they said she wasn't good-looking enough? Too fat? Kate's throat tightened.

'So you'd still like to meet someone tall, handsome, dark-haired . . . ?'

'Yes.'

'. . . with a strong jaw and blue eyes . . . ?'

'Yes!'

'. . . and a job in management, who takes regular holidays and has a nice car? Someone sporty, with a good physique . . . ?'

'*Yes, yes!*' Kate could hear her voice becoming shrill. 'Why are you asking?' She looked sharply at Alice for clues. Was she being told to lower her standards? Was she being told she was substandard for this kind of man?

Alice blushed and put down her teacup. Despite her pinkening cheeks, she still looked pale and drawn.

'I just wanted to check I was still on the right track.'

Kate felt relief surge through her body.

'Yes, that all sounds perfect. Just the kind of man I'm after!'

'So you wouldn't consider anyone who isn't a high earner and all those other things?'

'Er . . .' Kate felt confused, like she was being tested. She tried to laugh. 'I know that being rich and handsome won't make him a better person. Money isn't everything, of course. It's just that: well . . . little girls want to marry princes, don't they? Not dustmen. Not that there's anything wrong with dustmen, it's just that . . . well . . . a dustman was never part of my life plan.' She smiled weakly.

'OK.'

Kate relaxed.

'So I'll just keep looking for more of the same?'

'Yes!' Kate said certainly. Except that a bit of uncertainty was beginning to creep in. More of the same as Sebastian and Michael? She'd hated her dates with them. But they *had* ticked all the boxes. She'd just been unlucky. Sebastian and Michael were right on paper but wrong in person. That didn't mean that *all* tall, dark and handsome men were wrong. Tall, dark and handsome was just what she wanted! Tall, dark and handsome and with a car. And a big bank balance and nice teeth.

'Yes,' she repeated as she picked up her teacup and looked at Alice. 'More of the same, please.'

ALICE

When Alice got back to the office the first thing she saw was the florist leaving.

'Oh, Audrey,' Bianca gasped. 'What fantastic flowers. Are they from John?'

'Mmmm-hmmmm.' Even Audrey wasn't usually this disinterested in receiving a mountain of blooms that took both arms to hold.

'Not many men still send their wives bouquets like that after twenty years of marriage!' Bianca enthused sweetly. 'It's not your anniversary, is it?'

'No.' Audrey dumped the bouquet on Hilary's desk for her to arrange into a vase. Audrey's eye caught Alice's as she hovered by the door. She seemed to puff up her chest. 'They're just for being me,' she said stiffly, and turned and headed back into her office.

Alice scuttled to her desk. Audrey had been in a strange mood all day. She'd taken every possible opportunity to put her in her place. She'd even sent her out in the rain to get her lunch, which was something she didn't normally demand of anyone. She was probably angry with her for not coming back to the table last night. With a quick rush of shame Alice remembered how she'd run off home. Why hadn't she had more backbone? She could at least have said goodbye!

But Audrey hadn't actually *said* that this was what was upsetting her. And she *had* been quite drunk. Maybe she couldn't remember, Alice thought hopefully. But her hope instantly evaporated. More likely she *could* remember, and she'd seen John follow her out and give her his handkerchief. Maybe that was what was angering her: her husband being nice to the black sheep of Table For Two.

Alice sneaked a look at Audrey's bouquet as Hilary attempted to stuff it into a vase. It was even more enormous than usual. And it was *just for being me*. Alice had to hand it to Audrey: she must have done something pretty amazing after she'd left. John hadn't seemed like a man in the mood to blow fifty pounds on flowers for his wife. He'd actually seemed quite angry.

Trying to look as invisible as possible, Alice sidled over to Hilary, on the pretext of helping her arrange the flowers.

'Can I ask you something?' she whispered. She nervously looked over in Audrey's direction, but her boss had already sealed herself into her glass office and was frowning heavily at her computer.

'Do I look like a sodding florist?' Hilary muttered as she stabbed another hyacinth into the vase. 'Kevin never sends me flowers. Do you think she does this just to torture me?'

'You've worked here a long time . . .' Alice started delicately.

'Too bloody long!'

'Did you ever meet the first five clients? You know: the ones who all got married?'

'I hadn't joined when Audrey matched them,' Hilary replied, ramming in a handful of fern. 'She hired me a few months after. But I did meet them later on; she was forever rounding them up for photoshoots with the local paper.'

Alice sneaked a glance at Audrey's office to double-check her door was firmly closed. 'Did they seem happy?'

'Of course not – they were married by then!'

'What I mean is – do you think they stood the test of time? Do you think they're all still married?'

'I doubt it. Actually, at least one of the clients came back to us a few years later. She wanted help getting back into the scene after her divorce.'

'Divorce?' Alice felt the hairs on the back of her neck stand up.

'Audrey never mentions it, of course. She didn't want to take her back on as a client. I think she was terrified in case anyone remembered her from all the publicity.'

'So just *one* couple got divorced . . . ?' Alice whispered hopefully.

'Oh, at least! There were rumours about one of the other couples too.' Hilary paused in her flower-arranging, trying to remember. 'She was African; from Nigeria, I think. She only had a few months left on her visa.'

Alice gasped. 'Are you saying Audrey matched a marriage of convenience?' She couldn't believe what she was hearing.

It was even worse than Sheryl had said. She wished she'd never started digging.

Hilary shrugged. 'It was only a rumour; who knows? And I'm not saying she'd have done it deliberately. Knowing Audrey and her ability to read people, which is precisely zilch, she probably never had a clue. But it certainly made the chances of hitting the matchmaking jackpot a lot higher if one of the parties wanted to get a ring on her finger within the fortnight.' Hilary frowned heavily at her lumpy floral display.

'You didn't hear any rumours about any of the couples already dating before she actually matched them, did you?' Alice asked innocently, barely able to breathe as she did so.

Hilary suppressed a snort of laughter.

'No, but I *did* always think there was something fishy about Audrey's cousin.'

'Audrey's cousin?' Alice echoed in dismay, her head beginning to spin.

'Yeah, he was a second cousin once removed, or something like that. Whatever, he never looked too enamoured with his wife. I don't think I ever saw him exchange two words with her. He was a strange-looking bloke; looked like he'd hit hard times. I don't reckon he had a penny to his name. He was the kind of guy you wanted to take home and give a damn good meal. I think Audrey had to buy him his suit for the photos. I used to wonder if she'd paid him to get married; you know – to help bump up the statistics and get her into the papers? Your first four matches getting hitched doesn't quite have the same ring as five!'

Alice reeled in shock.

'Of course, it's probably not true,' Hilary continued as she picked up another handful of flowers and looked at her overstuffed vase in exasperation. 'Most likely the other four couples are in a state of permanent ecstasy and are all living on Utopia Avenue . . .'

Alice returned to her desk and sat down, the room reeling around her. So Sheryl had been right about the divorces. And if she'd been right about that, what about everything else she'd said? Alice looked at Audrey, who was angrily trying to swat a fly against her desk with a copy of *Brides* magazine. Was Sheryl right? Was Audrey in on the bad-matches-for-extra-fees scam too?

Numbly, Alice's hand crept into her cardigan pocket. Her fingers brushed against something soft. It was John's handkerchief. Alice had washed it last night, intending to return it to Audrey today. But something had stopped her – fear, probably. How would any woman react if her employee handed back her husband's hanky – let alone Audrey? And how could Alice explain having it without admitting she'd been crying? She could imagine Audrey's scorn. And then she'd peer at Alice's eyes and notice how puffy they were. It wouldn't take a genius to work out that Alice had spent most of the night sobbing.

What Alice wanted most was to wipe the whole evening from her memory forever – in fact, the whole *week*! Ever since she'd had that coffee with Sheryl, everything had gone into free fall. First of all Sheryl had made her doubt the integrity of her chosen profession. And then the ball –

206 Alice Brown's Lessons in the Curious Art of Dating

supposedly the best night of her life and the apex of her matchmaking career – had ended in humiliation. And now Hilary had unwittingly turned her world on its head, and everything she thought she knew about her boss suddenly seemed like it might just be a lie.

So Alice couldn't bring herself to return John's hanky to Audrey. Instead she let it nestle, cosy in her cardigan pocket. The truth was, she was beginning to like having it there. In amongst all the confusion and the tumult, the hanky felt soft, comforting, simple. It was the only thing she could think of that actually felt nice.

JOHN

'Drink?' asked Geraldine as she waved a bottle of red towards John and fumbled in the drawer for a corkscrew. 'I don't know about you, but I feel I deserve one. It's been a long week.'

She expertly pulled out the cork, poured the wine into two enormous goblets and carried them over to the sofa. Geraldine's office was large, tatty and shambolic, yet John had never known her to misplace anything, and it never failed to astonish him how many strange and wonderful things she conjured from her cupboards. She'd once served him an impromptu afternoon tea of scones, cream and jam, all courtesy of her filing cabinet.

'All meetings after 5.30 should be conducted over a large glass of wine,' she said amiably as she flopped onto the couch. 'It's the law. Or at least it should be.'

John laughed. Geraldine was right: it had been a long week.

'So.' Geraldine slapped the sofa between them cheerfully. 'I'm sure you've got better things to do than schlep all the way to the office on a Friday night for a chat. Not that I'm complaining: you're the best view I've had all week. But seeing as I have it on good authority that you do actually own a telephone, I don't need to be Miss Marple to work out there's probably something serious on your mind.' She peered at him curiously.

John gave a little laugh. 'Guilty as charged. Look, Geraldine, I'm afraid there's no easy way to say this . . .'

'. . . but . . . ?' Geraldine helped him along.

'. . . but I'd like to talk to you about a particular client,' John said carefully, 'and how I don't want to take any more bookings from her.'

'Riiiiiight. So I'm presuming the client in question is a certain lady businesswoman?'

John gave a rueful smile.

'A certain lady businesswoman with red hair and her very own dating agency?'

Despite everything, John couldn't help but chuckle.

'And an epic-sized crush and an inability to take "no" for an answer?'

'I wouldn't put it quite like that!'

Geraldine sighed. 'Well, I can't say it's not going to be a bit awkward, but I can't say I blame you either. Actually, you've been quite a saint to stick her out as long as you have. She'd have sent lesser men running to the hills years ago!'

'Look, I'm really sorry if this puts you in a difficult position. She's been a client for years and, at the end of the day, you're the one who's going to have to tell her. But I can't escort her any more. I just can't do it.'

Geraldine topped up his glass in a gesture of solidarity.

'Fair enough. Did something happen at the ball last night?' she asked lightly.

'No. Yes. No, not really. I've just reached my limit with her, that's all.' An image of Alice trying to hide her tears at the taxi rank flashed back into his mind, followed by Audrey's pursed lips as Sheryl won the prize.

'OK,' said Geraldine pensively as she sipped her wine. 'Look, you don't need to explain why you don't want to escort Audrey Cracknell any more. She's a funny old stick and she will insist on wearing her heart on her sleeve. It must have been hard to come up with diplomatic ways to sidestep her advances for the last ten years.'

John gave a small smile.

'Losing Audrey's business doesn't concern me,' she continued kindly. 'But what does concern me is potentially losing you. If you're just cheesed off with Audrey Cracknell, then fine. Let's write off our losses and move on. But if it's bigger than that, then I'm worried. So tell me: is there anything else I should know about?'

John looked at Geraldine, taking in her kind expression, her friendly face and her comfortably battered office. They'd been friends for years. She knew everything there was to know about him, and she'd been looking after his bookings ever since he'd started out in the business eleven long years ago. They'd been through thick and thin together. But could he tell her about the doubts he'd been having recently? About the thoughts that had crept into his mind on quiet Sunday mornings? He wasn't sure.

'No,' he replied firmly. 'It's just Audrey. I've done all I can for her. I can't give her what she wants. I used to think she understood, but recently I'm not so sure.'

Geraldine gave a small nod.

'Then it's definitely time.' She sat back. 'Of course, I'll offer her someone else in your place, but I'm sure she'll tell me where I can stick him!'

They both contemplated their glasses. Outside the window John could hear the stressful sounds of the Friday evening rush hour. He felt a weight leave his shoulders.

'Are you going to tell her soon?' he asked. 'Or are you going to wait until she next phones with a booking?'

Geraldine sighed. Her shoulders slumped.

'That, my darling, is the question. Sooner is probably better, but cowardice is such an inviting option.' And she finished her glass and gave him a wink.

ALICE

It was half past eleven, and the woes of the ball and the trials of the day were now nicely numbed and suitably far away. The restorative powers of an evening of food, wine and good company had worked wonders. Baby Scarlet was finally sleeping peacefully upstairs, and Dan was snoring in his armchair, his beer bottle still nestled upright in his lap.

Silently Ginny beckoned Alice into the kitchen.

'Let's leave him in peace,' she said quietly and reached into the fridge for another bottle of wine. 'Top-up?'

Ginny poured the wine.

'So, now that it's just the two of us you can tell me about this John guy,' she said with a mischievous grin.

Alice felt her cheeks pinken.

'What do you mean?'

'Oh, come on!' Ginny laughed quietly so as not to wake Dan. 'You can't fool me. You like him!'

'Like him?' Alice echoed in surprise, aware that Ginny was watching her like a hawk. She could feel the colour in her cheeks deepening. 'He's my boss's husband!'

Ginny raised an eyebrow.

'Well, of course I like him,' Alice admitted. 'He stuck up for me and then came out to the taxi rank to check I was OK. He's obviously a *likable* person.' Now didn't seem like the right time to tell Ginny how startlingly handsome he was, or how taken aback she'd been that he was younger than Audrey – at least five years younger, maybe even ten.

Ginny grinned knowingly.

'But he's a married man,' Alice insisted chastely. 'I don't like him *like him*, if that's what you're getting at.'

'Oh?'

'No!' Alice had to turn away; Ginny was unnerving her. 'Besides,' she added indignantly, 'I'm not the kind of woman who fancies other women's husbands.'

'Even if that woman's Audrey Cracknell and it's debatable whether she actually qualifies as a woman at all?'

'*Especially* if that woman's Audrey Cracknell! She's scary enough as it is, without anyone having designs on her husband. *And* she's my boss, for goodness sake. It would be career suicide.'

Alice thought about it rationally for a moment.

'Besides, it would be a totally implausible match,' she reasoned. 'Audrey and I are complete opposites, so whatever a man loves about her he wouldn't find in me. We're very different.'

'Are you?' Ginny asked mischievously.

'God, yes! Audrey and I have nothing in common. Nothing at all!'

'Except John.'

'Gin! Stop stirring! What a thing to say! And I thought I was supposed to be the one with the overactive imagination!'

'So, you're going to give Audrey back his handkerchief, then?'

'Um, well. It's complicated.'

'My point exactly!' Ginny grinned and topped up her wine glass. 'Oh, I'll be honest with you; I'm just jealous.'

'Jealous?' Alice put down her glass in surprise.

'Going to a ball, having a handsome man spring to your defence and then chase after you to check you're OK – it sounds exciting to me. More exciting than anything that happens in my life.'

'There's nothing exciting about being a laughing stock and sneaking home early in tears.'

'Yes, but all that stuff he said about you – about you having a good heart and how some man was going to be lucky to meet you. That's romantic.'

Alice looked at her friend. Ginny was beginning to look wistful.

'You've got romance in your life. You live with it every day. Dan's fantastic.'

'Is he?' Ginny asked.

The conversation suddenly felt darker.

'What do you mean? Dan's wonderful. My clients would give their eye teeth for a man like him.'

'Hmmmm.' Ginny picked up her glass and looked at it sceptically.

'What do you mean? You've lost me.'

'Of course I've lost you,' Ginny said with a sudden harshness. 'You think the sun shines out of Dan's arse! You think he's a perfect husband and a perfect dad!'

Alice recoiled in shock.

'Yes. Yes, I do. Dan's a good man. And you love him.'

There was a long pause. Alice began to feel a rising sense of panic. Ginny was staring at the table. Alice's statement hung heavily between them.

'Gin, you love him!' Alice repeated a bit more forcefully.

'Do I?'

'Yes!'

'Do I really?'

This wasn't good. This wasn't good at all.

'Ginny, what's wrong?' Alice asked softly. She immediately started berating herself. She should have known something was up. Ginny hadn't seemed very happy recently. And right now she looked miserable.

'You're probably just having a bad patch, that's all,' Alice said gently when her friend didn't answer. 'You need to talk things through with him.'

'Is that what I've got to do?' Ginny looked strange. 'No disrespect, Alice, but you've got no idea. You think your perfect man is just around the corner: a knight on a white charger. You think it's a fairy tale: that you meet, fall in love and live happily ever after. Well, life's not like that. Fairy tales don't exist, or they don't exist for very long. All the Prince Charmings turn into ball-scratching, beer-drinking, telly-watching slobs in the end.'

Alice felt numb with shock. Dan wasn't those things. He was lovely!

'Be careful what you wish for, Alice,' Ginny warned darkly. 'You might get to kiss the frog and discover he's nothing more than just that: a frog.'

'Dan's not a frog,' Alice said quietly, feeling dazed by Ginny's outburst. What on earth was going on?

'No. No, he's not,' Ginny said wearily, the fight suddenly gone out of her. She sighed. 'You're right. It's probably just a bad patch. I'm tired; I think it's time I went to bed.'

Alice nodded dumbly and gave her friend a hug.

'I'm here if you need me,' she said as she squeezed her tight.

Ginny nodded, gave a watery smile and headed towards the stairs.

Alice let herself out. Deeply troubled, she picked up her bike and pedalled hard in the direction of home.

LOU

'On Friday night, babe, it's going to be just you and me,' Tony had said. 'Suze thinks I'm out of town on business, but I'm going to pack my bag, shoot down here and wait for you in the office. You're going to bring me a beer and I'm going to watch you on the monitor, and check out your juicy little ass shaking its way round the bar putting smiles on everyone's face. I'll be stiff as a board watching you bend over to pick the Stellas off the bottom shelf of the fridge, your skirt pulling tight and your tits jiggling in your shirt. I might even have a wank whilst I'm waiting. And then, when the shift's over, we'll send the staff home early – fuck the clearing up – and I'm going to whisk you off in my BMW to a penthouse at the White Hotel where I'm going to slowly strip off your clothes, carry you to the hot tub and massage you all over with hot soapy suds. And then I'm going to take you over to the king-sized bed, throw you down and fuck you harder than you've ever been fucked in your life!'

And then he'd raised an eyebrow and given her his filthiest look.

Lou wouldn't let on, but she'd been pretty excited. A whole night with Tony, and the morning after too! He'd never offered her this before; things had never progressed beyond a few hours after their shifts before he scuttled back to Suzy with the smell of Lou on his skin. He'd certainly never taken her anywhere in his car, let alone shelled out for a posh room at the city's hippest hotel. In fact, Lou wasn't sure she'd even seen Tony in daylight before. Their business and pleasure had all taken place at work, in the basement bar with no windows. Maybe it was finally happening, she thought. Maybe he was thinking about leaving Suzy . . . for her! Lou had felt a delicious tingle of power, packed her best, tiniest underwear and headed to the bathroom for a night of diligent depilation.

But now it was one o'clock on Saturday morning, and the last of the Friday-night drinkers had staggered up the stairs and out into the street. Jake had bolted the door and Paul was cashing up. There was no sign of Tony.

Lou furiously started to collect empty glasses, beer slops spilling unnoticed as she slammed them onto the counter. He wasn't coming. He'd fed her all those lines about having a special night together, about how he couldn't wait to feel her naked skin against sheets rather than their usual upright shuffle against cold bottles and sharp-cornered packets of crisps. He'd got her hopes up. She'd let herself imagine. She was plucked, buffed and moisturized to perfection and her overnight bag was waiting expectantly in the office. But Tony wasn't here. She'd kill him. With her bare hands! Or failing that she'd administer a serious, hard-to-explain-to-Suzy injury with a forcefully applied slops bucket.

She clashed two towers of pint glasses together and marched around the bar on another circuit of glass-collecting. She could see Jake and Paul exchanging glances. Well, they could think what they liked. She was buggered if she was going to calm down. Being a rational, unflappable deputy manager wasn't all it was cracked up to be.

Despite herself, Lou couldn't help looking in the direction of the stairs, hoping to see Tony bounding down them, car keys and erection at the ready. Every time she looked she got angrier, not just with Tony but with herself. She wasn't the kind of girl who got taken in by blokes. She knew men weren't to be trusted; they were good for one thing only. And Tony wasn't even much good at that. Didn't she frequently have to suppress the urge to tidy the optics halfway through?

Eventually the tidying up was finished, and Lou had no more reasons to keep them all there.

'Right, well, thanks lads,' she said tersely. 'You can go.'

Jake and Paul looked at each other with relief.

Lou grimly went to the office to fetch her overnight bag. The monitor was on, its camera trained at the bar. She swore. So much for watching her all night in a state of suspended, tongue-hanging-out lust. She switched it off and left the room.

She made her way up the stairs, set the burglar alarm and locked the front door. She looked down the street. There was no waiting BMW; just her nightly minicab, its exhaust puffing into the night. She was going home. Alone.

Wearily she opened the cab door, nodded to the driver and immediately wished she'd had a cigarette before setting off.

'Good night?' the driver asked cheerily.

'Does it look like it?' Lou muttered sarcastically. She looked out of the window and unseeingly watched the city speed past.

'Here . . . it looks like you could do with one.'

She looked round. The taxi driver was waving a cigarette over his shoulder, keeping his eyes fixed firmly on the road.

'Are you sure?' she asked in surprise. 'Won't the fag police bang you up for crimes against lungs?'

His eyes met hers in the rear-view mirror. 'You're my last fare; I think I can risk it!' His eyes crinkled up to show he was smiling.

Lou took the cigarette. She lit and inhaled. As the smoke made its way into her lungs she felt a warm prickle of content- ment. It was amazing, the power of cigarettes, she thought. The anti-smoking brigade would never get it. They thought they could change smokers' minds by printing scary words on the packet, or by making revolting TV ads with black- ened innards or cigarettes oozing pus. As if that was going to work! Any blithering idiot knows fags are bad for you. But what the do-gooders fail to grasp is that fags are *good* for you. Cigarettes make you feel better, plain and simple, she thought. Smoking is one of the best feelings in the world.

She sat back and puffed indulgently. She looked at the driver, or what she could see of him in his rear-view mirror: his eyes, eyebrows and the bottom of his forehead.

'You look familiar.'

'Yeah, well, I take you home three times a week. You're normally a bit happier than tonight, though. Wanna talk about it?'

'No!'

'Wanna hear a joke?'

'No!'

The taxi pulled up at some traffic lights. Lou's attention was suddenly drawn to three drunken girls in miniskirts, weaving their way home. Two of the girls were holding the other one up. All were staggering as they struggled to balance on their four-inch stilettos, which didn't look so sassy with half a kebab spiked on the heel. The drunk mate with puke on her shirt wasn't such a hot accessory either.

'England's green and pleasant land, eh?' the taxi driver said sarcastically.

Lou looked back at him. He was laughing to himself. How old was he, she wondered? It was hard to tell with her limited view. But he looked to have a full head of hair, and his top looked modern and OK. And he had nice eyes. From her position in the back she could see the left side of his face, shaded red from the reflected glow of the traffic lights. He had a bit of stubble, but good skin. Young-looking skin. And a strong jaw.

Could she?

Should she?

Well, why the bloody hell not? Tony had had his chance and he'd blown it. He was too busy playing house in the suburbs with Sunbed Suzy and their gruesome 2.4 kids.

She was going to kill him when he next showed up at the bar. How dare he mess her around like that! Who did he think he was? Well, fuck him! She'd show him.

She leant forward in her seat, letting her coat fall open to show the low V of her blouse. She took a long drag on her cigarette, tipped her face to the car ceiling and then slowly exhaled, her mouth a deliberate Cupid's pout.

'What did you say your name was again?' she asked the taxi driver with a vampish smile.

ALICE

Alice stood outside Greenfingers garden centre, frowning as she waited for the doors to open. Her trip was normally reserved for Sundays, but after the stresses of last night she felt the need for the immediate soothing balm of plants.

'Problem?' asked Dudley as he unlocked the door and let the early-bird enthusiasts trickle in.

'Hmmm? No, I'm fine. Thanks, Dudley. How are you?'

Alice hadn't slept much last night. She couldn't believe Ginny and Dan's relationship was in trouble. She'd always thought of them as a perfect couple. Miserably she'd watched the red numbers on her alarm clock flick to 4 a.m.

But now it was morning and it was uncharacteristically sunny. She rushed to the outdoor courtyard and surveyed the scene. She always took a few moments to drink in the restorative powers of the calm natural picture before her: the gorgeously healthy rows of plants and the constant gentle babble of the water displays. Her pilgrimage never failed to wash away the problems of the week.

But today as she looked at the courtyard her whole body felt heavy. What with Sheryl's accusations, her terror of going to the ball and then the terrible reality of being at it, it had been one hell of a week. Every night had been a sleepless one. But last night . . . *last night* had been the worst of the lot. Her own unhappiness was one thing; the unhappiness of her friend was quite another.

She moved into the first row of plants. The tulips were beginning to bloom, like giant upside-down purple droplets balancing on the end of plump stalks. She picked one up, noticing how reassuring the cool pot and earth felt within her palm; how simple in comparison to her spinning, overheated head.

Alice wandered up and down the rows of budding cowslips and violets. Bit by bit all thoughts of Ginny, Audrey and Sheryl seeped away and she began a delicious descent into being well and truly lost in the world of the plants. Tiny rivers of soil began to form in the skin on her fingertips as she caressed the plants, carefully checking the earth for moisture levels and stroking the downy leaves. It was her own version of therapy, and infinitely cheaper. Slowly, without her realizing, her tension lifted, her eyes brightened and everything creaked and twisted back into place. Twenty minutes later she stood tall again, her shoulders opened up and her face lifted to the sun.

Alice turned into the final row of greenery, gently humming to herself as she hugged several plants to her body. At the end of the row she noticed a fellow early-bird gardener, bent over what looked like a Stachys byzantina. Alice smiled in recognition of a like-minded garden-lover. He was definitely a gardener, not just a dabbler. He was delicately stroking the plant's leaves between his thumb and forefinger, savouring the velvety touch, and looking for all the world as though he were kneeling before it in reverential worship. Alice hugged her plants closer, feeling a sudden warm glow of happiness. This was what mattered. Not office politics, or worrying about what people thought of her. This was where Alice was Alice and nothing could touch her. It was her special place. She smiled and turned back to her inspection of the row. She reached out to touch a plump daisy.

'Alice?'

A voice broke the tranquil quiet. Alice jumped, as the world rudely barged back in. Reluctantly she turned to see who it was.

It was the garden-lover at the end of the row, who had turned to face her. With a shock she realized she knew him.

It was John.

'Alice! It's good to see you!' He was smiling at her warmly.

Her brain whirred at breakneck speed. It was John Cracknell! What was he doing here? Did he like gardening? He looked different from before – more relaxed. And, wow, she'd forgotten how incredibly handsome he was. *Those eyes!* She quickly looked away from his face, and with surprise she saw his old, faded jeans with a patch of dried earth on one knee, his muddy boots and his fleece, ripped on the arm. He looked like a gardener. He *was* a gardener.

But then Alice's mind darkened ... Was Audrey with him? What if her boss suddenly stepped from the rows of greenery, ruining her special place forever ...? And what if John was – at this precise moment – having a mental flashback to her snot and tears at the taxi rank? But as she looked at him something flashed at the front of her brain in big red capital letters. 'He's just like me!' it said. And then it vanished.

'Er, hi,' she stuttered, suddenly aware that she'd forgotten to brush her teeth that morning.

'I was just admiring this Stachys byzantina. It's great to see them in bloom again.'

She was aware that he was looking at her, expecting her to say something. She tried not to look at his face; something about looking at him directly seemed to make her blush.

'I didn't know you were a gardener,' she blurted. 'I mean, Audrey never mentioned it.'

She noticed a funny expression flash across his face and then disappear.

'I *love* my garden,' he said. 'It's the most important room in the house.'

Alice nodded. What a great thing to say! But how weird that John Cracknell should say it. And what did this mean? Surely Audrey couldn't be a gardener too? Impossible! Alice tried to imagine her watering her garden, talking to her plants, or diligently kneeling in muddy earth as she lovingly planted a freesia. Surely she couldn't have got Audrey so wrong? She hoped not. She didn't like to think of herself as being in any way the same as her boss.

'Is, uh . . . is Audrey with you?' She tried to keep her voice light.

John laughed.

'No.'

He sounded very definite. So Audrey wasn't a gardener after all! Alice tried not to let the relief show.

'So, you're here first thing on a Saturday morning, and you're holding those clematis as though your life depended on it,' John continued lightly. 'I take it you're a gardener, then?'

'Yes, yes! Very much so.' Alice gave a quick laugh and relaxed her grip on the plants.

'Good!' he smiled. 'I've never met a gardener I didn't like.'

Alice looked at her feet, her cheeks flaming again.

'What I mean is ...' he added hastily, 'just that I think gardeners are easy-going, nurturing kind of people.'

Alice looked up and nodded dumbly. She knew what he meant but she didn't know what to say. She hoped he wouldn't come any nearer; she didn't want him within smelling distance of her breath, just in case.

'Look.' John stepped closer towards her. 'I know we didn't get off to the best of starts. Thursday was ... well, I'm sure we've both had better nights ...'

Alice stared back at her feet. Yet again she could have kicked herself for her behaviour at the ball. And how embarrassing that John Cracknell had witnessed it all.

'... but I'd really like to put it behind us, make a fresh start,' she heard him say.

There was a long pause while Alice tried to think of a reply.

'Look, Alice, do you have anywhere to go?'

'Go?'

'I mean, do you have to hurry off? I was wondering whether we could get a coffee. You know, chat about perennials and optimum pruning times.' He gave a small, awkward laugh.

Alice took a sharp intake of breath.

'No!' she said quickly. 'I don't really think it would be appropriate, do you?'

'Appropriate?'

Alice was surprised. He'd seemed like a thoughtful kind of man. Of course she couldn't have coffee with him! What was he thinking?

'*Audrey!*' Alice said meaningfully.

He looked blank.

'I just meant a coffee. And Audrey really isn't an issue . . .'

Alice hugged her plants primly. She couldn't believe he'd shrugged off his wife so casually! Did he really think it was OK to go for coffee with his wife's employee, and that Audrey wouldn't mind? Or maybe he was after something . . . ? Something else entirely. She'd obviously got him all wrong. She had a rare flash of anger. What kind of man dismisses his wife as not being 'an issue'?

'I've got to go!' she blurted. She turned on her heel, put her head down and accelerated as fast as she could. She heard John call out her name, but she kept on going, hurtling towards the exit. As she neared the tills she realized she still had the clematis in her hands. She really wanted them but couldn't risk stopping to pay. What if John caught up and tried to carry on talking? She quickly thrust them into a display of garden gnomes and charged towards the doors.

'Bye, Alice!' Dudley called as she rocketed past. Alice raced towards her bike and pedalled home as fast as she could, kicking herself for not buying the clematis and wondering over and over how she'd got John and his gentlemanly kindness so wrong.

KATE

Kate laughed. She liked him.

In front of her sat Steve, and he'd just come to the end of a very funny story about a series of epic blunders he'd made at work, each gaffe more embarrassing than the last, that had ended with his boss branding him *the most useless turd ever to have floated past my desk.*

Kate's face ached from laughing. He was certainly different from the other men Alice had matched her with. And the multiple gin-and-tonics helped. She felt relaxed, like she could kick back and be herself. It was a good feeling.

As her laughter faded Steve scooped up their glasses, loudly declared 'my round', and headed back to the bar.

Kate snuggled into her chair and watched him. He was great, but she didn't fancy him.

It wasn't that there was anything *wrong* with him. He ticked a lot of her boxes, like having a good job, and being close to his family. And unlike the other men Alice had matched her with, he was interesting and funny, and actually listened to what she had to say. So in many respects Steve was a great catch.

But he had two big minus points, and she couldn't wait to phone Lou to analyse them.

The first was hard to put her finger on, but it was a definite feeling, and it was getting stronger as the night progressed. Something about him didn't add up. There was something that Steve, for all his openness and self-deprecation, wasn't saying. Like his funny stories. They were brilliant. But there was something about them that was just too slick. They felt . . . what was it? *Rehearsed!* Like he'd told them before. A lot.

But repetition's not a crime, Kate reasoned. Everyone does it, women especially. Something hasn't really happened until you've told at least ten of your friends all the gory details. No, it was more that Steve's stories seemed *perfect*. He never got anything muddled or in the wrong order. It was like he was a comedian going through his set. Only it was for an audience of just one . . . her.

Kate saw Steve get the attention of the barman and order their drinks.

The second thing that stopped her fancying him was his face. She hated to admit it, but he just wasn't good-looking enough. OK, so that sounded really bad – and it was something she'd only ever admit out loud to Lou, for fear of anyone else thinking she was being shallow – but she couldn't help it. She wanted a drop-dead-handsome boyfriend, and Steve was more drop-dead than handsome. Besides, if she was looking for Mr Forever, then he had to have a face she'd want to look at . . . well, *forever*.

It was strange that Alice had put Steve forward, Kate

thought suddenly. After all, she knew what Kate wanted in a man, and looks had always been top of the list. And Harvey, who Kate had met last night, had been just as gorgeous as Sebastian and Michael, although slow on the uptake, and not very aware of the world around him. Kate had been surprised to discover that he never read newspapers or watched the news.

'How do you know what's happening in the world?' she'd asked curiously.

'What's there to know?' he'd replied with a slow smile.

Harvey knew everything about who'd won the latest reality TV show or which pair of Dolce & Gabbana jeans had the longest waiting list. But which political party was in power, which novelist was currently making waves or what topical scandal was dominating the papers totally escaped him.

So when Kate met Steve she'd found herself feeling relieved he wasn't like her other Table For Two dates. He wasn't self-obsessed, arrogant, rude, a workaholic, work-shy or an airhead. He didn't take calls on his mobile in the middle of their date, and he didn't make her feel stupid or fat. For the first time Kate began to wonder if she'd been barking up the wrong tree with the criteria she'd given Alice. But then she looked at Steve with his pale, shiny skin, barely there eyelashes and sticky-out ears and she knew it was a face she could never wake up next to.

Besides, there was still that funny feeling she just couldn't shake . . .

Steve made his way back from the bar and placed a jumbo-sized gin and tonic on the table with a flourish. Kate smiled. He was nice. But not boyfriend material. Or husband material. Or father material. He was a good laugh, nothing more. And after her recent dating disasters she was going to bloody well enjoy the moment.

She picked up her glass and drank.

ALICE

There was a disgruntled sigh from the other end of the telephone.

'I don't see the point of these post-mortems,' Maurice grumbled. 'It either worked or it didn't, and this one – just like all the other ones – didn't.'

He was beginning to sound angry.

'Anyway, even if I did answer your ridiculous questions, you'd still send me exactly the same kind of woman for my next date regardless; you lot always do. Where's your imagination? I joined Table For Two to meet *different* women – not this tedious stream of bland, bottle-blonde divorcees.'

Alice opened her mouth to speak. Her clients were normally happy, so she didn't know what to do when somebody wasn't; and Maurice clearly wasn't. All the girls had looked after him at some point over the years, and they'd all passed him on in exasperation. His diatribes were office legend. Even Audrey, who liked a good confrontation, only agreed to keep him on the books at all because he was a rare-as-gold-dust male client, and because Alice had promised to take him off everyone's hands. Alice couldn't bear for Table For Two to fail him. Everyone deserved to find love – even Maurice.

'So,' she summarized carefully, 'you're after someone unusual – someone who doesn't fit the mould.'

'At last!' he cried sarcastically.

'Someone with an interesting job ... with strong opinions or an unusual hobby ... Someone who's not shy of having a good debate?'

'Well, that would make me feel like the exorbitant fees I've been paying for the last four years haven't been completely wasted!'

'I'm sorry for the questions, but I've only just taken over your case and I want to make sure I completely understand the kind of woman you'd like to meet.'

'Yes, yes, but I've told so many of you Table For Two girls I feel like a parrot. Can't you just talk to each other? Communicate?'

There didn't seem much point in explaining that if all the others had got his ideal woman wrong, then getting a brief from them wasn't a good idea.

'I don't see why Ms Cracknell can't look after me,' Maurice grumbled. 'If her staff aren't capable of finding me a match then she should do it.'

'I'm sure she'd love to,' Alice replied delicately. 'But Audrey's books are full at the moment.'

'*Mauriced?*' asked Hilary sympathetically when Alice finally managed to put down the phone.

Alice nodded wearily. The difficult conversation had made her mouth completely dry. She took a sip of water and reached into her cardigan pocket for her lip balm. It was nestling against something soft and comforting: John's handkerchief. Alice felt a rush of excitement as she brushed it with her fingers.

By the time she'd made it home from the garden centre she'd wondered if she'd jumped the gun a bit. He'd only suggested coffee, not a dirty weekend in Amsterdam. And he probably *had* wanted to talk about optimum pruning times: after all, it's not often you get to meet a fellow gardener. And besides, he was a happily married man!

No, the more Alice thought about it, the more she was sure she'd got the wrong end of the stick. And what must he have thought when she ran off like that? *Again!* She felt embarrassed even thinking about it.

Alice shook her head. She needed to concentrate; she had to make a match – a *good* match – for Maurice. She made herself comfortable, looked out of the window and let herself drift ...

When Alice re-emerged she had several names written on her notepad: Felicity Dingle, Abigail Brookes and Rita Harrington.

Felicity was a vivacious, raven-haired taxi driver whose job meant she rarely had the luxury of free time in which to meet men. But the payback was that she could turn her hand to any possible conversation, from sport to politics to astronomy. If her evenings were her own to spend sociably then Alice had no doubt she'd be nabbed by a lucky suitor within the week.

Abigail was an artist whose dishevelled style Alice had always admired. She *was* a bottle blonde, but kept her dark roots at a defiant five centimetres. She was an ironic blonde with attitude.

And Rita was a headmistress and former head of her university debating society. If Rita couldn't blow away the cobwebs with a rigorous intellectual argument, then Alice didn't know who could. She'd certainly keep Maurice on his toes.

None of the women were divorced, and none could possibly be branded as bland.

Alice reached for the phone to call Maurice but something caught her eye. It was yet another outsized floral delivery walking through the door. Now that Alice knew how much John loved his garden, the frequency of the floral deliveries made sense. But something about this particular delivery didn't. Rather than being the usual collection of roses and lilies, this was an exotic cluster of bird of paradise. It was wild and vibrant, and could only have been chosen by someone who really knew about plants. Instinctively Alice rose to admire the bouquet more closely. But strangely it seemed to be heading her way. Every step taken by the human legs beneath the flowers brought them closer to her desk.

'Alice Brown?' asked the legs.

Alice nodded dumbly.

'These are for you.'

'Thank you.' Alice was astonished. The bouquet was thrust into her arms.

'Bloody hell! Who sent you those?' Hilary slammed down her phone and hurried over as fast as her pregnant body would allow.

Alice suddenly became aware of Audrey studying her closely from across the office. Numbly she delved for the card.

Dear Alice – she read.

From one plant lover to another, with the greenest of intentions. Please reconsider that coffee.

There was no signature, just an email address.

'It's a mystery admirer!' Hilary shouted excitedly, reading the card over Alice's shoulder.

Audrey was still watching her like a hawk. Alice studiously avoided eye contact. The delivery was obviously from John. But what if Audrey guessed? She was frightening enough when she didn't have a reason to be angry.

'Do you have any idea who they're from?' Hilary demanded.

Alice did her best to look casual.

'No one. Just a friend having a laugh, that's all.'

She placed the bouquet on the floor beside her desk, sat down and tried to look engrossed in her paperwork. Disappointed, the girls returned to their desks. Normal business resumed, and Alice finally felt the weight of Audrey's gaze shift away. But inside, her heart was thumping. John had sent her flowers! He didn't think she was an idiot for running away from him at the garden centre. Or for blubbing into his hanky at the ball. He didn't care that Sheryl had humiliated her, that she was a matchmaker without a boyfriend, or that she'd forgotten to brush her teeth before going to the garden centre.

John wanted to meet!

She forced herself to take a deep breath. She needed to forget all thoughts of those smiling eyes and that sunshine-coated skin. She had to be sensible.

It wasn't John who wanted a coffee; it was John *Cracknell* – Audrey's husband – and that was a whole different kettle of fish. Either he was a married man wanting a torrid affair or he was a married man wanting an innocent friendship with a fellow gardener to discuss drainage techniques for pot plants or the best way to get rid of slugs. Neither option was anything to get carried away with.

Alice longed to read the card again, but she daren't, in case anyone saw. So she tried to remember the wording and decipher its meaning. He'd said his intentions were green, but could she believe him? There was only one way to find out.

Though how on earth could she explain to Audrey that she was arranging a rendezvous with her husband . . . ?

But maybe Audrey already knew? Maybe she and John had laughed all through their Sunday lunch at the vision of Alice hurtling off, terrified by the proposition of a hot drink. Maybe that was why Audrey had been studying her so strangely when the bouquet had arrived.

Alice's head was beginning to ache. And time was ticking on. She still needed to talk Maurice through her suggested suitors. And then there was the round of Monday-morning phone calls to see how her weekend matches had got on. She didn't have time to daydream.

Alice reached for her phone again and dialled Maurice's number. She'd made her mind up. It was good manners to thank someone when they sent you a gift, so she'd send John a quick email. She wouldn't mention the coffee, but she also wouldn't delete the autosignature that automatically appeared at the bottom of her emails and included her mobile number. If John called her on it, it wouldn't be her fault. It would all be innocent and above board: totally greenly intended! Besides, she'd never had a gardening buddy before, and he might just have some suggestions to help save her geraniums from greenfly.

The ringing phone was picked up by Maurice, sounding calmer now. Alice opened her mouth and confidently began to talk him through her matches.

AUDREY

Audrey sat in her favourite position in the front row of the elevated section on the lower deck of the 119 bus. She never went upstairs; it was always full of teenagers and drunks. Instead she preferred her lower-deck vantage point from which she could cast withering verdicts on the alighting passengers.

But tonight, scathing judgements of the general public couldn't hold Audrey's attention. Her eyes kept straying to the grey, wet streets and her thoughts kept returning to John.

It had been six whole days since the ball and the awful conversation in the passenger seat of his Audi. For six days and six nights she'd gone over his words until they'd become embedded in her dreams when she was asleep and stamped before her eyeballs when she was awake.

I didn't know you were like that . . . hard . . . devoid of compassion.

So many times Audrey had almost picked up the phone to ring Geraldine and demand to know what he'd meant. Sometimes her hand had even touched the receiver, but she hadn't made the call. After all, how could she explain without admitting she'd somehow incurred John's disapproval? John, who was so equable about everyone.

No, it would be much better if Geraldine simply gave Audrey John's number so she could call him herself. She'd apologize, promise to change, donate to his favourite charity, anything that meant she'd be forgiven.

But she hadn't phoned to ask for his number either. She knew it wouldn't be given. She'd tried before, years ago. She'd been as persuasive as she'd known how, but John's number had remained firmly out of reach. It was agency policy. Audrey hadn't the heart to try again. She couldn't face refusal, not when she was feeling so weak.

Instead she'd forlornly hoped John would get in touch with her, apologize, and implore her with his Paul Newman eyes to forget the whole unhappy incident. Audrey's hopes had soared when the unscheduled floral delivery had arrived today. She'd held her breath whilst the delivery man pulled his paperwork from his pocket and was pointed towards the correct desk. By the time it was clear he wasn't heading for her glass-walled office, Audrey's breath had been held so long that her vision was peppered with small black dots. She should have known John wouldn't apologize that way. Besides, he'd never have chosen such a disagreeable bunch of flowers.

But if she wasn't going to phone Geraldine, and if John wasn't going to phone her, then what was she to do? Could she live in limbo until another professional occasion arose? What if John's feelings hardened during the wait? What if last Thursday's discontent got stronger? Was it a risk she could take? And just when she'd been sensing a break-through in their relationship too! The last few times she'd seen John she'd felt him inch closer towards a declaration of love. But now the thought of sliding back down the ladder made her want to cry with angry frustration.

No, she couldn't just leave everything to sort itself out. If there was one thing she knew, it was that men could *never* be left to their own devices.

Audrey began considering another option. She could book John for a night – not to accompany her to a function, just a normal weeknight date for them to enjoy each other's company. They could go to dinner. It would be the kind of night that other couples took for granted, and without the withering spotlight of a formal function maybe their love could blossom again.

But it was a big step to take. Firstly there would be the embarrassment factor of making the booking. Geraldine was bound to ask the purpose of the date. She'd see straight through Audrey's request and know she was desperate. And there was also the hit to her bank balance to consider. An evening with John didn't come cheap, and she wouldn't be able to disguise this one as a business expense.

The bus veered into Sidwell Street and she hit the bell. She swept through the double doors and onto the pave-ment. It had begun to drizzle.

What choice did she have about John? she asked herself as she quickstepped up the road, the light spots of rain already turning her hair to frizz. She'd have to do it. She'd have to brave Geraldine, book a restaurant and stump up the cash for a functionless night with John. It was a risk, but maybe her gamble would pay off. John would see that she wanted to spend time with *him*, and not just book him for professional reasons. And this could be the spur he needed to make his feelings known. To hell with the money! If all went to plan she might never have to pay for his company again! It could be the first of hundreds of functionless nights with John. It could be the night when eleven years of dreams finally came true!

Audrey's step became springier. That was it, she thought to herself, the weight of inaction lifting from her shoulders. She had a plan!

ALICE

Alice surveyed Steve from behind her orange juice. Kate was right; there was definitely something going on. He'd barely made eye contact; instead his eyes kept flitting around the pub or darting to the door, waiting for his mate to arrive. And that was another thing. Steve had known for a full week that they were having a drink to discuss his progress at Table For Two, so why had he arranged to meet his mate at exactly the same time? This wasn't the sweet, earnest Steve Alice remembered. Something was up.

'So, you're completely happy with how things are going?' Alice clarified, interrupting Steve's umpteenth visual journey around the interior of the pub.

'Yeah, yeah. It's great,' he enthused distractedly, still not looking at her.

'It's just that you've been on first dates with quite a few women but you haven't wanted to meet any of them again.'

'Yeah, that's right.'

Alice felt confused. Clients weren't usually so nonchalant. Normally, if Cupid hadn't shown up by date number three they were straight on the phone to complain.

'So . . . it's not great then really, is it?' she pushed.

'Eh?' His eyes flicked momentarily to her. 'No, really. It's fine.'

'But aren't you getting frustrated?'

'Frustrated?' he snorted. And then he quickly recomposed himself.

'That we haven't cracked it yet?'

'No, no. I mean, well, it's a hard job, isn't it, matching people up. You're bound to get a few duds before you hit the jackpot.'

Alice was amazed. Clients never said stuff like this!

'Look.' Steve briefly turned his attention to her. 'If you're here because you're worried I think you're doing a bad job, well, don't be. Worried, I mean. I'm sure you're doing your best.'

His tone wasn't conciliatory, or praising, or even patronizing. It was simply . . . what was it? It didn't make sense!

'So that's that then,' Steve concluded.

'Well, not exactly.'

Steve froze slightly. For a moment he looked caught.

'Look, I don't want to keep matching you with . . . "duds".' Alice forced herself to use his description. 'It's my job to find your perfect woman – the woman you said you wanted to grow old with, remember?'

Was it Alice's imagination, or did Steve blanch?

'I don't want to waste your money or let you down,' she rallied. 'I've got your happiness to think about! So let's stop wasting your time on dates with women you're not interested in, and let's find you "the one" and get you off the market.'

Steve studied the table. Alice tried to swallow her amazement.

'That is what you want, Steve. Isn't it?'

Her question hovered between them. She saw his cheeks flush, the blush spreading across his face, swallowing up his pale features and lighting up his ears. There were a few long seconds of silence. And then, just as he was opening his mouth to reply, his attention was caught by someone coming through the door and an expression – relief ? – flashed across his face.

'Tommy!' He jumped up. 'All right, mate? This is Alice from Table For Two. Alice, this is my mate Tommy.'

Reluctantly Alice drew her eyes away. A burly, friendly looking man was bowling towards them, a smile on his face and laughter in his eyes.

'So you're the lady who's been tasked with finding someone desperate enough to fall for this idiot!' he grinned, pumping her hand in greeting.

Tommy was a big rugged bear of a man, solidly built, and with an easy charm. As Steve moved to stand next to him Alice noticed he looked smaller and paler than before.

'Yeah, well, just because you only have to look at a woman for her to drop her knickers,' he mumbled bitterly.

There was a sudden silence. Tommy stifled a laugh. Alice noticed Steve's blush surge back across his face with even more force than before.

'Keeps his inner poet well hidden – don't you, mate?' Tommy glossed over the pause. 'Now, Alice: what can I get you? You must need a stiff drink after putting up with this plonker!'

Alice watched as Tommy strode towards the bar, Steve scuttling behind him, the tips of his ears glowing a painful pink. She sat back in her chair and thought. The pieces were suddenly fitting together.

LOU

Ever since Tony had stood her up, Lou had been feeling vicious. And when she felt vicious she liked a drink.

'So,' Kate interjected as Lou finished describing her boss with a list of the most venomous adjectives known to the English language. 'That *was* his last chance, right?'

Lou and Kate were halfway through their first bottle of laughably expensive wine in a swanky new bar on the fashionable side of the city. It had only opened a week ago, and they'd been lucky to get the last table, even if it *was* squeezed next to the loos.

'You can't shag him again,' Kate continued. 'He's made it clear where his priorities lie.'

Lou frowned. Kate had a really irritating way of hitting the nail on the head.

'As if I'd give that spineless, small-dicked arse-wipe the time of day,' she replied blithely.

'So it's over, then?'

'It never even started,' Lou said dismissively.

'But that's it? No more sex with Tony?'

Lou took a large sip of wine. No more sex with Tony. It sounded strange.

'Lou! Come on!' Kate cried. 'He chose Suzy!'

'As if I'd want him to leave his wife anyway!' Lou snapped. 'I'm only *shagging* him. Christ!'

There was a pause.

'So, like I said ... No more sex with Tony.'

'Sometimes I want it and Tony's just there!'

'Well, you'll just have to exercise a bit of self-control.'

'I don't believe in exercise.'

'I didn't mean that kind of exercise!'

'Look, the small-dicked arse-wipe's history,' Lou said dismissively. 'That's why I wanted to come here tonight. Check out the fish in a new pond. See if there are any good rods to nibble.'

The women sipped their drinks and looked around the bar.

All in all, it wasn't bad pickings, Lou thought. They were all well-heeled, suited types; not the bits of rough she preferred, but good enough for a Thursday night.

'Fuck!' Kate cried suddenly.

'That's the plan,' Lou deadpanned.

Kate thrust her head down and hunched her shoulders. 'Oh no! Fuck, fuck, fuck!'

Lou looked at her friend in alarm. Kate didn't swear much, and if she did she usually just splashed about in the shallow end with the bloody hells and an occasional bugger. It took quite a lot for her to wade into the deeper waters of the F-word.

'It's him!'

'Who?' Lou peered around the bar enthusiastically.

'Don't look! The idiot! The horrible man I had the date with. The one who said I was fat and made a big deal about my surname.'

'What, Sebastian?'

'Shhhhh! Oh God, no, this can't be happening.'

'Where is he? Which one?'

'Over there . . .' Kate gestured with her eyebrows, keeping her head angled away from the rest of the room.

'What, the cute one?'

'*Lou!*'

'What? I'm just saying! He's hot!'

'We've got to go,' Kate begged. She sounded close to tears.

'OK, just let me finish my drink.'

'I mean, *now*! I can't let him see me. He'd only make some horrible comment about my size.'

Lou looked at Kate sharply. '*You*, Kate Biggs, are gorgeous and *he* is a class-A twat. And he's smarmy. And fake-looking, and not that hot at all. Actually, he looks like he's got bad breath and a pencil dick.'

'Not helping,' Kate hissed from beneath her hair.

'Fuck him, Kate! Don't let him stand between you and your booze.'

'Lou, *please*!' Kate was almost crying now.

'OK, OK! I just need to pay for our drinks. You go and wait outside and I'll settle up. I'll only be a minute.'

'Promise? Don't be long. He might come out and see me.'

'I promise. Go and wait round the corner. Check out the window of Partridges'. I'll be there in a minute.'

Kate sidestepped awkwardly across the bar, keeping her back to Sebastian and her hair tipped over her face. Eventually Lou saw her reach the front door and escape.

Lou pursed her lips, narrowed her eyes and looked at Sebastian. He was wearing an expensive suit and quaffing a glass of champagne self-importantly. He certainly looked like a twat. The too-perfect tan and salon-immaculate hair were the giveaway. 'Wanker,' Lou thought viciously with a thrill of savage pleasure. How dare he upset her best mate?

'A bottle of Veuve, please.' She grabbed a passing waitress. 'And the bill.'

Lou smiled wickedly, not taking her eyes off Sebastian. And then she delved into her handbag for her purse, lipstick and pen.

'Excuse me!' Lou summoned the waitress back a few minutes later. 'I ordered this champagne, but I've just had an important call and I've got to leave. Would you mind giving it to the gentleman over there with my compliments?' She smiled sweetly and handed her a note and the champagne.

'Sure!' The waitress glanced at the paper and smiled conspiratorially. 'He's gorgeous, isn't he? Good luck. I hope he rings!'

'Oh, he will!' Lou rose from her table and sashayed towards Sebastian. As she got closer, he abruptly stopped his conversation and appreciatively eyed her up and down. Lou slinked her hips, fixed him with her most X-rated smile and lightly brushed against him as she headed for the door. Behind her she could hear the waitress make her approach.

'Thank God!' Kate breathed as Lou rounded the corner to Partridges' department store. 'What kept you?'

'Let's just say revenge is a dish best served bubbly.' Lou smirked cryptically.

'Wha—? Oh my God, you didn't speak to him, did you?' Kate panicked.

'Of course not! I sent him over a bottle of champagne!'

Kate looked like her heart had stopped beating. 'That man was so horrible to me. So rude, and cruel and nasty; and you sent him over *champagne*?'

'Well, it was a bit more than just champagne.'

Something in Lou's expression caught Kate's eye. She stopped hyperventilating. 'What've you been up to?' she asked suspiciously.

'I've just taken an old Sharon Osbourne classic and given it a Lou twist. She's a goddess, that woman. Rewrote the rule book on man-control. Young women ought to study her autobiography like a textbook. She should be on the national curriculum. GCSEs in Shazza's arts of ball-breaking and revenge!'

'What are you talking about? The only revenge-thing I know about Sharon Osbourne was that she pooed in someone's ... Oh my God. What have you done?'

'I pissed in his champagne!'

Kate clamped her hand over her mouth in horror.

'I took the champagne bottle to the Ladies, poured half

down the toilet and then topped it up with a little *eau de Lou*. And then I got a waitress to take it over to Sebastian with my compliments.'

'And he took it?' Kate asked, fascinated..

'Of course he took it! He's a vain, self-centred prick! He's too narcissistic to be suspicious.'

'Oh my God!' Kate thought for a moment. 'So Sebastian's in there *drinking your wee*?'

'Uh-huh!' Lou laughed. 'And it doesn't stop there. I also got the waitress to take him over a telephone number.'

'What, yours?'

'No!'

'Oh my God, not mine?'

'Don't be daft! Tony's. Tony's home number.'

Kate looked confused. 'I don't get it.'

'Ah, well, this is my second stroke of genius. Tony's hardly ever at home, but if he does happen to be there when Sebastian calls . . . *and he will call* . . . he's going to be totally flummoxed. Sebastian's enough of a big-head not to be put off if a man answers the phone. He's bound to ask for Suzy.'

'Suzy?'

'Yeah. I wrote her name next to the number. So, anyway, at the very least Tony's going to be suspicious and freaked out about what his precious wife might be up to. But hopefully that's not going to happen. Hopefully it'll be Suzy who answers the phone, and Sebastian will thank her for the champagne and, presuming she's got the hots for him, he'll ask her out for dinner. And Suzy, being every bit as narcissistic as Sebastian – and probably bored rigid by her pointless, flaccid husband – will say yes. And they'll meet up and that will be that. Those two are made for each other. She's a gold-digging airhead and he's a woman-hating wallet-on-legs.'

She grinned evilly.

'So I get to go to bed with a smile on my face knowing there's a very big chance Tony's wife will make a fool of him,' she continued triumphantly. 'And you get to go to bed knowing that Slimy Sebastian drank your best mate's piss!'

'Lou, you're a very, very bad person,' Kate scolded. 'But I love you very, very much!'

Lou tutted. 'You know I don't do the L-word.'

'Sorry, forgot!' Kate grinned. 'Well, here are a couple of words for you . . . "My" and "round".' She slipped her arm into Lou's. 'I'm buying you a bottle of the best plonk Luigi's can muster!'

And the two women headed off down King Street, giggling as they went.

ALICE

From the safety of her living room Alice logged into her Hotmail account and opened a new email. With a flutter of nerves she rummaged in her bag, fished out her notebook and typed Kate's email address. She stared at it as the TV chattered quietly in the background. Audrey would kill her if she ever found out. Goodness knows how much of her contract she was about to contravene. But she was going to do it anyway. She had a very strong feeling about this. And besides, love was love. It wasn't going to be stopped by a piece of paper.

She began to type.

Kate
I've found someone _perfect_ for you! But he's not on the Table For Two books. How do you feel about a black-market date?
Please don't reply to my work email. If Audrey found out I'd be flipping burgers within the hour.
Alice
P.S. He doesn't tick all your boxes, but trust me on this one!

She sat back nervously and reread what she'd written. A moment later she stretched forward and hit the *send* button. It was done. Her heart was racing.

Suddenly her mobile sprang to life, making her jump violently. It couldn't be Kate already, surely? Alice looked at her watch. Most of her friends wouldn't phone so late, unless it was Ginny needing to talk. She hoped it was. She'd thought about her constantly since Friday night. She'd phoned several times but the answerphone was always switched on.

But it wasn't Ginny. It was John.

'I hope it's not too late to call.'

She felt a thrill rush through her body. Her plan had worked.

'Thanks for the flowers!' She tried to sound calm and normal.

'Did you like them?'

'I loved them! So much better than roses!' She winced. Trust her to namecheck the universal floral shorthand for a declaration of love. Luckily John didn't seem to notice.

'Well, you didn't deadhead them and send them back to me,' he teased, '. . . and you haven't hung up – so I'm hoping you're not angry with me any more.'

'I wasn't angry with you,' Alice replied hurriedly. 'I was just . . .'

'. . . affronted because you thought I was making an indecent proposal via coffee?'

Alice floundered. It sounded so silly when he put it like that.

'I must admit, I was a bit surprised to see you vault the

dahlias and tear through the shop like that,' he laughed. 'As knockbacks go, it was pretty spectacular! Obviously it could simply be that you're a woman of taste and couldn't get away fast enough. But I realize it might also have been how I came across.'

Alice's brain whirred to keep ahead of him.

'Look, really, please.' John suddenly sounded nervous. 'I'm not like that.'

'Right. Good,' Alice replied, trying to sound like she knew what he was on about. 'Like what?'

'Well, you know. I'm not some lecherous Lothario who hangs around garden centres trying to pick up women.'

They both laughed awkwardly.

There was a small pause.

'Although I'd be lying if I said I only wanted to go for coffee with you to discuss the merits of herbaceous borders,' he added sheepishly.

There was a longer pause. Alice tried to digest what he'd just said. So he wasn't a lecherous Lothario on the lookout for a cheap extramarital fling. But he didn't just want to talk to her about gardening either. So what exactly did he want? A semi-lecherous affair with the odd horticultural aside? Alice was confused. She wasn't sure whether to feel outraged or not.

'Does Audrey know you're calling me?' she side-stepped. 'Is she there with you now?'

'Ah, no! Audrey is most definitely not with me now,' John laughed. 'And unless she's got my phone tapped then no, she doesn't know I'm calling you either.'

'So, you're, um, you're going behind her back, then?'

She waited nervously for his answer.

'It's none of Audrey's business who I call, or who I invite for coffee.'

'Oh!'

There was another pause, broken by John sighing.

'Arghh, I wanted to clear things up but I'm digging myself an even bigger hole. Am I about to get cut off?'

'I'm not really sure what to do. I've not got very much experience in handling late-night phone calls from my boss's husband.'

'Husband? Yes, I wondered if that was why you ran off.'

'Look, John.' Alice tried to be plain. 'You were very kind to me at the ball. A knight in shining armour, in fact. And I'm very grateful. And for the flowers too.' She took a deep breath before ploughing on. 'Obviously you heard all the stuff Sheryl said about me. She made me sound tragic and desperate. But I'm not. The bit about me being single was true, but that doesn't mean I'm easy pickings or that I'm going to fall into bed with the first man who buys me a cappuccino. Especially if he's married. And extremely especially if he's married to my boss!'

She felt dizzy with the effort of being so upfront.

'I'm sorry if that makes me sound like a prude,' she added timidly.

'Far from it. It makes you sound ... Look, it's like I said at the garden centre; I think we both might have got the wrong end of the stick. What I'm asking is for us to start again. With a clean sheet. I'm not sure who you think I am, but there's no way of telling you the truth without sounding like I'm spinning you a line. And I'm a very honest person. I'm a gardener, for heaven's sake!'

Alice thought for a moment. Her mind whipped through a series of flashbacks: of John standing up for her at the ball; of him hurrying to the taxi rank to apologize for everybody else's bad behaviour; of him pushing his hanky gently into her hands when she thought she'd managed to hide her tears.

'OK,' she mumbled. 'A clean sheet.'

'Good . . .' He sounded relieved. 'So, I'd like to tell you something in confidence. It's really important that you don't tell anyone at Table For Two, or at any other dating agency. You strike me as the kind of person who keeps her word.'

'I am.'

There was a long pause.

'I'm not married to Audrey,' he said finally. 'Actually, I'm not married to anyone.'

There was another pause.

'What, you mean you and Audrey never got married?' Alice asked dumbly. 'You're just long-term . . . partners?'

'We're long-term . . . *friends*.'

'So the fizzle has gone out of your relationship and now you see other women?'

'No!' There was a hint of a laugh in John's voice. 'I mean there has never been any fizzle. It's not – and has never been – a fizzling kind of relationship. It's a . . .' – he searched for the right word – '*special* relationship. But it's not what you think.'

'So you and Audrey aren't . . . ?'

'No.'

'But . . . But . . . all those beautiful bouquets you send to our office!'

'Flowers for Audrey? Nothing to do with me.'

'What about your anniversary? You took her to Paris.'

'No, not guilty. I've never been any further with Audrey than the Town and Country Golf Club.'

Alice struggled to make sense of it.

'But the ball? What about the ball? Everyone thought you were her husband.'

'They may have thought it, but I've never said it.'

'So you and Audrey aren't together?' Alice still couldn't believe it.

'Not in the conventional way, no.'

'Right . . .' She thought for a moment. Was there an unconventional way to be together? Like those permissive, partner-swapping relationships she'd seen on late-night TV? But weren't they all about sex parties and nasty rubber clothing with straps and harnesses? She didn't want to begin to think about Audrey like that.

'Would it do any good to ask you to trust me? To tell you I'll explain everything when the time's right?'

'Ummm . . .' Alice didn't know what to say. She didn't have a clue what he was going on about.

'Look, Alice, I like you. I liked you from the moment I met you. You were a breath of fresh air at the ball; natural and beautiful. You shone out amongst all the lipstick and back-stabbing. After you left I couldn't stop thinking about you. And then, when I bumped into you at the garden centre, in your jeans with your hair all scruffy, I liked you even more. And you're a gardener! How fantastic is that? You're *that* good *and* you're a gardener!'

Alice's body was slowly lighting up with the magic of his words.

John continued carefully.

'My relationship with Audrey is complicated and there are things between us – confidences – that I can't betray. But I can say, hand on heart, I've never so much as kissed her. And I never will.'

Alice was astonished. Audrey wasn't married to John! She was always bragging that she had the perfect marriage. But it was a lie! Why?

On the other hand, John wasn't married to Audrey! Handsome, gentlemanly, I-think-you're-natural-and-beautiful John wasn't married at all! And he was still speaking.

'I'm not trying to trick you, and I'm not trying to have an affair. I'm single. I like you.'

There was a pause. Alice's mind was too busy for speech. Luckily John's voice filled the void again.

'So, Alice,' she heard him say, 'would you *please* reconsider and let me buy you that coffee?'

AUDREY

Audrey breezed into Partridges' department store, consulted the store map and headed to the escalator, bound for the lingerie department on the first floor. Lingerie departments were rarely visited territory for Audrey. She preferred to do her shopping by catalogue, thereby escaping the double helping of hell that was high-street changing-room lighting and the spiteful elbows of competitive lady shoppers.

But today was an exception. On this particular Friday lunch break Audrey ventured defiantly into the hostile zone of Partridges' lingerie department with only one thing on her mind: support knickers.

Ever since the night of the ball Audrey had been tortured by two visions. The first was Sheryl Toogood's silver-wrapped, immaculately presented and unfairly proportioned body. And the other was her own, sagging and dimple-ridden, in her bedroom mirror. Every time she remembered herself she shuddered. If she was serious about winning back John, then she needed to take herself in hand. And the right underwear, it was claimed, could make you lose ten pounds.

As Audrey stepped off the escalator she armed herself

with her don't-trifle-with-me scowl. She was going to get this over with as fast as possible.

If it hadn't been for the matter of Jason and Jennifer's wedding tomorrow (as the architect of their union she was bound to be snapped with the happy couple for the local newspaper; which was not only excellent publicity for Table For Two, but there was also a chance that John might see it), then she probably would have put off buying lingerie for another few weeks. But needs must, so she bustled into the first row of underwear, eyeing the flimsy fragments of satin and lace with suspicion.

Was this modern-day support underwear? she wondered. Her own, purchased when she was twenty years younger and two dress sizes slimmer, was now threadbare. Surely support underwear had come on in leaps and bounds since then? Audrey poked a pair of pretty turquoise knickers and wondered if they were it.

'Can I help you, madam?' a voice enquired.

Audrey jumped guiltily.

'Yes!' she barked officiously, doing her best not to look ruffled. 'I want some support pants. To make me look thinner.'

'Certainly, madam,' the shop assistant said smoothly. 'Follow me.'

She led Audrey through the shop, the delicate pinks and lemons gradually giving way to sturdier blacks and beiges, as the waistbands grew higher and the gussets drooped lower. Eventually the assistant stopped before a display of items that looked more like jodhpurs than knickers. Surely these weren't underwear, Audrey thought. These were for old women in nursing homes with no bladder control.

But sure enough, the sales assistant's mouth was moving, and words like 'smooth lines' and 'better than a tummy tuck' were permeating Audrey's disbelieving ears. Audrey eyed the pants with dismay. Some of them were so long you had to hoist them over your shoulders. Were they *really* going to help her win back John?

But she reminded herself of the importance of her mission and dismissed the sales assistant. She quickly snatched a pair of beige jodhpurs and powered towards the tills.

But something stopped her dead in her tracks.

A cascade of blonde hair was standing at the tills. Its owner was rummaging in a large crocodile handbag and rocking on a pair of garish stilettos.

'When will you be getting in more of the purple marabou G-strings?' A coarse, familiar voice emanated from under the hair. 'Well, I'll just have to make do with the hot pink till then. Still, I don't suppose it matters. It's not like they stay on for long!'

The blonde emitted a raucous guffaw.

'They drive him wild!' she continued crassly. 'I don't know if it's because they're so tiny, or whether it's the feel of the fluff, but as soon as he gets a glimpse of them he just has to rip them off!'

Audrey's stomach turned queasily as she darted behind a row of tights. Sheryl Toogood! She felt a prickle of perspiration on her upper lip. Had she seen her? Surely not! Sheryl never lost the opportunity to gloat, and if she'd seen Audrey perusing the pensioner underwear she'd have been straight over to plunge the knife in.

Audrey squatted awkwardly, scrunching the support pants into her fist.

'I'm telling you,' Sheryl confided loudly to the shop assistant, 'you really must get yourself one of those sheer bras. So cheeky, seeing the nipples when the underwear's still on! My fella goes nuts for it. Turns him into a real animal. When we go out for dinner he's barely got his fork in his mouth before he's asking me if I've got it on. All hot under the collar, he gets. Can't eat a thing. You must buy one. You'll never look back!'

Audrey felt sick. The last thing she wanted was a mental picture of Sheryl and Brad in the bedroom, or at the dinner table, or anywhere at all for that matter. And she especially didn't want to imagine Sheryl's nipples. Was John the kind of man who turned into an animal? she thought with a sudden panic. Would he be the type who liked a bra so flimsy he could see right through it?

Eventually Sheryl paid for her goods and headed to the ground floor. As the last glimpse of teased blonde hair vanished down the escalator Audrey ventured out from her hiding place and scuttled over to the tills. She thrust the limp, sweat-dampened jodhpurs onto the counter and started frantically pulling out her money. Cash would be quicker than a card, and the faster she got away the better in case Sheryl came back for another X-rated purchase.

'Brazen woman!' she muttered to herself. 'Common little whore!'

'Pardon?' The shop assistant sounded affronted.

'Not you!' Audrey said brusquely, as she grabbed her purchase and headed for the nearest fire exit. She'd take the stairs, thank you very much. There was no way she was running the risk of bumping into Sheryl. No way on God's earth.

JOHN

John looked at Alice as she sipped her cappuccino. Her eyes were bright and her cheeks pink from riding her bike. She'd been adamant that they meet on the opposite side of the city to Table For Two. She'd burst through the door on the stroke of six o'clock, her bicycle helmet in her hand and her hair unruly. The women John usually met were always immaculately dressed for a formal function. But Alice looked wild, scruffy and full of energetic life. She'd almost taken his breath away.

He cleared his throat. He'd just taken a sip of his coffee but his mouth still felt dry. He was surprised by how nervous he was. He talked to women for a living. Wasn't he supposed to be good at this?

'So, what made you decide to become a matchmaker?' he asked awkwardly.

Alice smiled and stirred her coffee. 'It was the only thing I ever wanted to do. I don't think of it as a job; it's a privilege.'

'I'm interested.' He leant forward in his chair and then, realizing his knees were touching Alice's, leant back again.

'What makes you put people together? How do you know they'll get on?'

Alice laughed. 'It's going to sound strange . . .'

'Strange is good.'

She told him how she stared out of the Table For Two window and drifted into an imaginary world.

'Have you ever set people up who really hated each other?'

'A couple,' she said confidentially. 'But they were deliberate.'

'Deliberate? But matchmaking's your passion!'

'It is!' she replied earnestly. 'That's why I did it. Sometimes I *need* to make a bad match for the sake of the client. Like this one lady I've got at the moment.' She wriggled forward in her chair. 'She's lovely; pretty, successful, a nice person, good fun. She shouldn't have any trouble in finding someone. She doesn't realize it, but she's stopping herself from meeting a man. She's got two big obstacles in her way, and she's put both of them there herself!'

'What kind of obstacles?'

'Well, the first is her job. She's a workaholic,' Alice explained, her face alight with passion. 'She hides behind long working hours as an excuse for not getting out there and meeting men. Actually I think she's scared to, in case she tries and fails. She's used to working hard and succeeding. Falling flat on her face frightens her.'

'And the second?'

'She's got unrealistic expectations about the man she wants to meet. Lots of women are the same. It's as if she decided on her ideal man when she was thirteen and hasn't updated her fantasy since. She wants the works: looks, money, a fancy car, a perfect body, a family man. A Hollywood dream-man with no imperfections. But these men don't exist, not even in Hollywood!'

'So you set her up on a bad date deliberately?' John asked, enthralled.

'I had to!' Alice replied emphatically. But then she faltered for a moment, and her face seemed to crumple. John watched in fascination as she appeared to debate something within herself.

'But that doesn't make me like her!' she insisted suddenly.

'Like who?' he asked, confused.

She looked at him strangely as though suddenly remembering he was there. 'Like ... It doesn't matter.' And then she was back on track. 'But you have to understand – I only made bad matches to *help* this woman,' she explained earnestly. 'Because she has to see that what she's looking for isn't right for her. So I matched her with the richest, best-looking men on our books. But just because they're rich and handsome doesn't mean they're interesting or caring or fun! Don't get me wrong; they're perfect for someone. But not for her.'

'But how can you be so sure?' he asked. 'I mean, if she's telling you she wants one thing, why are you convinced she needs another?'

'If wealth and beauty were right for her I'd be able to tell.'

'How?'

'By everything! By what she wore, how she had her hair, the way she carried herself, the things she said ...'

'You can tell what somebody wants by what they're wearing?'

'Of course!' Alice nodded enthusiastically. 'Money attracts money, and the women chasing rich men know that. So they dress accordingly, with designer clothes and immaculate hair, manicured nails . . .'

'And how does your lady dress, then?' John asked.

Alice thought.

'Perfectly. Her clothes really matter to her. But her outfits are her protection – like armour. I think, beneath it all, she's actually underconfident. The heels and suits are there to give herself a boost.'

'So she's not dressing to attract a rich man?'

'No; she's dressing to make herself feel better. You need to be extremely confident to partner a rich man. And thick-skinned too. That's not the life for her.'

'And who do you dress for?' John heard himself asking.

Alice laughed and pulled at her simple dress and long cardigan.

They both blushed.

'So.' He tried to steer the conversation back to safer ground. 'You've sent your lady into the lion's den knowing she's going to have a bad date. And you do this so you can then put her on the right path with the right kind of man?'

'Yes!'

'But will it work?'

'Definitely!' Alice smiled confidently.

'And have you found someone who *is* right for her?'

'Yes, I think I've cracked it. She's not met him yet, and

he's certainly not rich, nor conventionally handsome. But he'll make her feel rich.'

'It's a risky strategy, though; it could backfire on you.'

'I know.' Alice smiled. 'But isn't love worth taking a risk for?'

John looked at her. She emanated warmth and kindness. It was hard to imagine her working in the same world as Audrey and Sheryl. She seemed like a beacon of purity, full of honesty and zest for life. She wore hardly any make-up, but far from looking plain, it lit her up. She looked natural and alive. And she had a habit of pulling her jumper around her and snuggling into it. It made him want to scoop her up so she could snuggle into him instead.

'So,' she was saying, 'we've established that you're not married to Audrey, but have you ever been married?'

'Once,' John replied honestly. 'I was very young – too young. It ended.'

'I'm sorry.'

'Yes, so was I. But it was a long time ago.'

'Do you have any children?'

'Yes, a daughter.' John's face broke into a smile. 'Emily. She's twenty-three and as wise as the hills. She's like her mother that way.'

'Is she very close to her mother?'

'No. Her mother died – car accident. Emily was only eight.'

'Oh, that's awful. I'm sorry, I didn't mean to pry.'

'No, it's fine. After my wife – her name was Eve – after Eve died I brought Emily up on my own.'

He never normally told anyone about Eve, but then, he

never normally went on dates of his own choosing. And suddenly it felt good to talk about the past.

'It was a tough time. Sometimes it felt like Emily was more grown-up about it than me. But we survived. And now we're very close.'

'That's good,' said Alice simply.

'Yes, it is.'

They smiled at each other.

'So, how about you?' John asked. 'Have you ever been married?'

'Er, no!' she laughed.

John looked at her. How could she not have been snapped up? She was lovely – the archetypal girl next door. Wasn't she just what men wanted? All the blokeish posturing men made about wanting girls with blonde hair and big breasts . . . but beneath the bravado, didn't they all, deep down, not really care about the Sheryl Toogoods of this world? Didn't they all *really* want someone just like Alice?

Their date was at an end, and he helped her into her coat. He didn't want her to go. He suddenly felt tongue-tied. He'd never been lost for words on a professional date. But here in the cafe, watching Alice fiddle with the strap of her bicycle helmet, he felt like he was floundering. It felt exciting, like he was out of his depth.

'I've been so rude,' Alice said suddenly. 'I haven't asked you what you do for a living!'

'It's a long story,' John fudged. 'One for another day . . . hopefully.'

'I'd like that.' Alice smiled nervously and looked him in the eye.

'So would I,' John replied, meeting her eyes and holding their gaze. 'I'd like that very much.'

ALICE

'Can I get the matchmaker, please? The matchmaker?' the *Gazette* photographer hollered.

'Yes. Here I am!' Audrey parted the wedding guests like a torpedo thundering through the sea.

'Oh!' The bride's face froze as Audrey barged into position alongside her and the groom. 'Maybe we should get Alice too?'

'Is she another matchmaker?' The photographer clearly wanted to get the shot in the bag and head home as soon as possible.

'She's one of my assistants,' Audrey interjected authoritatively.

'But she really was pivotal,' the bride added.

'Alice!' the photographer yelled grumpily across the chatting congregation. 'I need Alice!'

Moving as fast as she could in case the photographer shouted her name again, Alice joined the threesome in front of the lens.

'Congratulations!' she whispered happily to Jennifer and Jason. Ten seconds later the photographer grunted he had all he needed. Audrey immediately stepped forward and started issuing him with print instructions.

'We're so glad you could make it!' Jennifer took Alice's hands and smiled radiantly. 'We've so much to thank you for!'

'Hear, hear!' agreed Jason. 'We'll name our firstborn Alice in your honour. If it's a girl, of course!'

'Well . . .!' Alice laughed. 'But really, you don't have to thank Table For Two. You both did all the hard work.'

'Ah, but without you . . .' Jennifer said with a twinkle. 'I'll be aiming this at you later,' she added conspiratorially, nodding towards her bouquet and winking.

Alice blushed, but luckily both bride and groom were immediately surrounded by a group of well-wishers.

'Well, that went swimmingly.' Audrey rejoined her, adjusting her hat and straightening her suit jacket. 'Another victory for Table For Two!'

'It's the happy-ever-afters that make it all worthwhile,' Alice murmured, her eyes drinking in the glow emanating from Jennifer and Jason.

'Yes, well, let's not stand around gawping,' Audrey chided tartly. 'The place is chock-full of potential clients! Circulate!'

Alice moved into the crowd, happy to put some distance between her and her boss, who was already handing out business cards. If Audrey thought she was going to start soliciting clients, Alice said to herself, she could think again. This was the happiest day of Jennifer and Jason's life, and there was no way she was going to use it as a business opportunity. So she busied herself by chatting to a collection of elderly aunts, much to Audrey's obvious irritation.

All too soon Jennifer called for the single women to gather so she could throw her bouquet. Alice hung back, trying to make herself invisible. There was no way she was going to venture into the heaving throng of women, hands emptied of drinks for maximum catching ability, elbows pointing at fierce angles for the best jumping trajectories.

As Jennifer turned and threw the bouquet, Alice noticed Audrey rise from the crowd and make a muscular effort to catch the falling flowers. But she was beaten by a springy twenty-something who squealed with delight and trotted over to her boyfriend to show him her winnings. Alice saw Audrey's fleeting expression as the bouquet was whisked from her reach, a few tantalizing centimetres separating her from her happy-ever-after. For a moment she looked despondent. And then, a second later, her old expression resumed, and she loudly declared that she shouldn't even be in the bouquet throng, being the happily married lady that she was.

Alice turned away, filled with guilt. She almost wished she didn't know Audrey's secret. Ever since John had told her, it had felt like a blessing and a curse. A blessing because John was single. The memory of yesterday's meeting, of him leaning forward in his chair, smiling his lovely crinkly-eyed smile right at her, made her so happy she almost laughed out loud.

But then there was the curse. Why had Audrey lied about John being her husband? If she was single, why didn't she just come out and say so? Audrey never mentioned any friends, just told endless stories about John. But if John wasn't really in her life, who was? Maybe the nine-to-five of Table For Two *was* her life?

And what if – a nagging voice kept asking – what if Audrey pretended she was married to John because, in her heart of hearts, that was what she wanted? What if she was hopelessly in love with him? What if the thought of that love being fulfilled was the only thing that got her through each day?

Alice zigzagged through the guests to the ladies' toilet. She closed the door and leant her head against the mirror, willing the image of a lonely, lovelorn Audrey to disappear from her mind. But then her vision flooded with a fresh image from the dream she'd had last night – a dream where John was slowly leaning towards her and she was just moments away from his kiss. Guilt and happiness inter-twined confusingly. Alice exhaled shakily, her breath forming a small cloud on the mirror.

JOHN

John pulled up at the Four Seasons hotel, walked around the car to the passenger door and helped Janey step out of the car. She smiled gratefully. She was scared stiff. He tucked her arm into his and guided her up the steps and into the lobby.

Tonight was his second booking with Janey, and it was her long-dreaded annual company do. Janey worked in insurance and her colleagues sounded particularly cut-throat. When her husband suddenly left her and their three small children to take up with a woman half her age and two-thirds of her dress size, she hadn't wanted to tell her co-workers that her world had fallen apart. It wasn't the sympathy she'd been afraid of; there wouldn't be any of that. It was how her personal circumstances would inevitably be used against her. Any meetings she might miss would be attributed to childcare issues and her priorities would be questioned; if her sales targets weren't reached it would be put down to her fragile state of mind. All this was ample ammunition for her to be overlooked for promotion, a promotion accompanied by a salary rise that she needed now more than ever. So she'd decided to keep her marital problems private, and struggled on without anyone knowing her misery.

And she'd done well. Her colleagues were none the wiser, she'd not missed a day of work and her targets had been achieved. But life was about to throw two more obstacles in her way.

The first had been the wedding of an old, dear friend, to which her ex and his new partner were also invited. Non-attendance wasn't an option. Humiliation by attending alone and seeing her ex canoodle with a woman with a taut, childless body and eyes that weren't crêpey from crying seemed inevitable. But then another friend had suggested Janey stick two fingers up at her ex by booking herself a handsome, pretend new partner for the day. And that gentleman escort had been John.

The second obstacle that had loomed ominously in Janey's calendar had been the unavoidable matter of the company party. Spouses always attended, and for Janey to turn up solo would have caused a stir. But if her colleagues were to find out her marriage was over *but simultaneously* meet her hot new man, Janey would seem strong. Promotion might still be on the cards. So Janey redialled Geraldine's number and retained John's professional services again.

And here they were, on the day Janey had been dreading for so long.

John heard her take a deep breath as they stepped into the function room, so he put a calming hand on the small of her back to reassure her. He knew his mission. He was

Janey's devoted new boyfriend, and he was happy to play his role. Women like Janey – ordinary women who, through the hard knocks of life, had lost their confidence – were why he did his job. He wanted to help women who'd been dreading attending a can't-get-out-of-it event without a partner; women who'd lost belief in themselves and their own attractiveness; women who'd lost the security of being one half of a couple. John's job was to see them through whatever event had been causing them sleepless nights. Showing them affection, assuming a role they needed him to play, was part of the deal. These women were compliment-starved; nobody noticed what they wore or how they did their hair. But praising their appearance, holding their hand or stroking their back when someone important might see – these things helped bring them back to life, helped them hold their heads higher and shine again. Seeing a woman begin to believe in herself was the greatest job satisfaction ever.

Of course, when he explained to friends what he did for a living – that he was a gentleman escort – the reaction was always the same:

'Oh my God, *you're a rent boy*!' they'd shriek. 'So you *have* to have sex with the women, right?'

The truthful answer, which invariably disappointed the questioner, was no. Clients had to sign a strict contract of behaviour. In it Geraldine carefully set out the parameters of John's services: his ministrations were to be strictly gentlemanly. Hands might be kissed in greeting, brief kisses on the lip or cheek might occur, but clothes were to remain on and sexual contact was strictly forbidden. He was not to enter the client's home either before or after the date (if the lady was not ready when he arrived he was to wait on the front step or in the car). If the event took place in a hotel he was to stay on the ground floor. Bedrooms were not to be visited under any circumstances.

The contracts were there for John's benefit. In eleven years he'd only ever had a couple of clients who'd tried to overstep the mark, and he'd been grateful to refer them to the terms of the contract and point out that he wasn't *allowed* to take things further. Such a refusal was less demoralizing for the client. It wasn't personal, it was the contract!

But the overwhelming majority of women were happy to keep the relationship as intended; John was an attentive partner for the night, who turned up when needed and disappeared when not. Usually he'd be booked two or three times by a client, after which her life would have moved on and she'd no longer need him. Nobody blurred the lines or believed his role-playing was anything more than just that.

Nobody except Audrey Cracknell.

John smiled lovingly at Janey as she introduced him to her colleagues. He pretended not to notice them ogle him in surprise. He slipped into his role, buying everyone drinks, joining – but not dominating – the conversation and letting Janey shine. Her colleagues would later compliment her on her brave handling of her marriage collapse and her immediate bagging of a new man, and Janey would leave the event walking taller than she had on the way in, with the sparkle in her eyes reinstated and the feeling that, deep down, no matter what her husband had said and done, she, Janey, *still had it*!

As Janey chatted to her colleagues, John didn't see a browbeaten career woman, an exhausted single mother, or a heartbroken divorcee. He saw a woman – an intelligent, beautiful, independent woman. He smiled. He didn't think he'd be hearing from Janey again.

KATE

Kate stood outside the Seven Eleven and checked her watch again. It was 7.30 p.m. and she was now officially on time. She could finally enter the pub.

She'd been loitering for ten minutes to make sure she wasn't early for her date with Tommy. Lou had instructed her to arrive at least twenty minutes late, but that didn't sit right. What if he got fed up and left? And anyway, since when was Lou an expert on dating? A world authority on no-strings sex, yes. But on dating?

Kate checked her reflection in the Seven Eleven window, and took one last look at her silk tea dress and Mary-Jane heels. She smoothed down her hair, took a deep breath and walked the last few steps to the pub, trying to look confident as she swung open the door and stepped inside.

A man who could only be Tommy was sitting near the door, engrossed in a book. She looked at him, taking advantage of the few moments before he sensed her presence and looked up.

He wasn't her kind of man at all, but despite that, he looked *good*. His suit jacket was thrown on the seat next to him, his tie was off and his sleeves were rolled up revealing muscular forearms. He filled out his shirt in the best possible way, the material pulling tight over his wide, strong chest and the neck open to reveal a tuft of chest hair. Kate couldn't see much of his face, but he looked as though he'd once broken his nose, and his jaw was strong and shaded with five o'clock shadow. He certainly wasn't model pretty, not like Sebastian. He looked like a fireman or an off-duty rugby player – one hundred per cent alpha male.

Something stirred in Kate. She had a bizarre urge to lean forward and stroke the roughness of his stubble. She suddenly imagined being enveloped by those muscular arms and held tight against the wall of his chest.

'Kate?'

Tommy was smiling at her.

Kate jumped guiltily.

'Wow, hello!' He looked surprised. He stood and kissed her on the cheek. 'Now I see why Steve does it! I wasn't expecting . . . I mean, it's one thing having a laugh mucking about with internet dating, but I thought women who joined *actual* dating agencies would all be a bit . . . you know, *desperate*. But, wow . . .!'

Kate blushed furiously and felt lost for words.

'Not that you are, of course . . . Desperate, I mean. A woman like you . . . far from it,' he offered in embarrass-ment. He laughed. 'Anyway, I'm going to put my spade away now. I got you a glass of champagne.'

It was only then that Kate noticed a glass of champagne fizzing energetically next to his pint.

'Thank you,' she said in surprise.

They sat down.

Kate's mouth felt dry. She tried to think of something to say.

'So, you're a friend of Steve's?' she asked nervously.

''Fraid so!' Tommy grinned mischievously. 'He was really annoyed when Alice told him you weren't interested! And he's not happy that I'm seeing you tonight either. Reckon I'm off the Christmas card list.'

Kate sipped her champagne, feeling quietly chuffed that she was a subject of rivalry. She could feel Tommy's eyes taking her in, moving across her face and body. She felt strangely excited. She sat up straight and tried to suck everything in.

'So, what made you give it a go? Be set up, I mean?'

'I met Alice the other night, with Steve. She came to the pub to see how his dating was going – although I think she was really just checking up on him . . .'

Kate couldn't stop peeking at the small bit of chest at the top of his shirt. Normally she didn't go for hairy chests, but far from being a turn-off, it just made Tommy seem even more manly.

'. . . She asked if she could set me up; and I thought, why not? It's only one night. And I wanted to see what kind of woman an expert thinks is right for me. My beer goggles aren't exactly twenty-twenty.'

'Oh!' Kate fought a sudden sinking feeling. 'You, er, you wear them often, do you?'

'Beer goggles? I've updated my prescription, but it's still always a nasty shock when daylight sets in!'

So he was promiscuous, Kate thought in dismay, mentally unticking a box. But she still couldn't help but blush as he smiled at her.

'Well, you've tried to impress me by buying me champagne,' she heard herself saying flirtily. 'So, let me guess. I bet you're a stockbroker. Or maybe something big in oil.' She gave what she hoped was a sassy smile.

'I'm a salesman for a company that collects credit information.'

Kate struggled to hide her disappointment.

'Oh, that's . . .'

'. . . the most boring job in the world?'

Kate tried to smile. She didn't know what to say.

'I can see you're impressed!' Tommy joked. 'But I'm sure you're far too open-minded to judge someone by their job. Only shallow people and air-kissing media types do that. As if what you do between nine and five has any bearing on whether you're an interesting person or not!'

'That's so stupid!' Kate agreed hastily. And she did agree. It certainly sounded stupid when he put it like that. She remembered with an inner wince the rigid partner criteria she'd given Alice. What had she said about her perfect man's job? Didn't he have to be a top-earning manager with board potential? She hoped Alice hadn't mentioned it to Tommy.

'Do you like being a salesman?' she asked politely.

'It's a job. What about you? What do you do?'

'Ah, well, I'm an air-kissing media type.' Kate laughed. 'I work in PR. I haven't kissed an actual cheek in years!'

'Whoops!' Tommy grinned sheepishly. 'And do you like working in PR?'

'I love it!'

'It's weird meeting people who love their jobs. I thought you were an urban myth. I don't think I could love *any* job. When I was ten, our teacher asked the class what we wanted to be when we grew up. I told her I wanted to be a playboy. I didn't know what it meant. It was the word "play" that hooked me.'

An image swamped Kate's vision of Tommy in a jacuzzi with a bevy of scantily clad babes. She wasn't going to be his type, she thought with a pang. He clearly liked easy women with big boobs and tiny morals, even if he had only been ten at the time.

'So, what made you become a salesman?' she wondered aloud.

'It pays the most money for the least effort. I just go in, do my stuff and get out! I'll never be rich. I'd rather be happy ... You know, work-to-live not live-to-work.'

Kate froze. A tower of ticked boxes suddenly turned blank. He was lazy.

'I'm not lazy,' he laughed, as though reading her thoughts. 'I just don't see the point in working unpaid overtime when there are so many better things you could be doing!'

Kate wasn't so sure. What other things were there? She was more of a live-to-work kind of girl. But even as she thought it, she realized she didn't like the description. Nobody wanted to be a live-to-work kind of girl. Certainly not the sort of woman Tommy would want for a girlfriend. And looking at him, with his strong arms, laughing eyes and easy manner, she suddenly realized that – despite herself – she *did* want to be his girlfriend.

But did she really want to be with a womanizing under-achiever?

But how many underachievers had bodies like that? He looked like he could lift her up with just his left hand – and still keep his pint steady in his right. Kate spent every day feeling just that bit too curvy. But sitting across from Tommy she suddenly felt small and dainty and feminine.

She was confused. She couldn't stop smiling, and her body felt tingly, like she'd put her finger in a plug socket.

When their drinks were finished Tommy suggested dinner. As they left the bar, he took her hand in his. It felt warm and strong and big around hers.

They arrived at the restaurant and sat in the window, a candle flickering between them. Tommy ordered the wine whilst Kate studied the menu, quickly ticking off the dishes she shouldn't pick. Spaghetti was out: too messy. So were the garlic mushrooms: breath death. Lobster was definitely off the agenda. And salads were too insubstantial after all that champagne. She ordered steak and chips with a Béarnaise sauce.

'Good choice!' Tommy approved. 'I like a woman who likes her food. I've never gone for skinny women. It winds me up when they order a perfectly good dinner, take one mouthful and then pretend to be full.'

'God, yes! It drives me *nuts* when skinny women say, "Oh, I forgot to eat lunch,"' Kate agreed hotly. 'It makes me want to batter them with a chunky Kit Kat. I've never forgotten to eat a meal in my life!'

'Glad to hear it,' Tommy appeared. 'You look good on it too. You've got a great figure.'

'Oh! You think so?' Kate was taken aback. No man had ever complimented her figure before.

'Absolutely! Curves in all the right places. It's the kind of figure men really want.'

They chatted easily. Kate told Tommy about her job, and how she was on a mission to make dog food sexy. And then she told him about Lou and how she wished she could be more like her; how Lou was the crotchless knickers type, but that Kate was stuck being a pyjamas girl at heart.

'I've met Lou's kind before,' Tommy observed. 'They come over all confident and man-eating, but they're just over-compensating. I'd bet she's a softie underneath and really wants a boyfriend. You say you'd like to be more like her, but she probably wants to be like you!'

'No, not Lou,' Kate said certainly. 'I'm the last person she'd want to be like. We're total opposites. She'd be bored out of her mind being me. And she thinks I'm a real idiot for joining Table For Two.'

'Well, I wouldn't say you're an idiot,' Tommy said smiling, '. . . but I have been wondering why.'

He looked at her intently. Kate felt her breath get shorter.

'I don't get it, Kate. You're beautiful! You've got a cracking figure, you're good company and you like your food. You could have any man you want. So how come you're single?'

'I, er. I don't know. I guess I've just not met the right man.'

'Or Lou's scared him off.'

'No, it's not that.'

'Isn't it?'

'I probably work too much. I don't get out enough.'

'Ah!' Tommy exclaimed confidently, refilling her glass. 'Well, I can help you with that one.'

Later, at home, Kate was too excited to sleep. Her chin still tingled from the roughness of Tommy's stubble and her lips felt exotically bruised. She sat on her bed, hugged her knees to her chest and grinned.

The night had flown by in a whirr of drinks and compliments. Eventually, after they'd both gorged on highly calorific puddings, Tommy had guided her out of the restaurant and into a taxi. It had been most unlike her, but she'd let herself be pulled onto his lap, enjoying succumbing to his hard, muscular arms and not even worrying if her hips were crushing his legs. Tommy's legs were as strong as tree trunks.

They'd snogged deliciously as the taxi sped across the city centre. Kate's nipples had felt like fizzing bullets and she'd been so turned on she'd wanted to ignore the taxi driver, throw caution to the wind, rip off her clothes and demand instant ravishment.

As the taxi pulled up outside her flat Tommy had looked her in the eye and said:

'You know you're going to be my girlfriend, Kate. Resistance is futile.'

She'd felt her whole body light up at his confident assertion. *He wanted her to be his girlfriend!* He'd just come right
out and said it!

'I'm going to ring you,' he stated meaningfully and the
taxi whizzed off, leaving her grinning girlishly on the pavement.

She had to hand it to Alice, she thought as she snuggled
happily into bed, not caring that her silk dress was in a
pile on her bedroom floor, her teeth were unbrushed or
that for the first time in ten years she hadn't cleansed,
toned and moisturized. She really knows her matchmaking
stuff. And she turned out the light, falling into a contented,
dream-filled sleep within seconds.

ALICE

'At last! I've been so worried about you!' Alice had finally got through to Ginny. She twisted in her seat, trying to block out the noise of the office. 'Is everything OK?'

'Not exactly,' Ginny answered tightly. Something in her voice made Alice suddenly feel more worried than ever. 'A few days after you came round, Dan and I had a huge row. Everything came out: all the ugly things I'd been thinking. I can't believe the nasty stuff I said, like how he wasn't the person I'd fallen in love with, how I hated him for not making an effort any more, for not taking me out, telling me I'm attractive. I even told him I was only with him because of Scarlet, and given half a chance I'd run off with the milkman – or anybody who bothered to look at me twice.'

'Oh my God, Gin!' Alice was stunned. 'I'd no idea things had got that bad.' But as soon as the words came out of her mouth she remembered the clues she'd missed. Looking back, hadn't it been obvious? Ginny had been so weird in her kitchen the other night. And she'd been making odd asides for months now, implying that everything wasn't exactly peachy at home. Guiltily Alice realized she'd dismissed her friend's distress signals, writing them off as Ginny just being sleep-deprived because of Scarlet. But why hadn't she caught on; dug a bit deeper? Ginny was her best friend in the world, and she hadn't done a thing to help her. And now her marriage was in trouble – big trouble. 'But you wouldn't though, would you?' she asked tentatively, almost scared to hear Ginny's answer. 'Run off with another man, I mean . . . ?'

'Of course not! I just said it to hurt him. I was being a cow.'

It was a small crumb of relief.

'What did Dan say?'

'Not a lot, at first. But then he got angry. Told me he'd been pretty miserable too, that he loved Scarlet and that he thought he still loved me, but sometimes it was hard to remember why.'

'Ouch!'

'He said I'd been a right royal pain in the backside for the last year. He said he knew it was because I was tired and that Scarlet could be a handful, but he was tired too and he never took it out on me. And then he said he was disgusted with me for threatening him with an affair – that he thought I was a better person than that.'

'Oh, Ginny!' Something in Alice's insides was sinking, knotting uncomfortably into a hard and unpleasant lump. It wasn't just the agony of realizing her friend was utterly and painfully miserable – it was the very *wrongness* of it too. Ginny and Dan were perfect for each other. They'd fallen in love at first sight and had been inseparable ever since. Their relationship made such utter sense; they were such a team. They weren't fluffily romantic about each other, or gushingly sentimental, or suffocatingly joined at the hip; they had a long-lasting, realistic love based on friendship, respect and fancying each other rotten. She'd always believed their marriage was so strong that she held up it up and savoured it as her shining example whenever she tried to match her clients. Ginny and Dan *couldn't* be in trouble. If they were in trouble, anyone could be in trouble. The world suddenly felt a less safe place.

'It's really shaken me up,' Ginny admitted in a small voice. 'I didn't realize he was unhappy too; I thought it was just me. But now I know he's been having doubts ... It's really frightening, Alice. I can't believe I said such horrible things to him. I didn't mean them. But now the damage is done and I can't take them back.'

'What can I do to help? Can I come over?' Alice offered earnestly.

'Thanks, but I think we just need to spend some time on our own. You know – be a family.'

'Yes, of course. But it sounds like you and Dan could also do with some quality time together, just the two of you. Go on a date night; be Ginny and Dan for a few hours, not Ginny and Dan and Scarlet. If you want to go out, just say the word and I'll be straight over to babysit Scarlet.'

'You'd really voluntarily spend time with our perpetually screaming devil-child?' Ginny asked incredulously.

'In a heartbeat.'

'You're a very brave lady and a bloody good friend,' Ginny said, her throat tight with emotion. 'Anyway.' She did her best to lighten the tone. 'Enough about me; I'm sick of thinking about myself. Tell me about you. Did anything happen with Prince Charming?'

'Are you sure you really want to know?' Alice asked doubtfully.

'Yes, one hundred per cent! Come on, spill the beans. I could do with cheering up.'

'Well . . .' Alice quickly cast her eyes around the office to double-check Audrey was still out. And then, as discreetly as she could, she filled her in.

'We met again for lunch yesterday,' she finished quietly but with unmistakable excitement, 'and he's taking me to dinner tomorrow night.'

'Hurrah!' Ginny cheered, sounding almost like herself again for the first time in the conversation. 'Three dates! That's almost a relationship!'

Alice grinned happily.

'So what's it like dating an older man?'

'He's not old!' Alice protested. 'He's forty-one!'

'That's ten years older than you! And didn't you say he's a silver fox?'

'*Bits* of his hair are grey. Just like *bits* of George Clooney's hair are grey!'

'I suppose at forty-one he's lucky still to have hair!' Ginny teased.

'I like it that he's older.' Alice could barely get her words out for the enormous grin plastered across her face. 'It makes him more interesting. He's not trying to show off or prove anything. He's confident and articulate and intelligent, and he knows how to listen.'

'So you're not worried about Audrey, then?'

'What do you mean?' Alice's smile froze.

'Well, you believe they're not married?'

There was a pause. Alice could tell that Ginny was listening intently for her answer.

'Yes, I do,' Alice whispered. 'I believe him. But, yes, I do worry about her. I feel really bad about what I'm doing.'

'You've only had a coffee and a sandwich!' Ginny scoffed. 'It's hardly Sodom and Gomorrah!'

'You know what I mean.'

'But why? If they're not married, you're not doing anything wrong!'

'Apart from going behind her back and breaking her heart?'

Ginny snorted.

'You can't break something that doesn't exist!'

'That's not fair,' Alice said quietly.

'Audrey's never been fair with you.'

A little while later Alice put down the phone. Despite all her worries, and despite feeling bad for Ginny, she couldn't help herself – she was so excited about dinner with John she could barely concentrate. But it wasn't fair to put her clients' love lives on hold just because she had a date of her own tonight. She needed to buckle down. Her eye fell on a pile of paperwork. Admin, she thought decisively. It was probably all she was good for.

She started sorting through a pile of papers, carefully putting the invoices to one side before carrying them into Audrey's glass-walled office and placing them in her in tray. But as she turned, her eye was caught by the framed picture next to the computer. She'd seen it hundreds of times before, but it was still a shock to see it there. It was John, smartly dressed in his dinner jacket and looking just like he did on the night of the DIPS ball. Alice paused. He looked so handsome; she felt her inner geyser of excitement begin to bubble again. But what was he doing on Audrey's desk? Why did she keep his picture there, right where she'd see him a thousand times a day? She *must* be in love with him. John said he didn't have feelings for her, but why did he take her to the ball every year? Why did he let everyone think they were together?

Alice drifted back to her own desk, her face fixed into a frown. What was really going on? she wondered. What was it that she wasn't being told?

JOHN

There weren't many things that John was proud of: his work, if he thought about the women he'd met who were now confident and happy, his garden and his daughter Emily, who sat in front of him at the dinner table.

Emily, he often thought, was simply the best thing ever to have happened to him, and even now she'd reached the grand old age of twenty-three he still couldn't help but feel absurdly proud of her. She'd grown into a fine young woman; clever, sensible and beautiful, just like her mother. For years the similarity had haunted him. But now when he looked at Emily and saw a fleeting echo of Eve he felt only pride. He'd raised the best daughter in the world.

He looked at her as he carved the roast he'd just taken out of the oven. Emily was a charity worker and had just returned from a stint in Africa. Her face was covered with a fresh smattering of freckles that set off her long, curly auburn hair.

'You're looking thin,' he observed kindly.

'You always say that.' She laughed.

'I worry about you when you're abroad. You work too hard and forget to eat.'

'Yes, Mum!' She mock-saluted.

John smiled, but put an extra-large portion on her plate.

'So, what's going on in your life?' she asked as they started to tuck in.

'Nothing much,' John replied casually. 'I've been on a few dates.'

'When have you ever *not* been on a few dates, Dad?' Emily replied sardonically. But something in her father's face made her stop.

'D'you mean *date* dates? Dates that Aunty Geraldine hasn't set up for you?'

John couldn't help himself. He broke into a grin.

'I can't believe it! Really? Why didn't you tell me?'

'You were in Africa!'

'Yes, but this is big stuff. Kind of like the Berlin Wall coming down or man landing on the moon. So, you've really had some dates?'

John nodded happily.

'So, come on! Who with?'

'She's called Alice.'

'And?'

'And what?'

Emily threw up her hands in excited exasperation. 'What does she do? What's she like? And does she know you're a rent boy?'

'Oi!'

'It's got to be asked,' Emily grinned. 'It *is* the elephant in the room!'

John gave up trying to eat and filled her in on everything.

'So she doesn't know?'

'About the escorting? No.'

'But you're going to tell her, right?'

John sighed. 'I suppose I'm going to have to.'

'Of course you have to!' Emily cried. 'I mean, you *like* this woman, you want to have a relationship with her. So tell her the truth!'

'I know,' John replied reluctantly.

'If Alice is as good as you say she is, she'll understand.'

'But what if she doesn't?' John looked at her nervously. 'What if it scares her and she calls the whole thing off?'

'Well, you'll just have to explain it properly. Don't just let her hear the headline. Tell her why. Tell her what a sad sack you are.'

'That'll help!'

'Dad! You've got to stop hiding from life!' Emily scolded. 'You're an escort, not an axe murderer. And whilst you're at it, you've got to stop beating yourself up too! The past is past. Why don't you go crazy and tell her the whole hog? It's about time you got everything out in the open!'

'I told her you were as wise as the hills.'

'Too right! And you should be a good dad and do as I say!'

John laughed, before falling silent and looking glum again.

'There's another complication.'

He told her about Audrey.

'God, that Audrey!' Emily crashed her fork down angrily on her plate. 'She's been nothing but trouble for as long as you've been escorting her!'

'If Audrey found out that Alice and I were together, she'd

make life . . .' – John groped for the right word – '*awkward* for Alice. Alice loves her job; I mean *really* loves it. And a relationship with me might cost her her job.'

'So you think that's a reason not to tell her the truth?'

'Maybe.'

'Dad, come on!' Emily admonished. 'Alice is a grown woman. If you tell her, and she decides to give it a go, then that's her decision. But if you don't, she'll find out eventually, and then she'll be angry with you for keeping things from her. And it'll be curtains! You'll have cocked up and you'll be back on the shelf for another fifteen years.'

John looked at his plate unhappily.

'And Dad, you don't want to cock up!' she continued sagely. 'You've spent too long being a martyr and hiding behind Aunty Geraldine. It's time to live a bit. Tell her!'

John looked at her sparkling eyes and self-righteous fervour. He knew she was right. She was always right. He felt like such a beginner when it came to this relationship stuff. If it was organized dating, he could date like a pro. *He was a pro!* But doing it for real was a minefield.

'Mum would have wanted you to tell Alice,' Emily said bluntly, delivering the killer blow. 'Mum would have given you a kick up the backside, told you to stop hiding and get on with life. Mum would say that happiness is worth taking a risk for.'

John nodded. Emily was right.

He picked up his fork and ate his cold dinner.

KATE

It was 4 p.m., and Kate was at the Corn Exchange, wearing a starched white shirt and apron. She and the rest of the Julian Marquis PR team had been dressed as waiters and waitresses all day, running between stalls and making sure everything went smoothly for the inaugural Pedigree Pooch Gourmet Dog Food Festival. She'd been rushed off her feet since 8.30 a.m., erecting stalls, delivering fresh ingredients to the chefs and setting up microphones so the festival-goers (and their dogs) could hear the live cooking displays.

The first festivalgoers had arrived at ten, their dogs straining at their leashes as they caught the scents of the gourmet goodies being created in their honour. By 11.30 the area was packed.

Lots of journalists had turned up too, including several national newspapers and an ITN news crew looking for the day's 'and finally' item. The crew had kept serious faces all through their interview with Geoffrey Laird from Pedigree Pooch, and had even spent a po-faced forty-five minutes trying to film a range of enthusiastic responses from the dogs.

Now that everything was winding down Kate felt a sudden rush of happiness. The festival couldn't have gone better. The client was delighted, the journalists had been amused, and she'd helped bring a wag to the tail of a thousand local canines. All in all, it hadn't been a bad day at the office.

Julian sidled up behind her.

'Nice work, Katy darling. You've excelled yourself again.'

Of course, Julian had insisted on going one step further than dressing as a mere waiter and had come as a maître d', complete with a badge pointing out his hierarchy in the restaurant staff pecking order. Kate had initially raised her eyebrows in bemused irritation but she had to concede he'd more than pulled his weight. He'd schmoozed journalists, public and canines alike and had even waded in to split up two snarling St Bernards who'd been scrapping over the last rum-and-raisin pudding.

'Thanks.' Kate couldn't help grinning with pride.

'Let's get this wrapped up by five,' Julian muttered. 'Then it's drinks over the road in the Star Bar. I think we deserve a little celebration!' He shot across the square to bid an extravagant farewell to the *Daily Post*'s features editor who was leaving with Xavier, her nauseous-looking poodle. Xavier, it seemed, had embraced the festival a little too enthusiastically. Kate would put money on the editor having to scrape an accident off her carpet later.

Kate tried to quell her smile and went to help distribute the doggy bags.

By half past five the Julian Marquis PR team were ensconced

in the Star Bar, knocking back their second round of mojitos and loudly congratulating themselves on another roaring success. Giddy from his brush with fame, Geoffrey had joined them and was waving his company credit card high in the air and leading the call for champagne.

'To gorgeous food, greedy dogs and their pretentious owners!' he toasted loudly. He'd even loosened his tie; the man was clearly ready to party.

Everyone clinked glasses and roared in agreement.

'I must say, Julian, my man.' Geoffrey manoeuvred over to Julian and Kate. 'Great show today. Well done.' He threw a fatherly smile in Kate's direction. 'What a clever little assistant you have to come up with an idea like that. You'd better hope she doesn't sneak off and have babies.'

Kate stiffened. How did Geoffrey know she wanted a baby? And *an assistant*? Was that what people thought she was? She looked at Julian, waiting for him to put Geoffrey in his place.

'Babies?' Julian scoffed. 'She's a bit long in the tooth for all that, aren't you, Katy?'

Kate felt like she'd been punched. How could Julian say that? She was only thirty-three! And why didn't he tell Geoffrey she was an account director, and almost second in command of the whole agency?

She shot Julian a murderous look. He didn't notice; he was too busy fishing a mint leaf from between his teeth.

Suddenly a loud cheer went up as several bottles of champagne arrived at their table.

'Evening all!' came a familiar voice from the door. 'Is this a private party, or can anyone gatecrash?'

'Lou!' Kate cried out in relief. 'I'm so glad you could make it!'

'Free booze at a swanky members' bar? What could possibly be more pressing?' Lou replied dryly. 'Ooooh, is that for me?' She swept Geoffrey's glass of champagne clean out of his hand with a pout.

Kate turned to hide her smile. Lou was dressed in her customary tight, dark, dominatrix style; Dita Von Teese crossed with Sarah Palin, and heavy on the lipstick. Kate saw Geoffrey go pink in her presence.

'So, how did it go?' Lou asked.

'Fantastic!' Kate said happily, steering her friend away from the group. 'We made a lot of dogs very happy.'

'Amen. And Mr Marquis?'

Both women turned to look at Julian who was heading purposefully towards the Gents, his hand fumbling in the inside pocket of his jacket.

'Wait for it . . .' Kate quietly observed, and sure enough, exactly ten seconds later an excited Geoffrey followed him in, his nose twitching expectantly.

'A boss's work is never done,' Kate said archly.

'So . . .' Lou turned her attention back to Kate. 'How was last night? Didn't you have your black-market date with the Table For Two impostor?'

'Tommy? Yes, I did.'

'Is that the remnants of a snoggers' chin I can see?'

Kate's hand flew up to her face.

'Does it still show? I've put nearly a whole tube of cover-up on it!'

Lou laughed.

'So the date went well, then?'

Kate went dewy.

'Lou, it went so well, I can't believe it.'

She filled Lou in on the details.

'But hang on a minute,' Lou interrupted, refilling her glass from yet another bottle of champagne that someone had ordered at the absent Geoffrey's expense. 'Isn't he the complete opposite of what you're looking for? What happened to well groomed, well heeled and well positioned? I thought you wanted a trophy husband?'

'Oh, that!' Kate waved away her old criteria with the sweep of a hand. 'Rules are there to be broken.'

Lou looked surprised.

'But following the rules is your number one rule! You've got more goals and spreadsheets and timetables than anyone alive! You're the only person in the world who keeps a gallery of their most successful outfits on their iPhone.' Lou's attention was suddenly diverted. 'Oooh, watch out. Someone's ready to play!'

Julian and Geoffrey had returned from the Gents looking even more intent on celebrating. Both had flushed cheeks and shiny eyes. Julian had shed his jacket and tied his cashmere jumper around his shoulders.

'Lou, Lou, Lou.' He grabbed the nearest bottle and started topping up the girls' glasses. 'Good to see you. This party needs a few more party animals! I can't do it all on my own.'

'Looks like you're giving it a go,' Lou observed dryly.

Julian laughed. 'And may I say, Lou, you're looking as

delectable as ever. You're definitely my favourite friend of my favourite staff member.'

'I should think so!' Lou replied coquettishly, tipping her glass so Julian could fill it to the very top. 'And you're looking very ... dashing ... yourself.' She eyed his jumper ambiguously. 'Those classic catalogue looks never date. And I do love a man who smells of Chappie!'

Kate gasped. Only Lou could come out with an insult and still sound suggestive. Chappie was the smelliest dog food on the market.

Julian laughed loudly.

'At this very moment I'm probably irresistible to bitches.' He eyed Lou wolfishly.

'Woof, woof!' Lou drawled, her eyes locked on Julian's.

Kate turned away in horrified embarrassment. Surely Lou couldn't be coming on to Julian? She had to be joking! And Julian? She knew Lou had no standards, but she'd never thought of Julian as being sexual before. He was a dreadful flirt with clients, granted, but that was just business. Besides, surely Lou wouldn't be his type? He was posh and ridiculous; his girlfriends must be inbred Camilla types who rode ponies and wore caramel. But, Kate noticed, he *was* standing rather close to Lou. And as she looked she saw him stretch out his hand behind her friend, his fingers deliberately brushing her backside. Oh God, no, Kate thought with a sinking feeling. Please, no!

She looked at her watch. It was 5.45 p.m. Tommy had promised to call at six. Six o'clock couldn't come a minute too soon.

'You know, there's no style like doggy style,' Lou purred to Julian.

'Mmmm, tickle my tummy and call me a bad boy,' he replied lasciviously.

Kate quickly edged away.

At a minute past six Kate's mobile rang. She grabbed it gratefully and shot outside where it was quieter.

'I've just been watching the news headlines,' Tommy greeted her cheerfully, 'and they've got a special report coming up from the world's first gourmet dog food festival!'

Kate shrieked happily.

'Congratulations! You're the queen of spin!' Tommy cheered. 'So how about granting me another evening of your time?'

Kate wriggled with happiness, her stomach suddenly deliciously full of butterflies. She felt a stone lighter, like she was hovering above the pavement. Tommy was certainly better than any diet she'd ever been on.

'Pick you up at eight?'

'Eight's perfect!'

As she hung up she caught a glimpse of Lou and Julian through the window. Lou was sitting on Julian's lap, her champagne spilling slightly as she leant close and told him a story. Julian was wide-eyed with appreciation, his nose on a direct level with her breasts.

Kate jiggled her phone in her hand and wondered if she really had to go back in.

AUDREY

The afternoon had started badly. Audrey had been halfway through a Marks & Spencer prawn mayonnaise sandwich when Cassandra had bellowed across the office that Sheryl Toogood was on line three. Audrey swallowed painfully, shooting Cassandra a disapproving look. Why couldn't she get off her rectangular backside, walk over and quietly inform her that Sheryl was on the phone? She spent too much time with her horses, that girl. It was making her coarse.

Grumpily Audrey picked up her phone.

'Sheryl,' she said coolly, putting down her sandwich and sucking a chunk of prawn from her teeth.

'Auuuuuudrey!'

It was the sound of indigestion.

'Listen, darling, I won't keep you. I'm terribly busy and you sound like you're snuffling for truffles.'

Audrey's hackles rose. She wasn't sure what offended her most – being compared to a rummaging pig, or Sheryl calling her 'darling'.

'I know you like to be the first to know news, so I thought I'd give you a quick tinkle with the latest.'

Audrey felt her sandwich sink awkwardly down her oesophagus. She tried to sound uninterested, but her mind was already racing.

'Go on.'

'You're speaking to the new owner of Cupid's Cabin!' Sheryl crowed triumphantly.

'You've bought Cupid's Cabin?'

'For a song!'

'But I didn't know Nigel had put it up for sale.'

'He hadn't! But everyone knew his heart wasn't in it any more. "Take Marjorie on a cruise," I said to him. "Forget about all this matchmaking nonsense. Work on your own marriage." Well, Auuudrey, let me tell you, he almost bit my hand off!'

'But if he'd let everyone know . . . put the business on the market . . .' Audrey protested.

'You'd have put in an offer?' Sheryl gave a long, sceptical laugh. 'Businesswomen don't wait for situations to present themselves; we go out and make them happen. And besides, we all know you've got your hands full trying to cope with your little agency as it is. How's Alice, by the way?'

'Fine,' Audrey shot back automatically.

'Do make sure you pass on my news to her, won't you? I'm sure she'd be most interested to hear about my acquisition.'

'Right.' Audrey was lost for words and her prawn sandwich was already repeating on her. She could kick herself for missing such a glaring business opportunity.

'So, aren't you going to congratulate me?' Sheryl gloated.

'I mean, it's not every day you get to speak to a mogul, is it?'

Audrey put down the phone and simmered with indignation.

Why hadn't Nigel told her he wanted to sell up? They'd always got on so well; she couldn't believe he hadn't come to her first. But now Sheryl had got her hands on Cupid's Cabin, and that meant she was in charge of both of Table For Two's closest rival agencies. This was very bad news indeed.

There was a knock on her door. Bianca stood in the doorway.

'I've got Maurice Lazenby on line one. He's insisting he speak to you.'

'Oh, for heaven's sake!' Audrey snapped. 'Give him to Alice!'

She saw Bianca blanch at her tone.

'Alice is out.'

'What do you mean, "out"? Where?'

'Meeting a client.'

'Just get rid of him!' she barked angrily. 'Do I look like I want to speak to Maurice Lazenby?'

Bianca backed out looking pale.

Where the hell was Alice? And what, exactly, was the point of Alice? If she wasn't out racking up Table For Two's expenses by having unnecessary coffees with clients, then she was staring moonily out of the window, no good to man nor beast.

Audrey was struck by a sudden memory.

Why had Sheryl been so keen for Alice to know she'd bought Cupid's Cabin? Was Sheryl laughing at Audrey again? Hadn't she called her a 'little spinster' at the ball? Was that what people thought about her and her Table For Two staff . . . a bunch of little spinsters?

Audrey scowled at the remains of her sandwich and dropped it angrily into the bin.

The afternoon dragged on. Indigestion made its inevitable appearance. Audrey had two cups of chamomile tea and tried some deep-breathing techniques. But they only made her chest burn more viciously and her head throb. Eventually she decided to put the cumbersome business of work aside. Instead she'd attend to an altogether happier, personal matter. She was going to book John for a functionless date.

Audrey carefully closed her office door, took a deep breath and dialled Geraldine's number.

'What do you mean, you're unable to accept my booking?' Audrey bellowed a minute later. 'This is outrageous!'

'It's like I said,' Geraldine explained patiently. 'Regretfully John Marlowe is no longer available to you. I'm sorry. It happens sometimes.'

'But why?' Audrey snapped, panic beginning to grip. 'Why? Why?'

'It's a personal decision, taken by John, and one that we must both respect,' Geraldine continued calmly. 'I'm sorry, my love. But he felt he'd given you many years of good service, and that it was time for both of you to move on.'

'No, no, no!' Audrey's voice was shaking.

'Really, Audrey, you should be grateful to have enjoyed his company for as long as you have. You were his longest-standing client by quite some margin.'

'But I don't book him often,' Audrey pleaded, 'just a couple of times a year. Why can't we just go on as we are?'

Audrey's emotions were all over the place, fury, fear and incomprehension whizzing around her like the plastic balls in the National Lottery machine. The indignation ball was picked up by the scooper and served through the hatch.

'This is utter madness!' she thundered. 'Totally unacceptable!'

'Nevertheless,' Geraldine continued evenly, 'it's John's decision.'

'I *need* him!'

'I've got plenty of other interesting gentlemen on my books.'

'No!' Audrey cried out hysterically. 'Another man won't work. It has to be John!'

Why was this happening? Why was John turning his back on her? She felt like she couldn't breathe, like the life-support machine that had kept her alive for so long was suddenly being turned off. She had to grasp at the flex, fight tooth and nail to plug her life back in.

'But I have to have him. I have to! You don't understand. Everyone knows him. They expect to see him. How can I do things without him?'

'I'm sorry, Audrey.'

'But I'm the client. The client's always right. I haven't done anything wrong. It's not fair. I have rights!'

There was a short pause before Geraldine's composed voice came back on the line.

'How about you have a little think about things? Take a bit of time. I realize this has come as a bit of a shock. Let it sink in for a few days and then see how you feel. And in the meantime I can send you a link to our website so you can look through my other gentlemen. I think you'll be pleasantly surprised.'

'I don't want to be pleasantly surprised,' Audrey snapped. 'I want John. What am I supposed to do? Tell everyone I'm divorced?'

There was a long pause.

Audrey let out an agonized moan and slammed down the phone. The walls of her office felt like they were zooming in towards her, crushing her and making it hard to breathe.

She put on her coat, picked up her bag and steamed out of the office. When she hit the cool afternoon air she gulped, trying to get her breath back.

She cried out in anguish.

John was refusing to see her. Her life was in turmoil.

She pulled her coat around her and was about to set off for the bus stop, anxious to put her own front door between her and the world. But before she'd taken a step, her eye fell on something leaning against the railing. It was Alice's bike.

Audrey felt a surge of terrible anger, venomous and uncontrollable. The bike was a carbuncle, perched like a fungus outside the entrance to Table For Two. It was nothing less than a personal insult, a defiant two-fingered salute at her from the overgrown Von Trapp sister. Well, she wouldn't put up with it any longer.

She took two steps forward, swung her heavy handbag back and crashed it heavily into the spokes of the front wheel. Ten pounds of Filofax, make-up and a hardback library book thwacked into the spindly metal. It sounded strangely satisfying. She swung back her handbag again and took a second shot. *Thwack*. The bike's spokes were now sporting two definite dents. Audrey felt a violent thrill of triumph.

ALICE

'You know, it's just like you said when we first met,' Kate grinned over the corner table of the tea shop. 'You have to be open-minded. Life *is* more exciting when you let yourself be surprised!'

She looked bright-eyed and full of sparkle as she chased the last remnants of chocolate cake around her plate with her fork.

'So, I take it I don't need to set you up with any more dates for a while?' Alice smiled.

'No, thank you!' Kate beamed. 'I want to see how things go with Tommy. I know he doesn't tick any of my stupid boxes but you were completely right about him!'

'I'm very glad to hear it,' Alice replied, trying to keep the full extent of her delight from spilling out and engulfing the tea shop. Nothing felt better than making a successful match. 'Sometimes it's good to take a risk, isn't it?'

Kate nodded fiercely.

'And remember: not a word to anyone at Table For Two.' Alice tried to strike a note of caution, but it was hard to look serious with a joyful smile plastered across her face.

* * *

A few hours later Alice was still beaming happily as she sat in front of John at a candlelit restaurant in a quiet part of the city.

It had been a great evening. Alice had never met anyone who made her feel as attractive and comfortable as John did. She felt she could say anything to him, admit anything – even wear anything, from her baggiest cardigan to her tattiest gardening clothes. But something about John made her want to look nice, put on a dress, apply a bit of lipstick. He made her feel like a woman. And they hadn't even had sex yet!

Every time Alice thought about the possibility of going to bed with him she felt weak with excitement. Sex, or what she could remember of it, had always been a perfunctory exercise for her, something to get over and done with. She'd never felt like she knew what she was doing, so she'd held back and let the man take the lead. But with John . . . she couldn't wait to have sex with him, to fall asleep in his arms, for those eyes and that smile to be the first thing she saw when she woke up the next morning. She hoped it would happen soon; she hoped it would happen tonight!

'So you did it,' he said warmly, taking her hand across the table and entwining her fingers in his. 'You found the career woman her perfect match!'

Alice felt a delicious shiver travel up her arm from his touch.

'It's early days, but I think so.' She couldn't stop smiling. 'She definitely had that look. She looked like a woman falling in love.'

'And it was all because you took a risk,' John said emphatically.

Alice looked into his eyes. They were exactly the same shade of blue as forget-me-nots, she realized. How perfect that the thing she found most attractive about him was something he shared with one of the world's most gorgeous and uncomplicated flowers.

'But it was more than just that, wasn't it?' he continued, squeezing her fingers. 'It was because you made her realize she needed to be more open-minded and give people a chance.'

He leaned forward, looking earnestly at her. Alice felt herself slowly melt into his gaze, like ice cream oozing onto warm apple crumble. Is this what it feels like? she asked herself. Is this what falling in love feels like? It certainly felt good. Better than anything she'd ever felt before.

'You're making me sound very clever, but I'm not really.' She tried to shrug off the weight of his praise. 'I just think we all believe our perfect partner has to be a certain way. But it's not true. Perfect partners come in all shapes and sizes.'

'We've got to let ourselves be open to surprises.'

'Exactly!'

She felt him pull back his hand. He suddenly seemed on edge. She watched him pick up his dessertspoon and fiddle with it thoughtfully.

'John, are you OK?' she asked tentatively.

'Yes, yes,' he replied, but his face said otherwise. 'Look,' he said suddenly. 'I know we've only had a few dates and it's early days . . . But hopefully you know how much I like you.'

Alice tried to smile, but she suddenly felt nervous.

'I see a future for us, I really do.' His forget-me-not eyes met hers. 'I haven't had a relationship for a really long time, and now that I've met you I don't want to lose you.'

Alice's smile froze. Why would he lose her? What was wrong?

John sighed heavily. 'There's something I need to tell you. I want you to know the truth so that we can move on . . . together.'

'Oh, God, you *are* married . . .' Alice blurted in a panic.

'No.'

'It's Audrey, then. You're having a relationship with her after all.'

Alice was beginning to feel sick.

'Kind of,' John said haltingly. 'That's what I need to talk to you about.'

Something hard settled in the pit of Alice's stomach. She should have known this was too good to be true. John was too good. Women like her didn't get to go out with men like him.

'Things are complicated,' John admitted.

He stared at the table, apparently lost as to what to say next.

'So, you and Audrey are more than just friends?' Alice heard herself ask. She could barely stand to hear his reply.

There was a long pause.

'Audrey and I have a . . . *business* relationship,' John said quietly.

'What?' In her surprise Alice forgot her nervousness. 'Do you work in matchmaking as well?'

'I work in a . . . related industry.'

'I don't understand.'

'Please, Alice. *Please* don't jump to conclusions.'

His eyes begged her. She nodded dumbly.

'Audrey and I have a business relationship . . . where I agree to . . . *accompany* her on certain evenings.'

He looked at her to see if she understood. She looked back at him blankly.

'Like the evening you met me. I wasn't there as Audrey's friend. I was working.'

'What do you mean, working? Are you something to do with DIPS?'

'Women – women like Audrey – can book me to come to functions with them. To be their surrogate partner.'

She still looked blank. John waved away the waiter who had approached their table, and took her hand in his again.

'These women are single,' he explained gently. 'And usually their function is a work do or a wedding that they can't get out of; they *have* to go to it. But they're really worried. They're embarrassed about going on their own. Or maybe they don't want people to know they're single. And so they book me to go with them.'

There was another pause.

'I don't understand.' Alice's voice came out small, almost a whisper.

John held her hand more tightly.

'Alice, taking these women to functions, well, that's my job. I escort them.'

'Escort them?' she echoed hollowly, her brain racing to keep up with the truth, but her heart already urging it to slow down and not get there.

'Yes. They book me through my agent, and I accompany them wherever they need to go.'

She looked at his hand as it gripped hers tightly.

'Alice, I'm a . . .' He took a deep breath. 'I'm a professional escort.'

There was a pause. The words fell on Alice's ears. Something began to sink in. A cold, numb feeling crept through her body like a poisonous anaesthetic, shutting parts of her down as it went.

'So these women pay for your company?' Her voice was tight and strange.

'Yes.'

'And you do whatever they want?'

'Well, not exactly. They pay for my company, nothing else.'

'But you act like their boyfriend? You're theirs for the night?'

'I suppose so, yes.'

'And this is your job? To go out with women for money?'

'Yes.'

'And that's what you do for Audrey? That's what your "special relationship" is? You pretend to be her husband, and she pays you to do it?'

He gave a small, silent nod.

Gently, Alice pulled her hand away.

'Alice, please ... Let me explain. It's not as bad as it sounds.'

'I'm not stupid,' she said quietly, her voice shaking. 'I might be easy to mock because I'm single and I like gardening and I don't follow fashion. But I'm not an idiot. I know what this means.'

'But it doesn't mean what you're thinking!' John tried to reach for her hand again.

'I do live in the real world, you know.'

'I know, of course. But I promise, hand on heart, I escort them, nothing more.'

Alice struggled for breath, careful not to let John touch her. If he touched her she'd crumple, and she couldn't risk that. If there was one thing she knew in the midst of this confusing, terrible wreck of an evening, it was the absolute certainty that she must not cry. She couldn't look at him. She couldn't even get the air into her lungs. 'I need to go home now,' she managed to force out. 'I need to think.'

'Yes, of course,' John said reluctantly. 'But please, don't think too much. This isn't what you imagine. I'm still the same man.'

Alice stood up.

'Be open-minded,' he implored. 'Just like you tell your clients. *Please*, Alice! Take your own advice.'

Quietly, Alice headed for the door.

AUDREY

It was midnight.

Pickles had gone for a protracted nocturnal prowl and Audrey lay in bed feeling utterly, dreadfully alone.

She couldn't sleep.

Nothing worked: not hot milky drinks, nor counting sheep, nor a second glass of sherry. Nothing.

She hadn't slept properly since the night of the ball, and things had only got worse since her terrible phone call with Geraldine. Questions kept swirling around her head, silently but deafeningly filling her mind, like an irritating advertising jingle stuck on repeat. Why was John refusing to take her bookings? What had she done wrong?

She lay unmoving, stiff within her nightie like a stone effigy on the lid of a tomb. It didn't make sense. She hadn't *done* anything. She didn't look any different. She hadn't said anything different. She'd just been as she always was.

So why was he doing this?

The only possible explanation was that he needed space to make sense of his feelings. He must have become confused, realized she was no mere client – that she was someone special. Maybe that was why he'd put some distance between them? To pave the way to a new kind of relationship. That would explain his coldness when he'd dropped her off after the ball, and why he wouldn't let her book him again. That must be it! He wanted to unmuddy the waters, clear away the debris of their old arrangement before coming to her, offering a new way; offering himself – his love – for free.

It was the only rational explanation.

JOHN

John was tired. It hadn't been a good night's sleep. After Alice had walked out of the restaurant he'd paid the bill and walked home, hoping to see her somewhere on the way.

When he arrived home he'd realized he wasn't ready to go in, so he'd kept on walking. He'd found himself outside Greenfingers garden centre, where he'd first bumped into Alice. He didn't know what he'd been thinking. The place was shut; it was midnight! He'd turned round and come home.

John sipped his coffee and absent-mindedly stroked Buster.

He was just going to have to hope for the best, he thought to himself. Alice believed in happy endings. Surely she'd give him a chance to explain? He should sit tight and give her space.

Shouldn't he?

He grabbed the phone and called Emily.

'Just relax,' she counselled calmly. 'Give her the weekend to think about it and then call her on Monday.'

'But what if the weekend's too long? What if she comes to the wrong conclusions?'

'She just needs time to digest why it is that you got into escorting – what your higher purpose is.'

There was an awkward silence.

'You did tell her about Mum dying, didn't you, and how lonely you were?' she demanded suddenly.

'Um, I've sort of mentioned it before. A while ago,' John mumbled.

'But not in connection with the escorting? You didn't mention how it helped bring you back to life? You didn't tell her how you help women win back their confidence, how you make them feel attractive again?'

'I didn't really get the chance,' John interjected dolefully.

'*Dad!*' Emily used the same stern, exasperated tone that he remembered using with her when she was a child. 'I told you to explain it properly, remember? It's no wonder she walked out. She probably thought you were some stud for hire; that half the ladies in the city have had their wicked way with you!'

He heard her sigh.

'Look, forget about waiting till Monday,' she instructed brutally. 'Too much damage will have been done by then. You need to call her now. Tell her you're not the disease-ridden Casanova she probably thinks you are . . .'

John blanched at her frankness.

'Tell her the truth!' she commanded. 'Tell her you haven't had a date of your own choosing in over a decade. Tell her you haven't had sex for even longer! Tell her you haven't loved anyone since Mum, but that you think you might be falling in love with her!'

There was a pause. Emily's words echoed between them.

'Well, it's all true, isn't it?' she asked forcefully.

'Yes,' John conceded quietly. 'It's all true.'

He contemplated his coffee.

'I've cocked up, haven't I?' he asked.

'Yes, Dad,' Emily said bluntly. 'You've cocked up.'

LOU

When Lou opened her front door she could see Kate doing what she always did: surveying her messy flat and quickly covering her horrified expression with a smile.

'Hi,' Kate said brightly, giving Lou a hug.

Lou let herself be hugged without bothering to lift her arms. She knew her flat was a tip, but she liked it that way. She'd never seen the point of wardrobes when there was a floor to drop your clothes on. Tidying up was a waste of time. Kate's flat was so clean Lou felt like she'd be squirted with Dettol or tidied into a cupboard at any moment. Kate's books were shelved alphabetically and the tins in her cupboards were turned so their labels were all at the same angle. That wasn't a way to live. That was a psychosis.

'Glass of wine?' she asked flatly.

'Why not?' Kate replied, her bottom narrowly missing last night's takeaway as she flopped onto Lou's sofa.

Lou rummaged in the kitchen for her last clean glasses.

'Actually, I do feel like a celebration's in order,' Kate confided happily. 'I had another date with Tommy last night.'

'Right.' Lou did her best to sound uninterested. There was something very irritating about Kate when she talked about Tommy, she'd decided. She lit a cigarette so she wouldn't have to look at her.

'It was brilliant!' Kate gushed. 'He's amazing. So funny and interesting and kind and strong. And really confident. And manly. The kind of man who can put up shelves, or pick you up without worrying he's going to slip a disc.'

'Mmmm,' Lou said blandly, and blew out her smoke in a long misty column. She was sick of all this dating agency stuff.

There was an awkward pause. Kate looked confused.

'I thought you'd be pleased for me,' she said quietly.

'What, because you've decided Tommy's the best thing since sliced bread?'

'Don't be like that. I really like him.'

'Do you? Really, Kate, do you?' Lou flashed her eyes angrily. 'Because last week you wanted Adonis-on-a-career-fast-track. You had the agency hunting high and low for someone educated and loaded. Mr Perfect with a seat on the board and a six-figure salary!'

'Tommy's educated,' Kate protested.

'So's the rest of the developed world,' Lou replied scornfully.

'Anyway,' Kate reasoned, sounding hurt, 'isn't it better to be open-minded? Maybe all that prerequisite stuff was holding me back. Maybe what I should've been looking for wasn't Mr Perfect, but Mr Perfect For Me.'

'Oh, very sweet! Very self-help.'

'Tommy's what I want now.' Kate lifted her chin defiantly.

'Whatever!' Lou drew on her cigarette. She knew she was being cruel, but she couldn't stop herself. She was sick of being nice. She was sick of having to listen to Kate's supposed problems with her actually quite perfect life. 'Ever since we went to that Meeting Mr Right talk you've been strange, shelling out all that money to join that stupid agency.'

'You know why I signed up,' Kate said patiently. 'I want to meet someone, get married, have kids. It's quite normal, you know.'

'Well, bully for you, then.' Lou gave her sarcasm a free rein. 'You've compromised your standards and found a Mr Average to take you up the aisle and get you up the duff. How wonderfully *normal!*'

'I'm not saying I'm going to marry him! We haven't even had sex yet,' Kate added with a lame smile.

'Well, at least something's business as usual.'

'Meaning what, exactly?'

'Meaning at least you haven't changed beyond all recognition. You're still wearing those cast-iron knickers and walking around like you're on day release from the convent.'

Kate gasped.

'Lou, what's wrong with you today? It's like you're looking for a fight.'

'I'm just sick of hearing about your never-ending quest to get a ring on your finger.'

'I don't talk about it *that* much!'

Lou snorted.

'Yeah, right! Still, at least you've moved on from talking about work. Five years of obsessing about Julian really was enough for anyone to stomach.'

'I don't obsess about Julian! And besides, who else am I supposed to talk to but you? It's not as if either of us have *boyfriends* to talk about this stuff with.'

'Oh, we're back to boyfriends, are we?'

Kate threw up her hands in exasperation.

'Maybe we should just leave it for today.' She rose from the sofa. 'I'm going home.'

'What, to phone Tommy?' Lou sneered. 'To moan about the friend you think's beneath you now?'

Kate stopped in her tracks. 'Lou! What on earth gave you that idea?'

Lou drew sulkily on her cigarette.

'Isn't it all about your parade of rich boys nowadays? Isn't having a drink with your friend and letting life just happen a bit "over" for you?' She knew she was being unfair but she couldn't stop now.

'What's this *really* about?' Kate asked. Lou shrugged and concentrated on smoking.

'Look, you're great, Lou, but you're not there when I go to bed at night or get up in the morning. You don't make me a cup of tea after a hard day at work, or rub my back in the bath.'

Lou snorted in derision.

'I'm sick of being lonely!' Kate exclaimed in exasperation. 'Is that so wrong?'

There was a sudden silence. Kate's words seemed to hover between them.

'Did you shag Julian after the Pedigree Pooch event?' Kate asked suddenly.

'Does it matter?' Lou replied in surprise.

'You were all over him like herpes,' Kate said sharply. 'It was embarrassing.'

'You sitting there with your arms crossed and your mouth pursed was embarrassing. It was like having Mary Whitehouse at the table. Everyone else was managing to have fun.'

'Oh, what, you mean having fun by fornicating with my boss? What is it with you and bosses anyway? Do you have to shag every single one of them? Well, if you want to shit on your own doorstep with Tony then fine, but don't shit on mine.'

'Why so territorial about Julian, Kate?' Lou's voice was like cold acid. 'Are you after him? Because if you are, I've got news for you: you're not his type.'

'Of course I'm not after him. Don't be ridiculous!'

'*I'm* being ridiculous? I'm not the one who's turned into the sex police! Grow up, Kate. Adults fuck. Get over it!'

'I've got to work with him!' Kate cried indignantly.

'So? You didn't shag him. What's the fucking problem?'

'The problem,' Kate replied, her voice tight with fury, 'is that all this maneater stuff was funny in your twenties, but now it's fast becoming pathetic. You've got no self-respect, no ambition, no self-worth. Your only significant relationship of the last decade has been with a married man. Don't you want to be loved? Don't you want someone to care about you, to actually give a shit about whether you've had a bad day?'

Kate paused, somewhere between anger and pity. She looked at Lou, waiting for a response. Lou was trying to hide the fact that she was shaking. She grabbed the wine bottle and refilled her glass.

Kate sighed, and suddenly sat down.

'You're clever, Lou,' she said gently. 'What are you doing working in a bar? What happened to having a career? And if bar work is your career, why don't you own the bar by now? You're thirty-three. You shouldn't be the deputy manager; you should be the owner!'

'I'm happy as I am,' Lou mumbled defiantly.

'No, you're not,' Kate replied softly. 'If you were, you wouldn't be living off junk food and having meaningless shags with men who don't care about you.'

'Oh, and you're so bloody perfect!' Lou snapped viciously. 'What the hell do you know about shagging? When did you last have sex, Kate? Actually, when did you last get *screwed*? Sex isn't all about flowers and poetry and being worshipped on a bloody pedestal, you know. Sex is about excitement and exhilaration and pain. It's about being fucked to within an inch of your life, not stagnating in the missionary position with the lights off! And relationships?' Lou felt herself shaking even harder now. 'I'm not taking advice from someone who has to pay a professional to sort out her love life. It's tragic! And work? You've turned yourself into the busiest person in the western world, not because PR's so bloody important, but because it gives you an excuse not to go out. Because, who knows, if you did, *you might actually have fun*! You might actually have sex and get married and have kids and get all those things you want. But if you want it all so badly, why don't you switch off your computer at six o'clock like any normal person and actually engage with the world? You need to go out and get shagged senseless, Kate! You need to be fucked until you wake up and see what you've become!'

A silence suddenly fell.

And then Kate picked up her bag and headed for the door.

'We're not twenty any more,' she said quietly. 'We shouldn't be living in each other's pockets still. I need to get on with the next stage of my life. We both do.'

And she slipped through the door, closing it gently behind her.

'The sooner you bugger off with a boring husband and 2.4 kids the better!' Lou bellowed after her viciously. 'Put us all out of our fucking misery!'

She heard Kate's footsteps echo in the stairwell. She dragged on her cigarette. Her flat fell depressingly silent.

ALICE

Alice was finding it hard to be positive. As she plodded through her list of Monday morning calls, listening to her clients recount the wonderful dates they'd had at the weekend, she found herself zoning out.

It had been a terrible weekend. John's bombshell had left her not knowing what to think, or how to feel. Her instinct was to ring Ginny, but she and Dan had gone away for a 'working on it' weekend. Normally gardening cleared her head, but that didn't help either. She couldn't even make her usual pilgrimage to Greenfingers in case John was there. Besides, even if she'd wanted to go she couldn't. Someone must have accidentally bumped into her bike. The spokes on the front wheel were bent and it wouldn't ride straight.

So instead she'd sat stiffly on her sofa, numbly watching black-and-white movies; not taking anything in, just going over and over everything in her head. She wouldn't let herself cry; she refused to allow herself a single tear. Every thirty minutes her phone rang, but she didn't move a muscle to answer it. She knew it would be John, wanting to explain. But what could he say?

The man she'd been falling in love with was a prostitute.

She'd been such an idiot. More than an idiot: a fool. She'd actually dared believe a man like John could have been interested in a girl like her. What had she been thinking? John was handsome, urbane, at ease with everyone and everything. He was *sexy*; women wanted to be with him. Whereas she, on the other hand, was a plain, mousy frump; the most exciting thing she ever did was go round to Ginny's of an evening. And she was so far from sexy it was a joke. Of course he wouldn't have been interested in her; anyone with half a brain could see that. How had she let her romantic imagination get so out of control? Was she so pathetically desperate to find her own Prince Charming that she couldn't see logic and reason?

She'd even been deluded enough to think John might be falling in love with her! But actually, his love was for sale; his embraces could be booked by whoever waved their credit card. The kisses that had felt so magical now seemed dirty. She'd have been just another pair of lips to him, with the same taste as half the other women in the city. Why on earth would she be special, when he had so many other women – elegant, sophisticated, *experienced* women – to compare her with? How could she possibly compete?

Miserably, she wrapped her cardigan more tightly around her.

But what had John been playing at? What had she been to him exactly? She couldn't help but torture herself as the movie soundtrack swelled and the happy couple fell into each other's arms. An amusing diversion? A strange experiment? Some sick kind of bet? Had someone – Sheryl, maybe – been paying him from the start, getting him to string the sad little matchmaker-spinster along so everyone could have a good laugh? Or maybe Ginny had been right. Maybe she did have something in common with Audrey after all ... a one-sided crush on a man too polite to spell things out.

Whatever the answer, one thing was clear: it was over. She and John were over. If Audrey wanted him, she could have him.

And if *that* was settled, then something else became obvious too. Finishing with John sucked. And of all the many reasons *why* it sucked, it sucked most because it was *she* who'd been such a sucker. She'd brought this misery upon herself by getting carried away with her own sugar-coated imagination, she told herself harshly as yet another set of movie credits rolled. Ginny had told her she was daft to think a knight on a white charger solved anything. Well, she needed to stop dreaming, get her head out of the clouds and live in the real world. What kind of grown woman still believed in happy endings anyway? Life wasn't like that. Ginny had warned her that she might get to kiss the frog only to find out that he was nothing more than that: just a frog. Well, she'd kissed her frog and now she'd learnt her lesson. From now on she, Alice Brown, was going to be practical. All that love stuff was for other people: her clients, not her. She obviously couldn't handle it.

She lifted her chin and tried to jut it out defiantly, just as she'd seen her boss do so many times before. Yes, she needed to become hard-headed. Maybe Sheryl was right after all. Maybe love really was just a business and she was just a businesswoman. Love wasn't something to do on your own time, on evenings and at weekends. If she could just stick to Sheryl's way of thinking, she'd be OK. John and her broken heart and smashed dreams wouldn't matter. Life would go on, and in a few weeks' time she'd be perfectly fine. After all, she had been before – before the ball and the flowers and the coffee shop. She'd have her friends, her job and her garden; that was all she needed. Life would be settled . . . safe. She tried to ignore the fact that the dazzling, colourful world John had opened up to her had suddenly switched back to grey.

After a weekend of miserable self-flagellation and pep talks, it had been a relief to come back to work. But now she was here – surrounded by hope and romance – it didn't feel like much of a refuge.

And then Maurice Lazenby arrived without an appointment.

Despite the mildness of the day, Maurice was dressed for the cold, his coat fully buttoned and his scarf folded neatly around his neck as though his mother had dressed him. Beneath his immaculately combed hair and the perfect white line of his parting, his face was as wintry as his attire.

'Miss Brown,' he complained, 'I put my misgivings aside and went to the three lunch dates you organized for me. I met that scruffy artist woman who looked as if she'd just rolled out of bed. And the coarse lady taxi driver who kept trying to engage me about sport. The head teacher was passable, but not what I'm looking for. So you've failed.'

Already feeling weakened, Alice was shocked. She'd been so positive that one of her matches for Maurice would be perfect – but her judgement was obviously failing all round. She'd thought she knew about people – she'd prided herself on seeing people's true characters, on getting the *real them* – but it was becoming clear that she knew nothing at all.

'I don't know what to say. You really didn't like *any* of them?'

'No.'

'But they were different from the other women you've been matched with? More individualistic?'

'Well, yes. But they still weren't right, and that's all that matters.'

'Of course. But I thought . . . I was so sure . . . It's just that I'm . . .'

'Wrong! Again!'

'. . . sorry,' Alice finished softly, looking forlorn.

'Look,' Maurice offered, 'you seem like a nice girl, and I can see you gave me more consideration than most.' He looked critically around the office. 'But the point is, you haven't found me the woman I'm after, and so you leave me with no option.'

'Oh, Maurice . . .'

'I really must insist on being handled by Ms Cracknell. She's the expert. I need to be her personal responsibility.'

'But please, I . . .'

'No, really, Miss Brown. The time for buts is over. Ah, I see Ms Cracknell's in her office. Well, in which case, there's no time like the present . . .'

If it was possible, Alice's battered heart sank even deeper. Audrey was irritated by interruptions at the best of times. But her standard irritation turned to bad-tempered alarm when she saw Maurice striding into her office. She threw Alice a murderous look through the glass. But then she regained her composure and Alice heard her say, 'Maurice! How marvellous to see you!' in a tone that sounded fractionally genuine. And then Maurice closed the glass door behind him.

Alice bent her head and watched them through her lashes. This was a disaster. In fact, her whole life was a disaster. Everything she'd thought about everyone was wrong, and now, to cap it all, Maurice was giving Audrey both barrels. If the circumstances hadn't been so bad she might have found the sight of Audrey being royally ticked off funny; she'd never seen Audrey fail to get a word in edgeways before. But this was bad. Very bad. Audrey might be taking the punishment now, but the minute Maurice left, she'd be sure to punish Alice harder. She'd be furious with her for getting her accosted like this, and Alice didn't know whether – today of all days – she was strong enough to take it.

She grabbed her mobile and texted Ginny.

Are you back? Really need to talk . . .

And then Audrey's glass door swung open.

Alice straightened in her seat, tried to force her face into a bright, professional smile, and ignored the sick feeling creeping up from her stomach.

AUDREY

Maurice finally left. Audrey shut the door behind him and closed her eyes in relief. That man really was unbearable, with his petty moaning and search for a perfection that didn't exist. And even if such a perfect woman did exist, she'd hardly stoop as low as Maurice. But most annoying of all was that somehow, in the middle of his diatribe, Audrey had agreed to take on his case herself. She couldn't believe she'd done it! Maybe it was the professional flattery he'd been piling on, or maybe it was just to get him out of her sight as quickly as possible. Whatever, it was a complete disaster. As if life wasn't appalling enough with John refusing to take her dates, she'd just banged a nail into her own coffin by condemning herself to regular – and no doubt lengthy – conversations with Maurice Lazenby until she managed to find him a partner. Which realistically would be never.

'Poor you, Audrey,' Bianca called across the office sympathetically. 'That was the worst Mauricing I've ever seen!'

Audrey turned away from the door and targeted her eyes on Alice.

'Alice Brown, are you determined to lose me all my clients?' she asked in a voice that could cut glass. 'Or are you just concentrating on ditching the male ones?'

Bianca and Cassandra let out horrified gasps. Matchmakers would rather ditch their own grandmothers than their male clients.

Alice froze. 'Oh God, has Maurice quit?'

'If he had, it would be down to you,' Audrey sniped. 'Thankfully I was on hand to persuade him to stay.'

Alice slumped in relief, but Audrey thundered on.

'Not only have you upset Mr Lazenby, but I also received notice this morning of another of your dissatisfied clients leaving.'

Alice looked confused.

'But what I don't understand is – what could possibly have prevented you from making a match for an upwardly mobile, perfectly acceptable-looking young man like Steve Walker when we have dozens of desperate women on our books who'd settle for anything?'

'Steve's gone?'

'Yes, Mr Walker's gone! Why would he stay? You weren't sending him on dates!'

Alice squirmed. 'I . . . I had my reasons.'

'I don't give a fig about your reasons! He's a client. You're a matchmaker. You find him women to meet. It's not rocket science!' She was in no mood to be fobbed off. This was serious. Her neck flushed with the seriousness of it all. 'If I've told you once I've told you a thousand times. We have to cherish every single man on our books. They're more valuable than the women. We can afford to lose dozens of them!'

'Actually, I think Steve leaving could be a good thing.'

'Good thing?' Audrey thundered with maximum sarcasm. 'How could it possibly be a "good thing"?'

'I don't think he joined for the right reasons.'

'He joined for £300 and £100 a month. They sound like jolly good reasons to me.'

'But he's had loads of dates. Fifteen! And he didn't want to meet a single one of them again for a second date. Doesn't that strike you as odd?'

'Not especially. You obviously made fifteen poor matches.'

'My matches were good,' Alice asserted with surprising conviction.

'Not good enough,' Audrey shot back.

'I just had a funny feeling about Steve,' Alice offered lamely. 'Something about him made me suspicious, so I phoned all fifteen of his matches to ask them again about their dates. And do you know what? They all said exactly the same thing . . . That the date was going well, that they were flattered by how interested he was in them, and that he seemed incredibly keen. So keen, in fact, that he pushed to go home with every single one of them.'

Alice was clearly waiting for Audrey to be outraged by this news of his ungentlemanly advances, but Audrey was damned if she was going to give her the satisfaction. Instead she growled, 'You're supposed to be a matchmaker, not Miss Bloody Marple. So fifteen matches didn't work? Big deal; match him with fifteen more.'

Alice pushed on.

'. . . And when the ladies said no, he suddenly cooled. By the time I'd phone him the next morning, he'd have cooled so much that he didn't want a repeat date with any of them. Now, doesn't that make you question his motives? Doesn't that make you think he wasn't in this for real? And if he wasn't for real, what about all those women he disappointed?'

Alice's eyes were saucer-large with earnestness. In another world, Audrey thought suddenly, a world with no employment laws, consequences, or staff members to act as witnesses, she would have slapped her.

'So Mr Walker wasn't as keen on your ladies as their vanity led them to believe,' she snarled viciously. 'But what about all the women who now *can't* be set up with him? What about the loss to our male–female ratio? What about the loss to my bank balance? Who am I supposed to set our female clients up with now – *Mr Fresh-bloody-air?*'

Something she said made Alice stand to attention. Through the mist of her rage Audrey could see her studying her peculiarly.

'Are you saying I should have sent Steve on inappropriate dates just to make up the numbers?' she asked strangely.

'What I'm saying, you imbecile, is that Mr Walker was an asset to this agency, and thanks to you, he's gone.'

'Asset?' The bunny nose wrinkled up.

'God, give me strength!' Audrey snorted angrily. 'Have you learnt nothing all these years?'

'I can't make matches I don't believe in,' Alice declared

primly. 'The client has to find love; and if they can't find love, they at least have to learn something about themselves that will help them on their journey.'

'Journey? We're a dating agency, not the path to spiritual bloody enlightenment. And now we're one man down, and everyone's job just got harder.'

Very evenly Alice said, 'I'm sorry, but I can't be held responsible for Steve's unethical behaviour.'

'Just like you can't be held responsible for Maurice barging into my office to complain about yours?' Audrey spat venomously. The more calmly Alice protested her innocence, the more furious Audrey felt. And right now, she felt fit to burst.

'I've been thinking about Maurice as well,' Alice said quietly. 'I don't think anyone we match him with will be good enough for him.'

'So what are you suggesting? That we "lose" him too, just because he won't settle for your shoddy, second-rate matches?' Audrey drew herself up, ready to explode. She'd had enough of Alice Brown with her high ideals and her big eyes and baggy cardigans, her spinster bike, her unbrushed hair and her offensive footwear. She, Audrey Cracknell, was only human, and she'd had as much as any decent person could be expected to take. This was the final straw, the nail in the coffin, the fat lady waddling once too often onto the stage to sing. She felt a well of fury rising in her chest, about to erupt.

'Oh!' came a voice from the other side of the office, diverting Audrey's rage and knocking her off kilter.

'Oh!' said Hilary again. 'Fuck!'

'Shut up, Hilary!' Audrey bellowed irritably. 'I won't tolerate foul language in my office.'

'Sorry, Audrey.' Hilary didn't sound the least bit sorry. She sounded positively excited. 'It's just that, fuck; my waters have just broken!'

Audrey swung towards Hilary in alarm.

'Not here!' she barked. 'Not on the carpet!'

'It's a bit too late for that!' Hilary said cheerfully.

'Right, well . . . Hold the rest in!' Audrey ordered uncertainly. Childbirth was an alien area for her and she suddenly felt out of her depth. But she couldn't let it show – not when the troops were watching.

Hilary's face contorted suddenly in a most unladylike fashion.

'Fucking hell!' she exclaimed inelegantly. 'That was a contraction!'

'Maybe I should call a taxi, take Hilary to hospital?' Alice suggested quietly.

Audrey turned back to face her, rage being jostled for supremacy by panic. She wasn't even sure whether she could claim for the carpet on the insurance.

'Yes, maybe you should,' she managed to utter gracelessly. 'At least if you're out of the office you can't lose any more of my clients.'

She headed towards the sanctuary of her glass-walled office and closed the door. Despite her nightly diet of cop shows and murder whodunnits she'd never been able to stand the sight of blood . . . or semi-naked bodies, come to that. Bodies should remain clothed at all times and birth should happen behind closed doors – not glass ones. She grunted unhappily and tried to ignore the sight of Alice helping Hilary out of her sodden tights.

KATE

Kate landed sweatily on the bed, her cheeks flushed and her hair a mess. She swiftly pulled the sheet over herself and set about catching her breath.

'That,' panted Tommy, 'was brilliant!' He rolled over towards her and drew her close with a strong, sweaty arm. 'You're hot stuff, Miss Biggs!'

Kate grinned. Nobody had ever called her hot stuff before. But then again, nobody had ever made her *feel* like hot stuff before.

'And I'm liking this sweaty look,' Tommy teased, letting his hand slide over her wet skin. 'It's very next season.'

She laughed.

Tommy brushed her hair away from her face with his fingertips and looked at her closely. She felt herself tingle at the gentle firmness of his touch.

'You're beautiful,' he said softly.

Shyly Kate's eyes met his. She was surprised by how tenderly he was looking at her.

She hadn't expected to jump into bed with Tommy so quickly. She'd broken her six-date rule. Years ago she'd decided it wasn't good to have sex too early; women who gave out too soon never made the transition from a 'bit of fun' to a girl-friend. In her twenties, ending a night out with drunken, pornographic sex with a random stranger was almost the law. But taking your clothes off in front of a stranger had never been Kate's idea of a good time, and imposing the six-date rule had been a relief. However, she hadn't anticipated that the consequence would be almost no sex at all. The few men she did meet had all melted away by a fruitless date three.

Also, Kate thought as she nestled happily into Tommy's warm body, she hadn't expected sex with Tommy to be quite so good. It had been so long since she'd had it, she'd almost forgotten what it was like. She had memories of awkward encounters in squalid bachelor bedrooms; quick, unsatisfying fumbles that ended with her partner spent and snoring and Kate creeping to the bathroom to floss her teeth and smooth down her hair before positioning herself prettily on the pillow and dreaming of being brought breakfast in bed. When morning came, her hungover partner barely remembered where his own kitchen was, let alone served up coffee and croissants.

But tonight, with Tommy, everything felt different. They'd had such a great time at the comedy club. And in the taxi, any thought of going back to her place hadn't even crossed her mind.

And then there'd been the sex itself. When Tommy had pulled away her shirt she'd felt a succession of tiny elec-tric shocks as his naked skin brushed against hers and her body suddenly ached to be touched again. She'd forgotten just how good skin on skin felt – how dizzyingly erotic. As he gently pulled her half-naked body to his chest, she'd almost lost her breath. She could have let him slowly touch her skin with his all night.

But of course she hadn't. Things had gone much further than that. And in the candlelit bedroom she'd been unembarrassed about her naked body. Tommy's own body was so manly and muscular, she hadn't worried that her hips might be too wide, that her weight might crush him, or that he might change his mind and send her home when he saw the size of her bottom. She actually felt sexy! Tommy ran his hands through her hair and bit at her breasts, his big hands cupping her buttocks and smoothly lifting her up and onto him. His groan of appreciation made Kate feel foxy for the first time in her life. A thought suddenly entered her head. This must be what Lou felt like when she had sex. No wonder she did it so often.

She suddenly fell back to earth with a bang. As Tommy stroked her face and the sweat started to dry on her body, Kate felt something sink within her stomach.

She hadn't spoken to Lou since their argument. Lying in Tommy's bed with his arms wrapped around her, Kate suddenly felt lonely. Normally if something great happened she rang Lou straightaway. It was as though it hadn't really happened until she'd told her every tiny detail.

Kate looked at Tommy, her body still tingling deliciously from their exertions. She knew she wouldn't be telling Lou about this. Something had changed and there was no going back.

'I don't normally do this sort of thing,' she heard herself whisper.

'What, have sex?' Tommy joked.

'No! Yes! I mean, I don't normally, you know, *do it* so soon.'

Tommy looked confused.

'Not until the sixth date.'

'Why?' he spluttered.

'Because nice girls don't . . . too soon.'

Tommy threw back his head and roared with laughter. 'And that's what men want, is it? Nice girls?'

'No!' Kate said primly. 'They want bad girls who do it on the first night.'

Tommy propped himself up on an elbow and looked at her closely.

'So, you're saying that your strategy with men has been *not* to give them what they want?'

'They get it eventually,' Kate reasoned. 'Men respect women who make them wait. And besides, things are better if you've looked forward to them. It's delayed gratification.'

'It's why you've stayed single!' Tommy laughed. 'Kate, trust me; men aren't that complicated! We've got the attention spans of goldfish. If we wait too long for anything we've forgotten what it was we wanted in the first place. It's why we love our TV remotes so much. Otherwise, by the time we'd got as far as the telly, we'd have forgotten why we got up in the first place.'

Kate felt confused.

'But if you really wanted someone, you wouldn't forget

her,' she insisted. 'You'd want her more because you'd had to wait.'

'You're mad!' Tommy laughed and rolled away. 'You *do* know that, don't you?'

Kate's face froze. She panicked. She'd given away her body too soon, and now she looked an idiot by giving away too much of her mind.

'Have I blown it?' she asked nervously.

'Don't I have to wait for the seventh date for that?'

'Oi!' Kate laughed and punched him with her pillow.

'It's just as well I've always had a thing for nutty girls, isn't it?' Tommy teased, stretching out across the bed and pulling Kate towards him. 'Especially nutty girls who give out so quickly.'

And he wrestled her into a hug.

ALICE

Alice opened her front door and placed her keys in the dish. It was half past midnight and she was utterly shattered.

It had been a draining few days. As she'd held Hilary's hand in the delivery suite, shouting words of encouragement and supporting her as best she could until her husband, Kevin, could find a babysitter and make it to the hospital, she'd managed to forget the sleepless nights of the weekend just passed. She had a new and powerful burst of energy that pushed aside all thoughts of John and his double life and the aching gap he'd left behind. She'd been a pillar of positivity as she praised, roused and rallied her friend. But by the time the baby was crowning and Kevin arrived, Alice started to back out of the room.

'Oi, where do you think you're going?' Hilary demanded fiercely, breaking away from her gas-and-air and eyeballing Alice like a woman demented.

'I thought I'd give you and Kevin some privacy . . .'

'Privacy my arse! You've already spent the last couple of hours peering up my lady bits. You might as well stay to see me shit myself, cry like a schoolgirl and pop this enormous bastard!' Hilary bellowed.

Realizing that she was no match for a woman in labour, Alice stayed and joined Kevin in holding Hilary's hand though the last few minutes of labour and having all the bones in their fingers crushed by the primeval force of Mother Nature at work. And when Kevin held his brand-new baby boy, father and son blinking at each other in bewildered recognition, Alice sat back and smiled her first real smile in days. But when an exhausted Hilary tenderly took her son to her chest and kissed the top of his waxy head, something suddenly switched itself on in Alice's head, with a click so loud she couldn't believe that the nurses couldn't hear it. Everything suddenly made sense. Here, in this room, was what life was all about: partnership, childbirth, family. This was what really mattered. But this was what she was never going to have.

Hilary and Kevin were too happy to notice the light dying in Alice's smile. She stayed with the besotted parents a few more minutes and then discreetly slipped out of the room.

As she fell into a taxi, she couldn't hold the tears at bay any more. She sobbed indiscriminately, alarming the taxi driver with her barely concealed wails. She cried for Hilary and Kevin and the baby. And she cried for herself and for John, and for the future she'd lost and the dreams she'd had shattered. And she cried for Kate and her determination to find Mr Right and have kids. She'd never thought about having children before; there'd never been a man in her life to have them with. But could that have been her and John one day in the delivery suite, just like Hilary and Kevin? Would they have made it that far? Could they still?

She pulled her phone from her pocket and scrolled through her texts until she found the one from Ginny.

Trust your instincts, Alice, it said *They've never been wrong before.*

The trouble was, she didn't know what her instincts were any more.

For the first time she wondered if she'd made a mistake in walking away from John and out of the restaurant. Maybe she should have heard him out, been open-minded, given things a go? Maybe she'd have got used to spending nights in on her own, waiting for him to come back from his dates with other women. Maybe, in the end, she'd have got used to the sharing. But no: in her heart she knew she never could. Some women might; they could be cool and rational and dispassionate about his job. But not Alice. Not the romanceaholic. She had far too active an imagination for that. Every time John left for work her mind would send her to hell and back.

Back in her flat she pulled off her coat and made her way to the kitchen, not bothering to turn on the lights. The curtains were still open and the full moon lit up the room. She filled the kettle and sat down at the kitchen table, exhausted. She was asleep before the kettle boiled.

KATE

Kate woke to something hard pressing on her tummy. Blearily she opened her eyes a fraction, blinking at the sunlight. She was confused; her bedroom didn't get any morning sun. But as her eyes forced themselves open, Tommy's bedroom came into view. She suddenly remembered where she was. And she suddenly remembered how she always woke up with totally terrible morning breath.

'Morning, gorgeous!' Tommy was sitting on the bed looking right at her. 'I thought you might like this.'

'Hi,' Kate croaked, trying not to breathe out. She tried to remember where the bathroom was. Maybe Tommy would have some mouthwash. She sat up.

'Ah-ah!' Tommy cried out in warning, lifting a tray from Kate's shifting tummy. A breakfast tray. 'Watch the coffee! I thought you might like the fresh stuff. If I'd known I was having a guest I'd have got croissants in. But I didn't, so you'll have to make do with boiled egg and soldiers.'

'Boiled egg and soldiers sounds great,' Kate mumbled happily from behind her hand.

Tommy leaned forward, lowered Kate's hand and kissed

her on the mouth. She grinned. He really did look gorgeous this morning in his boxer shorts and nothing else. The sun warmed his dark brown hair, lit up the bits of stubble on his face and made his eyes glitter. She looked at the sheen of the sunlight as it hit the muscles in his arms and danced on the hairs on his chest. She felt like hugging herself with happiness. Two weeks ago she didn't even know this fantastic man existed; and now here she was, waking up in his bedroom, having amazing sex flashbacks and being served breakfast in bed.

'I could get used to this,' she smiled happily.

Tommy stretched out beside her, putting one arm around her shoulders whilst with the other he helped himself to toast.

'Couldn't have put it better myself,' he grinned. 'I think I'm going to like this having-a-girlfriend malarkey.'

Kate's egg soldier stopped halfway between her plate and her mouth.

'So I'm your girlfriend now, am I?' she joked. Her body felt on high alert for his answer.

'Isn't it my duty to save you from the world of organized dating, with sharks like Steve chatting you up, peering down your shirt and plying you with gin and tonics?' he grinned.

'Well, when you put it like that . . .'

'I'm just doing the gentlemanly thing.'

'. . . it sounds like a tempting offer.'

'What kind of man would I be if I just walked on by and left a damsel in distress? And Steve's enough to cause considerable distress. And you're quite some damsel!'

'That's so romantic!'

'That's me! The romance king! Haven't you heard? We credit information salesmen are romance's best-kept secret. You've got to pity those poor misguided women who find themselves saddled with boring, yacht-owning billionaires. They're missing out on so much!'

'Breakfast in bed, for starters.'

'Exactly!'

And then Kate said something she never thought she'd hear herself say.

'You know, breakfast in bed is all the romance I need.'

And she smiled happily at him.

'Good, well, that's sorted then!' Tommy sealed the deal with a long, lingering kiss that made Kate's stomach flip and her knees go wobbly even though she was lying down in bed.

'Eat up, girlfriend!' he laughed when he eventually came up for air. 'Skinny minnies get thrown back to the sharks!'

AUDREY

Audrey breezed through the doors of Table For Two, a smile playing on her lips. For the second day in a row there was no sign of Alice's bike, no eyesore to get the day off to a bad start. Audrey felt her spirits lift. She knew she should have taken her handbag to it years ago.

But although Alice's bike was absent, sadly Alice wouldn't be. She'd still be polluting the office with her moon face and bobbly jumper. *And* Audrey was now burdened with the headache of managing the online dating service, thanks to the unexpectedly early start to Hilary's maternity leave. *And* John still hadn't got in touch. But at least the bike was gone. It was a tiny glimmer of sunshine in her otherwise battleship-grey sky.

And then she noticed a man in Alice's seat. It was Max Higgert, her classiest client.

'Ms Cracknell,' he greeted her apologetically. 'I'm sorry to startle you. Bianca let me in. I was just, er. Well, I was just writing a quick note. For, ah, my mother. Whilst I waited for you.'

Audrey saw him slip a folded piece of pale-blue paper

into his pocket. Just behind him was the damp patch where Hilary's waters had broken yesterday. She hoped Max hadn't noticed. What if it smelt? What if the aroma of the amniotic fluid of one of her staff members had troubled Max's sensitive architect nostrils? And she'd left such strict instructions to the cleaner that the stain should be tackled with every disinfectant on the market.

'It's always a pleasure to see you!' she cried. 'Do come into my office.' She tried to usher him away from the damp patch.

'No, I'm afraid it's just a flying visit,' Max said apologetically, not moving. 'I just called in to say thank you and goodbye.'

'Goodbye? Whatever for?'

Max grinned, suddenly looking like a little boy who'd just found a pound. 'I'm taking myself off your books!'

'But . . .' Audrey started. Did this have something to do with Alice? she thought with a sudden fury. Is that why he'd been sitting at her desk?

'I'm delighted to say that Table For Two has another success on its hands!' Max beamed.

'We do?'

'Hayley!'

'Hayley?'

'Hayley Clarke. You matched me with her. Five foot four, blonde hair, a smile that lights up the room? The veterinary nurse?'

'With the funny finger?'

'Er, yes, I suppose so.'

'So it worked?' Audrey tried not to sound incredulous. 'You and the veterinary nurse?' She couldn't believe a man of Max's standing would be happy with a woman like that. She'd only made such a ridiculous match in the first place because Bianca had begged her to.

'Worked? That's an understatement!' Max laughed happily. 'Hayley's the most wonderful woman I've ever met. I feel like I've won the Lottery!'

'Oh!'

'I can't thank you enough.' Max beamed. 'I've met the woman for me!'

'Well, that's wonderful,' Audrey said gruffly, 'but are you sure you wouldn't like me to set you up with a few more dates? It's just that we have so many' – she managed to stop herself saying 'better' – '. . . *other* women interested in meeting you. I'm sure you'd find them quite delightful.'

'And I'm sure they are! But they couldn't be half as delightful as Hayley. Anyway, I just popped in to say thank you and to ask you to remove me from your books. I think Hayley has already had a word with Alice and done the necessary with her.'

'I'll bet she has,' Audrey flashed darkly.

'So, thank you and goodbye.' Max held out his hand.

'What, that's it?' Audrey blurted. 'You've only just joined! We have a minimum membership period of three months, you know. I couldn't possibly give you a refund.'

Max broke into a hearty laugh.

'Every penny I spent finding Hayley was worth a thousand

more. I'm very grateful. I wouldn't dream of asking for any money back!'

And he turned and left, leaving Audrey open-mouthed in the middle of the office. She couldn't believe such a prize male client was leaving so soon. She'd hoped to spread him around her lady clients for another few months at least. And why on earth was he settling for a two-bit piece of council-estate fluff like Hayley the veterinary nurse when there were so many nice Penelope Huffingtons and Hermione Bolton-Kings around? Men were such fools. They didn't know what was good for them.

She turned and headed into her office, cursing herself for not having had the presence of mind to ask him to recommend Table For Two to his single architect friends. They were just the kind of men she needed on her books. She didn't notice the pale-blue square of paper that Max had slipped back onto Alice's desk.

ALICE

'Well?'

Bianca and Cassandra were peering at her in excited anticipation.

'A boy!' Alice smiled triumphantly, letting the office door swing closed behind her. 'A beautiful, bouncing, perfect baby boy!'

Bianca and Cassandra whooped in noisy celebration whilst Audrey nodded, pursed her lips and retreated into her glass-walled office.

'Good old Hilary!' Bianca cheered. 'She's finally given Kevin an ally in a house full of women! How many daughters does she have?'

'Two!' Alice pulled off her coat. 'And according to her last night, there won't be three. She told Kevin she'd sue if he ever came near her again!'

'She says that now . . .!' Cassandra laughed.

Alice sagged down into her seat, exhausted but trying to let herself be buoyed by the infectious good news.

'What's this?' she asked, holding up Max's note.

The girls shrugged and turned away. She opened it.

Dear Alice,

You're a genius! I don't know what you said to Audrey, but the very next date she sent me on was perfect! It was with Hayley Clarke and I'm smitten – head-over-heels, taken-leave-of-my-senses smitten! Thank you so much for getting Audrey to see the kind of woman I really wanted. Both Hayley and I are eternally grateful.

Max Higgert

Alice closed her eyes and held the note to her chest. She felt tears prickle the insides of her eyelids. *She wasn't wrong.* She wasn't losing her marbles after all. She'd been right to go out on a limb. She'd made a match: a brilliant match. She'd helped two people find love. She suddenly felt weak with relief.

'Yeah, hello?' a voice cut across the office.

Alice opened her eyes. A young woman – a beautiful young woman – was standing by the door.

'Table For Two, right?' she addressed the room.

Out of the corner of her eye Alice saw Audrey stir in her glass office. She could see why; the woman was certainly eye-catching. She was classically beautiful, like a pre-Raphaelite painting, yet at the same time totally modern, in a trenchcoat and sparkly trainers. She had a sprinkle of unseasonal freckles across her perfect English complexion, and a mane of untamed auburn hair. Everyone in the office sat up. If she was a new client, they all wanted her on their books.

Audrey moved first, like a speeding bullet.

'Yes, yes, this is Table For Two. Please, step this way. Do come and take a seat in my office. I take it you're here to find love? I'm the agency owner; delighted to meet you. Would you like a cup of coffee? *Cassandra . . . kettle!*'

But the young woman didn't move a muscle. Instead she eyed Audrey up and down.

'You . . .' she said, her voice brimming with disdain, '. . . have *got* to be Audrey.'

Audrey paused mid-ushering.

'Er, yes. Yes, I am.'

She looked bamboozled. The whole office looked on in bafflement.

The woman gave a little nod as though confirming something to herself.

'That figures,' she said curtly. 'No, not you.'

There was a sharp collective intake of breath. Nobody ever spoke to Audrey like that. Audrey's cheeks flushed as though slapped.

But the young woman was scanning the room, scrutinizing the other women. 'I want Alice,' she declared loudly. 'Word is, she's the best.'

Suddenly, all possible sound seemed to be sucked out of the room. Cassandra's eyebrows rose to her hairline and Bianca's mouth froze in a noiseless 'oh'. Andrey stood as silent as the grave. Slowly, falteringly, Alice scraped back her chair and rose to her feet.

'I'm Alice,' she said quietly, instinctively wrapping her cardigan around her for protection. But the young woman's face suddenly cracked into a delicious grin.

'Brilliant! Can I have a quick word?'

For a moment, Alice was too dumbstruck to move. Who was this woman, and why had she dismissed Audrey like that? And more importantly – *how had she had the bottle?* But then Bianca coughed discreetly and Alice stumbled into action. She ignored the weight of Audrey's injured stare, and led the young woman into the interview room, carefully closing the door behind them.

The young woman looked around the room.

'This the heartbreak room, is it?' She grinned and pointed at the box of tissues that sat on the table between the two wicker chairs.

'Some people find it difficult talking about who they want to meet, especially if they've been looking for a long ...' Alice explained on autopilot before nervously petering out. The woman was examining her keenly.

'Yes,' the young woman confirmed, clearly pleased with something she'd seen. 'You're just as he described you.' And she sat down.

Alice felt herself blush. Just as who'd described her? And why had this woman asked for her specifically?

'Look, I'm sorry,' she said, as she sat in the remaining free seat. 'I'm confused. Are you interested in joining Table For Two?'

'God, no!' the woman laughed. 'I'm not here to be matchmade ... I'm here to matchmake you!'

'Sorry?' Alice almost choked.

The woman sighed.

'Men ... They can be right muppets sometimes, can't

they? All very good at the tricky stuff like fan belts and rewiring. But when it comes to the simple stuff . . . like *talking* . . . they're rubbish! All these years of evolution and they still can't quite get the hang of opening their mouths and making the right words come out.'

Alice's brain was whirring nineteen to the dozen. What was she talking about?

'Particularly my dad,' the young woman continued.

'Your dad?'

'Yeah, you know him. Blue eyes, greying hair; kind fella. Quite handsome, I suppose, if I think about it.'

'John . . .' The word escaped Alice's mouth like a whisper. Could she really mean John? Was this . . . was this *John's daughter*? She looked about the right age, and she was certainly beautiful enough to be his. '*Emily?*' she asked.

'The very same!' Emily grinned. She wriggled forward in her seat, her voice softening. 'Look, Alice, I'm sorry to barge in on you at work, but I had to do something. Dad would totally freak if he knew I was here, but hey, I'm twenty-three; it's not like he can ground me! And you know better than anyone that sometimes love needs a helping hand. The thing is, I love my Dad, and I want him to be happy – and he thinks you're the woman to do it. It's too bloody frustrating just to sit back and watch him mess everything up. He can't help it; he's just a bit . . . out of practice.'

'Out of practice?'

'With women.'

Despite herself, Alice couldn't help but raise a watery smile.

'I'm sure that's not strictly true.'

'Yeah ... look, about the women ... I know about the other night, and what he told you ...'

Alice blushed and dropped her eyes to her lap.

'Sounds like he made a right balls-up of it,' Emily declared bluntly. 'But it's what he *didn't* tell you that was the important stuff. I don't blame you if you want to run a mile in the opposite direction. Christ, I would! I'd be imagining all sorts of things, and most of them disgusting. But trust me: Dad's not what you're thinking.'

'But he's ...' Alice started, and then quickly stopped herself. What should she say? She didn't want to be rude about his profession in front of his daughter.

'... an escort; yeah, I know.' Emily decided for her. 'And I know that if I were you I'd be reckoning that "escort" is just big fat code for "rent boy".'

Again, Alice found herself blushing. It was as though Emily had peered into her head and read out her thoughts. John had been right: she *was* as wise as the hills.

'Well, I'm guessing that's another thing he wasn't quite clear about,' Emily continued. 'Trust me, if Dad was a rent boy, he'd have been made redundant within the week. I don't think abstinence is on the job description.'

'Abstinence?' Alice momentarily forgot her awkwardness and stared at Emily in confusion.

'Look, I know I'm just a complete stranger who's gatecrashed your work, but could I ask you a really big favour?' Emily was looking at her earnestly. 'If he tries to explain, would you hear him out? Please? And then, if you still want to run a mile, fair enough. But – sisterhood solidarity and all that – I wouldn't ask you to give him a chance if I didn't think he was one of life's good guys. There are plenty of crap men out there, but I promise you, my dad isn't one of them.'

Alice wrestled with herself. She was naturally hard-wired to make others happy, and always preferred to tell people 'yes' rather than 'no'. And goodness knows, her heart wanted her to tell Emily yes. But she caught herself. She remembered her weekend resolution. She *had* to stop listening to her heart; her heart only got her into trouble. She needed to remember her head.

'I want to believe you, I really do,' she said awkwardly. 'But he's your dad; you're bound to say good things about him. And I have to protect myself. I can't let myself be made a fool of any more.'

'Listen, Alice' – Emily was looking at her kindly – 'I know you don't want to get hurt … *more* hurt,' she corrected herself. 'But ask yourself this. Deep down – in your core – you *know* Dad would never want to make a fool out of anyone, don't you? And he especially wouldn't want to make a fool out of you.'

Alice squirmed. She couldn't look at Emily. Instead she tried to concentrate on the pointed, piercing pain of the last few days, the crush of disappointment in her chest that had made it so hard for her to breathe, and the horrible taste that flooded her mouth whenever she thought about John's job.

Emily got up to go.

'He's totally nuts about you, you know,' she said softly. And then she closed the door gently behind her.

LOU

'For fuck's sake, Lou!' Tony exploded. 'Whaddya mean you're not coming in? We've got that Premiership club party tonight – their in-house do; all blokes, no WAGs. I need all hands on deck, and more specifically, I need *you* behind the bar in something low-cut. How else am I going to keep sixty testosterone-pumped blokes happy?'

Sitting on her sofa in her oldest dressing gown with a coffee stain on the front, Lou gripped the telephone tightly. 'I told you, Tony; *I'm ill.* And I'm a deputy bar manager, not a stripper!' Tony was unbelievable. There was no way Julian would ever speak to Kate like this. Perfect little Kate. *Perfect little Kate who'd probably never thrown a sickie in her whole disciplined little life.* Christ only knew why she ever moaned about *her* boss. Julian paid her by the truckload and never expected *her* to whore it for the clients. 'You *have* booked them a stripper, haven't you?' she quizzed her own boss sceptically.

'Of course I've booked them a fucking stripper!' Tony snapped, sounding less than convincing. 'But that's not the fucking point. Suze and the kids are staying at her sister's tonight. I thought you could nip round to that sex shop, buy yourself that nurse's outfit. I was going to film us on the CCTV before we opened up; thought we could watch it back in the office later; have a little X-rated lock-in after we've sent the rabble home. But if you can't be bothered to come in . . .'

'Tony, *I'm ill!*'

'*And I'm horny!* Christ, Lou; if I'd known you were going to be this much hassle I'd never have bothered . . .'

'You've *ever* bothered . . . ?' Lou interjected sharply. 'I must have missed that.'

It was no wonder she was skiving off. Tony wasn't the most nurturing of employers and pulling pints (or Tony, come to that) was hardly worth getting out of bed for. She just wasn't up for it today. She couldn't be arsed to be sociable. That was the trouble with her job – you had to be pleasant with the punters, and since her run-in with Kate, pleasant was something Lou definitely wasn't. There was no way on God's earth she was going to cover herself in slap, drag herself to work and smile for the morons today.

'I don't know what's got into you lately,' Tony was rattling on. 'You're so mardy; and you were as frigid as a nun's tit the other night. Christ . . . !' Lou could practically hear the creak as Tony's brain turned over. 'You're not bloody pregnant, are you? You'd better not be; that'd be a total fucking disaster. Suze'd crucify me.'

'No, Tony,' Lou said grimly. 'I'm not pregnant.'

'Oh, thank fuck for that!' He sounded almost limp with relief.

'I've got the flu. The doctor told me to rest for a week. I'll be back in on Monday.'

'*Monday?* But we're showing the football tomorrow! You know what it's like – we'll be packed to the roof. And what about the stag we've got booked for Saturday? Jake and Paul'll never cope.'

'Jake and Paul will cope just great. And thanks for your concern. Great managerial skills, Tone . . . Really, the best!'

Lou hung up the phone and tossed it across the room. She was sick of Tony and she was sick of Kate. Well, they could both stuff it. She had a packet of fags, two bottles of red and hours of daytime TV stretching before her. As far as she was concerned, the world could take a running jump.

ALICE

'Oh my God, it's so good to see you!' A pale-faced Alice threw her arms around her friend and embraced her on the rain-soaked doorstep.

A few minutes later Alice and Ginny were sitting, tea in hand, in the warm kitchen, Ginny's coat drying on the side. Several packets of biscuits lay on the table between them.

'How long can you stay?' Alice hoped she didn't sound as desperate as she felt.

'As long as you like!' came Ginny's heavenly reply. 'When you said you'd taken a day's holiday, I knew it had to be an emergency; normally wild horses wouldn't keep you from your clients. So I've left Scarlet with a babysitter. It's part of our new regime: more quality time with adults!'

'New regime?' Even though Alice felt lower than she'd ever remembered feeling, the faintest whiff of positive progress in the Ginny/Dan situation instantly lifted her. 'So, how did your weekend away with Dan go?'

'Good!' Ginny laughed happily. 'We talked . . . a lot. And drank . . . a lot! And then we cried a bit, and then we shagged . . . *a lot!*'

'Well, that's great, isn't it?'

'God, yes! We hadn't done it for a while ... any of it! I think that was the problem.'

'And how do you feel now?'

'Better. We both do. It made us realize we both want to make the marriage work; not for Scarlet's sake, but for our own! So we've decided to go to Relate. Our marriage is precious, and if we're going to fix it we're going to fix it properly; a quick papering over the cracks won't do. We're in this for the long haul.'

'Wow, well done; that sounds like the perfect plan.'

'Cheers! Well, it's about time we started acting like grown-ups!' Ginny grinned and bit into a biscuit. 'Oh, and talking of growing up, I've realized something: *you* were right and I was wrong.'

'I doubt that,' Alice said sadly. She couldn't remember the last time she'd felt right about anything. In the last few weeks, everything she thought she knew about life had been stood on its head.

'I *am* lucky to have Dan,' Ginny continued earnestly. 'And the sun *does* shine out of his backside; I just got distracted and stopped being able to see it! In fact, whilst we were away I decided to take a leaf out of your book.'

'*My* book?'

'Yes: I'm going to start believing in happy-ever-afters!' Ginny was too evangelical to notice Alice's stricken expression.

'Really?'

'Why not? Self-fulfilling prophecies and all that. Isn't it better karma to believe good things are going to happen?'

Alice's lip trembled. She saw Ginny's radiant smile and had to look away. 'It's just . . . I'm not sure mine is the best advice to be taking,' she said weakly. 'My book's had a bit of a rewrite since you've been away.'

'What do you mean? Are you saying the great Alice Brown no longer believes in happy endings?' Ginny joked. But then she saw her friend's face and the penny slowly dropped. 'No! No way! That's not allowed. If *you* don't keep the faith, how are the rest of us supposed to? You not believing in love is like tea without biscuits, or snow in the summer. Is this why you've taken a day's leave?'

And so Alice told her everything, from John's confession to Emily's surprise visit. As she spoke, the day grew darker, the rain got heavier and the girls' tea went cold.

'Well . . .' Ginny said shakily when Alice finally finished speaking. Alice could see she was shocked. 'You've always said nobody's perfect!' she offered limply.

'I don't mind him not being perfect. I just never thought he'd be a . . .' – she hesitated, hating to say it out loud – 'a *rent boy*.' And she hadn't. Of all the thousands of different Prince Charming scenarios Alice's imagination had vividly conjured, she'd never pictured her man dating other women for money.

'He's not a rent boy; he's an escort.'

'Same thing,' Alice replied miserably.

'Is it?' Ginny mulled it over. 'I'm not an expert on all this rent-a-man stuff, but surely what he said isn't out of the realms of possibility?'

'What do you mean?' Alice was astounded. She'd

expected Ginny to tell her to forget John and his very existence. She hadn't expected her to mount the case for the defence.

'Well, there've got to be some women who *do* just want a pretend partner for the night,' Ginny reasoned. 'I totally get that it could be embarrassing to rock up at certain events single, especially if your ex is going to be there. Why not hire yourself a good-looking man as a bit of armour? It doesn't mean you're going to have sex with him.'

'Doesn't it?'

'No! Besides, I don't think women really go for the paying-for-sex thing. Women want relationships and romance; they want to feel special, for sex to actually *mean* something. You should know that; you know more than anyone about what women want in a man. So why shouldn't there be such a thing as an above-board gentleman escort? Especially nowadays when the whole world's divorced and everything's a "plus one".'

Alice looked out of the window and thought. Ginny did have a point. If all the years of matchmaking had shown her anything, it was that – when you boiled it all down – women wanted love. None of her clients were motivated by sex. Besides, if all they wanted was a one-night stand, wasn't it supposed to be easy? Weren't there millions of men out there looking for a no-strings quickie? Wasn't that why women came to her in the first place – to find someone who was looking for something more?

'Look, Alice,' Ginny said, interrupting her thoughts. 'It's your life. I can't tell you the right thing to do, but I know two things for sure. One: John made you happy, and two: you're never, ever wrong about people.'

Alice bit her lip and looked into her lap.

'Don't you think you should just hear him out?' Ginny asked gently. 'You wouldn't be promising anything; you'd only have to sit and listen.'

Alice frowned to try to keep the tears at bay. Ginny made it sound so easy, but it wasn't. Nothing about it was easy. It was more complicated than a grandmasters' game of chess.

'Besides,' Ginny prodded her, 'didn't you say his daughter was nice?'

Alice nodded. 'Very.'

'There you go: conclusive proof he's telling the truth!' Ginny declared. 'Rent boys can't possibly have nice daughters.'

There was a knock at the door.

With a watery smile, Alice wiped a runaway tear from her cheek and stood up.

'Alice Brown?' asked a man wearing a waterproof coat and an enormous grin. 'These are for you.' And he handed her a supersized bunch of chrysanthemums. Their immaculate white blooms shone in the gloom of the day.

'Thank you.' Alice sniffed in surprise.

'Blimey; who are *they* from?' Ginny asked as Alice returned to the kitchen table.

'I don't know. There's no card.' She examined the flowers. 'Chrysanths . . . they're a bit grannyfied, aren't they? They always remind me of the hats the Queen Mum used to wear.'

'They're beautiful.' Alice immediately leapt to the flowers' defence. 'Simple and unpretentious. They're supposed to symbolize truth and loyalty.'

'And they're yours for £2.99 from any garage forecourt.'

'Not these ones,' Alice said admiringly. 'They're Pavilion chrysanthemums. Look how flawless their petals are. They're brilliant specimens – perfect. They look like they were picked just a minute ago.' As she inspected the flowers she felt herself being sucked in by their gravitational pull. Despite her heavy heart and spin-cycle head, just a few seconds in the presence of nature was all it took for her shoulders to feel a fraction lighter.

'So, they're from John, right?' Ginny asked.

'But how would he know I'm at home?' Alice puzzled.

'How would anyone know you're at home? The only people who know are Audrey and the gang, and I can't exactly see that old trout sending you flowers, even if they *are* old-lady ones!'

Alice's mind was whirring. Could the flowers really be from John? He was the only likely candidate. And if so, should she accept them? Maybe she should run after the delivery man and ask him to take them back? But she looked at the flowers and at the protective way each snowy petal curled inwards as though guarding the middle of the bloom, like the world's most exquisite layer of defence. It would go against her DNA to return them. So instead she put the kettle on and hunted for a vase.

Half an hour and another cup of tea later there was another knock at the door. The same delivery man stood on Alice's doorstep, still wet, still smiling, and this time brandishing a second bunch of flowers.

'For you!' He gave her a bow.

Alice took the bouquet in astonishment. 'Thank you!' she called after him as he retreated up the path, his feet splashing in the puddles as he went.

'More flowers!' Ginny exclaimed as Alice carried a huge bunch of carnations into the kitchen, their petals sprinkled with raindrops. 'And more white! Any card?'

Alice shook her head.

'Must be from a neat-freak,' Ginny surmised knowingly. 'Someone who doesn't like colours messing things up. Either that, or the bloke's got the deliveries muddled and these should be going to a funeral.'

'You *can* send carnations in sympathy,' Alice murmured thoughtfully, 'but that's not their normal meaning.'

'Meaning? Flowers are just flowers, aren't they?'

'Well, yes. But traditionally flowers were symbolic. People understood what each variety stood for, and what it meant if you gave it.'

'Yeah? So what do these mean, then?'

Alice looked at her bouquet. It was a simple arrangement: just plain carnations, surrounded by lush green fern.

'Carnations – or rather, white carnations – are the flower of innocence,' she explained. 'Different colours stand for different things. A striped carnation means a refusal; a yellow one means disappointment. But these are the purest white. And the ferns around them – they mean something too. They're supposed to symbolize sincerity.'

A silence fell on the kitchen as Alice drifted into thoughtful reverie.

'He's not moving,' Ginny said suddenly. She was peering out of the kitchen window into Eversley Road. Alice followed her gaze. Sure enough, the flower delivery man was still there, sitting in his van, the windows beginning to steam up.

'He's probably just programming his satnav for his next delivery.'

'Mmmm, probably.' Ginny wasn't convinced.

And sure enough, five minutes later he still hadn't moved.

'Something tells me you're going to be getting his next delivery.' Ginny frowned.

'Don't be silly. I don't even know who these two are from.'

'Of course you do!' Ginny scoffed.

Twenty minutes later there was another knock at the door. This time both women scurried to answer it.

'Here you go,' the delivery man grinned.

'Definitely for me?' Alice asked in confusion. There was still no card.

'You *are* Alice Brown, aren't you? Yes, definitely for you!'

'OK, Columbo: what do this lot mean?' Ginny pounced the moment the front door was closed.

The women examined the colourful, rustic bouquet.

'Irises are a faith flower,' Alice explained. 'Roughly translated, they mean "Don't give up; have faith".'

'And the little pink ones?' Even Ginny sounded excited.

'They're dogwood,' Alice replied, her eyes beginning to shine. 'Dogwood's all about love and durability. It means something along the lines of *love lasting the distance . . .*' She faltered. Her face began to fill with colour, a soft hue of pink spreading across her cheeks as if in sympathy with the colourful blooms.

Suddenly she shot out of the front door, not bothering to stop and put on her coat. She sploshed along the path and rapped on the van's window. The electric window wound down with a gentle hum.

'But who are they from?' Alice asked breathlessly.

'Can't say,' the delivery man smiled. 'Florist/client confidentiality.'

'Well, why aren't you moving?' she demanded. 'Don't you have other deliveries to make?'

'I'm under strict instructions.'

'Instructions for what?'

'A bouquet – for you – every thirty minutes.'

'Every thirty minutes?' Alice echoed incredulously. 'How many bouquets have you got?'

He checked his sheet. 'Seven.'

Alice's mouth fell open. 'All from the same person?'

The delivery man grinned knowingly.

'Can't you just give the rest to me now?'

He shook his head. 'Strict instructions, remember?'

'So, it's a message from John, right?' Ginny said slowly when Alice returned to the flat. 'He's sending you a love letter, isn't he? A love letter through flowers.'

Alice nodded tightly, too dizzyingly intoxicated with the romance of it to speak. She knew she shouldn't want this, shouldn't let herself be excited, but she couldn't stop herself.

A message through flowers ... it was the most amazing thing she could ever have imagined. It was literally beyond her imagination.

Ginny exhaled noisily. 'I've got to hand it to him; that's seriously classy!'

Half an hour later, Alice rapped on the van window again, this time armed with a cheese sandwich and a mug of tea.

'Here.' She pushed them through the open window. 'If you're going to be out here for the long haul, I might as well make sure you're fed and watered.'

'Cheers!' The delivery man grinned as he took Alice's lunch and placed it on top of the dashboard. He checked his watch. 'Right, well, I'd better sort you out with your next bouquet.'

He got out of the van and opened the back doors, carefully positioning them so Alice couldn't see inside. And then with a flourish he pulled out a single sprig of mistletoe.

'Easy!' Ginny appeared magically at Alice's elbow, her coat held over her head as a makeshift umbrella. 'Even I know this one. He wants a snog!'

'No, that's not it,' Alice's voice was quiet and distant.

'If you don't mind me saying ...' the delivery man interjected with a smile. He was clearly enjoying the floral mystery that was unfolding, '... that's just the idiot's idea of mistletoe; too many Hollywood movies and Christmas cards ... No, what mistletoe really means is ...'

'... *I surmount difficulties*,' Alice finished softly, the rain falling around them.

The delivery man grinned and hopped back into his van.

'So, he's saying he'll beat this; that he'll get you both through it,' Ginny surmised as the girls walked back into the flat and closed the front door behind them. She pointed at the first three bouquets, now arranged in vases and lined up in chronological order along the kitchen worktop. 'First he said he was telling the truth. Then, that he was innocent. And then the third bunch said *Don't give up . . .*'

'. . . *have faith in me*,' Alice interrupted, her voice filling with wonder. '*In us*.' She looked at Ginny wildly. She felt like she was going to burst.

'Boy, has he got your number!' Ginny marvelled. 'He couldn't have thought of a more perfect way to get your attention!'

Half an hour later, the delivery man carried the next bouquet right into the kitchen, along with his empty mug and plate.

'Talk about saying it with flowers!' he grinned as he saw deliveries one to four lined up along the kitchen counter. 'I wish all my clients were like this guy. This blows a dozen red roses out of the water any day!'

But Alice was focused only on the riotous cascade of tiny purple stars he was holding in his hands, her eyes devouring their petals, searching for their meaning.

'I don't know this one!' she cried balefully.

'They're violets,' the delivery man helped out.

'Yes, yes! But what do they mean?'

'Yeah, this one had me stumped too.'

Ginny pulled out her iPhone and quickly started tapping. A minute later they had their answer.

'Another faith flower,' she read out loud.

Alice gasped. 'I remember now. Lovers who would be parted used to give them to each other as a pledge not to play the field.'

The room suddenly went quiet.

'He's saying he's yours, Alice,' Ginny said gently. 'Yours, and only yours.'

Alice made a strange, muffled noise, and turned away.

'I just need a moment,' she said, her voice tight, and she quickly retreated to her bedroom. She had to get away from the flowers; had to remove herself from the lure of their intoxicating powers.

In the quiet gloom of her bedroom, she could hear the muffled sounds of Ginny talking to the delivery man, and the chink of china and spoons as she made him another cup of tea. She sat stiffly on her bed and tried to breathe deeply. She needed to focus. There'd already been five bouquets, which meant there were only two more to go. And they were only flowers. She could be tough; she could get through this. She could resist.

Two minutes later Ginny tapped on her bedroom door. Alice looked at her watch, and sure enough, half an hour had passed.

'He's just getting the next bunch,' her friend called softly. Feeling a little delicate, Alice opened the door and came out. Ginny smiled at her encouragingly but she didn't notice. She was too busy staring through the window, watching the delivery man delve in the back of the van before shuffling back up the path, his shoulders hunched against the rain.

'Just this little fella here . . .' he declared as he placed number six on the table.

The two women stared at it.

'Are you sure this isn't a mistake?' Ginny asked incredulously. 'This can't be right.'

The delivery man grinned. 'No mistake.'

'But it's a cactus! It's just a spiky, stubby cactus! He's not going to win anyone back with a cactus!'

'You shouldn't judge a book by its cover,' the delivery man said leadingly. 'The lady understands.'

All eyes turned to Alice.

'It's about survival,' she said slowly, her own eyes not straying a millimetre from the cactus on the table. 'It's about living in a harsh world, and making it against the odds. Cactuses endure; they're strong. They'll be there come rain or shine, famine or drought.'

'Wow!' Ginny marvelled. 'Just, wow!'

Alice turned to the delivery man stiffly.

'I need to see the last one. No more half-hour intervals. I have to see it now.'

'But what about John's instructions?' Ginny urged. But Alice was already out of the door and heading for the van, the delivery man trailing in her wake.

'What's next?' she demanded wildly as she surveyed the load of technicolour blooms. The back of the van was a wall of petals and leaves and hues. 'Which one's mine?'

The seconds seemed an eternity as the delivery man fumbled in the back to find her last link. Alice didn't notice the unrelenting rain, washing her cheeks with raindrops and methodically flattening her hair. It was all she could do to stop herself from tearing the van apart to find her final floral message.

And then he straightened up and turned towards her, and she saw it.

'A single red tulip!' Ginny declared disparagingly. She too had ventured out into the rain, her nose wrinkled up in disappointment. 'Shouldn't that be a single red rose?'

'No!' Alice cried out aloud. 'This is much, much better.' She held the tulip to her chest and made a strange, choking sound.

Ginny looked at the delivery man for an explanation.

'*Believe me, I love you,*' he explained softly. He smiled and then added, 'It's the gardener's way.'

Alice closed her eyes and tried to hold back the tears. She held her head to the rain-filled skies and breathed deeply. What was it that Emily had said? *Deep down – in your core – you know he'd never make a fool of you . . . He's one of the good guys.* Of course he was! John wasn't all the terrible things she'd been imagining. He was lovely and kind and upright and dignified. He wouldn't take Sheryl's money, or date her for a laugh. He was good and honest and faithful and true. It was so obvious to her now. But she'd walked out and left him at the restaurant, and ignored all his calls when he tried to explain. She hadn't even paid him the courtesy of hearing him out, hadn't given him the chance to say what he wanted to say. And now he'd said it the only way left to him, in a way that needed no words.

Alice pressed her free hand to her face. She couldn't talk.

Everything was whirring around inside her so quickly she didn't know which words would tumble out. She looked wildly from Ginny to the delivery man and back again.

'I've got to go!' she blurted, twisting away.

'But I haven't given you the letter!' the delivery man protested. 'My instructions were all the bouquets, then the letter. How else are you going to know where to find him?' But Alice was already running up the middle of the puddle-strewn road, away from the van and the flat, and towards the centre of town.

'I'll lock up!' Ginny shouted after her. 'I'll leave your key under the plant pot!'

But Alice was gone, her tulip still clutched to her chest and her cardigan already getting heavy with rain. She knew where he'd be. She didn't need a letter to know exactly where he'd be waiting. She didn't care that her shoes were sodden or that her hair was sticking damply to her cheeks; all she cared about was getting there faster than humanly possible.

As she ran the landscape got busier around her. Soon the roads were too clogged with traffic, so she ran on the pavements. She went faster and faster, dodging the city's commuters and weaving between bag-laden shoppers. She had to get to John. She had to feel him take her in his arms and kiss her.

Finally she reached the coffee shop. As she breathlessly reached to push open the heavy glass door she caught sight of him and stopped in her tracks. He saw her too. He left his coffee steaming on the table and came straight out.

'Thanks for coming. I didn't know if you would,' he said stiffly, almost formally, as they stood together on the pavement. He stood very close and for a moment Alice thought he was about to touch her. She felt herself go dizzy; she could barely breathe from all the running and the new, sudden proximity to him. It felt so good to stand next to him again. Her whole body ached for him to reach forward and touch her.

'I've been here for hours,' he said softly. 'I wasn't sure if the florist would stick to the schedule, and I couldn't risk you turning up early and me missing you.'

Imperceptibly they inched still closer together, as if drawn by magnets. 'This is where he kisses me,' Alice thought to herself. 'This is where he takes me in his arms and makes everything all right.' And she lifted her head in anticipation.

And then she saw it.

'Oh!' she exclaimed. Her eyes fixed on his chest. She couldn't believe she hadn't seen it before; John was wearing a dinner jacket.

'I'm working tonight,' he explained grimly.

'Oh!' Alice's face fell. She took a step back. What on earth was she doing here? What was she thinking? She'd let herself be blinded by hope and romance and flowers. Nothing had changed; not really. A shirt and jacket had told her more than all those clever bouquets . . . John had another, more important date tonight.

'Alice, *please*.' He saw the change in her face. 'I need you to see something. It's just a few streets away. You've come this far; please don't turn back now.'

Alice was too confused to argue. But as she walked numbly beside him, she was achingly aware of the few centimetres of air that separated them. Now that she was with him, could see him, could *feel* his presence – did the other women *actually* matter? At that precise moment, she wasn't sure she even cared about them any more. The only thing she knew for certain was how much she yearned, *hungered*, for John to touch her. Why hadn't he hugged her? Why wasn't he holding her hand? He'd gone to all that trouble to get her here, but he hadn't even tried to kiss her. Did he even want her at all?

The rain had stopped now, and John strode along the glistening street looking strangely exotic as he cut through the sea of commuters in his dinner jacket. Miserably, Alice watched women glance at him as he passed by. She remembered her red face and wet hair with shame. She was no match for John. She wasn't even in the same league.

Suddenly he stopped.

'This is it,' he said, pressing a brass bell next to a black door. Alice peered at the plaque. It said *G. Ashby Appointments*.

'Where are we going?'

'There's someone I want you to meet. My agent.'

Alice's mouth fell open and she was about to protest when a woman's voice crackled over the intercom, 'Come on up, John!' and the door swung open. John held it for her. Alice hesitated.

'At least hear what I have to say.' His blue eyes caught hers imploringly.

Powerless she stepped inside. What was she doing? she

asked herself, her heart thumping as she climbed the thickly carpeted staircase. She didn't want to meet his agent! What if Ginny *wasn't* right? What if he *was* a rent boy? 'Agent' would be code for 'pimp'? She wasn't ready for this; she wasn't prepared.

'Keep going,' he said. 'It's the top floor.'

Alice began to panic. She shouldn't be here. She was a nice girl – a gardener. Gardeners didn't meet pimps. And what, exactly, would be waiting for her at the top of the stairs? A room full of flashing neon signs and scantily clad women? Men with gold teeth and racks of rubber masks? Although she couldn't help but notice that the pile of the navy-blue carpet was luxuriously thick and the stairway walls were panelled in a dark, rich-looking wood. It wasn't quite how she'd have imagined the entrance to a pimp's lair. She'd seen the movies; weren't they supposed to be crack dens?

She stopped. The stairs had run out and there was a heavy mahogany door in front of her. She felt John at her shoulder and tried to ignore how her body tingled at his closeness. He leant around her and opened the door.

'John!' a woman's voice called out in cheery welcome.

Alice blinked and found herself being gently propelled into the room. A woman was walking towards them with a beaming smile. She was in her fifties and exuded matronly kindness. With her curly grey hair, crumpled linen suit and laughing eyes she looked like somebody's mum.

'I see you've brought a guest!' She smiled at Alice.

'Geraldine, may I introduce Alice?' John said calmly. 'Alice, this is my friend and agent, Geraldine.'

Wordlessly Alice let her hand be shaken. She looked at Geraldine. She must be the G. Ashby of G. Ashby Appointments. But she didn't look like a pimp; she actually looked ... well, *nice*.

Geraldine smiled and ushered them over to a sunken-looking sofa that had seen better days. Alice noticed a curling paperback copy of *Polo* hooked over the arm.

'Glass of wine?' Geraldine called from her desk. 'It's gone six, after all!'

'Definitely for me,' John replied. 'Alice?'

Alice nodded dumbly and watched Geraldine conjure three wine glasses and a bottle of red from her messy desk. She then pulled up an old, battered chair and joined them at the sofa.

'Cheers!' Geraldine toasted merrily.

Alice mechanically sipped her drink. What on earth was going on?

'So,' John said, 'I'm afraid this isn't a social visit.'

'Well, I did wonder,' replied Geraldine cautiously.

There was a pause. Despite her confusion, Alice noticed John become tense beside her.

'Do you remember a few weeks ago?' he asked carefully. 'When I told you I no longer wanted Audrey Cracknell as my client?'

'Of course.' Geraldine nodded. 'I asked you if there was anything wrong.'

'I lied,' John said awkwardly. 'There *was* something wrong. Well, not wrong exactly. Something very right, actually.'

'OK,' said Geraldine slowly, glancing at Alice. Alice stared at John, struggling to keep up with the day's ever-changing turn of events.

John cleared his throat and pulled at his collar to loosen his bow tie.

'Well, the thing is, I've been doing this for a long time. Escorting, I mean. Eleven years, give or take. And for a while now I've been thinking maybe it's not the job for me any more.'

Alice took a silent intake of breath. Her mind was whirring. What was John saying?

'I've been thinking: maybe I've been hiding in my job a bit. Using it as an excuse not to, well, meet people,' John said awkwardly. 'I know I meet people for a living, but it's not the same. I should meet people for myself. *As* myself. I've been thinking maybe it was time for me to stop trying to save everyone else from their loneliness and, well – ' he paused, suddenly looking lost – 'work on doing something about my own.'

Alice was shocked. Was John lonely? He'd never said. She shot a look at Geraldine, who was wearing a strange expression. It seemed to be saying 'at last'.

'And then I met Alice.' John suddenly grasped Alice's hand. She almost gasped out loud at the warmth of his skin. Touching John – *being touched* by John – felt amazing.

'Meeting Alice made me realize that all the thoughts I'd been having were right,' John continued. 'I need to break away from the – I don't know – *prison* I've built myself. I need to have a go at life, jump in. Let myself be happy.'

He turned and looked at Alice, his eyes filled with something she hadn't seen before.

'And so you're quitting escorting,' Geraldine said gently. It was a statement, not a question.

'Yes. I'd like tonight to be my last night. I was hoping you wouldn't make me work my notice.' He cracked a watery smile.

Geraldine beamed.

'Don't be daft, you old softie! As your agent I'm obviously sorry to lose you, but as your friend I'm cock-a-hoop!'

'Really?'

'Of course!' she laughed. 'Eleven years of penance is enough for anyone! Eve wouldn't have wanted you to be lonely for the rest of your life. It's about bloody time you fell in love again. I was beginning to worry it would only be me and Emily visiting you in the nursing home!'

John lunged forward and enveloped Geraldine in a giant bear hug. He then returned to the sofa and looked at Alice.

'So, that's it!' he said happily. 'Alice, do you think you'd consider going out with a *former* male escort? One who swears on his life that he never slept with any of his clients?'

'Too bloody right he didn't!' Geraldine harrumphed. 'I'm not running a knocking shop!'

'So he's definitely not a . . . ?' Alice started to ask Geraldine. They were the first words she'd said since she'd arrived.

'Goodness, no!' Geraldine exclaimed. 'Do I look like a pimp?'

'No!' Alice said hurriedly. She suddenly felt stupid. Why had she assumed the worst? Wasn't she supposed to be hard-wired for happy endings? 'But I don't get it,' she puzzled. 'What do you mean, eleven years of penance?' She turned to John. 'And what was that stuff about building yourself a prison?'

'Hasn't he told you?' asked Geraldine.

Alice looked blankly at John, but he was looking deep into his wine glass.

'John's wife died fifteen years ago,' Geraldine explained.

Alice looked at John. He was sitting as still as stone.

'He blamed himself. He was late picking her up from work one night, so she decided to walk home and got hit by a car on the way.'

'Oh! That's awful!' Impulsively Alice took John's hand.

'I'd been ... I'd been having an affair,' John admitted awkwardly, his face stricken. 'I was late picking up my wife because I was with another woman.'

'Oh!' Alice's hand went rigid in his.

'It's the only thing I've ever done that I'm ashamed of,' John said quietly, unable to bring himself to look at Alice. 'And I've spent the rest of my life regretting it. I didn't tell you before, because I didn't want you to think less of me. It was a terrible thing I did, and I would never, ever do it again.'

John looked into the distance miserably for a moment. Alice didn't know what to think or say.

'Eve and I married very young,' John said eventually. 'We hadn't intended to, but she fell pregnant and we wanted to do the right thing. I loved her, but looking back, I wasn't ready. And having Emily, well ... Don't get me wrong: I love my daughter, but having a child takes its toll on a relationship. It's hard, especially when you're practically a child yourself. I was eighteen. The problem was, the years passed but I still thought I was eighteen. I wasn't the best of husbands.'

Alice opened her mouth, but couldn't find any words.

'After Eve died I hid from the world,' he continued. 'I just looked after Emily during the day, and sat on my sofa at night. I didn't feel I deserved to go out and be happy.'

'Well, the affair was obviously very bad, but it wasn't your fault Eve died. *You* didn't run her over,' Alice reasoned.

'Try telling him that every day for fifteen years ...' Geraldine muttered.

'I know that now.' John smiled weakly. 'But it took a while. I just kept thinking "what if?" What if I'd been a better husband, a better man?'

'After a few years I staged an intervention!' said Geraldine. 'I'd just set up this business, and I needed more escorts on my books. John was the best-looking man I knew, and he was no good to anyone stagnating on his sofa. I knew he wasn't ready to meet anyone new or find himself a girlfriend. But I also knew he must be lonely. Just as lonely as my clients.'

'So she persuaded me to join,' John continued. 'She told me I'd be helping lonely women face their demons and feel better about themselves.'

'I told him he'd be making amends,' Geraldine interrupted, 'that Eve wouldn't want him rotting away at home. And that I'd babysit Emily whilst he was working.'

'Oh!' Alice said

'He still hasn't had a proper relationship since Eve, you know,' Geraldine told her.

'Ah, but I have my clients.' John smiled sadly.

'Emily calls them his surrogate girlfriends,' Geraldine laughed. 'She says he's dysfunctional with a capital "D".'

'Emily knows about all this,' Alice said, remembering back to their chat at the office.

'Every last bit,' John replied. 'Miraculously she forgave me for cheating on her mother. And she's known about the escorting for years.'

He looked at Alice and smiled.

'I've made mistakes,' he said. 'Big mistakes that I truly regret. But escorting isn't one of them. It's nothing to be ashamed of.'

'I know,' said Alice. And she did.

John squeezed her hand. 'Alice, you're the first person who's made me want to have a girlfriend again. Who's made me feel like I deserve one.'

His eyes met hers. Alice felt her breath leave her body.

'I'm not the same man as I was back then,' he said softly. 'I've tried to help women, not sleep with them. I've learnt my lesson; I've done my time.'

He smiled at her hopefully.

'Do you believe me?' he asked. 'Do I get a second chance?'

'Yes!' she cried. 'Yes, yes!' and she threw her arms around him.

'Well, congratulations to you both!' Geraldine grinned. 'You've got yourself a good man there, Alice.'

'I know!' replied Alice happily.

'And you!' Geraldine mock-scolded John. 'You'd better get out and give Lady Denham the date of her life! I'm not having a half-hearted job just because you've got one foot out of the door!'

'*Lady* Denham?' Alice echoed.

'No riff-raff for John!' Geraldine replied. 'Only the choicest lady clients for the most popular gentleman on my books. They all seem to be under the illusion that the man's got class, the poor devils.'

Moments later John and Alice were at the bottom of the stairs on the private side of the black door.

'You're really giving it up?' Alice asked. 'For me?'

'I should have done it long ago!' John grinned, suddenly looking drunk with happiness. 'I'm a one-woman man from now on!' he declared. 'John Marlowe is retiring! Long live John Smith!'

'John *Smith*?'

'Smith; that's my real name! You didn't think I'd escort under my own name, did you? It was bad enough Emily knowing what I did for a living whilst she was still at school. I wasn't going to open her up to ridicule from her friends by making it more likely they'd find out that Emily Smith's dad was the same Mr Smith who'd taken their divorced mum out to dinner last Saturday.'

'But what will you do for money?'

'Don't worry about that!' John wrapped her into a tight, warm embrace. 'I'm a good escort, but not that good! I do have a day job as well, you know! I'm a nude model.'

He laughed at Alice's stricken face.

'I'm joking! I'm a business adviser.' He leaned close to kiss her.

'Good!' Alice said in relief. 'Because I'm not sure I want to go out with a man who's retired. It makes you sound really old.'

'Yeah?' John murmured. 'But I'm not the one wearing a cardy!' he teased. And he kissed her for a very long time.

JOHN

Eventually John managed to stop kissing Alice, open the black door and re-enter the real world – a world where appointments had to be kept and business needed to be finished. After hugging Alice goodbye he straightened his dinner jacket, ran his fingers through his hair and rushed off for dinner at The Privet with Lady Denham. For the first time in his professional career he was late for a date with a client.

The maître d' ushered him to where Lady Denham was waiting, a large champagne cocktail before her, and her jewellery sparkling in the candlelight.

'Oh, there you are!' she said in mock annoyance. 'You're so late I thought you must have been run over. I was imagining a hit-and-run by a crazed, jealous client. The last words on your lips had been my name.'

John laughed, kissed her cheek and sat down. He liked Lady Denham. Rich and posh though she was, she was always good company. She'd been one of his regulars for years and he'd never seen her without an inordinate amount of jewellery dripping from every available surface of skin. He'd once asked whether she was worried about being mugged.

'Darling!' she'd exclaimed in her exaggerated, camp way. 'What's the point in having the pudding if you don't over-egg it?'

Lady Denham was an unusual client in that she never *needed* to see John. He was booked purely for her amusement. Her third divorce in her late fifties had finally left her so fabulously wealthy she couldn't give a fig who knew she was single. Well groomed, with a neat figure and a face that was still captivating, she firmly believed that having a merry-go-round of younger men on her arm was as good for her image as it was for her soul. John enjoyed escorting her enormously.

He settled into his seat, accepted a champagne cocktail from the waiter and allowed Lady Denham to order for them both. As the waiter turned to leave, John noticed Lady Denham check out his backside.

'Hungry?' he asked mischievously.

'Ravenous!' she declared archly, dragging her eyes away from the waiter's bottom. 'Still, despite your tardy time-keeping, which I'm going to choose to forgive just this once, I'm pleased to say you're looking as delicious as ever. Which is just as well, else I'd be straight on the phone to Geraldine to trade you in for a younger model!'

'Ah, well, seeing as you brought it up,' John interceded. 'I hadn't planned on telling you quite so early but I've got some news. You might be phoning Geraldine sooner than you'd thought.'

'Why?' Lady Denham straightened her poker-straight posture even further. 'No, let me guess ... Business is bad, so Geraldine's booked you in for a little surgical pick-me-up?'

John laughed and shook his head. Lady Denham guessed again.

'The furious husband of one of your clients has challenged you to pistols at dawn. This is your last supper!'

'Nothing as exciting as that, I'm afraid,' John smiled. 'I'm retiring. Tonight is my last night as a gentleman escort. And as my favourite client I thought it fitting that you were my swansong.'

'Oh!' Lady Denham said hollowly, looking piqued. She took a sip from her champagne cocktail before rallying herself and replying drily, 'Well, it's for the best. You're really rather tiresome and I've been racking my brains as to how I could let you down gently. I've been hoping Geraldine might find me a replacement with a tighter chin.'

'I'm sure she'd be only too happy to oblige. In fact, she's already got a selection of tight-chinned, tight-buttocked substitutes ready for your inspection,' John teased.

Lady Denham smiled in acquiescence.

'I'm very grateful to you for having suffered me for so long,' John added meaningfully.

'That's all right, darling!' Lady Denham sniffed. 'One likes to do one's bit.' She fiddled with her jewellery, suddenly looking lost.

'So what are you going to do with your life post-escorting?' she asked abruptly. 'It's going to be dull after all our high living at The Privet.'

John smiled.

'I don't really know, to tell you the truth. Dedicate myself to my own happy-ever-after, I expect.'

'Oh, how sweet,' Lady Denham said drily. 'Well, I'll spare you a thought when you're huddled in front of your television eating some miserable dinner from an aluminium tray and I'm feasting on *foie gras* with my latest toy boy. Although I'm sure you'll be quite forgotten by the time the season's out.'

There was a heavy pause.

'I'll miss you,' John said honestly, their playful tone momentarily put aside.

'I'll miss you too,' Lady Denham replied with equal candour. There was a moment of stillness between them. And then she looked away and pretended to survey the restaurant merrily. 'You little deserter,' she added cuttingly through her rigid smile.

John looked at her. Humour was both Lady Denham's greatest ally and her greatest weapon. It had got her through three high-profile divorces. For all her put-downs he knew she'd meant it when she told him she'd miss him. He saw a speck of a tear on her cheek as she pretended to be engrossed in her inspection of her fellow diners. He leant forward, took her face gently in his hand and wiped it away with the tip of his thumb.

'Just a little splash of champagne,' he said lightly, and smiled. He would truly miss her. She'd been a loyal client and a rare source of fun. In a funny way she'd been his good friend too.

Wrapped in his goodbye, John didn't notice a figure rising from her table at the far side of the restaurant. Her glossily lipsticked mouth fell open as she stared at the tender scene before her. She kept her eyes locked on him as she walked past and out of the restaurant door, her unseasonably tanned partner trailing vacantly in her wake.

LOU

Lou passed him his pint, took the twenty out of his hand and tried to make their eye contact last as long as possible. He was gorgeous!

'Take one for yourself.' He smiled politely.

'Thanks!' She threw him her sexiest grin and twirled off to the till, wiggling her hips to show off her bum in her figure-hugging skirt. She sneaked a look back at him, but he'd already turned away and was chatting to his mate.

It was a much busier Tuesday night than usual and she'd been watching him out of the corner of her eye as he'd patiently waited his turn to be served. Tempting as it had been to serve him first, experience had taught her that the longer a fit-looking bloke had to wait, the longer she had to eye him up at close quarters. It wasn't often men as good-looking as him wandered into her bar. And now that everyone else had been served she could take her time, give him the opportunity to chat her up and look down her shirt.

'I haven't seen you in here before,' she said, making sure her fingers stroked his hand as she gave him his change. 'I'd remember a face like yours.'

'I've just started a new job,' he answered, seemingly oblivious to her flirting. 'Round the corner, on Bateman Street. This is my first time.'

'First time?' Lou raised her eyebrow suggestively. 'Well, now you've popped your cherry I hope you'll come again.'

He laughed in embarrassment.

'Nice to meet you.' He semi-raised his pint and turned away.

'What's your name?' Lou called after him.

'Simon.'

'I'm Lou. Thanks for the V&T!'

He nodded, smiled and sat down with his friend. He didn't look back. Lou felt oddly put out.

So, his name was Simon, she thought. And if he'd just started work on Bateman Street the chances were he'd become a regular. She felt strangely pleased with this information. He wasn't the kind she normally went for. He was a bit straight. And he hadn't responded to her flirting. Most men she flirted with were mentally undressing her before they'd got their first pint in their hands. By their second they were trying to lure her up to street level and into the side alley. Somehow Simon didn't seem the type.

Her thoughts were suddenly interrupted by a finger snaking up the inside of her thigh. Tony had silently appeared behind her.

'You're looking hot,' he breathed lecherously into her ear. 'I think you should come out back; get some air on your skin.'

Lou edged away. He had a nerve! He hadn't bothered

asking if she was better from her flu, even if she had made it all up. *And* he hadn't apologized for standing her up the other week, *or* for being crappy on the phone. There was no way he was getting a shag. Besides, she didn't want Simon to see her being pawed by her boss. She wanted to make sure she looked available. To Simon.

'I'm busy. Things to do,' she said crisply, suddenly taking it on herself to clean out the nearest drip tray.

'I've got things to do too,' Tony persisted, pushing the length of his body against hers. 'You!' He rubbed himself against her.

'Not now.' Lou stepped away from him again, irritation creeping into her voice. 'I'm working.'

Tony stepped back in surprise.

'Since when did that ever stop you?'

Lou noticed his tone. It wasn't pleasant.

'Suit yourself,' he said curtly. 'Barmaids are two a penny.'

He turned on his heel and headed to the back room where Lou knew he'd be watching her moodily on the monitor, waiting for her to come in and make it up to him. Well, he'd have a long bloody wait. If there was any making up to do she was buggered if it was going to come from her. She continued to busy herself with the drip trays, sneaking glances at Simon.

Simon looked nice. The kind of man Kate was paying good money to meet. A man you could take home to meet your parents and not worry that he'd want to shag you in the conservatory or try it on with your mum. He was the kind of man, Lou thought, that Kate thought Lou could never have.

Thinking about Kate made Lou feel strange. They still hadn't spoken since their argument. They usually called each other several times a day, sometimes just to tell each other how massively they'd pigged out at lunch. But there was no way Lou was going to apologize first. Besides, some of the things Kate had said still sat awkwardly in her chest, like something heavy she'd eaten and couldn't quite digest.

She rinsed out the last drip tray, studying Simon through her eyelashes. Kate had made her life sound pathetic. Well, she was going to make Kate eat her words. She was going to show her she was just as capable of bagging a decent man as an indecent one. She wasn't stuck with the Tonys of this world. She could have any man she wanted, even the squeaky-clean suburbia-seekers that Kate was trying to pin down. That would shut Kate up. She'd show her you didn't need to join poncey agencies to bag yourself a 'proper' man. She'd show her she was wrong to think so badly of her best friend.

Lou was going to have Simon.

SHERYL

Sheryl stood outside The Privet, her whole body buzzing with the scent of scandal.

'Did you see that?' she hissed at Brad as he bowled up alongside her.

'See what, babe?'

'John Cracknell!'

Brad looked blank.

'Audrey Cracknell's husband, you idiot! He was in there. *With another woman!*'

Sheryl peered back into the lobby, looking as though she might march back in for a second helping of gawping.

'A much better-looking woman than Audrey!' she added gleefully. Her face broke into a sadistic smile. 'John Cracknell!' she declared to the night air. 'You sly old dog!'

Brad shifted uncomfortably.

'It's none of our business, babe.'

'Don't be ridiculous! He's fouling on his own doorstep; it's everyone's business!' She laughed cruelly. 'Well, well, well. It serves Audrey right, the sanctimonious old cow. She's forever going on about her "rock-solid" marriage and fawning over him like a teenager. But I knew something didn't add up. John never looked right for her; way too good-looking. And now he's dipping his wick outside the marital love nest. He's having an affair!'

Brad was eyeing up the nearby taxi rank.

'Just because he's having dinner with someone doesn't mean there's anything in it,' he said mildly. 'Maybe she's his sister.'

Sheryl snorted contemptuously, strode over to the window and peered in at the diners.

'I know this woman,' she said thoughtfully.

'Babe, maybe we should just get this taxi.'

Sheryl waved him away as though swatting a fly.

'Where have I seen her before?' she deliberated aloud. She'd got the bit between her teeth now. Her blood was up.

'Baby, come on. You promised we'd be home in time to watch that movie.'

'For God's sake, Brad,' she hissed viciously. 'You go home. I've got things to do.'

'You're not going back in there?'

'No,' she answered unconvincingly. She still hadn't taken her eyes off John and his companion. 'I've just remembered there's something I need to do in the office.'

She gave Brad a dismissive kiss on the nose before turning back to her view.

'Night, darling,' she muttered distractedly over her shoulder.

She vaguely heard Brad tut and get into a taxi. Not caring

how she might look to anyone passing on the street she stayed rooted at her spot at the window, her predatory breath clouding the pane as she racked her brains as to who the elegant woman in the jewellery could be.

ALICE

Alice thought she might literally burst with happiness. Surely such a flimsy thing as human skin couldn't hold in this much whirling excitement and the dynamite of glee? She felt like a joy bomb about to explode!

John was giving up his job!

And she also had it on very good authority – Geraldine's, who she'd decided was one hundred per cent trustworthy; she read Jilly Cooper, for God's sake! – that John had never been any of the nasty things she'd imagined. He was a gentleman – just like she'd wanted him to be!

Alice felt like pinching herself. Surely she, Alice Brown, couldn't be this lucky?

She arrived home on a cloud of happiness. She went straight to her bedroom, opened her wardrobe and took out the dress she'd worn to the ball.

'Thank you!' she whispered to her dress. 'Thank you, thank you, thank you!'

She hugged it to her. This was the outfit that had started everything. And to think, she'd almost not bought it! To think, she'd even tried to get out of going to the ball!

Thank goodness fate had known better than she had.

As she held her dress she decided to give it another outing. She was going to wear it – *and* her heels, handbag, earrings and make-up – on a date with John. She was going to wow him all over again. She was going to make him look at her and know she was worth giving up his job for.

She felt another wave of excitement crash over her. She had a boyfriend! And a better, handsomer, more perfect boyfriend than even she could ever have imagined! She slipped her dress back onto the rail and laughed at how it looked, a lone slick of glamour amidst a sea of corduroy and knitwear.

SHERYL

Somewhere in the middle of her filing cabinet, with dozens of old case files spilled across the floor in a fan of forgotten lonely hearts finally meeting years after the need, recognition hit Sheryl. Like a twisted thunderbolt or a rogue arrow from an off-colour Cupid, she suddenly realized who John's mystery woman was. Her face was smiling up at Sheryl from a faded Manila folder.

She was Lady Isabella Denham, formerly known as Isabella Alpine and before that plain old Isabel Jones. A long time ago, before her marriage to Lord Denham, she'd been a fully signed up and very active member of Love Birds.

Sheryl laughed out loud and kissed the file victoriously. She knew she'd known her from somewhere!

The file contained all the ammunition she needed on Lady Denham – from her age to her preferences to her divorces. She had a complete record of her dates throughout the two years she'd been a Love Birds client: a voracious catalogue of men, all of whom, Sheryl noticed, were considerably younger than her. Sheryl even had her mobile number! She wondered if it still worked.

Leaving her files scattered on the floor she took Lady Denham's folder to her desk. So she knew the identity of John Cracknell's mystery lady. All she needed now was a bit more evidence to establish his guilt as a philanderer. Just seeing him dining with a woman who wasn't his wife was not enough. She needed something more: an irrefutable, cast-iron nail for Audrey's coffin.

Sheryl reached for her telephone, her breath quick and excited. God, this was fun! She could already picture the look on Audrey's face . . .

'Yes?' Isabella Denham's clipped tones rang in Sheryl's ear. She sounded like she was in a car – presumably on the way home from her tryst at The Privet. Was John with her? Were they on their way to a hotel bedroom, about to make steamy, passionate love?

'Lady Denham, sorry to bother you. Sheryl Toogood here from Love Birds matchmaking bureau.'

'Love Birds? What on earth do *you* want? And at this time of night? It's been years!'

'I know. And I'm so sorry for the late hour.' Sheryl used her most ingratiating tone. 'It's just that a cracker of a bachelor has come onto our books – a real gem! And you know how it is when a good-looking, eligible man comes along,' she confided, enjoying her own yarn. 'There's always a fight as everyone scrambles to get their claws into him first. I'm trying to think of a suitable match for him, a *worthy* match, before word gets out and the feeding frenzy starts. And then it hit me! He would be absolutely perfect for you! And so I had to call you straightaway to see if you were interested. I wouldn't be able to sleep tonight if I hadn't tried to make this match!'

There was a long pause.

'I don't suppose ... I was wondering ... are you ...' – Sheryl tried to sound as casual as possible – 'looking for a date at the moment?' She held her breath for the answer.

There was another long pause. Sheryl's buttocks clenched her chair in anticipation. The seconds ticked interminably by. She could hear the sounds of Lady Denham's car droning discreetly in the background.

'Well, Ms Toogood,' Lady Denham replied eventually, her voice curt. 'Despite the rude hour of your phone call, your timing is surprisingly excellent.'

'Oh?' Sheryl replied excitedly. All she needed was for Lady Denham to take a couple of steps forward and walk into her net.

'As coincidence would have it,' Lady Denham continued crisply, 'one of my regulars let me down tonight. So, yes, I could potentially be interested in hearing about your new gentleman. Tell me more.'

Sheryl could hear her heart beating loudly in her ears. Lady Denham had called John a 'regular'. Something was definitely going on between them!

'Of course, Lady Denham,' Sheryl replied sweetly. 'But what rotten luck about your regular. What happened?'

'He's retiring from escorting.'

'From escorting?' Sheryl breathed giddily. 'What, is he an agency man?'

'Not from a dating agency, no. Obviously I gave those up when I met Lord Denham.'

Sheryl could hardly believe her luck. Lady Denham was as easy to squeeze as a tea bag.

'But you say this man was an escort? So you, um, you paid him, right?'

'That's right. Much simpler. Everyone knows what they're getting into that way. He was from Geraldine.'

'Geraldine?'

'Yes, Geraldine Ashby. Look, I'm really not sure whether I'd want to join your little agency again, Ms Toogood, but I suppose you might as well tell me about your gentleman anyway. Maybe some sort of arrangement could be made if he's up to scratch.'

Even as Lady Denham spoke Sheryl was already calling up the Google page on her computer and typing in the name 'Geraldine Ashby'. She blithely spun Lady Denham a few lines about her dazzling new bachelor, making sure he didn't sound too dazzling. After all, she was buggered if Lady Denham wanted to meet him. He didn't exist.

She quickly found a website for 'G. Ashby Appointments' and hit return.

'Hmmm, well, I'm not sure,' Lady Denham said doubt-fully. 'He's not exactly what I'm after these days. I think you might be losing your touch, Ms Toogood.'

'Oh well!' Sheryl hit the button for *gentleman escorts*. She whizzed through the blurb at the top of the screen. '*Escorting you through your vital events . . . Discreet and profes-sional service.*'

'We must catch up sometime soon,' Sheryl sang airily, her attention elsewhere. 'Do lunch.' She dropped the phone back onto its cradle without waiting for a reply. She had what she needed now, and it wasn't Lady Denham's custom. She clicked on the button that said *gallery* and held her breath as she browsed through the selection of male escorts.

And there he was. John Cracknell. His distinguished face, so familiar from the DIPS balls, smiled handsomely at her from the computer screen. Except he wasn't John Cracknell. He was John Marlowe. His interests were current affairs, sport and gardening. He was forty-one years old and yours for the night for G. Ashby Appointments' highest fee.

Sheryl leaned back in her chair and smiled victoriously.

'Gotcha!' she said out loud to her empty office.

JOHN

John beamed at Alice for the umpteenth time that evening and wondered yet again what he'd done to deserve to feel this good. He couldn't believe she was actually here, sitting in his kitchen, eating his cooking, drinking his wine and, hopefully soon, sleeping in his bed.

'You know,' he grinned, 'other than Emily and Geraldine, you're the first woman I've cooked for in fifteen years!'

Alice smiled, but she seemed distracted. She put down her fork. 'What are we going to do about Audrey?' she asked quietly, her voice sounding small and worried. 'We can't let her find out about us by accident; it wouldn't be fair.'

'Wouldn't it?' John had a flashback to Audrey's hard, cruel face at the ball.

'She'd feel humiliated, like we'd not only broken her heart but made a fool of her too.'

'Do you know,' John said lightly, 'for the first time in my life I don't care how Audrey feels, or how any of my ex-clients feel. I've worried about them for too long. It's time I worried about the people who are really important. You, me and Emily. Oh, and Buster, of course.' He looked at Alice and saw worry etched across her face. 'You don't owe her anything, you know. She's treated you pretty badly over the years.'

'She doesn't *mean* to be unkind.'

'She just does it automatically!'

But Alice still looked worried. She pushed her half-eaten food away.

'You're not having second thoughts, are you?' he asked suddenly.

'No!' Alice exclaimed emphatically. 'It's just that I can't stop imagining how she must be feeling, and how much worse it'll get for her when she finds out about us. She's going to have to explain your no-show at the next ball. I suppose she'll have to say you've divorced.'

'But will she?' John asked. 'I think she'll just say I'm away on business and can't make it. The lie's entrenched now. It's too big for her to get out of.'

Alice thought for a moment.

'If you ask me,' said John grimly, 'the sooner she finds out about us the better. It'll do her good to be set free from her lies. Believe me, I should know. Freedom feels fantastic!'

'She'll sack me,' Alice said sadly. 'She'll have no reason, but she'll do it anyway.'

John chose his words carefully.

'Would that really be so bad? You're better than Table For Two. You're a brilliant matchmaker. You should be running your own agency.'

'But I love my job.'

'There are other jobs.'

'I love my clients.'

'And other clients!'

'I know,' Alice replied uncertainly, looking glum. John abandoned his dinner. He pushed his plate away, reached across the table and stroked her face.

'Let's not worry about this tonight. You're the best thing that's happened to me in ages, and I don't want to ruin it by thinking about Audrey. I'm so happy you're here. So, now that I've finally got you, let me enjoy being with you. We'll think of a plan, a *kind* plan, for telling Audrey another day. I promise.'

He gave her a reassuring smile, stood up and led her away from the kitchen.

ALICE

It was 2.15 p.m. Alice shut down her computer, picked up her bag and followed Bianca and Cassandra as they trailed Audrey out of the building and across the city centre to the bimonthly meeting of the Dating Practitioners' Society. Spring had finally arrived at last. Alice sighed as the warm, mild air softly tickled her skin.

'Someone sounds happy!'

Bianca was smiling at her.

'Better not let Crackers Cracknell catch you!' Cassandra warned. 'You're not paid to be happy!'

Alice smiled in surprise. It was a rare moment of staff solidarity. Normally Bianca and Cassandra marched ahead, a fraction off Audrey's heels, with Alice and Hilary keeping up the rear.

'You're looking different.' Bianca was scrutinizing her thoughtfully. 'Blooming.'

Alice blushed.

'If I didn't know better I'd say you had a man!' Bianca said lightly, before turning her attention away. The idea of Alice bagging herself a man was obviously so preposterous that she didn't bother to see whether her comment had scored a direct hit.

'A man!' Alice mumbled in hot embarrassment, her mind whirring as to how she could deny it without telling an outright fib. She forced an awkward chuckle. 'That's funny!'

But Bianca and Cassandra had already moved minutely ahead. Relieved, Alice resumed her place at the back of the line.

Ernie tackled the agenda quickly. As business skipped along Alice felt her mind wandering. This was happening a lot nowadays. All she could think about was John's face, John's kiss, or some tiny thing John had said. It was as though every other topic had floated out of her brain.

Alice shook herself to attention and tried to concentrate. The DIPS meetings were a treasure trove of handy match-making tips. Besides, she only had to concentrate for a little while. Tonight John was taking her to Beckwith's, the city's most romantic restaurant. She couldn't wait! And in honour of the occasion, she'd carefully stowed her backless dress and high heels in the sports bag at her feet.

'Does anyone have any other business?' she suddenly heard Ernie ask. Alice felt shocked. Had she really daydreamed through the entire meeting? She couldn't recall a single item of business. Her notebook – normally brim-ming with news and ideas – was empty.

There was a silence. Nobody, it seemed, had anything to add.

'Well, in which case, that just about wraps things u—'

'Er, there *is* one little thing ...' Sheryl suddenly piped up, uncurling her legs from beneath her and slipping her bare feet back into their heels.

She rose imperiously. Ernie knew his place. He sat down.

'It's just a small matter,' Sheryl continued, taking a wodge of brown envelopes from her mock-croc handbag. 'But a very important one. Somebody in our Society' – she paused dramatically – 'has been lying.'

There was a collective intake of breath.

'Abusing our trust; engaging in a deception ...'

Alice's heart suddenly beat faster. Her whole body prickled with danger. Sheryl must have found out about her and John. But how? They'd been so discreet!

'... a *romantic* deception,' Sheryl finished meaningfully.

Shock ricocheted around the room. A romantic deception – to a group of professional matchmakers – was a crime against the very fibre of humanity. Alice felt her mouth go dry. This wasn't how she wanted everyone to find out; how she wanted Audrey to find out. She felt sick.

'I'd like you all to take one of these.' Sheryl handed the envelopes to Matteus. He grabbed one and passed the pile on.

'I should warn you,' Sheryl continued, 'you might find the contents shocking.'

The envelopes slowly made their way around the group, the sense of excited outrage growing. Alice was sitting a long way from the front. She was going to be one of the last to receive an envelope. She looked at the Society members who'd been served their envelopes first. Most were turning them over in their hands reverently, savouring the anticipation of scandal, not wanting to be seen to be the first to rip theirs open in an unseemly race for titillation. She racked her brains. What could be inside? What could Sheryl have seen? Was it a photo of her and John together? Surely that was impossible. They'd always been so careful about where they went, choosing out-of-the-way locations, making sure they never kissed in public. How had they got caught out like this? In a panic, her eye flew over to where Audrey was sitting. She too was going to be one of the last to receive an envelope, and her head was pivoting fast as she looked from Sheryl to Matteus to Ernie to the envelopes. Her cheeks were flecked with dark red blotches. Despite her racing heartbeat and nervous, sweaty palms, Alice felt a rush of pity. Audrey hated to be the last to know about anything, let alone a deception unearthed by Sheryl Toogood. Alice felt a sudden urge to protect her. She wanted to beg her forgiveness, to tell her she hadn't meant to hurt her; that she was sorry for falling in love with John, but she'd been powerless to stop.

A few seconds later an envelope was resting weightily in her hands.

'Oh my God! It can't be!' a wobbly voice rang out.

Bianca was gasping at the contents of her envelope. Her eyes were wide and her mouth was open, aghast. And then she looked up. But it wasn't at Alice. It was at Audrey.

Quickly Alice ripped her envelope apart. Inside was a picture of John.

Around her people were beginning to gasp and tut.

But it wasn't a photo of Alice and John together. Instead it seemed to be a page from a website. John's picture was in the middle and below was a catalogue-style description of his hobbies and a price code of 'A*'. Scrawled diagonally across the page in bold red letters were the words, 'John Marlowe, aka John Cracknell' and then in capitals: 'RENT BOY'.

Alice stared in confusion. And then gradually it dawned on her. It was a page from Geraldine's website. It was where visitors could browse through the escorts and pick a date. Alice hadn't seen it before – it hadn't occurred to her that Geraldine would have a website and that John would be on it. But somehow Sheryl had got hold of it.

Alice felt red-hot fury flood through her. How dare Sheryl treat John this way? What right did she think she had to expose him like an outlaw and brand him a rent boy? It wasn't like that. *He* wasn't like that. And besides, what business was it of Sheryl's anyway?

Alice got to her feet. Before she could think about what she was doing she heard her own voice cut across the whispers and gasps.

'It's not like that!' she cried out. Heads rotated and she felt the eyes of the group upon her.

'Alice,' Sheryl purred nastily. 'Sweet little Alice. So trusting.'

Alice swallowed awkwardly as she prepared herself for exposure at the manicured hands of Sheryl Toogood.

'So loyal,' Sheryl continued poisonously, 'so loyal to her deceitful employer – who's been lying to us all for years.'

The heat of Sheryl's attention suddenly swung away from Alice and onto the crimson face of Audrey. For the briefest of moments Alice felt relief. But then she saw Audrey. Her head was bowed and her jowls were wobbling strangely.

'Ladies and gentleman,' Sheryl continued maliciously. 'I present you with concrete evidence that the man our very own Audrey Cracknell has been passing off as her husband is not her husband at all. He's an impostor. In fact, he's worse than an impostor. He's an escort; a *rent boy!*'

Hands flew to bosoms as everyone in the room took an audible intake of scandalized breath.

'He's a man Audrey has been hiring and faking a relationship with. He's not Mr John Cracknell. He's Mr John Marlowe and he charges by the hour.'

There was a stunned silence.

'Surely not, Sheryl,' Ernie interjected reasonably. 'There must be some kind of mistake. I've met the man. He seems very decent. Audrey and John are in love!'

'There's no mistake, Ernie.' Sheryl quashed his objection contemptuously. 'And of course he *seems* decent. Pay him enough and he'll be whatever you want him to be! And in love? Pah!' She laughed, her eyes cruel and glinting. 'I'm sure he's "in love" with half the ladies in the city. And maybe half the men too!'

At this there was the largest gasp of the afternoon. Perfect Partner's David Bennett choked in disbelief. Loving Liaisons' Wendy Arthur spilt her cup of tea into her lap.

'Yes, that's right,' Sheryl continued harshly, 'our very

own Audrey Cracknell has been using the services of a *prostitute!*'

The DIPS members exploded into a cacophony of outraged gossip.

'He's not! He's not like that!' Alice shouted, silencing the chatter, the eyes of the room swinging back to her once again. She suddenly realized she was still standing up. 'And Audrey's not like that either!' she added vehemently. You've got it all wrong!'

'It's time you forgot your sugar-coated fairy tales, Alice, and joined the real world.' Sheryl's voice dripped acid. 'Face facts, Miss Brown. We've all been made a mockery of by a trusted member of our *own* Society.'

The group's collective gaze followed Sheryl's manicured finger to where it pointed at the shaking, mottled face of Audrey Cracknell. Audrey's eyes were still fixed on her lap. Alice could see ripples of emotion wobbling through her cheeks and into her juddering bosom.

'Ladies and gentlemen,' Sheryl continued mercilessly, like a big cat about to bite into the jugular. 'I put it to you that Audrey Cracknell is not married at all. Audrey Cracknell is actually *single*.'

Someone in the group whimpered. 'Single' was not a word they used about each other. 'Single' was a crime against their profession. Wendy Arthur stopped sponging her skirt and lifted her hand to her mouth in horror.

Alice started moving towards her boss, weaving between the chairs to get to her.

'She *hasn't* got a significant other,' Sheryl mocked. 'She's got no romantic qualifications to be a matchmaker at all! Audrey Cracknell, who has for years lived off the profits of her supposedly "expert" dating advice, is nothing more than . . .' – Sheryl paused before plunging in her final knife – 'a *spinster*!'

'Goodness!' said Ernie.

'Holy Moly!' said Barry Chambers.

'Fuck me!' said Cassandra.

Alice had reached Audrey. She put her hand on her shoulder. She could feel her shaking violently, like a volcano about to erupt.

'I've told you all today so we can work out – *as a group* – how to deal with this,' Sheryl continued. 'If the public got to hear about it we'd *all* be discredited. We'd be called frauds and romantic failures. We'd be ruined. I have no choice but to table a motion that *Miss* Cracknell be barred from our Society with immediate effect.'

The room broke into a roar of chatter.

Suddenly Alice's hand shot up off Audrey's shoulder and into the air. Audrey had finally blown. Her chair scraped back with an angry, injured yelp, silencing the room. Audrey was on her feet, her eyes pink and bulging with rage.

'This is none of your business!' she yelled like a wounded beast. '*My life* is none of your business,' she roared, her furious face framed by the fire of her ginger hair. Alice had never seen her look more terrifying. 'John and I are in love. *In love!*'

A few Society members had the grace to cough nervously. A fat tear rolled down Audrey's face, wobbled and then splattered onto her bosom. She scooped up her bag and nearly knocked Alice over in her rush to get out of the room, Sheryl's flyer flapping in her fist.

The door crashed behind her leaving an eerie silence. Alice looked across the sea of scandalized DIPS faces, cheeks pink with titillated excitement. And then her eye fell on Sheryl, and she saw the unmistakable look of triumph.

Alice turned and silently followed Audrey out of the room.

AUDREY

Audrey barely noticed the pain that bit at the back of her heels, let alone the blood that was seeping through her tights and onto the back of her shoes. For once, she hadn't considered the unsightly sweat she was working up as she marched, or that her professional reputation was in shreds behind her. She could think of nothing but calling John. Or rather, calling Geraldine to get his number and then calling John.

She bumped and pushed her way through the shoppers, Sheryl's exposé still clutched in her hand. She had to get home, and fast. Waiting for the bus wasn't an option; she couldn't stand still. So she puffed and panted her way across the city, dumbly turning over the same words in her brain: *It's not like that . . . It's not like that . . . We're in love . . . We're in love . . .* Everyone had got it wrong. She and John were going to live happily ever after. They were in love. *In love!*

Everything was out in the open now; there was nothing to hide any more, nothing to stop them being together. She *had* to tell him what had happened. She *had* to hear him finally say the words she'd been waiting for: *Audrey, I love you. I've always loved you.* And then he'd take her in his arms and shelter her from Sheryl and Ernie and all the doubters and make everything in the world make sense.

Finally, after an hour of desperate power-walking, she steamed up the garden path to home. She swung open the door. Pickles rushed towards her in unnoticed greeting as she lunged for the phone.

'Geraldine? Audrey Cracknell. I must speak to John. It's an emergency.'

'Emergency? Whatever's happened? Are you all right?'

'Never mind that, I need to speak to John right away.'

There was a confused pause at the other end of the phone.

'It's a matter of life and death!' Audrey harried.

'Has there been an accident?'

'Not exactly. Sort of. Look, come on! It's urgent.' Audrey jumped from foot to foot in agitation. She could see her reflection in the mirror. She looked wild, crazy, out of control.

'But you're not hurt?'

'I'm very hurt!' she cried out impatiently. 'That's why I need to speak to John!'

'Do you need me to call you an ambulance?'

'Christ, no! Not that kind of hurt. Look, stop wasting time!'

'Audrey, you're not making any sense. And, besides, you know I can't give you John's phone number. Clients can't make direct contact.'

'Bugger the rules!' Audrey cried angrily. 'The rules have already been broken.'

'What do you mean?'

Pickles began to purr loudly, winding around Audrey's calves and sniffing at the blood at the back of her heel.

'I mean, it's over! Everyone knows. John's been exposed!' she wailed.

'Ah, I see!' Geraldine's voice lightened with what sounded insultingly close to amusement. 'Well, I don't think John will be too worried about that. You see, he's taken the decision to retire from escorting. He's given it up.'

'Given it up? What – stopped? With *all* his clients?' For the first time since leaving DIPS HQ, Audrey stood stock-still.

'Yes.'

'So, no more dates? With anyone?'

'That's right.'

Audrey gasped. It was happening! It was finally happening! 'Well, then, don't you see?' she stressed excitedly. 'It's more important than ever that I speak to him! We need to get things straight so we can be together!'

'What things? There's nothing to get straight. And you're not together. Audrey, you need to let go!'

'Let go? Oh, for goodness sake! You don't understand. *Give me his number!*'

'You know our policy: we don't give escorts' numbers to clients.'

'But you said yourself – he's no longer an escort and I'm no longer a client!' Audrey cried in exasperated rage. She hadn't come this far, been through this much, to be thwarted by Geraldine and her blasted policy.

'Audrey, no,' Geraldine replied firmly. 'I'm not going to give it to you. Especially when you're in this state.'

'What state? What do you mean?'

'I mean, you're not yourself, Audrey. You might do or say something you'd later regret.'

'Regret? I'll tell you what I regret! I regret not sorting this out years ago. I regret all the time John and I have wasted.'

There was a long pause. Audrey gripped the phone in desperation. 'I'm sorry,' Geraldine said finally.

The words cut to Audrey's heart like a blade. The injustice of the refusal nearly took her breath away. If she couldn't speak to John, or book him for a date, how was she supposed ever to see him again? How were they supposed to tell each other they loved each other? How was anything in the world ever going to be OK again?

'Well, can you at least tell me where he is today?' she croaked, her voice sounding broken. 'Please? I'm desperate, Geraldine.'

There was a very long pause.

'You might find him in the conservation area, just south of the river,' Geraldine said eventually. 'That's all I'm prepared to say. But, Audrey . . . ?'

There was no answer. The front door slammed shut, its mottled glass revealing Audrey's misshapen silhouette hurtling away up the path. All that was left was a forlornly mewing Pickles and a small drop of blood on the carpet.

JOHN

John looked at his watch.

'I'd better make tracks.'

At the kitchen table Emily looked up from her computer.

'Do you mind if I stay and finish this? My internet connection keeps crashing at the flat.'

'Be my guest. Buster loves a bit of company.'

Emily smiled as she watched John check his reflection in the oven door.

'Are you sure I'm not underdressed?' he asked worriedly. 'I'm so used to having to truss myself up. I never thought I'd say it, but I feel lost without my dinner jacket.'

'It's dinner with Alice, Dad, not a client. I'm sure she'd be mortified if you dressed the same way for her as you did for all your other women.'

'I don't want her to think I'm not making the effort.'

'I don't think ditching your job and taking her to the most romantic restaurant in town could be misconstrued as not making an effort!' Emily laughed.

John rummaged for his coat.

'I know, I know,' he conceded. 'I need to relax, don't I?

I can't believe my luck, that's all! I'm going to dinner with a woman and I'm actually going to pay! And not only that, I'm dining with the most beautiful woman in the world.'

Emily threw him an arch look.

'Sorry, the *second* most beautiful woman in the world!'

'That's more like it,' Emily scolded.

John headed towards the front door.

'Look, stay as long as you like. Stay the night if you want. I'd love you to meet her.'

'What, she's doing sleepovers already?' Emily raised an eyebrow. 'I'm not sure you should be hanging out with that kind of woman.'

John laughed, gave Buster a farewell tickle and closed the front door behind him.

AUDREY

It was getting dark by the time Audrey spotted John's car. She'd spent two hours wandering the streets of the city's conservation area and had been on the verge of giving up. She was exhausted. It had been a long time since she'd fled the Dating Practitioners' Society meeting, a long time since she'd last sat down, and her feet were killing her. Towards eight she'd become aware of a sharp pain at the back of her heel and had discovered that her new suedette courts had given her a nasty blood blister that had erupted on her tights. She'd hobbled to a corner shop for a box of plasters, leant unsteadily against a road sign and stuck a plaster on top of her tights. She frowned. The back of her right shoe was now a rusty-brown blood colour. Blood was a devil to get out of anything, let alone suedette. They were probably a write-off.

As she straightened up she suddenly spotted it: John's car, parked quietly on the driveway of a large, attractive house with a lush garden. Audrey's heart missed a beat.

She scuttled across the road and onto John's driveway, peering through the windows of the car for anything she recognized. She tried not to steam the pane with her excited breath. This had to be his car! It had the same cream leather interior, the same unfussy dash, the same 'ACJ' letters in the number plate that served as divine proof that she and he were destined to be together. Audrey ached as she pictured herself in the passenger seat, John skilfully driving them to the latest Dating Practitioners' function, both of them excited about the night ahead. This was the car, she thought triumphantly. She was here! She'd found John's home! She'd found John!

Without thinking she rushed to the front door and banged on the knocker. 'This is it!' she thought as she heard a dog bark inside and footsteps coming towards her. This was the moment of truth: the moment she told John they had nothing to hide from any more and they were free to love as they pleased.

The door swung open.

A young woman, red-headed and beautiful, stood before her.

'*You!*' Audrey's smile froze.

It was the woman who'd come to the agency: the one who'd barged in and demanded to see Alice. But what the hell was she doing here, in John's house?

'Where is he? Where's John?'

'He's not in,' the redhead answered curtly, looking Audrey up and down. Audrey had a sudden vision of herself, wild-haired with bloody tights. She puffed out her chest in defiance of the young woman's neat figure and perfect skin.

But if this was the right place, then *who was she*? Why had she been at the agency? And why was she here now?

'Who are you?' she demanded.

The woman smirked.

'John's daughter.'

Audrey's mouth fell open. 'I didn't know John had a daughter!'

'Yeah, well, I expect there's a lot you don't know about him.'

Audrey was flummoxed. What should she say to this woman, this daughter – this future daughter-in-law?

'Christ! You're stalking him, aren't you?' The daughter suddenly laughed. 'You're *actually* stalking my dad!'

Audrey felt her neck flush.

'Of course I'm not stalking him! What a ridiculous suggestion!'

'So what are you doing here then? Clients aren't supposed to come to the house.'

'I'm not a client!' Audrey bristled. 'I'm ... Your father and I are ...'

'... are nothing!' the daughter said sternly. 'You're a business arrangement, that's all.'

Her words stung Audrey's cheeks. How dare she? The impudence of it! She drew back her shoulders; it was time to pull rank.

'Look, young lady. I'm in a rush. It's vitally important that I speak to John, without delay. Tell me where he is. He'll be most displeased by your obstruction.'

'I doubt that!'

Audrey nearly cried out in frustration. How could this daughter not see how important it was? She wanted to reach over the doorstep and shake her to make her understand.

'This is urgent. Critical! I have to speak to him *now*. Everything depends on it.' She couldn't believe she'd got so far – to John's very front door – still to be denied. 'I have to see him. I *have* to!'

But the daughter didn't move. She just stood on the doorstep with her arms crossed. And yet, something had changed in the way she was looking at her. She seemed to be weighing something up.

'OK,' she said suddenly. 'This has gone on long enough. Someone has to put you out of your misery, and it might as well be me. He's at Beckwith's.'

'The restaurant?'

'The very same.'

Audrey hurtled back down the garden path. As she regained the pavement she remembered the daughter. It was probably best to keep on her good side; they'd be seeing a lot more of each other in the future.

'Thank you, young lady,' she called out.

But the front door was already closed.

Audrey ignored her painful heel and limped back into the city centre, her mind whirring. After the horror of the Dating Practitioners' Society meeting, not only had she had the double bombshells of John giving up escorting *and* having a daughter, but she'd just found out he was dining in the most romantic restaurant in town. But why would he do that if he wasn't with a client? And why hadn't he come to visit her now that he was free?

A bus whizzed past but she made no attempt to catch it. She'd made it this far on leg power and shoe leather, so she'd make it all the way.

She was close to the bright lights of the city centre now, only a few streets away from Beckwith's. She tried to slow down so that her cheeks could return to their normal shade, but her feet wouldn't let her. She felt the gravity of John pulling her in. It was as though he was her twin magnet and she was powerless to fight the strength of his attraction. She'd waited so many years for this; how could she delay a moment longer?

And then she was climbing the steps to Beckwith's. The foyer was bright and busy, but Audrey didn't notice. She didn't see the receptionist approach to ask if she had a reservation. She just saw the archway into the dining area and she glided towards it, a bright light at the end of a long dark tunnel.

And then she was in the restaurant, her eyes sweeping across the diners in search of the man she loved.

And then she found him. Laughing. His beautiful blue eyes crinkling in the way they always did, making Audrey draw in her breath and buckle at the knees. And he was picking up a bottle – his hand so strong and familiar – and pouring a glass of wine. Somebody else's glass of wine. And then Audrey's eyes took in a figure seated opposite him. It was a woman. A woman in a backless dress.

'Can I help you, madam?'

A waiter had stepped in front of her, blacking out her vision like an eclipse. Entranced, Audrey stepped aside and the lights came back on and John and the woman swam into focus again.

'I'm looking for my husband,' she murmured.

Silently, as though in a dream, Audrey moved towards John's table. He hadn't seen her yet, hadn't sensed her presence. He was smiling at the woman in the backless dress, listening rapt to something she was saying. And as the woman spoke, she tucked her hair behind her ear, and a long, dangling earring glinted as it caressed the skin of her neck. Her bare back looked radiant, cashmere-soft in the candlelight. But still Audrey glided on.

And then John began to move. At first Audrey thought it was towards her, that he'd seen her at last. But he was gently leaning across the table, taking the face of the woman in his hands and slowly, ever so slowly, moving towards her to kiss her lips. As John's lips touched the woman's Audrey cried out, a high-pitched yelp of pain. John's eyes flew towards her and he pulled back in surprise, his face full of shock. And as if in slow motion, the woman looked at John and then turned to see what he saw. And as she moved her earring sparkled, and then her eyes were on Audrey and Audrey's eyes were on her.

Audrey gasped.

It was Alice.

The world went silent.

All she could hear was her own heart beating, and

then the slow arrival of John's words, as though through water.

'Audrey! What are you doing here?'

Audrey felt her mouth open and close, but no sound came out. She looked at John. She couldn't look at Alice. She couldn't look at the sophisticated beauty that mousy, cardiganed Alice had become. Alice the dreamer. Alice the waste of space. She couldn't look at *this* Alice sitting here with *her* John.

'I'm so, so sorry, Audrey.' The words came from Alice's direction.

But still Audrey couldn't remove her eyes from John. His shock was subsiding now. His face was regaining its composure.

'John?' Audrey thought she heard her own voice ask.

His face softened, and his mouth began to take a shape of kindness. For a brief moment Audrey thought he was going to tell her that everything was OK, that this was just a horrible misunderstanding.

'This isn't how we planned to tell you,' he said kindly. 'But maybe it's for the best.'

Audrey blinked. John's face was swimming out of vision and she wasn't sure why. Something was getting in the way of her seeing, flooding her eyes. It was getting harder to breathe. She'd been stabbed. Nobody had moved, but somebody, unseen, had taken a knife and plunged it between her ribs and was carving it up towards her heart.

And then her feet started to move and she was rushing through the foyer, down the steps and into the night. She collided with someone at street level and briefly felt the heat of their body. She thought she heard someone call out her name. But then that too receded behind her as her bloodstained suedette shoes carried her off in the direction of home.

KATE

Kate was quietly thrilled by the small but regular contraception risks she and Tommy were now taking. She knew she should be sensible; it was still early days for their relationship. But she just couldn't help herself. And neither, it seemed, could Tommy.

Take tonight, for instance, she told herself. They'd both been desperate to see the latest cop blockbuster at the cinema. But halfway through the movie, cuddled as closely as a chair arm and a jumbo box of popcorn would allow, Tommy had suddenly leaned in excitingly close and whispered hotly in her ear, 'I want you.'

Exactly sixty seconds later Kate had found herself locked inside a toilet cubicle, pinned to the partition wall. The box of popcorn tumbled to the floor, spilling out its sugary cargo like a cliché in a steamy B-movie as Kate surrendered to the moment. She briefly wished Lou could see her. Her eyes would probably pop out of her head. The Kate that Lou knew – the old Kate – would never have had sex in the ladies' loo at the local cinema, she thought deliciously. The old Kate wouldn't have made it to the cinema at all; she'd still be at her desk, writing and rewriting press releases until they reached the height of literary perfection.

'I'm going to come,' Tommy suddenly breathed in her ear.

Kate felt him begin to pull away from her. Firmly but gently she pushed his buttocks back into position and held them there.

'It's OK,' she whispered, feeling a dangerous tingle of adrenalin.

'You sure?' Tommy paused, drawing back his head to check. 'Isn't it a risk?'

Kate resisted the temptation to answer him honestly: that the risk was the most exciting part of all, and that if she should suddenly find herself impregnated by this gorgeous, rebellious, rugged man who didn't care about working his way up some pointless career ladder and who made her tummy flip and her breath go short every time she saw him, then that would be the sexiest thing imaginable.

'It's an OK time of the month,' she panted. 'Just fuck me!' And she pulled him hard to her, barely registering that the old Kate would never have used the F-word like that.

Afterwards it was far too late to go back into the cinema and watch the rest of the film. Besides, car chases and explosions had lost their thrill.

'I know what I want to do,' Tommy said as they left the cinema and reached the cooler night air. He tucked Kate's hand protectively under his arm.

'What?' she murmured dewily as she looked up at him.

Although she knew that technically she'd been truthful, it really was a safe part of the month (the old Kate still lived, and she'd scoured the NHS website that morning to look up which days in the cycle you couldn't conceive), she still felt wonderfully reckless and unmistakably turned on by the significance of what had just happened. They'd wordlessly passed into new territory.

'Go back to yours and pick up where we left off.' He grinned mischievously. Kate felt herself squirm with delight. They set off in the direction of her flat.

'We probably should get some condoms, just to be safe,' she said sensibly, trying not to let the disappointment she felt at the prospect be audible in her voice.

'Probably,' agreed Tommy mildly. He stopped suddenly and took her in his arms. 'Fuck it! You do know I'm crazy about you, don't you, Kate?'

Kate's heart leapt and time seemed to stand still. She looked up at him. He truly was the most gorgeous man she'd ever seen.

They'd stopped outside an expensive-looking restaurant, and the soft lighting of the foyer spilled out into the street and lit up Tommy's face.

'What I'm trying to say is ... I know we shouldn't be stupid, but ...' And then he grinned. 'You know me, Kate; I don't like playing games – never fancied learning the rules. I know you'd tell me I'm supposed to wait a certain number of dates before I say this, and that the moon needs to be aligned with Jupiter and that you should be wearing emerald green, but sod it; I'm not a rules kind of guy. So

I'm just going to come out and say it. I love you, Kate. I love you, I love you, I love you!'

And so, in a place she'd never have selected, to a man she'd never have thought possible, and wearing something distinctly last season – but with a full four hundred and ninety-seven days to spare before her thirty-fifth birthday – Kate's heart whizzed like a firework and she said those three magic words back. Well, eight, to be precise.

'I love you, Tommy! I really, really do.'

And they kissed the most delicious kiss imaginable.

'And about the contraception . . .' Tommy added when they finally came up for air. 'Obviously it's up to you. But if you're asking me what I think, well . . . what's the worst that can happen? You find yourself pregnant and we're saddled with each other for evermore. That doesn't seem so terrible from where I'm standing!'

'No,' Kate breathed, so excited she could barely speak. 'Not so terrible at all!'

'So, let's do it, shall we? Let's decide to live dangerously!'

'Yes,' she heard herself agree dizzily. 'Let's!'

And they both grinned ecstatically in the darkness.

Suddenly, a woman hurtled down the restaurant steps and into the street, shattering their moment as she ran blindly into them. She was sobbing hysterically, tears mixing with snot as she gulped the night air. Instinctively Kate held her arm to steady her.

'Audrey Cracknell?' Kate asked in surprise. 'Are you OK?'

But the woman was already speeding down the road in the direction of the cinema.

'Do you know her?' Tommy asked as he watched the retreating figure.

'I think so.' Kate stared after her in concern. 'I think it's the lady who runs Table For Two, but it can't be. She's normally so . . . regimented.'

'Hey, talking about Table For Two . . . I didn't tell you, did I?' Tommy said suddenly, his voice filled with excited amusement. 'You remember my mate Steve? Well, he only got found out by Alice!'

'Found out?'

'Yeah. Well, you see, Steve didn't actually join to find himself a girlfriend. He signed up because it'd been a year since his last shag and somehow he'd managed to be the only person in the universe to fail to pull on the internet. So his logic was, if a woman was desperate enough to pay good money to join a dating agency, then she might, *just might*, be desperate enough to sleep with him!'

'He signed up for sex?' Kate asked incredulously.

'With as many women as his fee would stretch to.'

'I *knew* there was something funny about him!' Kate exclaimed. 'He seemed, well, almost like he'd rehearsed.'

'That's because he had!' Tommy laughed. 'When he hit on a patter that finally coaxed some poor woman into bed, he'd repeat his stories verbatim on the next target. He still didn't have much of a success rate, though. One in twenty, he reckoned.'

'I can't believe it!' Kate said in wonder. 'It's so cynical. It sounds like something Lou would do!'

'So, anyway, our friend Alice rumbled him,' Tommy

continued, 'and Steve's supply of dates dried up. So he ditched Table For Two and moved on to the next agency. He's got it all planned out, you see. Six to twelve months at an agency, try it on with all the women on their books and then move on to a new pool of talent. He's signed with this other place now. Apparently it's run by a real maneater. Steve's only gone and convinced himself he's in with a chance with her!'

'The dirty dog!' Kate replied thoughtfully, her mind filled with fond nostalgia. And she suddenly realized how much she missed her best friend.

AUDREY

Audrey staggered through the streets, her tears rolling freely. She lurched unseeingly into the road, across red traffic lights and through dangerously dark parks. She saw nothing, heard nothing, felt nothing but the knife that John and Alice had plunged into her heart.

John and Alice.

Her John and *her* Alice.

When had Alice become attractive? When, exactly, had the ugly duckling turned into a swan? Her trysts with John must have been going on right under Audrey's nose. Her insides twisted painfully. Had John kissed Alice before? Had he touched her face, smoothed his hand down the velvet skin of her back, pushed his hands under the straps of her dress and watched it fall luxuriously to the floor? Had he . . . ? With Alice? With butter-wouldn't-melt, stare-out-of-the-window Alice? The Alice she'd employed and trusted and nurtured and supported? The Alice she – out of the goodness of her own heart – had taken to the ball? And how had Alice repaid her? By deceiving her; by lying. By hiding in cardigans by day and dressing like a vixen by night. By stealing Audrey's one true love and flaunting it in her face.

As Audrey neared home her whole body pumped with the poison of anger. How dare she do this to her! How dare she take John! She must have been laughing at her for weeks. Not a day must have passed when she hadn't smugly congratulated herself for getting one over on the boss, smiling sweetly to Audrey's face whilst sharpening the knife for her back and running her harlot fingers down John's.

Audrey stomped up her garden path breathing pure fury. She threw open her front door and steamed into the hallway, fists clenched. Well, she was going to show Alice! She was going to show that scheming little whore that she wasn't to be trifled with. She was going to fire her. She was going to expose her. She was going to string her up and run her out of town. She was going to . . .

In the background of her rage she was dimly aware of Pickles snaking between her legs and clamouring for food.

. . . She was going to smash that conniving bitch. She was going to ruin her. She was going to make John regret the day he ever clapped eyes on that duplicitous, evil little tart.

Audrey kicked out in fury. Her foot connected with something soft. There was a pitiful yelp, and then a sudden flood of silence. Audrey stood paralysed on one leg, her other still extended as her mouth filled with the taste of bile.

And then she looked down.

Pickles had landed where the floor met the skirting board. His ribcage heaved with raggedy, laboured breath and his hind leg was cocked unnaturally. His leg was broken. Pickles was broken.

Audrey cried out, a long anguished moan from the very gut of her being. She fell to her knees.

'Pickles!' she cried remorsefully. 'My darling Pickles. I'm sorry. I'm sorry!'

She tried to stroke him, but Pickles flinched in pain.

'I'm sorry, I'm sorry, I'm sorry,' she pleaded. Big fat tears dripped from her face onto Pickles's fur, disappearing into his luxuriant coat.

'I'm sorry, I'm sorry, I'm sorry.'

The tears poured out, her anger forgotten as she watched her friend fight for breath. After several long moments, Audrey clambered to her feet and ransacked the telephone cupboard in panic, pulling out free newspapers and old leaflets as she desperately hunted for a Yellow Pages.

'I'm sorry, I'm sorry,' she repeated over and over as she tried to focus on the tiny print and find an emergency vet. Her tears fell heavily onto the pages. The thin yellow paper soaked them up like blotting paper, their wetness obscuring the numbers below.

ALICE

Today had been the worst day of her life, Alice thought miserably as she lay in bed next to the man of her dreams.

Lying on her side, feeling the heat of John's body as he sleepily spooned behind her, Alice couldn't help but wonder if it was worth it. Of course, *John* was worth it. He was the best man she'd ever met and the thought of losing him made her feel like she couldn't breathe. But was *she* worth it? Was her own selfish happiness worth more than Audrey's?

Alice had looked at her boss's face in the soft candle-light of Beckwith's and she'd seen something inside her break.

She'd tried to go after her. She'd ignored John's warning and had run out into the night in her wake. But Audrey was nowhere to be seen.

'It's for the best,' John had said. 'This isn't some quick fling we're having. She had to find out sooner or later.'

'I just didn't want it to be like this. I wanted . . .'

'What?' John reasoned kindly. 'There's no *good* way of telling her. At least now we can come out from the shadows; enjoy being together.'

But how could she enjoy being with John when Audrey was suffering? It didn't seem fair.

'Tomorrow . . .' she started.

'. . . is going to be tough,' John conceded.

'What do I do? Do I go to work? Do I stay away? What would the kindest thing be?'

'Only you know what's best.'

'She must hate me.'

'She probably hates herself more. This is a problem of her making. My relationship with Audrey was clearly defined from the start. Only she chose to see it for something it wasn't.'

'She was in love.'

'No, she wasn't. She was no more in love with me than a teenager is in love with the pop star they see on TV. What she felt wasn't real. She didn't even know me.'

Alice pulled John's arm tighter around her, wishing it could shield her from tomorrow. She'd never come first at anything before. How was she to know that winning first prize could be anything more complicated than a straightforward delight? But in reality things were never black or white. They say there's a silver lining to misery, she told herself. And now she knew that there's an ugly side to joy.

She sighed heavily.

She *would* go to work tomorrow. And she'd get there early so she could speak to Audrey before the others arrived. She'd apologize. And then she'd resign. It was the least she could do. After all, she'd already won first prize. She should have the grace to leave Audrey her business. She could at least leave Audrey with that.

Oh my goodness, she thought suddenly. *I'm leaving Table For Two!*

And suddenly she felt even worse.

AUDREY

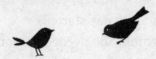

Audrey hadn't switched on the lights. Instead she sat stiffly on the edge of her armchair, her coat still on, her handbag still looped over her shoulder. It was four in the morning.

Now that she'd finally sat down her body was consumed with tiredness. She was more exhausted than she'd ever been in her life, but she wouldn't let herself relax into the chair's familiar folds. She couldn't. She didn't deserve a shred of comfort, not even from a three-piece suite. Her feet ached as if they were on fire and her heel throbbed as though it were clamped in a pit bull's teeth. But the physical pains were the least of it. The two daggers in her heart were worse. And the second one she'd put there herself. She'd stabbed herself in her cold, black heart when she'd kicked her most precious friend in the world.

She replayed the vision of Pickles lying broken on the vet's examining table. Her best friend; her trusting, purring companion. Pickles, who would curl up on her lap – in this very chair – and sit with her evening upon evening as she stroked his fur and rubbed his ears.

Every time Audrey remembered Pickles's leg, snapped

and sticking out, she felt a new flush of shame. But whenever the image receded it would be replaced by another horrible vision: of John taking Alice's hand, of Alice's earring falling against honeyed skin, of John moving forward to kiss her; and Audrey would feel a new lurch of despair.

What on earth was she supposed to do when the darkness faded and the new day started?

She needed to think. She needed to work out a plan, to see if anything could be salvaged from the wreckage of the last twenty-four hours.

Pickles, she'd been assured, would make a complete recovery. But it was hardly the point. He'd never trust her again. She didn't deserve his trust. She didn't deserve him.

But still, he *would* recover, and in the darkness of her living room Audrey vowed to be a better owner, a more patient friend. She'd cook him real dinners, rather than just spoon them out of a tin. She'd give him real cuddles, not half-hearted asides while she watched TV. She'd let him sleep in the middle of her bed, rather than inch him towards the wall with her knee.

Her own heart, however, wouldn't be as resilient. It would never recover from the fatal injury done by John and Alice. Why hadn't she seen it coming? And how was she going to sit in the same office as Alice and pretend nothing had happened? To know that Alice had won the heart of the man she'd loved – *she'd loved* – for eleven years?

But, Audrey thought with new-found penitence, maybe if she hadn't been so blinkered by her feelings . . . ? If she hadn't been so deluded by what she'd imagined, she'd *fantasized*, John was thinking about her? She'd been a fool, she scolded herself. An old, fat fool. Because that's what she was. Old and fat and foolish. Of course John couldn't have loved her. What was there to love?

And then there was the damage to her reputation too. She could barely remember as far back as the DIPS meeting. All she could remember was Sheryl calling for her disbarment. They all thought she was a liar. And worse, *a frequenter of prostitutes*. She could imagine what they were all thinking. She'd have jumped to the same conclusions too. Audrey felt her cheeks flush again in the dark.

How could she face them – any of them? John, Alice, Sheryl, Ernie, Barry Chambers, Wendy Arthur? Bianca and Cassandra? Pickles? How could she face any of the people in her life again?

And how was she ever going to do anything without the dream of having John?

But if this dreadful day had shown her anything, it had shown her that she needed to change. Become a better person. A *nicer* person. John wasn't hers.

John wasn't hers.

Around her the room's inky blackness started to turn to fuzzy purple, and small sounds of life began to emanate from the street. Audrey squinted at the clock on her old VCR machine. There was no point in going to bed. In an hour she'd put on a fresh outfit, paint on a new face and get the 119 bus to the office as though her world hadn't really imploded overnight. Today was the first day of her new life: a kinder life. And the sooner she went to work, the sooner she'd be able to bring home Pickles. They'd said she'd be able to collect him tomorrow evening, and it was already the start of tomorrow.

There was just the small matter of the day to get through first.

LOU

Lou strode defiantly past the morning commuters, cutting through their ranks and ignoring their disapproving glances. Nothing was going to delay her from her mission, which was to get home as fast as humanly possible.

She wanted nothing more than to shut her front door behind her, rip off last night's clothes and wipe away her make-up. Her outfit – so sexy yesterday – now itched toxically against her skin. But if she let herself imagine how good it would be to climb into a scalding hot bath she'd probably start crying now. And that absolutely wasn't going to happen.

Out of the corner of her eye she saw a businesswoman staring at her with open distaste, no doubt comparing Lou's leather mini and fishnets with her own A-line and triple-digit deniers. Lou eyeballed her squarely and then slowly raised her middle finger. As the woman looked away in pink-cheeked alarm Lou felt a savage pleasure. She hadn't given anyone the finger in years!

Suddenly she saw her bus and forced her four-inch stilettos into an awkward sprint towards the stop. She clambered on board, ignored the sea of disapproving eyes that greeted her and marched to an empty seat. As the bus pulled away she calculated how many minutes it would be until home.

Last night her plan had seemed perfect. As predicted, Simon had become a regular. He'd been hard work, but bit by bit Lou had discovered he was a middle-ranking manager who liked spy thrillers, cinema and cider. He visited his parents every month, his fingernails were always clean, and – most importantly – he was single. Operation Fornication-with-Mr-Nice-Guy was all systems go! She'd soon have Kate eating her words. Or she would if she ever spoke to Kate again.

And besides, despite her original motives she was beginning to like Simon. He was different; nice. He didn't drink himself senseless or ogle every woman who came into the bar. He was quiet and clever and asked Lou questions about herself. Maybe Kate was on to something with this 'proper boyfriend' malarkey. Maybe it *would* be nice to have Simon ask her about her day when she got in at night; pour her a glass of wine; introduce her to his mother. Why couldn't that happen to her, just this once? Why shouldn't the nice boy want her to be his girlfriend?

After several weeks of small talk Lou decided the verbal foreplay was over. She was going to make her strike.

She'd picked her outfit with extra care. Simon wasn't like normal men; he was shy, unassuming. He didn't seem to notice Lou's double entendres. Lou needed to spell things out, make sure there was no ambiguity. So she stated her intentions as clearly as she could. She wore her leather mini, fishnets and heels.

From the moment Simon entered the bar the regulars were ignored, excuses were made to swing by his table and she'd even dipped into her own purse to buy him pints when it looked like he might be leaving. Eventually, as the night drew to a close and the bar started emptying, she managed to corner him.

'Fancy a lock-in?'

'Um, well. I think I've had enough,' he answered tipsily.

'It's just that my regular taxi driver rang to say he can't pick me up tonight,' Lou lied. 'Would you mind walking me to the rank after my shift?'

'Ah.' Simon stalled reluctantly. Lou could tell he was fighting the urge to look at his watch. But his gentlemanly nature got the better of him. 'Of course,' he replied.

Round one to her. He was going to be putty in her hands.

She deliberately led him to the worst taxi rank in the city centre, the one with the longest queues and fewest cabs. After twenty minutes of fruitless waiting she turned to a yawning Simon and said:

'This isn't going to work. I'll just crash on your sofa instead.'

Simon choked. Before he could reply Lou looped her arm in his and steered him away from the rank.

'Come on.' She snuggled up to him. 'I'm freezing. Let's get walking.'

'Do you want my . . . ?' Simon politely offered his jacket.

'There's no point in both of us getting cold. Why don't you just put your arm around me instead?'

Obediently, Simon laid his arm stiffly around her shoulders and they walked awkwardly back to his flat.

Lou was banking on Simon being – underneath it all – as red-blooded as any other man. When they arrived at his flat (a loft apartment on the river; the kind Kate would die for her man to have) Lou led him straight to the bedroom. She was going to win him as a boyfriend. She was going to bring him to his knees and make him beg for more. She was going to ride him like a Grand National stallion. She was going to fuck him to within an inch of his middle-class life.

After an hour of X-rated foreplay during which Lou removed everything but her heels and leather mini, she finally decided he'd been teased enough. Besides, he was looking tired and she didn't want him falling asleep. So she pulled herself onto all fours, hitched up her skirt and begged him to take her from behind. As he timidly entered her, careful not to hurt her, she urged him to spank her – hard – on the backside. When his hand flip-flopped limply on the side of her hip with all the sexual aggression of custard she showed him what she meant, twisting her own hand into position and bringing it forcefully down onto her buttocks with an ear-popping crack.

The night wore on and still Lou wouldn't let Simon rest. She remembered reading that cults brainwashed their victims by denying them sleep and decided this was a good strategy. She pulled out her arsenal of tricks – moaning, writhing and pleading with him to take her harder, treat her rougher, be as wild as he wanted to be. Her throat ached from all the gasps of ecstasy. She lost count of how many orgasms she faked.

And Simon had enjoyed it. Hadn't he? OK, so he hadn't been as energetic as the taxi driver or as filthy as Tony. He'd seemed a bit embarrassed by her porn-movie patter and top-shelf positions. But he'd gone along with it. He hadn't said no. He'd come, for God's sake!

Yet still …

On the back seat of the 138 bus Lou winced as she remembered the mildness of his responses. He'd hardly thrown himself into it. He'd gone along with everything, nothing more. And when she'd finally let them finish he'd pulled the blanket right up to his neck, wished her an embarrassed goodnight and slept on the furthest edge of the bed.

Lou pulled her eyes from the bus window and looked into her lap in dawning realization. He hadn't enjoyed it. She'd just backed him into a corner and he'd been too polite to say no. She felt her cheeks sting. And then it caught her eye: a small, crusty patch of white on her leather skirt; an incriminating neon light advertising last night's behaviour. With a flush of shame she scratched the mockery that was Simon's dried semen off her skirt and brushed it discreetly onto the floor.

Eventually the bus lurched into her road. Lou lunged for the bell.

She'd woken feeling good. She'd done it! She'd won herself a nice boy! She'd woken up in his bed (nice boys didn't shag you in alleys, they let you stay over!) and she was going to be his girlfriend. She'd rolled over and gazed happily at

Simon's back, grinning with anticipation of the moment when he'd roll over and scoop her up in his arms.

Except . . .

He hadn't rolled over. He hadn't looked at her at all. Instead he'd slipped out of bed without turning around, hurriedly found his clothes and dressed. He was sorry about last night. He shouldn't have taken advantage. He'd call her a cab and give her the fare.

'But you didn't take advantage!' Lou replied incredulously. 'I wanted it to happen. And you . . .' She'd leaned over and tried to stroke him, but felt him recoil from her touch. 'You were fantastic. An animal!'

It won't happen again, he promised. He was sorry to have led her up the garden path.

'But what's the problem?' Lou demanded. 'You're single, I'm single. I thought we could, you know . . . go out.'

He was sorry, but it wasn't a good idea.

'But we had a good time!'

It was complicated.

'Complicated how?'

Maybe not complicated, exactly. It's just, he wasn't looking for a relationship right now.

'Of course you are! Your sort's always looking for relationships,' Lou insisted.

After a couple of minutes the truth came out.

He *was* looking for a relationship, just not with her.

'Bar managers not good enough for you?' Lou spat. 'Not respectable enough to introduce to Mummy?'

He started phoning a cab.

'But I thought this was different,' Lou heard herself plead. 'I thought we had a connection!'

Lou could see the front door to her apartment block and locked her eyes on it. She blotted out everything else, not hearing the scrape of her stilettos on the pavement, the car horn beeping her, or the wolf-whistle of a passing schoolboy. She only had tunnel vision for her front door. Once inside she could let everything go: pull off her clothes, smear her scarlet lips into some toilet roll and sink into a pile on the carpet.

Why couldn't men see her? Why couldn't they see *her*, not just her bum or her tits or her make-up? Why didn't they care that she was clever and interesting, had read all the classics, was a demon at *Countdown* and could be the wittiest guest at the dinner party? She had just as much to give as any other girl. More! She could talk politics and sport. She could do walks in the hills and afternoons at the cinema. She could cook her man a roast, chat to his mother, play with his dog.

But what hope did she have of men seeing all this, she thought miserably, if even her best friend couldn't?

Kate.

Why couldn't she be Kate?

If she were Kate there was no way she'd waste her life hiding at work or worrying about the size of her hips. She'd have a boyfriend in an instant. Kate was lovable. Not like her. She was just fuckable. Good for a shag but not for falling in love with.

Lou reached the apartment block's door. And suddenly the world was behind her and she was dashing up the stairs, not bothering to stop the tears from falling.

Why couldn't anyone see that what she wanted was the same as what Kate wanted? A man; a home; a family. She couldn't admit it, of course. People would laugh. She wasn't the type. But what was the type, exactly? What gave Kate and her kind the monopoly on being able to admit they wanted a happy ending?

Lou slammed her front door behind her, pulled off her clothes and dropped them in the bin. And then she cried for a very long time.

AUDREY

Audrey was doing one of the things she hated most in the world: fidgeting. But she couldn't help herself. The wait for the bus was lasting forever, and as each minute stretched interminably on, she tried to ignore her mounting paranoia.

Everyone knew, she was sure of it. Every set of eyes she'd come across since leaving the house bored directly into her. Normally nobody gave her a second glance in the morning; she was just one of the invisible middle-aged. But today was different. Today she was sure that every waiting bus passenger and passing driver knew, *just knew*, that she was the scandal of the matchmaking world.

Eventually the bus arrived. Audrey gratefully made her way to the back of the lower deck, pulled out her hardback and pretended to be immersed in its flimsy plot.

She tried to ignore the rising panic gripping her throat. Now that she was on the bus, she was closer than ever to work . . . and Alice. Her plan had been to arrive early and scuttle straight into her glass-walled office (why, oh why hadn't she opted for brick?). By the time the others arrived she could pretend to be ensconced in paperwork or in the middle of an important call.

But now she wasn't so sure. Maybe she should speak to Alice and get it over and done with? Not that she'd refer to last night's shenanigans, nor permit Alice to either. But maybe she could ask her to fetch her a coffee, or give her a client update: just a little something to show that she wasn't hiding.

Of course, she wasn't going to explain yesterday's bombshells from the Dating Practitioners' Society meeting to anyone. She needed time – much more time. Although she'd spent the entire night thinking, she'd only managed to scratch the surface of her crime against Pickles, the pain of her broken heart and the indignity of who it was that broke it. The ruins of her professional reputation had had to wait. So the temporary strategy was to instruct the girls to tell all callers that she was unavailable, thereby keeping the matchmaking world at bay a little bit longer. And if she could avoid the phone for *two* days, then it would be the weekend, and she'd have plenty of time to concoct a defence. If she could only hold on that long ...

'Audrey?'

Audrey jumped from her book with a start.

'I thought it was you! May I?'

A man was standing over her, his body lurching in tandem with the movements of the bus. It was Maurice Lazenby. If it was possible for Audrey's heart to sink any further, it did. Maurice gestured to the empty seat next to her and she nodded in weary submission. Maybe she deserved to be Mauriced.

'I'm so glad I caught you,' he declared as he settled into his seat and fussily straightened his mac around him. 'I was planning to call to see if I could arrange a meeting. I'm very keen to hear about any progress you've made in finding me a match. I hope you won't find it forward of me to tell you how very pleased I am – well, excited really – that you've agreed to take over my case personally. As I've been saying all along, you're the only woman for the job. Not that your staff aren't excellent, but *your* skills are far superior.'

Despite her public surroundings Audrey was surprised to find her eyes filling with tears. As much as Maurice was the last person she wanted to see this morning – or any morning – his blind faith in her and her matchmaking skills cut through her flimsy armour. He believed in her. He thought she was good at her job. He, at least, didn't know about yesterday's catalogue of indignities or her shame. Tears suddenly cascaded down her face.

'Is everything all right? Have I spoken out of turn?'

Audrey fumbled in her bag for a tissue.

'No, really, I'm fine. I'm just . . .'

'Please, take this.' A large, immaculately pressed white handkerchief loomed into view.

'Thank you.' Audrey submitted, and after tentatively dabbing at a few tears for a moment she gave up and buried her face in its comforting folds.

'It's just that I . . .' she heaved between raggedy breaths, 'I've had some bad news. Rather a lot of bad news. And I've been such a fool.'

'I doubt that very much.'

Audrey sniffed noisily and dabbed at her face with the handkerchief.

'I haven't slept.'

'Ah!'

'And I'm so worried about going into work today.' As soon as the words were out she felt a new onslaught of tears. This time she didn't bother dabbing them; she covered her face in the hanky again. Suddenly she felt Maurice's arm move protectively around her shoulders. She stiffened with shock. Audrey was never touched, other than by mistake. And she couldn't remember the last time anyone had touched her like this. *She was being hugged*, she suddenly realized ... *and by Maurice*!

But then the pleasant warmth of simple human contact began to seep through her coat and into her tired bones, and bit by bit she let herself unfreeze until her head was resting against Maurice's shoulder and her tears were seeping slowly into his tailored lapel.

They rode like this in silence for a few minutes, Audrey suddenly feeling every hour of her sleepless exhaustion as she permitted herself a few moments in the unexpected safety of Maurice's semi-embrace.

As her stop loomed nearer she began to mentally compose a few words of thanks. What on earth could she say? She was grateful for Maurice's kindness – and for the use of his handkerchief – but how embarrassing that he'd seen her like this, so weak! What were the chances of her bumping into a client this morning, let alone Maurice the moaner?

How on earth was she going to get their relationship back on a professional keel after this?

And then her stop was in sight and she could prevaricate no longer. She stood up. To her surprise Maurice rose too.

'I'm going to escort you to your desk,' he explained gallantly.

'That's very kind, but really not necessary.'

'Nonsense,' Maurice insisted. 'I wouldn't dream of letting you go into the office on your own.'

As Audrey followed him she couldn't help but feel deeply touched that he would put himself out for her. And it did feel better to walk through the doors of Table For Two and not be alone. Especially when she saw Alice already sitting at her desk. Audrey stiffened. As Maurice ushered her protectively through the open-plan office she forced herself to meet Alice's eyes briefly and give her a stiff nod of greeting. Her glimpse surprised her. Alice looked almost as wretched as she did.

'Morning, Miss Brown,' Maurice greeted Alice politely. 'Could you possibly make Ms Cracknell a cup of tea, please? With extra sugar.'

'Of course!' Alice replied in surprise, rising instantly. Audrey thought she heard a touch of disappointment in her voice. What was she doing in the office so early? Could it be that she wanted to catch Audrey alone?

But there was no time to think. Maurice swept her onwards, holding open the door to her glass-walled enclave, and once inside, closing it gently behind him. Aware that

Alice might be watching, Audrey self-consciously removed her coat, inwardly cursing as a flurry of scrunched-up, tear-filled tissues fell out of her sleeve and cascaded to the floor.

'Here, let me.' Maurice swiftly gathered them up and dropped them into the bin. He then delved into his own coat and proffered his business card.

'Now, I'm sure you'll be perfectly fine,' he said kindly. 'And I know you'll have dozens of friends you'd rather speak to. But sometimes it's good to offload to a stranger. Not that I'm a complete stranger, but maybe for these purposes I'm as good as. What I mean is, you would be more than welcome to offload on me. In fact, I'd like it. It would be an honour to help.'

Audrey took the card uncertainly. She didn't know what to say.

'We may not know each other very well,' Maurice continued formally, 'but I want you to know I have the utmost regard for you as a matchmaker, and a business-woman, and a woman, and it pains me to see you unhappy. Here are my contact numbers. I'm at your disposal any time, day or night. So if there's anything you need, anything at all, just call.'

Audrey felt the hot sting of tears prickle her eyes again at his kind words and she swallowed hard. She mustered a watery smile of thanks.

Maurice half-nodded, half-bowed and backed courteously towards the glass door. As he left, Alice entered with a cup of tea.

'Thank you, Alice,' Audrey croaked, trying to flatten any

crackle of emotion in her voice. She was aware of Alice hovering uncertainly but didn't look her way. Instead she watched the retreating figure of Maurice. As his coat disappeared out of the front door she suddenly felt a lot less safe.

'Audrey?' Alice asked hesitantly.

'Not now,' she replied quietly, her eyes on the spot where Maurice's coat had disappeared.

And then merciful distraction. Into the space vacated by Maurice burst Bianca and Cassandra. As Alice turned to watch them enter, Audrey quickly picked up her telephone and blindly punched in a fictitious number. Alice reluctantly backed out of the glass-walled office and into the noisy chatter of the girls.

Heaving a sigh of relief, Audrey swivelled on her chair and pretended to be busy on a call.

ALICE

It was fast approaching lunchtime and, other than a cursory greeting and a thank you for the cup of tea, Audrey hadn't acknowledged Alice at all. Or anyone, in fact. She hadn't even set foot outside her glass-walled office. She'd been absorbed in her paperwork or engaged on one of her important-looking phone calls. It was as though the world on the other side of her glass wall didn't exist.

Bent over her computer in what she hoped was a mirror image of Audrey's industrious concentration, Alice waited for an opportunity to slip into her office and apologize. Audrey looked tired, she thought. But other than that no one would guess the trials she'd been through yesterday.

The ins and outs of Audrey's love life were all that Bianca and Cassandra could talk about. Alice had tried to stop their gossip several times, but after the filthy looks the girls had thrown her, plus the hissed reminder that she wasn't the boss, she'd given up. Between them they bought a dozen gossip magazines each week, so to stop them talking about a real-life scandal that had unfolded under their very noses was probably impossible. Besides, matchmakers across the county were probably *all* inspecting Audrey's dirty linen this morning. The thought made Alice want to run into her office and cover her boss's ears.

Unhappily Alice turned back to her half-written resignation letter.

She had no doubt her resignation would be accepted. Audrey had wanted rid of her practically from the moment she'd hired her. Maybe that was why she was so busy today, Alice thought suddenly. Maybe she was compiling a case for her dismissal. Why else would Maurice Lazenby have arrived with her first thing this morning? Alice didn't have many dissatisfied clients, but Maurice was certainly one of them. So it was Maurice who was going to provide the ammunition for her Table For Two firing squad, she thought sadly.

An email popped into her in-box, distracting her from her professional funeral. It was from John.

Sweetheart, it read.

> *I hope it's all going OK. Or as OK as can be expected. And if she*
> *fires you, fear not! I have a plan for both our professional*
> *futures. Dinner at mine tonight so I can explain? I'll pick you up*
> *from the hospital at 8 (presuming you're still going to visit*
> *Hilary and the baby – not that Audrey will have put you there!).*
> *J x*

Despite herself, Alice couldn't help smiling. God, it felt good to finally have a boyfriend. She hadn't realized how much she'd been missing out on all these years. It was all going to be worth it, she told herself. She'd get another job, somewhere else, away from the territory of Table For Two. After all, it would feel like the final act of betrayal to battle Audrey for her clients as well as her man. And besides, who around here could she bear to work for? Not Sheryl. Nor any of the other DIPS members. None of them had had the decency to stick up for Audrey at the meeting.

No, she would have to go to another city. It'd mean leaving her clients behind, she thought with a pang, but it had to be done. She and John would go somewhere new, where neither of their old jobs could haunt them. And once they were gone then maybe, just maybe, Audrey's heart would begin to mend. And in a couple of years Alice and John would be forgotten, a mere ghost of a bad dream that Audrey could barely remember. The glass is always half full, Alice reminded herself.

She lifted her shoulders and concentrated on finishing her resignation letter.

LOU

Lou paused, ignored the fear churning unpleasantly in her stomach, lifted her head defiantly and went inside. It had been a difficult walk to work, not least because her feet were unaccustomed to flat shoes (surprisingly awkward after years of heels). But that hadn't been the worst of it. She'd felt horrible, naked: caught in the middle of a bad dream – the one where you went to work but forgot to put on your clothes.

It was the first time she'd left the flat since the morning after her night with Simon. And it was the first time she'd been anywhere without make-up since she was twelve. It wasn't easy. It was beyond a big deal. Her hefty layer of cosmetic colour had been her protection. Without it she felt exposed and nervous. She wasn't sure she was cut out for this relaxed, natural look. It felt distinctly unnatural to her.

But she'd made it this far without turning back . . .

As she descended the stairs she concentrated on keeping her eyes fixed firmly ahead – studiously avoiding the big mirror that greeted drinkers on arrival – and made her way across the empty room to where Tony, Paul and Jake were bottling up.

'Fucking hell!' exclaimed Tony as he caught sight of her. 'Look at the state of you! Are you ill again?'

He peered at her, making sure he kept his distance. In Tony's world it was a medical fact that germs couldn't leap distances of more than thirty centimetres.

'No, I'm fine,' Lou replied. She noticed there wasn't any concern in her lover's voice.

She could feel Tony's eyes boring into her as she pushed open the door to the back room and disappeared momentarily to stow away her bag. Out of sight for a few seconds she brushed her hand through her hair nervously, bit her lip (no worries about lipstick on her teeth any more) and then walked back into the bar.

Tony hadn't moved. He was still staring at her, his mouth gaping and his face full of his natural suspicion of illness. Behind him, Paul and Jake were also staring, although a lot more kindly.

Ignoring them all, Lou busied herself with setting up the till, tipping the plastic bags of coins into their allotted segments.

'Listen, love,' Tony's voice had softened. Lou stiffened as she recognized his 'be nice to the lady staff, they're probably on the blob' voice. 'Are you sure you should be here? You're not contagious or anything, are you? I'm just thinking of you!' he added quickly, holding his hands up as if in surrender to an imminent menstrually aggressive attack. 'Besides, me, Suze and the kids are off to Marbella at the weekend. I don't want any of your lurgy.'

'I've told you, I'm perfectly all right, thank you,' Lou replied, not looking up from her work.

In her peripheral vision she saw Tony turn to Jake and Paul and pull a face.

'Right, well, in that case' – his voice was back to its normal bullish tone – 'you'd better pull yourself together. That face could curdle beer. The regulars want eye candy, not sauerkraut.'

He turned angrily and headed to the back room. Something in the way he stropped off made Lou realize their relationship had only been as deep as her make-up. Their up-against-the-optics quickies were over.

'Are you sure you're OK?' Paul asked quietly, his voice full of concern. 'We can always cover for you if you need to go home.'

'Cheers, Paul, but that won't be necessary.'

'Right. If you say so,' he replied, but he didn't sound convinced. 'You just don't look yourself, that's all.'

Lou sighed. She might as well get it over and done with. After all, this wasn't supposed to be an experiment for just one day.

'Look, if you must know,' – she raised her voice slightly so Jake could hear too – 'I'm not wearing any make-up, that's all.'

'Oh!' Paul sounded embarrassed. 'Shit! Sorry Lou!'

'Don't be,' she chirped. Maybe cheery optimism was the

way to get through this. 'Make-up costs a bomb. The amount I used to trowel on, I'm going to save a bloody fortune.'

'You look great!' Jake called over. 'Younger.'

'Thanks! I just thought it was time you all got the chance to see me,' she said brightly. 'I mean, really *see* me.'

Jake and Paul looked puzzled. Lou couldn't be bothered to elaborate. Instead she turned to the optics and started to replace the empty bottles, smiling as she caught a glimpse of her freshly scrubbed reflection peering back at her from the steel.

AUDREY

It was nearly four o'clock, and Audrey was pulling on her raincoat to go to the vet and pick up Pickles when something extraordinary happened. She got a delivery of flowers.

The arrival of a bouquet of flowers was not unusual in itself. But this particular delivery was extraordinary for two reasons. Firstly because it was the smallest, simplest posy she'd ever received: a modest bunch of clean, yellow marigolds. And secondly because it was the first bunch of flowers she'd ever received that she hadn't sent to herself. The shock was so great that she sat back down in her fully buttoned coat to admire them.

If you ever need a friend . . . Maurice Lazenby, read the card.

A nugget of warmth kindled in Audrey's chest. After hours of maintaining her rigid iron mask she felt an almost happy prickle of tears at the unexpected kindness Maurice had shown her yet again. For the first time in years human nature had pleasantly (rather than unpleasantly) surprised her and she felt a flush of shame for every time she'd rolled her eyes to hear Maurice was on the phone. How she'd misjudged him! He wasn't a moaner at all. He was a gentleman. Old fashioned, fussy and with ideas of a suitor that were well above his station. But beneath it all, a kind and thoughtful gentleman.

She picked up the phone to thank him. It was her first genuine phone call of the day.

'You're welcome.' He dismissed her thanks. 'In fact, I was wondering if you'd permit me to buy you lunch tomorrow . . . to give you an escape from the office.'

Audrey paused, unsure of how to proceed into such unknown social territory. She looked at the flowers and remembered the relief of his handkerchief and the warmth of his arm around her shoulders.

'Well, I suppose it would be nice to get out of the office for once,' she conceded.

'That's settled, then. Shall I come to Table For Two for 12.30?'

Audrey was about to tell him to meet her outside – the girls might laugh if they knew she was lunching with Maurice – but she stopped short. *A nicer me*, she reminded herself.

And then just as she stood again, gathering her handbag and Pickles's travel basket to her, something else unexpected happened. Alice shot into her office.

'Not now, Alice,' Audrey said as neutrally as possible. 'There's somewhere very important I have to be. I can't be late.'

'Oh! Right.'

Alice looked as though the wind had been let out of her sails. Audrey noticed how tired and pale she was; all traces of last night's glamour-puss were gone. The cardigan was back. Some sort of order had been restored.

'Well, can I give you this? Maybe you could read it later.' Alice nervously held an envelope towards her. Audrey nodded and folded it into her pocket.

'I really mustn't be late. It's my cat, you see.'

'Yes, of course.'

Audrey made her way to the glass door.

'Audrey . . . ?' Alice asked.

Something in her voice made Audrey stop and turn to face her.

'I'm sorry,' Alice said softly.

There was a short, silent pause as the complexity of meaning of the two simple words settled upon both women.

Audrey nodded, and then sailed out of the room and out of Table For Two. It wasn't until she was on the bus on the way to the vet's that she pulled out Alice's envelope and realized it contained her resignation letter. And then she didn't know what to think.

SHERYL

Sheryl slid into her red convertible, checked her lipgloss in the rear-view mirror and fired up the engine with an unnecessarily ostentatious roar. She checked her watch. She still had plenty of time.

She began to weave her way through the early rush-hour traffic, tossing her hair and feigning ignorance of the heads she knew she was turning amongst the commuters. Sheryl loved spring. And summer and autumn, come to that. Winter was the only season she disliked, with its lowered hemlines and unspoken fashion law that cleavages should be buried under layers of repugnant wool. But now that the weather had finally turned, Sheryl took every opportunity to draw back the roof of her car and display herself to her fellow road users, even if it did mean turning the heater up to max.

A cycle courier pulled up alongside her at the lights and took advantage of the height of his bike to peer down her cleavage. Yes, spring was definitely a wonderful season, she smirked.

As she waited for the lights to change, her eye wandered

across the vista of drivers, lingering on a van containing three red-blooded labourers. She deliberately let her eye contact linger long enough for one of them to lean out of his window and call out a mild but complimentary obscenity. Sheryl rewarded him with a salacious smile, just as the lights changed. Her convertible roared and she leapt speedily towards the next red light.

Life is good, she thought sassily. Business was booming, profits were soaring and her acquisition of Cupid's Cabin had gone smoothly. When she factored in her ingenious exposure of Audrey Cracknell yesterday, and her carefully packed overnight bag nestling in the passenger seat, ready for a clandestine rendezvous at the White Hotel, life could barely be better.

When you're winning . . . Sheryl thought smugly. Everything was slipping into place like choreography, right down to Partridges' getting in more of their purple marabou G-strings, just in time for tonight. Her marabou G-strings (particularly the purple ones) always drove Ernie wild, and Sheryl had tried to hide her irritation when he'd slipped her previous pair into his pocket after their last hotel tryst.

'A souvenir,' he'd said with a smile that made his network of crow's feet shine in the artificial light.

Stupid old man, she'd thought, wondering whether men ever grew out of their inner teenager. Still, she had to acknowledge that the G-strings were doing their work. Ernie was already treating her like his DIPS deputy, openly deferring to her in meetings. And when the silly sod finally realized it was time to retire Sheryl had him right where she wanted him to make sure the succession to the presidency was hers.

Besides, her extra-curricular meetings with Ernie weren't all work. She'd always been a firm advocate of variety, and Ernie's age and gratitude were a refreshing foil to Brad's vanity and acrobatics. And despite what they said about not being able to teach old dogs new tricks, Sheryl had made Ernie bark in ways she'd never thought possible.

She drummed her scarlet talons on the steering wheel and idly turned to check out Partridges' window. But before her eye could reach the designer-clad mannequins her attention fell on a familiar figure clutching a cat basket at the bus stop. It took Sheryl a couple of seconds to realize that the unassuming woman lost in maudlin introspection was Audrey Cracknell. She looked different somehow. So much less. It was as if the fight had seeped out of her. Her chin no longer jutted like a private's on parade. Even her hair didn't seem so antagonistically orange. She barely looked like Sheryl's adversary at all.

Sheryl smiled a smug smirk of victory, deliberately over-revved her engine and sped forwards into a sudden clearing in the traffic. Maybe she'd put in a call tomorrow, she thought mercilessly; see whether the time was right for Table For Two to go on the market. After all, she reasoned heartlessly, business wasn't business. It was war. And everyone knows what they say about love and war.

AUDREY

It was over their apple crumble that Maurice dropped his bombshell.

'You do know why nobody from Table For Two has been able to find me my perfect match, don't you?' he asked suddenly.

'No,' Audrey replied, taken aback.

She hadn't expected this tangent in the conversation. So far, she'd done all the talking. She hadn't planned on telling Maurice everything, but there was something about him that made her suddenly decide to come clean. So she'd told him about her unrequited love for John, how she'd allowed everyone to believe they were a couple because she'd wanted it to be true. She'd told him how she'd been exposed by Sheryl and expelled from the Dating Practitioners' Society; she'd told him everything, right down to the moment she'd come across John and Alice having dinner together and how she'd lashed out at Pickles. And Maurice had listened to it all without comment or judgement. By the time they'd ordered dessert Audrey felt a stone lighter. She'd revealed all. And the person she'd done it to was still sitting before her, with neither pity nor disgust nor repugnance on his face. It felt good.

'No,' she repeated. 'I hadn't really wondered why we hadn't matched you. I just presumed that my girls were . . .'

'Incompetent?' he smiled.

'Well, yes, I suppose I did,' Audrey conceded, ashamed. 'And were they?' She held her breath as she waited for his answer. Suddenly it seemed very important to hear good things about her staff.

'Far from it,' he said matter-of-factly. 'They tried their best, and Miss Brown in particular gave my case a great deal of thought. Her matches were . . .' – he searched for the right word – 'inspired.'

Audrey felt a small but distinct flush of something. Was it pleasure? she thought. Pride? She wasn't sure, but it felt strangely good to hear Maurice's positive feedback about her girls. Particularly the praise for Alice, whose resignation letter still languished in Audrey's pocket and to whom she hadn't been sure what to say this morning. And so, to her embarrassment, she'd said nothing. She'd have to speak to Alice this afternoon. She'd have to acknowledge her resignation; accept it, even. She'd wanted rid of her for long enough. But now she finally had what she wanted – professionally, at least – she wasn't sure what to do. She'd only just realized what a phenomenal matchmaker Alice was. Could she possibly put all the other stuff aside and ask her to stay? She didn't know.

'You're a tough nut to crack.' She smiled at Maurice. 'A

man who knows what he wants and accepts no substitutes. You're a bit like me, in fact. We're perfectionists. I didn't realize it before, but we seem to have a lot in common.'

'A lot,' Maurice agreed, but he suddenly seemed nervous. 'Maybe more than you think. Actually, as we're putting our cards on the table today, I think it's time I also came clean. I've got a confession to make.'

Audrey looked at him quizzically. Maurice took a deep breath.

'I'm afraid I haven't been completely truthful with you, Audrey. My motives for staying with Table For Two haven't been entirely ethical.'

Audrey's spoon paused in mid-air and her face suddenly pinched tight. 'Oh, Maurice, you're not ... *married* ... ?' Her voice seemed to come out strangely. She hoped he hadn't noticed.

'No, no; nothing like that. What I mean is, I'm afraid I set you all an impossible mission. You've all been looking for my perfect match on your books, but I know for a fact she's not there.'

'Of course she's there!' Audrey replied in a rush. 'We have the best client list in the city. We have every kind of woman there possibly is. I refuse to give in and accept defeat, especially when you've been so kind to me. I gave you my word that I'd find her for you, and I will.'

'Will you?' Maurice replied. His question hung in the air for a moment. 'Well, you'll have to stop searching your client list and start searching your payroll.' He adjusted his napkin in embarrassment.

Audrey gasped.

'Bianca?' Again her voice came out funny: flat. Something seemed to sink in her stomach, and it wasn't the apple crumble.

Maurice waved her suggestion away. 'Audrey, why do you think I've made everyone's life a misery until eventually my case was passed high enough up the food chain to reach you?'

'I, uh . . .' Audrey wasn't sure what to say. It felt inappropriately vain to paraphrase back his assertion that she was the best.

'It's because *you* are my perfect woman,' Maurice blurted suddenly, his eyes fixing on hers. 'You're a magnificent woman: a flagship for your species, a *QE2* amongst a sea of working tugs and superficial liners. Why would I be interested in the Biancas of this world? Or the benign string of blondes your staff have matched me with? None of them holds a single interesting thought in their heads. None of them knows how to run a business, manage a team, empathize with a whole host of lonely clients and make each one feel special. Ever since I first heard you speak at one of your "Finding Miss Right" talks four years ago, the only woman I've wanted has been you.'

Audrey looked at him in disbelief. Could she be hearing this right? She'd had so many shocks in the last few days.

'I was hoping someone in your agency might spot it,' Maurice said with a wry smile. 'I almost thought Miss Brown might, for a while.'

There was a pause.

'Maurice, you've genuinely surprised me,' Audrey said after a moment. 'I don't know what to say.'

'Say you'll give it some thought.' He leaned towards her. 'Say you won't dismiss me out of hand, or hide behind some made-up rule about not dating your clients. Say you'll be open-minded.'

Audrey looked at him. And she realized that he looked different. What she'd always written off as irritating, overly groomed and twee now seemed caring, careful and comfortably old-fashioned. He wasn't a moaner; he was a listener. A good and kind and thoughtful listener. Everyone had got him so wrong; *she'd* got him so wrong. She wondered how on earth she – *she*, who prided herself on knowing everything about the complexities of men and women – had never noticed it before . . . Maurice was a gentleman.

'Yes,' she heard herself answer. 'I promise I'll think about it.'

And she found herself smiling back at him.

And then they both picked up their spoons and ate their apple crumble.

KATE

Making up was surprisingly easy in the end. Kate decided to make the first move, and she nervously negotiated the stairs down to Lou's bar on her way home from work.

She had her strategy in place. She didn't want to apologize fully; she still stood by what she'd said. Lou's behaviour *was* self-destructive and she *was* wasting her life working in Tony's bar. And if they were to be friends again – and that *was* what Kate wanted – then they needed to stop living in each other's pockets. A bit of distance was in order. They had to make space in their relationship to allow new relationships in. After all, it was no coincidence that when they'd had their bust-up Kate had finally fallen in love.

But it was definitely time for a partial apology. She'd missed her!

'Hello, stranger!' Lou's face broke into a smile as Kate approached the bar.

Kate felt a flood of relief. She hadn't known what to expect, but Lou looked genuinely pleased to see her. And unusually radiant too.

'Wow!' Kate said honestly. 'You look amazing!'

She thought she saw Lou blush slightly.

'Ah, well, I've been easing off on the slap. Thought I'd let the inner me get an airing.'

'You look good on it.'

'Thanks.' Lou smiled and handed Kate a glass of wine. 'Actually, you're lucky you caught me. If you'd left it another week I wouldn't have been here.'

'Oh?'

'I've handed in my notice.'

Kate opened her mouth in shock.

'Because of what I said?'

'Partly,' Lou admitted. 'You were right. I *do* need to get away from Tony. I deserve better.'

'Hear, hear!'

'And you were right about something else too! I *do* need to get my arse into gear, else I'll be the oldest barmaid in town! So I've got myself a job at that new bar we went to near Partridges'. I start next week. As manager!'

'That's fantastic! Congratulations!' Kate clinked her glass with Lou's enthusiastically. 'You'll be a brilliant boss!'

'Thanks.' Lou smiled and looked at her watch. 'So, a late lunch, is it?'

Kate grinned.

'No, I've just finished work for the day. I was on my way home.'

'But it's not even six!'

'Ah well, I thought I'd take a bit of your advice, too. Break the shackles to Julian, catch up on a bit of life.'

Lou grinned and ushered Kate to a table in the corner.

'It's good to see you,' she said warmly as they sat down.

'You too.'

'So how've you been?'

And Kate filled her in, enjoying the chance to gossip at long last.

'So let me get this straight,' Lou summarized. 'You've started leaving work at 5.30 and the sky hasn't fallen in.'

Kate grinned.

'You've seen sense about Julian and realized he's just a bloke and not PR's answer to Donald Trump. You've fallen in love with a man who makes you see life beyond the office and has persuaded you to break a few rules. And you're looking dangerously like someone who's actually happy!'

'I am!' Kate admitted with a rush.

'I'm really pleased for you,' Lou smiled. And she seemed to mean it.

'And I've got more news,' Kate teased, looking carefully at Lou. 'I think Julian's got the hots for you!'

'For me?' Lou looked surprised and – if Kate wasn't mistaken – a little bit pleased.

'He came over to my desk this afternoon and asked for your phone number. He even seemed a bit shy. He muttered something about you being even more beautiful in the morning light; compared you to a Klimt painting, the daft sod. And then he asked me if I thought you'd be interested.'

'What did you say?' Lou asked, studiously casual.

'I said I didn't know.'

Kate noticed that Lou looked disappointed.

'I said he should phone you and find out for himself,' she continued. 'I told him he'd be lucky to have you, and that if he messed you around I'd put all his nasty habits in a press release and fire it off to every journalist in the country.'

Lou grinned.

'But I thought Julian was off-limits,' she said delicately.

'Yeah, well, it's like I said. I've taken your advice. I'm trying to let go a bit,' Kate conceded with a smile.

Lou reached across the table and clasped her hand. They smiled at each other.

'You know, you shouldn't be so hard on Julian,' Lou teased archly, pulling her hand away. 'He's obviously a man of taste. OK, so he knocks off early every day, but who wouldn't if they owned the company? And it's not his fault his mother never taught him to keep his mouth closed when eating croissants!'

'Ah, so you *do* like him then!' Kate laughed. 'I thought you might!'

'It's a posh thing . . .' Lou continued, deliberately ignoring Kate's comment. 'If you close your mouth, what happens to the silver spoon? Eating with your mouth open is the curse of the upper classes.'

'Get you!' Kate laughed. 'What happened to your taste for a bit of rough?'

'I'm an equal opportunities shagger, me,' Lou grinned. 'It's the only politically correct thing about me.'

'You know, maybe you and Julian wouldn't be such a bad

match after all,' Kate mused. 'You're both heavy-drinking tarts with a complete lack of shame. Maybe you'll be doing the world a favour by taking yourselves off the market and stopping any other poor innocents straying into your paths. Actually, I can't think why I didn't see this before. You two might just be a match made in heaven!'

Lou winked.

'He's loaded!' Kate added helpfully.

'And not just in the wallet department.' Lou grinned wickedly, suddenly looking like her old self again. 'I'm telling you, Kate, your boss has got the biggest cock I've ever seen!'

Six months later . . .

ALICE

It was just a hundred metres from the seafront and had a red front door with a shiny brass knocker. Alice stood on the pavement, squeezing John's hand in excitement.

'It's Edwardian,' he said.

'It's perfect!' she cried. And it was. It was traditional and discreet and solid and safe; the sort of place clients would feel comfortable visiting.

'So we're really going to do this? It's definitely what you want?' he asked.

'One hundred per cent!'

'The top two floors have plenty of room for us to live in, and the office can be at street level. And it's got an enormous garden, south-facing, so it gets lots of sun. Just think what we can grow in it! Sunflowers, sweet peas, honeysuckle!'

'And mistletoe, and cacti and red tulips,' Alice added, grinning like the Cheshire Cat.

'Of course! They go without saying,' John grinned back at her. 'Tomorrow I thought we could check out the local pubs. And Ginny and Dan have already promised to visit.'

'They'd better be quick! Gin's due to give birth in two months!' Alice laughed as her eyes drank in the building. Everything felt different here: exciting. The people looked different, the gardens looked different. Even the air smelt different, and it wasn't just the tempting aroma of freshly fried fish and chips that was creeping deliciously into her nostrils. 'I feel so happy I could burst,' she said joyously. 'It feels so right. It's a brand-new start!'

John pulled her close.

'It's our happy-ever-after,' he grinned.

'That sounds like an ending!' Alice laughed. 'But this is a beginning. It's *our* beginning!' And she twirled him into a rapturous little dance on the pavement as the seagulls squawked overhead.

Everything about her life felt like a beginning now. Summer had flashed by so quickly, in a dazzling, exciting whirl. She'd quickly sold her flat in Eversley Road and moved in with John at his house. She'd always thought it would be a wrench to leave her flat and garden behind, but she'd barely glanced back. She'd only been at John's a couple of months before he too had found a buyer, and now here they were, setting up their lives together somewhere new.

'And look round here.' John took her hand excitedly and steered her to the side of the house. Alice peered up the stone passageway that led to the back garden. Something on the left caught her eye.

'My bike!' she exclaimed. And then she saw something else. 'You've bought me a stand! My very own bike stand!'

'It's just a little something to make you feel at home,'

John explained bashfully. 'Besides, now that you've got a better bike, it seems a shame just to lean it against a wall.'

'I love it!' she declared. And she did. She rushed forward to examine her bike and stand. The bike had, perhaps, been the biggest surprise of the last six months – or rather, the person who gave it had. Audrey had barely looked her in the eye the week she'd resigned, and Alice had reconciled herself to being given the silent treatment for the entire month of her notice. She didn't mind; she understood why Audrey thought she deserved it. But bit by bit Audrey had thawed. She'd started including her in office discussions, and had even bought her a coffee when she'd uncharacteristically popped out to buy the staff cappuccinos. But despite the rapprochement, Alice had never expected a leaving do, and much less a leaving present.

'It's second-hand,' Audrey had declared as she'd wheeled the bike into Luigi's. 'It was Maurice's idea.'

Alice had been so moved, it had been all she could do to blink back a tear. The bike was perfect, and the pannier was huge and roomy. Before she could even think to stop herself she'd heard herself ask aloud: 'Audrey, do you know if any of the first five clients you matched are still married?'

'Good heavens, I'm a matchmaker, not a miracle worker!' Audrey had replied in surprise. 'Actually, it turned out that one of the couples might only have married so the wife could stay in the country. I'd never have matched them if I'd known – I could have been an accessory to an immigration crime! No, the only couple I believe are still together are my second cousin and his wife. We haven't been in touch for years, but the last I heard they'd had three children, and I've no reason to doubt they're still going strong.'

Alice wished with all her heart she'd had the courage to ask Audrey before. And so, by way of relief and thanks, she'd taken Audrey into a quiet corner and shared with her the only thing she had to give: knowledge. Audrey's mouth had fallen open when Alice told her about Sheryl's moneymaking strategy. She'd been so astounded she couldn't speak for several minutes. Alice felt a deep flush of shame that she'd ever – even fleetingly – suspected Audrey might be capable of the same.

'That's appalling!' Audrey had finally spluttered. 'Unforgivable! The poor clients ...'

And she'd promised to use the information wisely. There'd been none of the power-crazed zeal Alice would have expected from her when handed a stash of ammunition to use against Sheryl. Just a serious nod, and a declaration that she'd see to it that things were put right. Alice knew Audrey would do the right thing. And because of the new *entente cordiale* she'd reached with her boss, there was no bitter aftertaste to her leaving.

John broke Alice's reverie with a squeeze of her hand, and they made their way back to the front of the house.

'So,' he teased her gently. 'All that's left is for us to decide on a name for this new business venture of ours.'

'Yes, I've been thinking about that!' Alice announced excitedly. 'You know how ours is going to be a dating agency with a difference? How we're going to use our experiences to offer the full service to finding love ... life coaching, confidence building, dating etiquette *and* matchmaking!'

John nodded, smiling at her animation.

'Well, I think that sounds old-fashioned – but in a good way! Our clients will get the personal touch. We'll go through the dos and don'ts of dating demystify all the unwritten rules to help people be confident, have fun and fall in love. We're going to look after them like their best friend ever, or a wise old aunt.'

John laughed. 'Please tell me we're not calling it "Auntie John"?'

'What I mean is, we'll be looking after our clients in a way that nobody does any more; really taking the time to get to know them. It's the kind of service people used to get before computers and profit margins. So if we're giving the personal touch, we should *be* personal. We're Alice and John: *Miss Brown and Mr Smith*!' She looked at him expectantly.

'You want to call our agency "Miss Brown and Mr Smith" ...?' John mulled it over. 'Well, it's not sugary. And it's not a nauseating pun like Love Birds, or A Fine Romance ...'

'It's honest.'

'It's certainly old-fashioned ...'

'It's us!'

'Yes ...' John mused. 'But I think we can do better.'

'Oh?' Alice tried not to sound disappointed. She watched him survey their new premises as he made a show of mulling things over. The street was quietening down for the evening and she thought she could hear the gentle lapping of the sea. The autumn evening sunshine bathed John's skin in gold. He looked exotic, like something precious – more precious than she could ever have imagined for herself. And then he turned away from the red front door, his blue eyes twinkled and his face broke into a wonderful smile.

'Forget "Miss Brown and Mr Smith"!' he grinned. 'I think "Mr and Mrs Smith" has a much better ring to it!' And he took both of her hands in his and dropped down on one knee on the pavement. 'I love you, Miss Brown,' he said softly. 'The day I met you was the luckiest day of my life. Would you please do me the honour of agreeing to become my wife?'

Alice's heart leapt and she fell to her knees and kissed him, down there in the evening sunshine on the pavement. She'd known she'd been right all along to believe in Prince Charmings, to have fantasies and be a shameless romance-aholic. She'd been right to believe that one day she'd find a man who wouldn't care that she wore cardigans, rode an old-fashioned bike and preferred gardening to nightclubs. And now here she was, happier than she'd ever thought possible, being pulled up into a standing position and being swept into the arms of her very own Mr Right. And they were about to head off into the sunset. She squeezed him ecstatically as she imagined the life they'd have together: Alice the matchmaking gardener and her perfect Prince Charming, John Smith!

ACKNOWLEDGEMENTS

Enormous thanks to the army of fantastic people who made this book happen . . . Maggie, Sarah and the team at Ed Victor; Charlotte, Nicola and everyone at Quercus; and Fiona Carpenter for the cover . . . you have been my very own *Jim'll Fix It* squad and I'm forever grateful.

Thanks also to the MTV Press girls, who first gave me the confidence to write by laughing at my press releases (in all the right places), and to Maddy, for matchmaking me with the world of books. Plus thanks to Mum, Dad and the myriad babysitters, without whom this book could never have been written.

Finally, extra big thanks to Nige for having enough confidence in me to stand back and watch my career disintegrate and our bank balance diminish, all in the pursuit of chick lit!